To: Mort & Gloria, my dear friends. Enjoy! Al

SATAN STALKS SINATRA DRIVE

SATAN STALKS SINATRA DRIVE

A. J. HARRIS, M.D.

Murder Mystery Press
Palm Desert • California

Copyright © 2011 Murder Mystery Press
ISBN: 978-0-9829361-0-8 (paperback)
    978-0-9829361-1-5 (hardcover)
    978-0-9829361-2-2 (ebook)
Published by Murder Mystery Press, www.murdermysterypress.com

Publishing Consulting and Product Development
BookStudio, LLC, www.bookstudiobooks.com

Line editing:
Christine Jones, Elan Press

Copyediting:
Lisa Wolff

Jacket and Interior Design:
Bill Greaves, Concept West Design, www.conceptwest.com

Library of Congress Control Number: 2010934434

Publishers Cataloging in Publication Data available from the publisher.

All rights reserved.

No part of this publication may be reproduced or transmitted in any form or by any means, electronic or mechanical, including photocopy, recording, or any information storage and retrieval system, without permission in writing from the publisher.

Printed in the United States of America

To the Children:
Elizabeth, Shelby, Marla, Larry, and Paul

Acknowledgments

A novel takes on a greater degree of realism when the author learns from those actively engaged in certain pursuits, professions, or industries. For instance, I learned about arrest procedures for criminals living outside the state in which the crime is committed by speaking with active and recently retired law enforcement agents. I became familiar with the serious injuries associated with the lumber industry from treating many patients while living in the Northwest timber country.

Despite all the information I've gathered for this story, I have modified some of the facts to accommodate the story line and strengthen the plot. For that, I apologize to my teachers and informants. All mistakes are mine alone.

The following people were exceedingly helpful in providing information and technical data: Dr. Joyce Wade-Maltais, Brad Oliver, Sylvia Selfman, Nina Markos, Jean Denning, Patricia Rothman, Danny Davis, David Weiel, Steve Powell, Clyde Walsh, Pat Martin, Jim Schmitz, Ralph Calafiore, Dennis Gillard, Karla Olson, Bill Greaves, Christine Jones, and Lisa Wolff.

ONE

The room stank of death.

Dr. Josh Harrington entered the hospital room with a sense of foreboding. No amount of disinfectant spray could mask the odor of decomposing tissue.

He nodded to Nurse Dudley, who stood on the opposite side of the orthopedic bed with all its apparatus, her face wreathed in worry. In front of him lay Chesley Upton Effingwell, who had been one of Josh's patients since his earliest days in practice.

Josh stepped closer to the bed. Lying within a complicated arrangement of ropes, pulleys, and splints, Effingwell already appeared corpselike. Whatever condition ravaged his body in the last seventy-two hours remained a diagnostic mystery. Josh swallowed back a curse. Why in the hell was Effingwell dying before his eyes?

As if he read Josh's thoughts, the man's bald, cadaver-like head moved slowly. One eye, then the other opened to look at Nurse Dudley, then at Josh. With his bony hand, its skin parchment-like and blotchy, he reached up and removed the plastic oxygen mask covering his mouth.

"Jesus Chris', Doc." His voice was a raspy wheeze. "Where the hell ya been? I'm dyin' here and nobody's doin' a goddamn thing. Fix this fuckin' hip so's I c'n get the hell outta here." He felt the roundness of the amputated end on his other thigh and shook his head. "Fer goddamn sure I can't walk on that, either." He attempted to expel the gurgling phlegm in his throat. The effort further wracked his painful body.

Chesley Upton Effingwell, an irascible seventy-nine-year-old, lay in an orthopedic bed with a four-poster metal frame to support the rigging of a Thomas splint for his fractured right hip. Three years ago, Josh had amputated above his left knee for an old luetic lesion.

Josh lifted Effingwell's skeletal wrist and felt for its almost imperceptible pulse. He counted quietly, then leaned close to his ear. "Chesley, unfortunately, your overall condition is—well—it's not optimum, and the medical specialist won't give his okay for surgery just yet . . ."

"Doc, don't renege on me. I don't know how much time I got left. If you don't operate soon, I'll die. Fer goddamn sure, I'll die."

Josh spoke softly and apologetically. "You'll probably die if we operate."

"I'll take that chance." Effingwell's eyes explored the paraphernalia around him. "I don't want to lay in this goddamn prison with all these fuckin' pulleys and ropes. I've got tubes in my arms, wires on my chest, and a hose in my prick. This ain't no way to live, fer Chrissake." Josh understood Effingwell's anguish but was not about to accept the consequences of a rash surgical decision. His lab tests were abysmally abnormal and becoming worse, mitigating the justification for surgical intervention.

"Look, Doc, I know you're a decent guy and wouldn't do nothin' to hurt me. I trust you a *hunerd* percent. Whatever ya say goes, but ya gotta get me better and outta here. Just layin' here I'm gettin' worse. Maybe I got no right to ask fer more years, but I'd like 'em anyway. Hell, I took chances all my life, and I ain't got much to show fer it. I'm flat broke. There's no way I c'n pay you a goddamn red cent." He hesitated to catch his breath. "But I c'n give you what I got."

Josh shook his head while adjusting the Thomas splint. "I'll accept whatever Medicare pays."

"Shit, what you get from them won't even pay fer your gasoline to come out here . . ." He motioned for Harrington to come closer, then grabbed his lapel. "Fer a year, I've been carryin' the deed to my old adobe house and the land around it off Frank Sinatra Drive in the hills." He paused to catch his breath as his withered neck muscles retracted.

Josh interrupted. "Chesley, the last thing I need is an old adobe house. Give it to a relative, or donate it to charity."

Effingwell's spidery fingers clutched the doctor's lapel more firmly. "Doc, I got no relatives, 'cept fer my no-account brother, Chester, who disappeared ten years ago. As fer charities—they never done nothin' fer me, not that I ever wanted 'em to."

Something about Effingwell's manner reminded Josh of a man on a mission, a mission based on desperation. The old man looked at Nurse Dudley. "Girlie, you be a witness to this. I want the doc to have that deed." He looked at Harrington. "Now, don't argue, dammit. Open the closet door and take the goddamn deed outta my jacket pocket. Go on. Do it now. There's a house key in there, too."

Reluctantly, Dr. Harrington removed a soiled envelope with dog-eared corners and reached inside. Written on yellow-lined, legal-sized paper in a barely legible hand was a crude quitclaim with blank spaces below for signatures and dates. A blackened key lay on the bottom of the envelope. Josh gave the form a cursory glance, shook his head, and replaced the envelope with its form in Effingwell's jacket.

"Sign the goddamn thing, right now," the old man croaked.

Badgered by the patient's insistence and not wanting to upset his fragile condition, Josh took the form and, in full view of Effingwell, signed his name. He gave the form to Nurse Dudley to witness his signature and to date the document. A rough map, not drawn to scale, designated the property lines and acreage. He refolded the papers and placed them and the key in the envelope, then put the envelope in the inner pocket of his suit jacket. Accepting the deed made him uncomfortable, but he forced a smile.

"Chesley, thank you for your generous gift. We'll do our best to make you comfortable. See you in the morning."

Effingwell nodded and waved them off. Then, as afterthought, he called out, "Doc, promise you won't sell the house. I don't give a damn what you do with the rest of the property."

Josh, though puzzled by Effingwell's request, did not want to engage in further conversation since he was running late. "Don't worry, old buddy, you have my word, the house won't be sold."

A half hour later, after completing rounds, Josh thanked Nurse Dudley, then walked into the ward station when a Code Blue was announced for room 312. Two nurses and an attendant stopped suddenly. One grabbed an emergency cart with a defibrillator just outside the nurses' station, and all three ran toward the room.

Room 312? Damn, that was Effingwell's room. Josh left his charts on the desk and ran behind them. He stopped at the door to observe the quickened choreography of attempted resuscitation: extension of the head and neck, exploring the airway with a finger, and initiating rhythmic and prolonged CPR.

Josh grabbed the defibrillator paddles, placed them on the patient's chest, adjusted the joule output, and ordered, "Everyone stand back!" A series of three jolts caused the patient gross spasmodic contractions. The jolts failed to restart his heartbeat. With wide-eyed determination Josh grabbed a syringe of adrenaline from the tray, located the proper intercostal space, and injected the cardiac muscle. All four watched expectantly—hopefully.

No response.

"Goddammit, Effingwell, start breathing!" Josh snarled. He hammered the man's chest several times—no response. He put his ear to the patient's mouth and nose. No breath sounds. Effingwell's pupils were fixed and the conjunctivae were glazed. The futility of further resuscitation was obvious. Josh ran his hand gently and respectfully over the head and neck of the jaundiced, emaciated body, which felt waxy to the touch.

His professionalism even in the face of obvious death forced Josh to perform further death verification tests. He placed the stethoscope on the patient's chest, felt for wrist and neck pulses, and inflicted normally painful pressure above the eyes; all signs were negative. He closed the lids over the staring eyes, then covered the corpse with the bedsheet. He noted the time of expiration: 11:15 a.m.

After reviewing Effingwell's records, Josh remained troubled by the man's downward spiral since his admission three days ago.

His initial tests revealed a moderate anemia and subsequent tests showed a worsening despite blood transfusions. His thin habitus was consistent with his reclusive lifestyle. While in the hospital he ate little and ignored or pushed his food trays aside. Hydration was maintained by IVs. An alcoholic, he had quit drinking several years ago on the advice of a doctor at the free clinic who'd diagnosed mild or early cirrhosis of the liver. He had smoked since age twelve and developed a hacking, productive cough with underlying emphysema. But his demise was not the result of a slow, disabling disease due to compromised lung function.

The underlying diagnosis baffled Josh as well as the medical consultant. What in the world would cause all of the organ systems to fail suddenly and completely?

TWO

In her crisp, white uniform, Nurse Maggie Harrington greeted her husband as he came through the rear door of the office. She responded with disappointment to his perfunctory peck on her cheek.

"Why so glum, chum?"

Josh walked to his desk and absently looked at the mail stacked on his blotter. "Effingwell, our crusty old seaman, died. For almost twenty years I treated him for various orthopedic problems, not the least of which was a left leg amputation three years ago. I liked the old guy, and I'll miss his spicy stories."

"I'm terribly sorry. I knew you enjoyed his company, and I knew he admired you. What was the cause of death?"

The question disturbed Josh. "Initially I thought perhaps some exotic disease had escaped detection, something like a tropical parasite or possibly exposure to a toxic substance from a manufacturing plant, but Effingwell insisted he hadn't been out of the country for a number of years and denied being in a chemical environment. The diagnosis would be determined by the final arbiter, the coroner—if we're lucky."

"Well, of course, he'll have the answer." Maggie helped Josh remove his jacket and saw the soiled envelope. She picked it up with her thumb and index finger at arm's length. "What's this?"

"Oh, that? Effingwell wanted me to have the deed for some land and an old adobe house as a kind of payment for services."

"You mean you accepted it, just like that?"

"I didn't want it. I refused it initially, but he insisted and left me no choice. What's more, he asked that I not get rid of the old adobe."

"That's the strangest thing I ever heard. What are we supposed to do with that?" Before Josh could respond, she added, "Well, I suppose the least we can do is look at it before we have to decide whether we want to pay taxes on it." She slapped the envelope against the palm of her hand, then opened the closet door and placed it in her handbag.

Josh smiled at her decision. In California, where property is held under joint tenancy, she had clearly staked her claim.

• • •

Two days later, on a bright Sunday morning, during the first week of the new year, Maggie suggested they try to locate their newly inherited property in Rancho Mirage.

"Let's go up Sinatra Drive. I hear there are magnificent homes and the median has gorgeous plantings," she said.

"I'm not sure we'll locate the property. This hand-drawn map is about as primitive as it gets."

An hour later, they were on their way in their SUV. Josh, who was more familiar with the community, explained its history to Maggie, "This road had been called Wonder Palms Drive before it was renamed. Sometime in the early 'seventies, members of the city council renamed the street for their most popular resident, Francis Albert Sinatra. Stories are told about how he would buzz the homes in his private plane and on occasion the noise from his late-night parties annoyed some of the old guard. But by all accounts he was an enormous asset to the community with his global popularity and generous charitable contributions."

Maggie took the crude map from her purse, unfolded it, and pressed it against her thigh. "Isn't it odd that Effingwell, a sailor, made his home here in the desert? You'd think he'd want to live in a coastal town."

"I asked the same question years ago. He said his father purchased the house with considerable acreage about seventy years ago to escape the harsh winters of the East Coast and to relieve Chesley's boyhood respiratory problems. The site was chosen after his father discovered this old adobe on two hundred and nine hillside acres about twelve miles east of Palm Springs. The house and land had been financed for about fifty grand."

Maggie whistled. "You couldn't buy anything around here for that now."

"That's for sure." Josh smiled. "Well, maybe an upscale outhouse."

"Ha, ha, funny man." Maggie turned toward him. "When did the Effingwells come here?"

"In the late 'thirties. Chesley told me about it once. He described the ten-day trek from New Jersey in a 1939 Ford sedan that was his father's pride and joy. It was loaded with everything his mother could pile into it. He was ten years old, and his brother Chester was thirteen. He said they fought constantly on the trip out here."

"Sounds typical of brothers."

Josh sobered. "It's sad, really. Chesley told me they remained unfriendly most of their lives. At best they learned to tolerate each other. When Chester approached his teen years he developed a limp and was unable to participate in vigorous sports, although he never was much of an athlete anyway."

A car ahead of them began to slow and its right turn signal blinked. Josh slowed the SUV until the car in front turned into a side road, then resumed his speed.

"Chesley, on the other hand, had become an avid sportsman. That difference, among others, had driven a further wedge between them."

"Okay, I see it all now." Maggie smiled. "Chesley was open and given to adventure; while Chester was calculating, more cerebral. I can understand those sibling differences, but don't stop now. I want to hear more."

That was one of the things Josh loved about his wife . . . her curiosity to know everything about everything. He took a deep breath and continued his story, adding his own embellishments.

"When the family arrived in the desert, they found a lonely, sand-covered two-lane road connecting Palm Springs with the territory extending about eighteen miles east to Indio. By this time, Palm

Springs was becoming a playground for the Hollywood set while Indio was an agricultural mecca. Chesley discovered that he was able to breathe more easily without wheezing."

"Aha! That explains it."

Josh glanced at his wife. "Explains what?"

"How Chesley with his breathing trouble had become such an outdoorsman. I wondered about that."

"Good analysis, Maggie. Chesley told me about his excitement when he smelled orange blossoms and saw date palms for the first time. He loved the valley, the brilliant sunshine, the wonderful desert flora, and the acres and acres of farmland. Best of all, he just felt better."

"He was lucky. Not every asthmatic responds well to this environment."

"Not today, that's for sure." Josh thought of all the patients he'd seen over the years with breathing problems. All aggravated by the increasing pollution.

"Go on with your story. I want to hear more."

"According to Chesley, he joined the Merchant Marines during World War Two when he was not quite sixteen."

"That young? He was just a kid. How did he manage that?"

"By forging false dates on a birth certificate. He told me he was tall and looked older. At that time there was an urgent need to get war materiel to England, so no one questioned his age."

"Did he ever marry? Were there children?"

Josh glanced at his wife and saw her eyes wide with interest. Trust her to think about a love interest.

"Well, Effingwell did talk about a marriage to a high school sweetheart during the war. He said a year after their marriage, she was ready to give birth when complications forced a hurried C-section that went horribly wrong—both mother and child died."

Maggie gasped. "Oh, how sad!"

Josh nodded. He knew what it meant to lose a loved one since he had lost his own wife, Sally, three years ago. He continued, "After the death of Chesley's wife and child he started to drink heavily. He laughed when he claimed that he was drunk half the time and whored around the other half—oftentimes doing both together."

"Not much of a life if you ask me," Maggie sniffed.

"Different times, different reactions, Maggie. Back then, help for grieving wasn't always available like it is today."

"I know, but still . . ." Maggie waved with a come-on signal. "Keep talking."

Josh stared ahead at the low flow of traffic. "After the Japanese surrender in 1945, Chesley returned to the desert for a rest before taking on another tour of duty in the Pacific. While he'd been gone, the adobe house had been leased to a family of mestizos who managed date farms in Indio, about five miles to the east. They also maintained a vegetable garden next to the house. Chesley was treated with the rights and privileges of the *padrone* whenever he returned to the desert."

"Really? That must have made living arrangements pretty crowded."

"Actually, the house was made available to him alone. The family went to stay with relatives. He planned to remain several weeks and do little more than soak up the sun, sip Jack Daniels, and read seafaring tales. On weekends he would ride to Palm Springs hoping to find a gal in a bar with whom he could shack up. But his sexual forays left him feeling depressed. He'd get so stoned that he said he didn't even remember whether he got laid. He yearned for a lasting, meaningful relationship with a good woman. Then one afternoon while he was lounging on the patio, his renters' daughter came by to tend the garden."

Maggie grinned. "You certainly remember a great many details."

"Many of his stories I'd heard more than once, but they were memorable, and I enjoyed them." Josh gave his wife a deadpan look. "Do you want me to stop?"

"For heaven's sake, no. What happened next?"

Josh smiled and continued. "The sixteen-year-old beauty Chesley described had an unforgettable grace and charm even as she labored in the garden. He fell madly in love with her, but she didn't reciprocate, at least not immediately. She was betrothed to a wealthy ranchero's son, Ramundo, a jealous kid with a hair-trigger temper."

"Uh-oh, that sounds like trouble. She probably had to be careful about the company she kept. What was her name?"

Josh paused. "You know, it's a strange name, but I remember it because Effingwell had a faded tattoo on his arm. He pulled his wrinkled skin tight to make the names legible on a red heart pierced by an arrow. His name, *Chesley*, was written above the arrow, and *Nydia* was written below."

"Oh, how romantic!"

"In time, Nydia succumbed to the flattering attention Chesley showered on her, not to mention all the gifts."

"Lucky girl." Maggie released an exaggerated sigh. "I wish I had that kind of attention paid to me once in a while."

Josh chose to ignore her. "As I was saying, even though she was expected to marry Ramundo, Effingwell ignored her dilemma and day by day pursued her more earnestly. One torrid afternoon, while Nydia was working in the garden, she fainted from heat exhaustion. Chesley ran to carry her limp body to his bed. With loving concern he applied cool, moist compresses to her head, bare arms, and legs until she regained consciousness. She looked into his caring eyes, caressed his face, and invited him to make passionate love to her."

"Josh Harrington!" Maggie reached over and punched him on the shoulder. "Something tells me you're embellishing the story a little bit here."

"Maybe . . . maybe not." He grinned at his wife. "Chesley did love to talk."

"Hmph. So? Did he?"

"Did he what?"

"Make passionate love to her?"

Josh laughed out loud. "Effingwell described the experience as the most wonderful sensation he had ever known. To Nydia, the act constituted a sacred commitment—a marriage pact."

"Really?"

"Really. Effingwell was so happy. He wanted Nydia to announce their engagement to her family."

"Oh boy, I bet that went over well."

"Right. Mama and Papa were furious. They didn't want their precious daughter who was promised to Ramundo to break tradition and cast shame upon both families. Nydia implored her parents to release her obligation of marriage to Ramundo and argued that her life with him would be tragic since she no longer loved him, and in fact, she feared him."

"After hearing that, were her parents more understanding?"

"Apparently not. They warned her it would be worse if she stayed with Chesley. They told her that her gringo husband-to-be would abandon her after getting her pregnant and would beat her when he was drunk. Also she would face long periods of loneliness while he was at sea. In spite of all their warnings, Nydia remained obstinate about wanting to marry Effingwell."

"Good for her. How did Ramundo respond?"

"He went plumb *loco*. According to Chesley, the man stalked him. One day he found Chesley alone at the house—or so he thought. Filled with rage, Ramundo kicked in the door and leveled a shotgun point blank at Chesley. He didn't see Nydia dash in from another room. Just as Ramundo pulled the trigger, she threw herself in front of Effingwell. The blast caught her right in the chest. She slumped to the floor peppered with shot, bleeding and dying. Chesley told me she died in his arms."

"Oh no. Not again." Maggie grabbed her purse and dug out a tissue. "I don't like the way this story is going." She wiped her eyes and blew her nose. "What happened to Ramundo? I hope he rotted in prison for this."

"Actually, he panicked and ran to his family's ranch. He scribbled a quick note begging forgiveness, then put a pistol to his head."

Maggie sniffed. "What a terribly sad story!"

Josh nodded. "What's even sadder, Chesley said Nydia was in the early stage of pregnancy."

More tears rolled down Maggie's cheeks. She pulled out another tissue and blotted her eyes. "No wonder Nydia's death as well as the death of his first wife, both of whom were pregnant, soured Effingwell on future relationships. It also explains why he became such a crusty old geezer."

Maggie didn't want to dwell on the sadness and sought to change the subject. "Whatever happened to Chesley's brother?"

"Chester remained in the East with a thriving business. Chesley said Chester made semiannual trips to the desert, where he owned other properties with his son. Then one day ten years ago while visiting out here, Chester disappeared and never was found, despite extensive searches by the local and state police and FBI. He was declared legally dead some time after."

Maggie sighed. "Seems like an awful lot of tragedy hit that family. How could Chesley insist on keeping the old adobe? Didn't he share that property with his brother? Even if he retained ownership as the last surviving member of the family, wouldn't he have to share that with his nephew?"

"The impression I got was that Chesley Effingwell owned the old adobe and the property it sat on wholly and completely. The official deed, I'm sure, will explain everything."

"What I don't understand is why Chesley insisted on keeping the old adobe. Why didn't he just sell it off?"

"The only reason I could think of," Josh said, "was Effingwell's cherished memories of his beloved Nydia. Chesley spoke wistfully of the adobe as a kind of hallowed ground, a holy shrine to her. Their brief time together, he said, was the happiest he had ever known. He had even painted on the lintel above the front door a sign decorated with red roses on a green vine that read, *Santa Nydia, todo mi amore.*"

Maggie turned and gazed out the windows at the majestic San Jacinto and San Gorgonio Mountains, their white caps contrasted against the cloudless azure sky. "How tragic, the way all this beauty was stolen from the young and lovely *señorita* just as she was coming into womanhood and with a baby. Chesley must have been devastated."

"I'm sure he was."

Maggie became pensive. "You're not serious about keeping that old adobe, are you?" Before Josh could respond, she looked at him incredulously. "Well, are you? That old dilapidated house, I would think, has questionable value. I'm sure it would require great expense to renovate, anyway."

Josh sighed impatiently. "It was Chesley's dying wish that I keep it. Never mind that it makes no financial sense—a promise is a promise."

Maggie decided not to argue, but to wait and hope that reason would prevail and he'd have a change of heart.

He drove on Fred Waring Drive to Highway 111, then turned west. Looking over his left shoulder in Rancho Mirage, he saw the ungraded hillside with rocky terrain and scrubby desert flora. If an adobe house existed, it had to be hidden by the undulating hills and vegetation, just as the old Ritz-Carlton had been.

Maggie picked up the wrinkled map she'd had on her lap earlier. With her finger she circled an area east of Sinatra Drive and south of Highway 111 as the approximate location of the property. When they reached the entrance to the winding, upward drive, she wasn't too surprised to see how elegant it was since it was also the road leading to the original Ritz-Carlton Hotel. She knew the hotel had been built about twenty years ago but was never commercially successful; she had heard that it was now undergoing a complete renovation by new owners. She went back to studying the primitive map.

Josh muttered under his breath at the sudden appearance of construction equipment on the road.

"What is it? What's wrong, Josh?

"All these orange pylons and yellow tape . . . too damn much construction here if you ask me. God knows how I'll avoid all the potholes and crevices."

The SUV bounced viciously and Maggie gripped the grab bars. "That was some pothole! Be careful." She looked up and stared in disbelief at the enormous houses being built near the shuttered hotel. "When did all this building activity start?"

"Who knows?"

A menacing deep rumbling from behind became louder. Maggie glanced into the side mirror to see the front end of a mud-spattered Mack truck, its aggressive bulldog hood ornament about to mount their back end. Josh must have noticed it at the same time. His foot came down hard on the accelerator. The SUV responded instantly. The back wheels spun and squealed as the vehicle skidded laterally. While he fought for control, Maggie looked forward and screamed,

"Josh, look out! There's another one. It's coming straight at us—it's on our side of the road!"

Josh swerved, and the descending tractor-trailer roared past, missing them by inches. Much to her relief, the truck at the rear veered off to a side and disappeared.

Maggie collapsed against the seat.

Josh drew a deep breath. "Damn, I think they're using us as a target! What the hell are they doing here on a Sunday?" As if to answer his question, two earth-moving Komatsus appeared on their right. Both were leveling the land in tier formation and disgorging their loads onto dump trucks that quivered with every release of earth and rocks. A dusting of dirt and sand already covered their SUV.

Maggie sat upright, gripping the console with her left hand and squeezing the armrest with her right. "Someone must be paying a lot of overtime to meet or beat a deadline. Just look at all the giant-sized equipment. Maybe the builder knows housing prices are plunging and wants advanced sales, ASAP."

"Whatever, we ought to get the hell out of here before we become fatalities." Josh adjusted his hand on the wheel to make a U-turn.

"Josh, wait! We haven't seen our property, and we're practically there. Why would you turn around now? If these trucks bother you, I'll drive."

"That's ridiculous. You don't even know where to look." There was no compromising in his voice.

Maggie folded her arms across her chest defiantly, not at all understanding her husband's sudden change of attitude. "For heaven's sake, what was the point in coming here if we weren't going to look at the property?"

"Maggie, calm down. I didn't know there'd be all this crazy construction going on, especially on a Sunday. I'm just not going to risk our safety here and drive willy-nilly around this deadly obstacle course. I promise to return after I've gone to the Riverside County Courthouse to get a copy of the official land plat."

Josh pulled over to the side as far as he dared and stopped away from the tumult of the heavy equipment. A change of subject, he figured, was wise, since Maggie was not mollified by his proposal to return. He pointed to the valley floor beneath them. "Look at this magnificent setting. It's like a picture postcard."

Maggie leaned forward and sighed. "It is lovely." She looked all around. "With the mountains behind us, they're like a protective shield for the valley, forming a kind of cove."

"Cove," Josh repeated. "Yes, and that's why these towns are called cove communities: Cathedral City, Rancho Mirage, Indian Wells, Palm Desert, La Quinta—and all within a radius of about twenty-five miles."

As Josh rattled off the names, Maggie eyed her husband affectionately. The desert had become her home only a year ago when Josh brought her from Chicago as his new bride. "You know, Josh, I just love learning about the area from you." She loosened her seat belt and leaned toward him. "I think you're right." She kissed him on the cheek. "We should go home and do this another day when we know where we're going to have more time to explore." She gave him a come-hither grin. "Let's go home and really enjoy the afternoon."

Josh smiled and his eyebrows arched. "Okay, home it is. You don't have to ask me twice."

She kissed him again and settled back into her seat. "While you drive, you can tell me more about the area. I just love your explanations."

Josh assumed the proprietary air of someone who enjoyed playing the alpha role. "Well, my little darling, the land adjacent to the mountains is formed from alluvial soil, washed and windblown off the mountains to form plains on which farms and homes were built . . ."

THREE

The following morning, Josh had the pleasure of Maggie's company as he made hospital rounds. Twice a week she accompanied him to familiarize herself with the patients and to do what she loved doing: assisting him in such chores as adjusting traction apparatus and making progress notes as he dictated. Patients enjoyed her ebullient personality, especially the elderly men with whom she flirted openly. After completing rounds, they stopped at the hospital café for coffee and toasted bagels and to discuss patients' problems.

Afterward they drove to the medical office and entered it through the rear door. Carmenita, the receptionist approached them anxiously.

"Dr. Harrington, a secretary from the coroner's office asked that you call as soon as you came in. It sounded urgent."

"Get him on the phone, please."

Maggie went to the supply closet to fetch a clean lab coat for Josh. When she returned with the coat to the consultation room, she stopped to watch him as he stood to replace the phone on its cradle.

"Josh, what is it? You look as though you've seen a ghost."

"Yeah, something like that." He grasped the armrests of his chair and lowered himself into the seat. "Effingwell died of radioactive poisoning." A numbing silence ensued before Josh continued. "The aplastic anemia and the cellular destruction of the organs was the result of a highly toxic substance. The Geiger counter went crazy."

Maggie sank into a chair facing him. "That doesn't sound likely, does it? Here's an old recluse and someone slips him a death potion?" Suddenly she straightened and sat on the edge of the chair. "You're not thinking his death had anything to do with our quitclaim?"

Josh shook his head. "I don't see that connection at all. He was terribly sick before he gave us the claim. What concerns me more is why anyone would want to kill Chesley, especially that way."

Maggie stared wide-eyed at Josh. "It's bizarre like some weird James Bond thriller."

The lines in Josh's face deepened. "I'm worried. How did they, whoever the hell they are, manage to slip the substance into him without anyone knowing?" He shook his head. "Did this happen in the hospital, or right before his admission? And why would anyone choose such a damned grotesque method? The whole thing makes no sense at all."

Maggie nodded. "You're right. None of this makes any sense." She put her arms around Josh. "This is frightening. I wonder if anything else is going to happen."

* * *

Sitting at her computer in the den that evening, Maggie scanned a long list of e-mails consisting mostly of stale jokes and pleas for charitable and political donations. Toward the end of the list, one message finally caught her attention. She clicked on it and squinted at the monitor. She read the words again. Still not quite believing what she read, she yelled, "Honey, come in here—you've got to read this!"

Josh stepped into the den and put on his glasses. "What is it?" He bent forward and read aloud the small print. "Mrs. Margaret Harrington, you have been named as a beneficiary in the will of the late Dr. Martin Simon . . ." Josh trailed off and looked at her with surprise.

Maggie backed her chair away from the computer and put her hands over her mouth. For several seconds she stared in shock. She lowered her hands and whispered, "Oh, my God! I can't believe this is happening."

Josh stood behind her and placed his hands on her shoulders while he read the instructions. "You are requested to appear at the law offices of Barker, Sellers and Vitz, at Ten West La Salle Street, Chicago, Illinois. Bring original or certified copies of your birth certificate, social security card, and driver's license within two weeks of this date. A written confirmation will be forwarded within forty-eight hours. If for any reason you are unable to . . ."

Maggie spun around and bolted from her chair. "Josh, can you believe this?" She bounced on her toes and clapped her hands in front of her face just like a little girl receiving a gift. "Nothing like this has ever happened to me."

"Whoa, slow down, baby. Who was this Dr. Simon? And how did you know him?"

Maggie's excitement subsided slightly. "I met Dr. Simon, a famous industrialist, twenty-five years ago when his granddaughter, eight-year-old Suzanne Simon, unconscious and bleeding, had been admitted to the pediatric intensive care unit at the Cook County Hospital following a horrendous automobile accident in which both her parents were killed. The child sustained severe head and abdominal trauma plus multiple fractures of both lower extremities. She had been extricated from the twisted metal of the wreck and was alive, but barely."

"Poor kid."

Maggie nodded. "She was rushed to surgery for decompression of the skull and skeletal traction to both legs. Despite the head surgery, she remained comatose for several weeks, was fed by gastric intubation and kept on IVs. A heart monitor was in place for days. Dr. Simon and his wife maintained an almost constant vigil."

She sighed. "Seeing how they grieved and worried for their granddaughter, I decided to make it my duty to attend to Suzanne's needs frequently, on and off duty. One afternoon while I was on duty, the unimaginable happened, Suzanne's heart stopped. The EKG flatlined, and the monitor buzzed its ominous message. I dashed into the room, leaped on the bed, and positioned myself over her, administering CPR. It was downright scary."

"I can understand that," Josh said sympathetically.

Maggie gave her husband a fond smile, knowing that he of all people would understand her emotions. "Finally the child gasped and coughed, and her heart resumed a normal rhythm. When I watched the blips on the monitor, I cried. Much of what had happened was just plain old luck."

"Luck, nothing, it was your good nursing," Josh boasted.

"Another thing I love about you, Josh." She kissed him on the lips. "You'll always be my cheerleader."

"Of course I will, just as you'll always be mine." He pulled her into his arms. "Tell me more about Suzanne."

"Miraculously, she came out of her coma several weeks later. Within two months she was using a walker. A weakness on her left side and a speech defect which surfaced when she first awoke disappeared. Her hair, which had been shaven, came back in thick black strands."

Josh gave her a hug. "She survived because of you. You deserve a great deal of credit. Did you ever see Suzanne again? After her discharge, I mean."

"I was invited to her bat mitzvah party at the Drake Hotel in Chicago on her thirteenth birthday." She grinned sheepishly. "I was treated like royalty. It was almost embarrassing. Dr. Simon proposed a toast to me in front of hundreds of guests and told the crowd that this happy celebration never would have occurred if I had not saved Suzanne's life."

"I would have been in complete agreement. What eventually happened to her?"

"Suzanne became a stunning young woman who graduated from the University of Chicago with honors. She married a prominent attorney, Carlos Grandee, who became the chief operating officer in her grandfather's corporation. They have three beautiful daughters, and she is head of the National Women's League for Orphaned Children. Every Christmas she remembers me with a gift and a photograph of her beautiful family. Remember? I had shown you the card last Christmas."

Josh nodded. "And what of her grandfather?"

"Dr. Simon was an engineer who immigrated to this country many years ago from England. He held patents on a number of inventions, including synthetic rubber, airplane designs, and armaments. His contributions to national security were legendary. President Johnson awarded him the Presidential Medal of Freedom."

Josh was impressed. "Maybe with what he left you, we can retire."

"You're such an optimist, my darling." She put her arms around his neck, and asked, "Will you come with me to Chicago? You have two weeks to make arrangements."

"I'd like to, but I have several joint replacements scheduled over the next week and a half, and I need to be around for the post-op care. Why don't you plan to visit with Judy? I'm sure your niece would like to take in a play or two, shop at Bloomies . . ."

She put her hand over his mouth. "Aha, sounds as though you're eager to get rid of me. Aren't you worried that I might take the money and run off with some gigolo?"

Josh removed her hand from his mouth, then dropped his hands to her rounded derriere and squeezed firmly but lovingly. "One wild night with you, baby, and that gigolo will be looking for another profession."

Maggie laughed and punched his arm playfully. "You give me too much credit."

Josh held his arm, feigning pain. "You know, while you're gone, I think I'll talk with Attorney Farquhaar about the quitclaim, then go to the Riverside Courthouse for a copy of the legal land description. I need to find out more of what's on that land."

Maggie's euphoria ebbed as she noted Josh's serious expression. "Speaking of the land, have you heard any more about Effingwell's death from the coroner's office?"

He shook his head. "No, but I'm sure some government agency will be calling soon. Having a patient die of radiation poisoning won't stay quiet for long. Once the word gets out, someone will be at my door doing their damndest to put me on the hot seat."

FOUR

The Riverside County Administrative Center was not as Josh had imagined. His point of reference for government buildings dated back to the turn of the century. He remembered the photos from his high school civics text and expected to see a red brick building with ivy-covered walls shaded by deciduous trees, like poplars, sycamores, and oaks. When he turned onto Lemon Street off Route 91, he was struck by the starkly modern, glistening white five-story edifices.

An enormous curved wall of paneled brick green glass formed a large part of the exterior. On a velvety lawn bordered by red and white geraniums, a monolith with foot-high letters spelled out the building's title. Tall palm trees evenly spaced around the building enhanced its verticality.

Beyond the broad white steps leading to the entrance, an armed deputy eyed Josh as he gawked at the spacious lobby. Josh approached him about information on property ownership and was directed to the fifth floor. He stood in a queue for ten minutes before explaining his needs to a seemingly disinterested clerk, who pointed toward the Viewing Room. His thanks to the clerk went ignored. A sign above a door projected into the hall and read "Assessor Maps, Property Data, Records, Tax Information." He opened the door to a room where a bank of twelve computers, six on either side, was positioned in the center of a long table. Eight computers were in use.

Observing Josh's bewildered expression, a pleasant-looking, soft-spoken clerk asked if she could help. Her name badge read "Sherri Aviloh."

He handed her his professional card, then asked for information on property in Rancho Mirage owned by a Chesley Upton Effingwell. She inquired about the spelling, then walked to a computer. Following, he asked, "Am I asking for privileged information—transgressing any laws?"

"No, not at all." She quickly explained that the information was in the public domain. She showed him what to enter on the keyboard and the data appeared on the monitor. "If you'd like a printed copy, you can pick it up at window number ten."

Josh thanked her.

At window number ten, he paid the required three dollars and scanned the sheet. Two names were typed in on the document that gave the legal description of the property: Chesley Upton Effingwell, his deceased patient, and Chester Uriah Effingwell. The brother? Josh frowned. He was dead, wasn't he?

"Is something wrong, Mr. Harrington?"

The woman behind the window must have noticed his frown. He gave her a slight smile and shook his head.

The clerk was tall, fiftyish, attractive and trim. Her low-cut V-necked black sleeveless dress was made more noticeable by a long single strand of pearls that dipped into a well-defined cleavage. Her badge read "Penelope Longfellow." She studied Josh's face for several seconds, then said, "Wait a moment. Don't leave."

Josh looked around, then stood still. Why? If he moved, would he set off an alarm?

The clerk appeared from a side door and ran toward him, her arms extended. "Josh Harrington, is this really you?" Her voice scaled upward an octave. "I can't believe this. Don't tell me I'm dreaming. Is it really you?"

She took his hands in hers; an uncomfortable warm sensation crept up the back of his neck. He knew he was blushing as he forced a smile. He looked into her eyes, blinked several times, then prodded his memory. Did he know her? Nothing in his memory conjured up one clue. Who *was* this woman?

"Josh, it's me!" She took a step back and waited, expecting recognition. "It's me, Prissy Schoenkopf, remember? I sat behind you in English 101, downstate, at the U of I."

In the murkiest recesses of his mind, emerged an image of a bucktoothed gal with a vicious case of acne who had openly flirted with him a hundred years ago—well, thirty-five, anyway. Josh examined her face, which had undergone major reconstruction, and a body that showed remarkable femininity. Was it possible that this once unappealing creature had morphed into this flower, this physically appealing woman? How kindly the gods of cosmetology, the wizards of transformation had treated her.

"Yes, yes, of course," he stammered. "How are you, Prissy? Er, I mean Penelope," he said, glancing again at her name plate. "I didn't recognize you with your married name." Truth was, he would not have recognized her under any name.

"Josh, I can't believe it," she repeated, tilting her head and surveying all of him. "You're still a gorgeous hunk. Are you in a hurry?" She looked at her watch. "It's almost lunch time. I'd love to talk with you. You'll share lunch with me, won't you?"

He smiled. "I'd be delighted." He was cautiously curious and did not want to appear impolite.

She hurried back to her post, where she grabbed her purse and a small brown paper bag. "I brought a low-calorie lunch we can share in the atrium cafeteria downstairs."

Josh pictured her having a lunch of wispy celery and carrot sticks sandwiched between Ry-Krisp wafers and said, "Prissy—I mean Penelope—this is a special occasion. Let me buy lunch; save your food for later."

"Why, thank you." She placed her arm in his and held it firmly as they walked to the elevators.

At the cafeteria food line, she walked in front of him with a youthful hip motion, rocking her firm buttocks, the probable result of a rigid exercise program, dieting, and a snug-fitting garment. Her clingy, dark satiny dress seemed a smidgen short and exposed tanned, well-turned calves befitting someone half her age. Several men greeted her with warmth bordering on familiarity. The food line reminded Josh of the army chow line, but then any cafeteria reminded him of an army chow line. He watched as Prissy chose three cooked vegetables and a slice of mock meatloaf.

"I see you eat healthy."

"I try, but every now and then I like a *really* good piece of meat."

When she turned and gave him a sexy smile, he wasn't sure whether she intended a double entendre.

As they approached the checkout stand, Josh chose a slice of apple pie and a cup of coffee.

Prissy looked at his tray. "Shame on you, Josh Harrington. You're a doctor; you should know better than to select all that sugary stuff and hydrogenated fat."

"What makes you think doctors are not capable of stupid decisions? It's their advice and treatment to others they get paid for."

Prissy chose a round table, where she angled the chair and crossed her long legs. The dress hiked to her upper thighs, revealed more than a discreet bit of femininity. Josh purposely concentrated on her face. She asked what he had done since leaving school, and before he could outline the major events that shaped his life, she interrupted to ask whether he was married. When he said he was happily married, she responded with a casual, "Oh." But then, when he stupidly mentioned that Maggie would be out of town for a few days, her eyebrows skyrocketed. "Really?"

Everything about her suggested a sensual presence, from her subtle perfume to the low cut of her dress. Even the string of pearls, which she continually caressed, called attention to her well-defined cleavage. Every time she spoke, she leaned closer, gazed into his eyes, and wet her lips with a provocative roll of the tongue. Thinking he had been sufficiently courteous, Josh made an effort to leave as soon as they finished eating.

As he was rising out of his chair, Prissy grabbed his arm. "Wait, I've hardly told you anything about me."

He looked at his watch to indicate time constraints, but she was unfazed. She pulled him back into his chair and continued her narcissistic monologue, outlining her life after leaving Illinois with a degree in Home Economics. She related how she went west to the land of golden opportunity. However, she said the real purpose in leaving her small hometown in southern Illinois was to change her face and body and to have some degree of anonymity.

"Remember how awful I looked? I had the worst case of adolescent acne, which clung to me into adulthood. I was a real mess. I could never get a man even if I wore a sign advertising free sex."

"Well, I'm sure that's no longer a problem."

She smiled and reached for his hands. "After a year and a half of painful facial resurfacing, having my pearly whites realigned, and ballooning up my boobs, I looked so gorgeous I hardly recognized myself," she laughed. "I joined a gym, got a trainer, firmed up my abs and glutes, and *voilà*! Suddenly, I had everything I wanted—everything, except a good man. You didn't know, of course, but when we were in school I used to fantasize about swooning in your arms and having you make love to me, again and again. God, how I wanted you! And you didn't even notice me. You were completely oblivious."

Josh responded softly and with embarrassment, "No, I guess I never knew."

She squeezed his hands more firmly. "Well, anyway, with my new persona, a beautiful face and rock-solid body, I was on the prowl for Mr. Eligible. He must have been looking for me too, because when we found each other we collided like two speeding locomotives. Pow!" She made a loud clapping sound that startled Josh.

Although eager to leave, Josh was compelled to ask, "Who's the lucky guy?"

"Peter Brickman Longfellow," she said. "That's his honest-to-God name, and he turned out to be just what the doctor ordered—at least for the first few years."

"Do I dare ask what happened?"

She went on to explain that among other things, Peter got tired or couldn't keep up with her pace. Their love fizzled to an indifferent and infrequent routine. Eventually, they became intolerant of each other and developed differences in business philosophies. She grew more aggressive; Pete, after some business reversals, became more cautious and conservative. Their differences led to frequent bickering.

Josh wanted to leave but could not, since Prissy kept her hand on his wrist. He interrupted the uneven flow of conversation. "You're still married?"

"Legally, yes. He'd have to give up too much in a divorce. We share the same house but live in different rooms. Actually, we have a kind of symbiotic relationship. We get together once a week or so to discuss deals of mutual interest, but our meetings are impersonal. I keep the books, and he does the outside work. You met my friend Sherri Aviloh in the property data room. Her husband, Dan, does the same kind of work as Pete. They grew up together in the Coachella Valley. In fact, the four of us have been quite chummy for years."

"What kind of work?"

"They're contractors who build single-family dwellings, condos, office buildings, even hospitals. You must have seen our billboard ads along the I-10. *Longfellow Homes Mean Homes Long on Quality, Long on Value.* Pete is a good builder, and we've done very well financially. We live in an estate in Rancho Mirage on Frank Sinatra Drive. I swear the place is large enough to house half the community, and since we have no kids, we can really rattle around in it. By the way, I noticed on your form that we're practically neighbors—there's only about four miles between us. We could see a lot of each other. You could come over some evenings for a drinky-poo, and skinny-dipping, and whatever." She tilted her head in a coy and cutesy manner.

Josh noted the invitation did not mention his wife, and he did not intend to respond to her proposal. "Incidentally, why do you work here in Riverside? You're about seventy miles or more from home."

"I don't mind the commute." She looked around, then leaned closer and in conspiratorial tones said, "Working here gives me firsthand information on building activity, and I can tell Peter what's hot in the valley. We've made a few good choices with my picks. Now this adobe home you acquired and the land . . ."

Their conversation was interrupted by a woman who approached the table with a message for Prissy. Josh saw the interruption as an opportunity to leave. He stood, but Prissy maintained a hold on his arm and said, "Josh, I can research your plat and give you some helpful information. Why not drop by the house tonight, say about eight? I'll make a copy of the plat, and we can develop some ideas."

Josh must have telegraphed an obvious reluctance, because she added quickly, "Oh, don't worry, you'll be safe. Peter will be home."

Even with that assurance, Josh was uneasy. Yet he really didn't want to travel the 140 miles to and from Riverside. After what she had told him about her marriage, he wondered if her husband really cared at all who called on her. She handed him a business card and wrote her home address and phone number on the back. The front of the card read, "Penelope Longfellow, Certified Agent, Residential and Industrial Properties."

He glanced at the card, then at her. "This certainly looks impressive."

"It's meant to be." She leaned forward and kissed him on the lips. "Tonight at eight, love."

• • •

Traffic on the I-10 eastbound to the desert was relatively light at 1:30 in the afternoon and the familiar music of the 'forties, 'fifties, and 'sixties on KWXY did not intrude on Josh's thinking. Prissy had sure come on strong. Maggie would have had an absolute fit if she knew about her. Josh smiled at the thought. He wondered how she was doing in Chicago and what she would receive from Dr. Simon's will. He hoped there would be at least enough to pay for her traveling expenses.

Approaching the Date Palm Drive off-ramp, he heard the sudden roar of a truck and a burst of Jake brakes. He glanced in the rearview mirror. *Jeezus*, the front end of an enormous Freightliner was bearing down on him! Before he could accelerate away, he was jolted from the rear. What the hell was going on? His speedometer read 75. He looked in the rearview mirror again. The sonofabitch was coming on to him again. Was he drunk, drugged, or dead? But Josh really didn't care; he just wanted out of there. He stomped on the accelerator, sped into the right lane, and raced up the off-ramp. Glancing to the left, he caught a glimpse of the tail end of the mud-spattered white dump truck speeding ahead. It bore the name of a construction company he couldn't read. That bastard could have killed him.

He pulled to the side of the road and got out to assess the damage—a ten-inch-long, two-inch-deep crunch with paint scraped off the rear bumper area. Running his hand over the dent, he estimated the damage at five hundred to a thousand dollars, and he had a five hundred deductible. No witnesses, no license numbers, nothing. *Shit.*

FIVE

Josh heated a small pot of soup and a container of stuffed cabbage Maggie had left for him in the freezer. She had been gone less than two days and he already missed her desperately. Making a mealtime choice could be as frustrating as making a surgical decision. Maggie made it all look so easy. He knew she spoiled him, and he enjoyed being pampered. Although the meal was tasty, his appetite suffered from the almost constant intrusion of Effingwell's death. Damn if the old guy didn't look like the end portrait of Dorian Gray. He berated himself for not thinking that a malignancy could have created such a sudden downward spiral . . . a vicious exotoxin maybe, or even a poison. And what about the responsibilities of the newly acquired property and the freaky freeway misadventure? Was there a connection?

He cleared the table, put the dishes in the dishwasher, and headed for the shower.

Later, while toweling himself, he brought his head closer to the mirror. His hairline had receded and his hair was more gray than brown. A small bulge in his abdomen was less than Adonis-like. Prissy might never have recognized him after thirty-five years if she hadn't seen his name on that request form. For sure, he never would have recognized her. He had lingering doubts about the necessity of seeing her in her home, although she had impressed him as being well informed and enthusiastic about offering help. Besides, there was no harm in reminiscing about their university days.

At 7:45, he drove up Frank Sinatra Drive in the Rancho Mirage community called Mammoth Rock Estates. Once again, he was in awe of the enormous homes, remotely resembling Mediterranean mansions with broad circular driveways, lawns of velvety grass, and base-lighted palm trees.

The entry to the Longfellow estate was recessed and spanned by an archway decorated with river-washed rock that gave it a kind of incongruous western jailhouse look. A mounted porcelain blue-and-white sign to the right of the entry warned of an alarm system. At the entry, two ten-foot, carved wooden doors with heavy wrought-iron hardware suggested origin from an eighteenth-century Mexican church or monastery.

Josh pushed the button beside the door and chimes played the theme to "Roll the Barrel." Not exactly a touch of class, he thought. One of the tall doors opened slowly to reveal Prissy in a sheer black gown that concealed very little. With the light from behind, the gown accentuated her sensuous form. Despite his resolve to remain aloof, Josh stood transfixed. Prissy reached forward and took his hand, pulling him inside. A recording of "I Could Have Danced All Night" emanated from a surround-sound system that bathed the room.

She led him into a great room with two-story cloister-type windows lavishly draped in red velvet and swagged with thick gold-braided ropes.

"This is amazing," he said, gawking. She laughed at his comment, which was neither clever nor humorous.

"Would you like a drink?" She sauntered toward a commercial-sized bar with a dazzling display of liquors and crystal stemware glistening against the backdrop of a floor-to-ceiling mirror.

He shook his head. Getting even the slightest bit tipsy here, he figured, was to be avoided.

"You don't mind if I have one?" She poured Scotch over ice, then moved to an oversized sofa. As she crossed her long legs, a slit in her gown opened predictably to reveal her smooth suntanned thigh. She patted the seat beside her. "Come, sit next to me. Let's talk."

He looked about, hoping her husband would appear and wondering why he had not.

"Uh, Prissy, er, Penelope—which do you prefer?"

"To my intimate friends, I'm Prissy; call me Prissy."

"Where is your husband?" Josh was feeling uneasy. He lowered himself slowly onto the sofa and looked around.

She tilted her head and smiled slyly. "Oh, that big galoot called a half hour ago and said he was tied up with a client for at least another three hours—not unusual for him. I hope that doesn't bother you."

"Prissy, maybe I should leave. Come back when your husband is home."

She laughed and tossed her head, shaking her long, shiny tresses like Angelina Jolie in a seduction scene. She looked at him with a kind of triumphant glow, took another sip of Scotch, and reached for his jacket. "Josh, relax, get comfortable. I promise I won't bite you—unless you'd enjoy that." She laughed again.

He hesitated, thinking that if he removed his jacket he would feel even less comfortable. "I was hoping you and your husband could give me some ideas about developing that land. I'm pressed for time, expecting a call from Maggie." He looked at his watch.

"All right then." In a conciliatory move, she unrolled an enlarged photostat of the plat and flattened it on the cocktail table in front of them. She turned to face him. The upper part of her gown draped loosely, revealing more than he cared to see. The phone rang. She hurried to answer it, listened briefly, then placed her hand over the speaker. "I have to take this call. I'll be just a minute or two."

Josh nodded and walked out of hearing range to view some large paintings on a far wall. Paintings by Lichtenstein, Neiman, and Warhol. He never could appreciate the beauty of cartoon-type characters or a two-dimensional display of stacked cans of Campbell's tomato soup, although he knew the signed and numbered lithographs had to be worth thousands. Neiman's explosive action sport figures were dazzling but dizzying.

Prissy quietly approached from behind, whirled around in front of him, placed her arms around his neck, and gave him a long, sensuous moist kiss.

"Josh, I'm so happy to be with you. It's like a dream come true."

He pulled her arms off his neck and took a step backward. "This isn't right, Prissy."

She continued, unfazed. "You can't escape me now after all these years. Besides, I'm in a position to really help you. If you're thinking seriously about doing anything with the house and the land, I can give you expert advice." She turned her back and took several steps. The scent of her lipstick reached his nostrils. He whipped out his handkerchief and wiped it off his lips. She turned slowly to face him again. "Of course, if you want to sell, I can help you there, too." She returned to him and placed her hands around his waist, making him feel even more awkward. "And, in the future, should you feel lonesome and want company, well, you have my number."

He wondered how many others had her number. Seeking to get back to the reason for his visit, he asked soberly, "What is the exact acreage in my parcel?"

She released him reluctantly and returned to the table to pick up the diagram. "Approximately two hundred and eight acres. At about a half acre per lot, that's a good four hundred building sites. The best lots will sell for anywhere from a half to one million."

"Dollars?" Josh whistled. "That much?"

She laughed. "That much, but it's not all profit." She started to count on her fingers. "You'll have to grade the land, put in streets, curbs, and sidewalks, sewers, water lines, electrical cables, street lamps, landscaping, and much more." She straightened her back, emphasizing her ample bosom. "Remember, if you don't want to fuss with this project, I can handle it completely." Her eyes became heavy-lidded and her smile suggestive "I have the means and equipment to make things happen."

Josh nodded; of that he had no doubt. "I believe you have."

Despite her less-than-subtle advances, she knew enough about land development and construction to impress him. She folded her arms across her chest. "We'll need a geologist's report on the soil and a construction engineer's figure on the number of footings to support . . ."

"Do what?" Much of what she said was beyond Josh's comprehension.

"Here . . ." She handed him a beginner's book on home building. "Study this. Our next meeting should be more productive." She walked him to the door, then suddenly took his face in both her hands and gave him another open-mouth kiss, pressing her torso against him. She took an embroidered initialed handkerchief from her sleeve and wiped the lipstick from his mouth, then placed it on the console in the foyer. Josh stared at it stupidly. Then, a second later, the initials on the handkerchief seemed to jump out at him. They were arranged in a triangular pattern. *dAd?* What in the hell did that mean?

Completely befuddled by the entire meeting, Josh left hurriedly with a barely audible, "Good night."

Once in the car he whipped out his own handkerchief and wiped his mouth again forcefully. He sped off for the emotional safety of his home.

While driving, he thought about Prissy's unabashed flirtations and the sudden windfall of the property and the increased responsibilities it would bring. He decided that he really did not want the involvement of the day-to-day details of developing a large project, of trying to get construction loans, dealing with contractors and subs, things he knew little or nothing about. All of that would take time away from his medical practice that he was reluctant to give. He'd discuss all this with Maggie, whose practical mind would put matters in proper perspective. However, he was not about to tell her of this meeting with Prissy. That would be matrimonial suicide.

* * *

Later that evening, stretched out in his favorite recliner, Josh was turning on the TV to watch the evening news when the doorbell rang. He looked at his watch: 10:05-. Who would be calling at this hour?

He ran his hands through his hair and lowered the leg support on the recliner. He lowered the volume on the TV and walked to the door.

Framed in the doorway like Paul Bunyan stood a hefty six-footer. His warm smile was bordered by a box-trimmed black beard. Worn Levis, work boots, and a flannel shirt with suspenders clothed the man, appearing as if he'd just come off a construction site.

Josh opened the door wider. "Can I help you?"

The man's resonant baritone said, "Dr. Harrington? I'm Peter—Peter Longfellow. Do you have a minute?"

Josh extended his hand. "Certainly. Come in, won't you?"

"No, thanks, Doc. I'm covered with dust and dirt. I'll stay out here if you don't mind. Sorry to be calling at this late hour. Just dropped by to see you after I talked briefly with Prissy this evening. I don't know for sure what all she told you about your property." He stopped, scratching his hairy chin before selecting his next words. "She might have given you good advice. She's smart about business, but you have to be careful when dealing with her."

Josh studied Longfellow's demeanor. "I beg your pardon? I don't understand."

"I wouldn't expect you to. Not right off. You see, there are some problems . . ."

The phone rang. Josh held up his hand. "Would you excuse me for a moment? I'd like to answer this call. It's probably my wife, calling from Chicago. I'll be right back."

Longfellow neither nodded nor shook his head. Josh took it as a sign to go ahead.

He hurried from the door and picked up the phone.

Three minutes later, after being dominated by Maggie's chattering about her wonderful visit and her eagerness to see him, Josh managed to interrupt and explain he was visiting with a building contractor.

By the time he'd returned to the front door, Longfellow had gone. The door was closed. Josh grabbed the knob, swung the door open, and stepped outside, but no one was in sight. The streets were empty except for a pickup in the distance headed for the exit gate.

SIX

Josh awakened early to complete a few chores before Maggie's arrival that evening. The house required a smidgen of order and cleanliness; not that he was slovenly, but some things needed attending, such as the unmade bed, clothes draped on furniture, and a sink with a few dishes. While vacuuming, he heard the phone ring. Before he could answer hello, a woman started speaking.

"Dr. Harrington? This is Sherri Aviloh, from the Riverside County Administration Building. We met the other day in the property tax division."

"Yes. I remember you."

"Someone phoned to inquire about your property in Rancho Mirage. I wondered if you wanted me to give him your phone number, or would you like to phone him yourself?"

"I'll phone him." Josh reached for his pen and a pad. "What's the man's name and number?"

She quickly recited the information.

When he had finished writing, he adjusted the phone closer to his ear. "Thanks, I got it. By the way, how did the man learn about my property?"

No response. "Hello?"

"Oh, sorry." Sherri Aviloh's voice sounded rushed and agitated. "Excuse me, please, I have a call waiting."

A click was followed by a cutoff signal.

Josh looked at the phone before replacing it on the cradle. He picked up the pad and studied the number. He recognized the prefix as a New York City area code.

Curious, he punched in the number and immediately got a busy signal.

• • •

Palm Springs International Airport was roughly forty minutes by car from home. Josh allowed himself an hour, including ten minutes to pick up a bouquet of roses and ten minutes to find a parking space. He placed the roses on the passenger seat so when Maggie entered the car he would hear her familiar squeal of delight, which always preceded a hug and a kiss.

Inside the terminal, Josh checked the overhead monitor for flight arrivals. Maggie's plane was on time. He paced the lobby for fifteen minutes until she came rushing though the exit gate into his arms, kissing him repeatedly. "Oh, Josh, I missed you so."

"It's good having you back, baby." Josh took her coat and overnight bag as they walked to the baggage area. "Tell me everything that happened. Who was there, and who got what?"

"I'll tell you everything, but you've got to be patient. There's so much to tell."

"Fine, start from the beginning." He pulled her wheeled luggage off the carousel, and they walked toward the parking lot.

Maggie wasted little time sharing the details. She began by telling what occurred when she arrived at O'Hare. She was met by a uniformed chauffeur who held a sign with her name. That made her feel quite important. She described how he escorted her to the baggage area, then how they passed the crowds waiting for taxies. He led her to the biggest, longest, plushiest Rolls-Royce she had ever seen. The passenger compartment smelled of leather permeated with colognes and perfumes. She told of a disappearing bar and anchored crystal glasses. Even a mini fridge with soft drinks that unfolded out of the back of the front seat. A large bolstered armrest divided the rear seat. The driver's compartment was separated by a glass partition, and a folded mouton robe lay on the seat beside her.

Maggie continued her recall with amazing minutia, describing her arrival at the estate in Kenilworth. She told her how Suzanne had rushed to greet her and how her husband, Carlos Grandee, a slender handsome man, kissed her hand in an oh-so-gallant gesture. He wanted to know all about us, where we lived, and whether we enjoyed living in the desert. He explained that his corporation was developing properties on El Paseo in Palm Desert. Properties that were to be more costly and opulent than those on Rodeo Drive in Beverly Hills. The principal part of their many-faceted corporation runs an airplane parts factory south of Los Angeles in El Segundo. He expressed a desire to be close to the new project on El Paseo. Besides, he said he would enjoy being in the desert during the winter.

"But getting back to their house, Josh—did I say house? That place was a fairy-tale mansion—more like a palace." Maggie placed her hands over her heart and closed her eyes in rhapsodic exclamation. "Oh, Josh, I wish you could have seen it. The foyer alone was the size of our entire home, marble floors with Persian rugs, Aubusson tapestries, Chinese porcelain vases from some Ming dynasty, taller than me, in separate alcoves, a crystal chandelier hanging from a two-story ceiling and . . ."

"Whoa, slow down." Josh smiled. "Tell me what happened at the attorney's office. Are we multimillionaires? What did the good doctor leave you?" Josh opened Maggie's door.

"Oooh, roses!"

As Josh had predicted, Maggie squealed when she saw the bouquet. She spun around and gave him a big kiss. "Oh, Josh, you're so sweet." Then she kissed him again.

The minute he was in the driver's seat, he tapped the dashboard clock. "Tell me what the doctor left you. I know you too well. You're incapable of keeping a secret for more than five minutes." He tapped the clock again. "See? You're overdue."

"Maybe I am." She tilted her head back and gave him that little-girl smile he loved so much. "What will you give me to know right now?"

"What would you like?"

"Well, you've already given me roses, so I can't ask for flowers. How about a restful evening, just the two of us? You can pour my favorite wine and tell me how much you love me."

"Not until you tell me how much the doctor left you."

"I'll give you three guesses. If your guesses are too high or too low, you'll have to do my bidding."

"For instance?"

"Mm-m-m, let's see . . . a complete body massage."

"And if I guess correctly?"

"I'll be your slave and do your bidding, for the evening."

It was a win-win situation, he thought. "All right, my first guess is ten thousand dollars."

Maggie laughed and elbowed him. "Oh, Josh, you're such a piker."

"Twenty-five thousand?"

"Nope." Maggie sat back with a smug smile. "I can just feel my body responding to your strong hands."

"Just a minute! I get one more guess." Glancing at Maggie, he gave a triumphant yell, "One hundred thousand dollars!"

"Get the body oil ready, big boy. You're not even close. I want you to massage my back and legs till I tingle."

"I'll massage you until you beg for mercy. Now tell me, how much?"

Hesitating, she inverted her lips to indicate complete silence—which piqued him further. Then she asked, "How does one million dollars sound?"

Josh said nothing. The full impact of what she'd said did not fully register for several seconds.

"Maggie, are you sure? That's like all the money in the world."

Maggie tossed her head back, threw her arms outward, and in a glory-be-to-God gesture sang, "That's right, we're now bloody millionaires."

Josh gave her a faint smile and started up the car.

Maggie looked at him quizzically. "I thought you'd be more excited. What is it? Are there any new developments in Effingwell's death and the land project?"

He backed out of the parking space. "Quite a bit has happened. I'll tell you all about that at home."

"Oh, Josh, this is all so exciting, I'm ready to jump out of my skin."

"I'll be grateful just to have you jump out of your clothes."

Maggie laughed. "You're so impractical. I'm talking *mucho dinero,* and all you can think of is making love. How did I get so lucky?"

*   *   *

The second Maggie walked through the door of their bedroom she whirled around like a child at play. "I love our little home. It's so cozy and warm. It even smells good."

"Glad to hear it."

As soon as Josh set her suitcase on the floor, she rushed at him with a force that squeezed the breath out of him. She shoved him onto the bed and jumped on top of him, rubbing her nose against his. "Did someone try to steal you while I was gone? Now tell the truth."

"How could anyone possibly get between us?" Josh had instant remorse about not mentioning his visit with Prissy, but there was no way he was going to recant . . . not now.

"They'd better not!" Maggie unbuttoned his polo shirt and had just released his belt buckle when the phone rang. "Damn, isn't that my luck? I no sooner get you in bed and the phone rings. All right, all right, hold your horses, I'm coming." She rolled over and pushed the speaker button on the phone. "Harrington residence."

"Mrs. Harrington, this is Millie at the doctors' exchange. There's a woman on the line who insists on talking to the doctor; she says it's urgent."

"Put the call through, and I'll give the phone to my husband."

Josh scooted closer to the phone. "Hello?"

"Hi, handsome. This is Prissy. So good talking to you again." In a smoky voice, her words slithered provocatively over the speaker phone.

Josh inwardly groaned and shook his head as though to negate the conversation that Maggie was also hearing.

Prissy continued, "Sherri Aviloh told me someone from New York is interested in your property. Don't be hasty about selling, darling. I can meet or beat any offer. Just give me an opportunity to bid. Besides, I'm sure I'm better looking. By the way, I so enjoyed being with you last night. I look forward to seeing you when we can spend more time together."

"Thanks." Josh kept his voice neutral. "I'll keep that in mind." He tapped the speaker phone's off button and straightened.

Maggie bolted upright as well. "Who in *the* hell is Prissy?"

Josh sighed, trying hard not to be frustrated and defensive at the same time. "Take it easy, Honey. Prissy is a woman who works at the Riverside County Administration."

Maggie's voice lifted an octave. "It sounds more like she's some love-struck floozy who's trying to put the make on you . . ."

"Maggie, calm down. Before you get too upset, I should also tell you she's someone I went to college with. We graduated from Illinois before I went to medical school. Her name at that time was Penelope Schoenkopf. I hadn't seen her for all these years until I ran into her at the administrative office at Riverside. She and her husband, Peter Longfellow, live in Rancho Mirage. He's a general contractor. Both are knowledgeable about developing properties in this area and could help us.

"Sounds as though she's already helped herself to you."

Maggie jumped off the bed and started to unpack her suitcase, throwing her garments haphazardly on a chair. "Sometimes I think you may be just a bit too damn trusting. Why would she call you at this hour, and what the hell happened last night?" Without waiting for an answer, she added, "Is she pretty?"

"Well, she's not unattractive."

"Josh, you're so gullible. Do me a favor, don't get involved with her. Talk with the husband if you need to, but stay away from her. You say they live close by?"

"About four miles from here."

"Why was it necessary for you to go to her home?"

Josh knew his response was going to evoke a fresh firestorm, but he was committed to honesty. "She had an official plat, and I went hoping to pick up some pointers on the development of our land."

She sighed. "Was her husband there?"

"He was supposed to be . . ." He trailed away when he noticed Maggie starting to bristle.

Maggie squared her shoulders and stammered, "Dammit, did she . . .?"

"Nothing happened, Maggie, I swear it." Josh felt as if he kept digging a deeper hole with every answer.

Maggie refused to hear any more. She stormed out of the bedroom and went into the den. Slamming the door behind her, she plopped on the sofa, folded her arms, and sighed deeply. Her anger mounted when she thought of that woman's voice on the phone, that bitchy tart who flirted so openly. The nerve of her! Eventually her fiery temper subsided; she knew Josh was too decent to carry on with another woman—she hoped.

Feeling a bit more in control, Maggie walked to the bookshelf and saw the large *Illio*, the yearbook for Illinois graduates of 1974, the year of Josh's graduation as well as that hussy's. Maggie remembered her first name, Penelope, but had forgotten the entire last name. The first part of her last name sounded like "Shane." She would go through all the female graduates whose names started with S. Her finger ran down the double column. "Schoene, Schoenbroeck, Schoenkopf." *Schoenkopf, that's it.* Maggie brought the book to the desk and placed it under the lamp.

She studied the picture of the home economics graduate. This rather unattractive woman with her chipmunk cheeks, protruding upper teeth, and rather prominent nose could not possibly pose a threat. Maggie was convinced that the woman's appearance would not have improved after thirty-some years. Perhaps Josh was just being kind when he said she was not unattractive.

Meanwhile, getting into his pajamas, Josh wondered if he should attempt to appease Maggie, but then thought he had better give her some space and time to cool down. He lay on his side of the bed and opened a worn edition of *The Adventures of Sherlock Holmes*, which he kept on his nightstand. Of all the mythical sleuths, Holmes still fascinated him and compelled repeated readings. The author, Sir Arthur Conan Doyle, a doctor himself, commanded Josh's respect because he endowed his hero with uncanny intuitive powers and deductive reasoning. Doyle's mentor, Dr. Boyd, was the author of an old pathology reference book Josh had used as a medical student. So there existed a kind of vicarious bond between Holmes, his author, and Josh. Sometime later with the book upon his chest, and his mind slipping into sleep, Josh felt the gentle lifting of the book, a rearrangement of the blanket, and a light kiss on his forehead.

*   *   *

Maggie had not yet adjusted to the two-hour time difference between Chicago and the desert. At 5:30 a.m., she leaped out of bed, ran to the kitchen to prepare breakfast, and then brought Josh a cup of steaming coffee. He lay in bed, eyes blinking until he could keep them open long enough to focus on the smiling Maggie standing beside him.

"Good morning, Doctor Millionaire, or should I say Doctor Don Juan?" she asked with just a hint of sarcasm.

Sitting on the edge of the bed and sipping his coffee, he thought how fortunate he was to have this lovely creature looking after him, and that an occasional note of sarcasm was quite tolerable.

Maggie suddenly put her face close to his, nearly jostling his coffee mug. "Darling, I'm sorry I blew up last night, but I can't understand in heaven's name how you managed to get involved with this woman! Not that I blame her altogether."

He placed the coffee mug on the nightstand, and from his sitting position on the edge of the bed, he embraced Maggie standing next to him. He nuzzled her breasts, covered by her silky nightgown. She took his head in her hands, then bent over and kissed the top of his head.

"You're a wonderful but naughty boy, and fortunately for you, I'm hopelessly in love with you."

He slid out of bed, pulled her toward him, and held her closely. With a mischievous smile, Maggie looked up at him. "Do you think you're entitled to take liberties just because you're a millionaire?" Then she looked down. "Let's save that hungry tiger for tonight when we have more time." She kissed him and pushed herself away. "You have hospital rounds and I have chores. Come, let's have breakfast and discuss our big money plans." With that said, she slipped into her robe and handed him his own.

The kitchen was transformed by her mere presence. Place mats, dinnerware, napkins, goblets of orange juice, toast with three types of spread. God, how he'd missed all that when she had gone, even for a few days. His appetite had been stimulated by their teasing sexual activity, but that aside, the food just looked and tasted better in her company.

* * *

Both had finished dressing and Maggie was brushing her hair when the door chimes sounded. Josh looked at his watch. "Eight o'clock, who's calling at this hour?"

Opening the door, Josh saw a ghostly specter in an ill-fitting black suit, his features partially obscured by the glaring sun behind, a vaguely familiar, disturbing figure. As the stranger stepped forward, his face became more distinct. He attempted a smile on a face unaccustomed to smiling. His sallow complexion, his sunken eye sockets overlaid by bushy brows, and his deeply hollowed cheeks gave him a kind of beardless Lincolnesque visage, mournful but without compassion.

Josh now recognized him. "Mannheim?"

"Well, Doc, we meet again." A deep monotone preceded a bony handshake. Following him was a shorter, heavier man.

Maggie walked up and stopped beside Josh. Seeing the taller man, she gasped and put her hand to her mouth.

Josh squinted. "Is that really you?" All the years he'd know the man, Josh had never been quite sure about Mannheim's mood. His expression was usually impassive or suggested a scowl but certainly never a smile. He seldom engaged in trivial or humorous conversation. Word at headquarters was that Mannheim would ticket his own mother for spitting on the sidewalk.

The relationship between Josh and Mannheim was tenuous at best. They had cooperated tangentially on two prior cases, before Mannheim's abortive retirement. They respected one another, but not to the extent of having a warm or comradely relationship. Mannheim suspected the doctor of having withheld information on previous cases, and Josh felt that Mannheim was not always forthcoming.

Josh stepped back and opened the front door wider. "What in the hell are you doing here? I thought you retired to Montana."

Mannheim walked farther into the room and directed his remarks to the wall. "I thought I would, until I froze my ass up there." Seeing that Maggie followed him, he stopped and said, "Sorry, ma'am." A slight crack at the corners of his mouth lifted. "Have you ever tried living in a deep freeze for six months?"

She responded only with a shake of her head, then watched as the other man entered.

The thin man made a quarter turn. "This here is Officer Harry Todd, my associate. He's been recently reassigned out of Riverside."

Todd, a man in his forties, rosy-cheeked, almost cherubic, smiled and extended his hand. "Ma-am."

After Josh shook Todd's hand, he turned his attention to the gaunt figure. "I take it, coming here isn't exactly a social call, is it, Mannheim?"

The smile the detective attempted became more like a sinister sneer. The action deepened the lines around his nose and mouth as he said, "You got that right." He took a small spiral notebook from the inner pocket of his jacket and flipped several pages. "You knew a Peter Longfellow?"

Knew? Josh stiffened. "Barely; I met him briefly two nights ago. Why?"

"Mrs. Longfellow told us her husband left the house after they argued and said he was going to your place to talk with you. What did you two talk about?"

Something about Mannheim's manner irritated him. "He came to the house, yes. But never came inside; he remained in the doorway. Why?"

Still looking at his notebook, Mannheim said, deadpan, "He was murdered sometime last night or early this morning."

Josh felt the blood rush from his face and reflexively reached for the back of a nearby chair. "Murdered? How?"

"The guy was found hanging by the neck in his home. Bludgeoned, too."

"What? Why?" Josh stared at the impassive Mannheim. "And what the hell does this have to do with me?"

"Where were you last night, Doc?" Mannheim didn't lift his eyes from his notebook. "From ten o'clock on?"

"Home with my wife." Josh turned to look at Maggie, who also appeared stunned. He walked over to her and gathered her hands into his. "Isn't that right, Maggie?"

"Yes." She looked over Josh's shoulder toward Mannheim. "Yes, that's right."

This time Mannheim did look up. "Is there anyone, besides your wife, who can vouch for you?"

The shock of hearing about Longfellow's death instantly disappeared. In its place anger surfaced. "C'mon Mannheim, cut the bullshit. You know if I said I was here, and my wife backs me up, then I was here."

"Maybe."

"Dammit! You know damned well I had nothing to do with the man's death."

The officer remained impassive. "You said you were with the deceased two nights ago, right?"

Maggie turned toward Josh. "What is this all about?"

"I have no idea."

Mannheim pointed his pen at Josh. "What did the two of you talk about, you and Peter Longfellow?"

"Nothing. Nothing at all. Just as he arrived, the phone rang. I told him I needed to answer it and would be right back. I knew it was Maggie, calling from Chicago. When I returned, Longfellow was gone. That's it. Nothing more."

"And what did you two discuss?" Mannheim persisted.

"Like I said, we had no time for conversation. Longfellow started to say something about not getting involved with his wife when the phone rang."

Mannheim's deep-set, brooding eyes continued to stare at Josh. "Uh-huh."

Josh's patience was almost gone. "Did you ask Mrs. Longfellow what she and her husband argued about?"

Mannheim snorted and shook his head. "I'll ask the questions, if you don't mind."

"Fine. Ask them. Only I won't be here." Josh looked at his watch. "I've got surgery at nine thirty."

Mannheim said nothing.

"I hope you're not trying to involve me in this murder." Josh deepened his voice, hoping it would get through to the detective. "You'll be wasting your time and mine."

He started for the foyer, drawing Maggie with him. When he reached it, he gave her a kiss on the cheek. "Don't let this upset you, dear. There's no way I'm involved in this."

Mannheim was suddenly beside them. "Can you tell me, Doc, what you and Mrs. Longfellow talked about when you saw her two nights ago?"

Josh grabbed his jacket and slipped into it. His jaw tightened and he gave the man an angry glance.

"Right." Mannheim flipped his notebook shut. "We can talk about this later."

Josh nodded and headed toward the kitchen, which led to the garage. "I'm sure we will. You'll see to that."

SEVEN

Mannheim and Todd left through the front door while Josh entered the garage and got into the car. When the garage door opened, Josh did a double-take. The two detectives stood in the driveway as though defying him to move. Mannheim, his shoulders slumped, his head bobbing slowly, entered the garage and came to Josh's side of the car. Reluctantly, Josh lowered his window.

"Just a couple more questions, Doc. What time did you leave Mrs. Longfellow's the other night?"

Josh sighed. "About nine thirty." He started the engine.

"What happened that night?" He looked around, then, in a near-whisper, asked, "Did her old man walk in while you two were at it?"

"Of course not! You're disgusting and you're really starting to piss me off." With the car in neutral, Josh stepped on the accelerator and raced the engine to show his impatience. "I saw Prissy—that is, Mrs. Longfellow—about developing a parcel of land; that's all."

Mannheim arched his brows. "Prissy, did you say, Prissy?"

Dammit, of all times for a slip of the tongue. "Yeah, that's her nickname."

"I see." Mannheim's eyes expressed all the cynicism of a cop who had spent a professional lifetime listening to a thousand stupid comments. "Was her husband around?"

"No."

"No?"

"That's what I said, no. Now, if you'll excuse me . . ." Josh closed the window and backed the car slowly. When he was sure both men were out of the garage and clear of the vehicle, he shut the garage door by remote and turned onto the street. In the rearview mirror he saw the two of them standing in the driveway, watching him drive away.

* * *

With his shoulder Josh shoved open the door to the surgeons' locker room, simultaneously undoing his tie. A bank of lockers lined all four walls. Long wooden benches in front of them served the doctors for changing clothes and putting on shoe covers.

Dr. Paul Schultz, who was to assist Josh, was already in his surgical scrubs. His usual grace and unhurried manner had changed to a slight edginess. Seeing Josh, Paul walked toward him. He lifted his index finger to his lips and tilted his head toward the L-shaped extension, which was cut off from their view.

"Who's there, a process server?" Josh whispered, trying to sound jocular.

One of Paul's eyebrows lifted. He cupped his hand near Josh's ear and said in a soft voice. "Not sure. Some dude asked for you. He got through security, so he must have official status."

Josh thought of Mannheim and undressed quickly. "Great! Just what I need before surgery. A subpoena."

"A what?" Paul waved a hand. "Never mind."

Just then, turning the corner and walking toward Josh was a handsome black man, six-one or two, about thirty-five, dressed in a dark suit. Seeing Josh, he pulled his credentials from a leather folder and flashed them. Then he handed Josh a professional card. "Dr. Harrington? John Sangamon, from the Federal Radiation Protection Agency, in from Phoenix. Do you have a few minutes?"

This time it was Josh's eyebrows that rose. His pulse rate quickened and he started dressing into his scrubs. "I'm due in the OR, so I won't have much time. What can I do for you?"

"I need information about your former patient, Mr. Chesley Effingwell."

Paul nodded his head toward the scrub room door. "I'll leave you fellas to talk privately while I scrub up."

Josh had anticipated a meeting of this kind. But it surprised him when, finally being confronted by an agent, it caused him some anxiety. Josh quickly outlined Effingwell's medical history and physical findings.

While he continued to talk, Sangamon nodded as though he had already read the records and was merely verifying statements. His brow furrowed when Josh finished. "Were you aware that he was poisoned with a radioactive isotope?"

"Not until the coroner mentioned something to that effect the other day." Josh tucked the hem of his surgical top into his pants and tightened the string around his waist. "I expected you fellas to be coming around. What took you so long?"

"We needed a few days to process information. We believe your patient died from a radioactive substance, specifically, polonium-210."

Josh eased himself slowly onto the bench. The air around him suddenly turned chilly, and not from the air conditioner alone. Goose flesh prickled the skin on his arms. "Polonium-210? Why would anyone want to kill him? This was an old guy, disabled and in poor health. He didn't have much more time to live as it was."

Sangamon placed his briefcase onto the bench, opened it, and removed a black spiral notebook. "We were hoping you might be able to provide some clues. Was there anything unusual in the patient's history? Did he mention any associations with foreign governments or agents? Do you know if he owned property, stocks, bonds, paintings?"

Josh started to mention the property in Rancho Mirage deeded to him when a nurse's head appeared around the scrub room door.

"Dr. Harrington, your patient is in room three. Will you start scrubbing, please?"

Josh nodded. "All right. I'll be there." He turned toward the agent. "I'm sorry, Mr. Sangamon. But I really do need to go."

"I understand, sir." Sangamon snapped his case shut. "If you think of anything that might be helpful, will you call me?"

"Of course." Josh headed for the scrub room, then stopped. "How could he have gotten the polonium-210 in his system, do you know?"

"Probably in his food or drink."

That shocked Josh. While Effingwell had been in the hospital, he'd personally monitored what the old man ate. "Where, when, and by whom?"

Sangamon shook his head and looked Josh directly in the eyes. "The FBI, CIA, National Security, and about two dozen other agencies would like those answers also."

* * *

While Paul and Josh scrubbed, Josh explained briefly the events preceding Effingwell's death and the shocking diagnosis of toxic radioactive poisoning.

Paul pulled his soapy hands away from the faucet and looked at Josh wide-eyed over his mask. "Jesus, that sounds like science fiction. Who made that hot-shot diagnosis, and how in the hell did they do it?"

"With a Geiger counter, I guess," Josh said facetiously. "I'll get more details later. Come on. Let's get our patient."

One hour and twenty-two minutes later, Paul put in the last metal clip, reached for the final dressing, and glanced up at the OR wall clock. "Skin to skin. Not bad. Not bad at all." He glanced at Josh, who stood across the operating table watching him do the final wrap-up. "You can do surgery on my hip anytime. Man, you are good."

Josh chuckled. "You didn't do so bad yourself. The feeling's mutual."

While the patient was transferred to a gurney, both doctors removed their surgical gloves and followed the gurney into the recovery room. Josh wrote post-op orders at the nurses' desk and Paul leaned against the desk. "When I called the other day, Maggie told me you have a parcel of land you're going to develop in Rancho Mirage."

"We're thinking about it."

"Do you have someone in mind to help you?"

"I've been talking to a Mrs. Longfellow . . ."

Paul jerked his head back, surprised. "Prissy Longfellow? Her husband Peter was just murdered. It's been all over the morning papers and on TV."

Josh stopped writing. "You knew the Longfellows?"

Paul winked. "I knew Prissy pretty damn well."

"What's that supposed to mean?"

Paul went to the gurney to check the patient's foot pulses. "Before either of us got married we had a thing going." He grinned. "Old buddy, let me tell you this, you'd better be careful. Any guy around her will wish he had an extra pair of gonads to satisfy that vixen. She'll have you gasping for air and smother you in her boobs, then squeeze you so hard you'll need a resuscitator."

Josh shook his head and continued to write orders. "My, my such eloquent medical terminology."

"I'm not joking. Take my advice, when ever you're around her, put your libido in low gear. And keep Maggie away from her. Prissy is a sick gal—suffers from sex addiction."

Josh frowned. "Is that a verifiable diagnosis?"

"It's my clinical assessment based on personal experience."

Josh finished the last post-op order and slid the chart away from him. "You need not expand on how much personal experience, thank you very much." He looked up at his friend. "How well did you know her husband?"

"Seemed decent enough, but I really didn't know him all that well. Can't imagine Prissy keeping any man for long. Hell, no man could keep up with her damned marathon of orgiastic demands."

"That bad, huh?"

"That bad. Look, I'm going to the locker room. What are you going to do?"

Josh looked at his patient. "I think I'll stick around here for a while and monitor her post-op condition."

Fifteen minutes later, Josh removed his surgical cap and gown and walked into the surgeons' locker room. Standing directly in front of him, like a dark inquisitor, was Agent John Sangamon.

"Are you still here?" Josh stepped around him. "I thought you left long ago."

Sangamon turned and followed him to his locker. "It's a long way back to Phoenix and I have more questions regarding Effingwell. Can you spare those few minutes now?"

"Sure. I'll help any way I can."

"Good." Sangamon again set his briefcase on the bench. "I think I'll be able to understand the radiation poisoning better if I talk to you personally. We've already made arrangements to have all personnel tested who came in contact with Effingwell."

"I can understand that."

The agent opened his notepad. "Did Effingwell have any medical findings that would have suggested radiation poisoning?"

"No." Josh removed his scrub suit and threw the top and pants in a hamper. He walked to a basin and splashed his face. When he straightened and looked into the mirror, he found Sangamon standing directly behind him. "Radiation poisoning isn't an everyday occurrence, if you know what I mean. It's not something one would think of immediately."

"Yes, I understand."

Josh reached for a towel and dried his face. "Effingwell was anemic and going downhill rapidly. I have to admit that concerned me. I talked with the internist. Like me he was unhappy with the blood tests, but neither one of us ever thought about radiation poisoning." He looked at the agent. "In fact, to my knowledge and reading, I've never come across a case where a patient has been intentionally poisoned with radiation. At least not in the United States." Josh tossed the damp towel into another hamper. Effingwell's case was probably causing a furor in Washington and a near calamity in international diplomacy.

Sangamon referred to his notes again. "If I mispronounce some of these terms, doctor, please bear with me: The corpse displayed cerebral edema, inflammation of the bowel, swelling of the liver, kidneys, and spleen, the bone marrow was aplastic, and a blood smear revealed a pancytopenia." Sangamon looked at Josh. "What is that, pan-cyto-penia?"

"That's a picture of severe anemia, meaning all blood elements are depressed."

"You said you weren't aware of anyone dying of radiation poisoning in the United States. Are you aware of the former KGB spy who was poisoned and died in a London hospital?"

Josh nodded. "I've read the newspaper and magazine accounts."

"Then you know about as much as we do." Sangamon stepped closer to Josh, his eyes darting about as if to insure confidentiality. "There's been an effort here to keep it hush-hush. Everyone who handled the corpse, or learned of the diagnosis, has been sworn to secrecy by the hospital administration. The only reason you weren't called in was that I had been ordered to speak with you personally. As far as I know, everyone has cooperated."

"I'm not surprised. The staff here is very loyal to the hospital." Josh headed for his locker.

Sangamon followed. "We can't have pandemonium if the news escapes."

"Certainly not."

"Our department is one of several conducting a full-scale investigation. I understand you have already been examined for radiation contamination."

"Yes and no measurable radiation was found when the nuclear radiation department tested me." He knotted his tie and turned to face Sangamon. "I still would like to know who did this and why."

Sangamon shrugged.

Josh got the message. When the man had no answer, or preferred not to answer, he would just shrug.

Grabbing his comb, Josh returned to the mirror and began combing his hair.

Again Sangamon followed. "Dr. Harrington, I hope you don't mind my asking, but did Effingwell pay or promise you anything for medical services?"

Josh didn't stop his combing. Aha, was this the *ringer*, the *nugget*, the big *question*? The reason why Sangamon waited almost two hours to ask it?

He had no reason to hide the truth. Besides, if Sangamon had poked his nose around the hospital, he probably had already learned of Effingwell's generous gift in the form of the deed.

Josh lowered the comb. "Yes, Effingwell signed over a deed to some property to me and insisted upon my taking the quit claim just before his death. I tried to talk him out of it, but the man wouldn't hear of anything else. Nurse Dudley was in the room and witnessed the signatures. You can speak with her if you wish."

"I see. Thank you." Sangamon scribbled something in his notepad.

"Agent Sangamon, I'm curious, how does this concern you or your organization?"

"We need to explore every possible source of that radioactive poison. Asking tangential questions sometimes yields a clue. This kind of crime is unprecedented, at least in this country, and concerns us greatly."

Josh nodded but withheld comment.

"If the only thing of value Effingwell owned was the property he gave you, then his death—more properly, his murder—may possibly be tied in with that land."

Josh frowned. "Effingwell said he had no heirs."

"Things of value don't exist in a vacuum very long, Dr. Harrington." Sangamon smiled. "The State, for one, sees to that."

At that moment, a nurse opened the door partially and called Josh's name.

"Yes?"

"The administrator, Mr. Yamamoto, asked if he could see you in his office for a few minutes."

"I'm sorry. I'll have to go. When the hospital's administrator calls, I'm told one must go. If I happen to remember anything more, Mr. Sangamon, I'll call you."

"Sounds good." Sangamon picked up his briefcase and walked out of the room.

Josh looked in the mirror, patted his hair, then straightened his tie. Going to Yamamoto's office was a new experience. He had never had occasion to talk with him, although he had heard him address the staff with pep talks and the customary appeals for donations to the hospital foundation.

Gerrick Yamamoto, in his mid-fifties, five foot nine, had a rugged face lined with concern, abundant steel-gray hair, and horn-rimmed glasses. When Josh entered his office, Yamamoto stood ramrod straight behind his desk and extended his hand. His weary smile indicated a troubled preoccupation.

"Please have a seat." When they both sat, he said, "Thank you for coming in." He hesitated, then brought his folded hands forward onto his desk. "I think you know why I wanted this talk. It's about your patient, Effingwell, who died of radioactive poisoning. This is a matter of grave concern to all of us. Let me say at the onset that there is no criticism from the medical review board about your management of the case. Your reputation has never been challenged. I need your cooperation in a related matter, one which may trouble you, at least initially."

Josh listened and remained quiet.

Yamamoto said the hospital had managed to keep a lid on the calamity to prevent it from becoming a community catastrophe, and not until there were definitive answers would the public be informed. Even then, there might be an attempt by the State Department to limit disclosure. "We would prefer that you say nothing to anyone about the cause of death until we advise you otherwise." Yamamoto leaned back in his chair, tilted his head, and looked at Josh quizzically. "Do you have any notion why Effingwell was murdered, and by whom? Did he have any connections with the Russian Mafia or KGB?"

Josh shook his head. "I have no knowledge of that."

Yamamoto paused. "I see. Why do you think Effingwell gave you that property?" Before Josh could answer, Yamamoto added, "That's quite a valuable parcel."

Josh's eyes locked on to Yamamoto's. "How did you learn about that? And what concern is that of yours?"

Yamamoto closed his eyes and nodded slowly with clasped hands on his abdomen. "This hospital is a small community and magnanimous gifts don't go unnoticed, especially those given to doctors by their patients."

Only Nurse Dudley knew about the will, as far as Josh was aware. Heat rose up the back of his neck, along with a pulsing knot forming in the middle of his forehead. He slid forward in his chair and leaned on Yamamoto's desk. "Let's set the record straight. I didn't want any gifts from Effingwell. He insisted that I take the property even after I objected." With nothing more to add, he stared stonily at the administrator.

Yamamoto smiled tightly. "Don't take offense. You must understand that people might misconstrue the gift as a sort of, well, an offer made when your patient was not capable of thinking clearly. He had, after all, been medicated for pain, which might have altered his thinking. We wouldn't want people thinking that any of our staff preyed upon—"

Josh stood, the muscles in his jaw tightening. "I find this conversation insulting and demeaning. You have no right—"

Yamamoto held up a hand to stop him. "No one is accusing you of any wrongdoing. If I've offended you, I did so unwittingly. Hear me out." He stood and walked toward a walnut credenza with a display of several golf trophies. On the wall, a picture of three past presidents—Bush, Ford, and Clinton—in golf attire smiled agreeably. An autographed picture of Arnold Palmer shaking hands with Yamamoto was set aside, as in a place of honor. He opened the doors of the credenza, looked at Josh, and asked, "Drink?"

"No, thank you."

Yamamoto placed ice cubes in a tumbler and poured a liberal amount of Crown Royal. He walked toward the window, swirled his tumbler, and spoke, his back to Josh. "I come from a family that is keenly aware of the virtual theft of valuable property. My radar remains sensitive to such matters, even to this day."

Josh made no comment.

Yamamoto returned to his commodious chair. "My grandparents and parents lost a large tract of farmland in the Monterey area at the start of World War Two when the government, in its infinite wisdom, practically confiscated land belonging to Japanese farmers." Yamamoto stared at Josh and his voice rose. "Japanese farmers who were *American citizens*."

Finally it dawned on Josh that Yamamoto had his own demons. "I'm aware of that injustice. It was deplorable."

Though Josh tried to sound diplomatic, the administrator's face darkened. "You can't begin to know about that kind of injustice." An awkward silence followed before he resumed a more moderate but patronizing tone. "So, valuable parcels of land that trade hands without reasonable compensation are of special interest to me and make me wonder what, if any, foul play has transpired."

Josh's anger simmered again when Yamamoto used the term "foul play." "Let me remind you again, there's been no foul play. That piece of land is really none of your goddamn business." Josh knew he was being irrational, but the way the administrator acted made him angry. He'd think long and hard about donating the land to the hospital. Maybe later once he'd cooled off, but now, no way.

Again, Yamamoto put up his hand to quell Josh's agitation. "Forget what I said; I was out of line. My primary concern is that no mention be made of the radioactive poisoning death until we get clearance from the authorities. Of course, the safety and protection of our patients and personnel from further exposure . . ." He trailed off. "Well, you understand." The administrator smiled perfunctorily and extended his hand as though he intended no ill-will.

Josh hesitated, then reached out to shake his hand. Just as their fingers touched, Josh's cell phone rang.

"Excuse me. I'll take this outside your office."

Though his anger was not entirely mollified by Yamamoto's apology, he smiled when he saw who was calling. "Hello, Maggie, what's up?"

EIGHT

By the time Josh finished talking with Maggie, he had arrived at his office.

The instant he walked in the door, his receptionist informed him that Detective Mannheim and Detective Todd were sitting in his consultation room.

Sighing, Josh headed there and opened the door. Mannheim stood by Josh's desk and was finger-tapping a slow, rhythmic beat on its surface. Todd lounged in one of the chairs.

Josh forced himself to present a happy demeanor. "Fellas, to what do I owe this pleasure? Are you here to tell me that Longfellow's murder has been solved, and you owe me an apology?"

Mannheim turned slowly to look at him. "Not quite, Doc, we just want to go over some of the details of your meeting with Peter Longfellow and your relationship with Mrs. Longfellow."

Josh looked back down the hall, hoping that Maggie was still in the outer office. He stepped inside and shut the door behind him. Pointing at Mannheim, he said in a deliberate and distinct voice, "Listen to me clearly, I had *no relationship* with Mrs. Longfellow—other than a short business meeting. Why is it so hard for you to understand? As for Mr. Longfellow, I talked with him for perhaps a minute. I've never seen or met him before that time. Nor did I see him again. Is that clear? What must I do to convince you guys, submit to a polygraph?"

"Easy, Doc. Don't get your dander up. It's just that we think you might have been one of the last persons to talk with him."

"Oh, really?" Josh walked around his desk and sat down. "You're not making any sense. Why would you even link me remotely to his murder? However, now it's my turn. I want to ask the questions. Who discovered the body? Who reported it? Do you have fingerprints, shoe prints, blood samples? Do you have any clues at all? What did his wife tell you?"

"Doc . . ." Mannheim held up a hand. "We'll ask the questions, if you don't mind."

"I do mind, and don't treat me like a demented criminal. You expect me to cooperate, but you insist on grilling me as though I were guilty of something. Get off your collective asses and start looking for probable suspects."

Mannheim folded his arms across his chest and took a deep breath. "Fine. Any suggestions?"

"Have you talked with Longfellow's business associates? His construction workers? Unhappy home owners? Creditors?"

Mannheim stifled a yawn. "Thanks for the valuable suggestions."

"I'm not talking with you guys unless you fill me in on some details, and if you insist on harassing me, you'll talk to my attorney."

Mannheim's bushy brows arched as he groaned. "Oh, Jesus, not Roscoe Farquhaar. Okay, let's make a pact: you tell me everything you know, and I'll tell you what I can. That's going beyond protocol, understand? I can't tell you everything. And for Chrissake, don't tell anyone what you heard from me, not even the Missus." The detective shook his index finger at Josh. "And keep that fuckin' shyster Farquhaar away from me."

That amused Josh. Mannheim never did like the lawyer. Exactly why, Josh had no idea. "Who discovered the corpse?"

Mannheim in his usual deadpan said, "The maid."

"The maid?" Josh frowned; he hadn't remembered seeing one there. "What maid?"

Mannheim glared at him. "She comes in five days a week. That morning she got to the Longfellows at seven thirty. Has her own set of keys. She walked into the living room, saw the body hanging, and fainted. When she came to, she called nine-one-one. Todd and I buzzed right over from headquarters in Thousand Palms. She was outside pacing hysterically. Wasn't she, Todd?"

The ever-silent Todd nodded in agreement.

"Anyway, some neighbors noticed her and gathered around trying to comfort her. When she saw us, she practically pulled us out of the car and ran us into the living room, where we found this goddamn grisly sight. Longfellow was strung up to the chandelier by a drape cord. Streaks of blood had poured out of his skull and were caked on his hair, his face, beard, and neck. Poor bastard's eyes were bugging out."

Mannheim took a small spiral notebook from an inner pocket of his jacket. Consulting his notes, he said, "The coroner figured he was dead or unconscious minutes before he was hanged. Autopsy confirmed a deep skull fracture over the left parietal area, resulting in massive brain damage. The blow was delivered by a blunt object. A dislocation of the neck with compression of the cervical cord was noted, but that was postmortem." Mannheim stopped, closed his notebook, and waited for Josh's response.

Josh shook his head. "Somebody with a goddamn twisted mind went through a lot of trouble to create that scene. Do you think they were trying to send a message?"

"To whom?" Mannheim asked nonchalantly . . . too nonchalantly.

Josh shrugged. "Hell, I don't know. Just a thought. Does Mrs. Longfellow have a rock-solid alibi?" Mannheim started to open his mouth, but Josh stopped him. "How is it possible that *she* didn't find the body before she left the house that morning, and why didn't she hear any noise or commotion?"

Mannheim perched his skinny behind on the corner of Josh's desk. With slumped shoulders, and his head and neck flexed, he resembled a brooding vulture. "She claims she left at six in the morning, her usual time. Never once looked in the living room."

"Wasn't that unusual?"

"That's what I said to her." Mannheim referred to his notes. "Told me she took the back stairs down to the kitchen, then left through the garage. Doing that, she wouldn't have seen the living room."

"Are you satisfied with that explanation?"

"Frankly, I'm skeptical, but I checked the layout of the house. Her route description seemed credible, but that's all." Mannheim hiked his trousers by pulling up on his belt. "Doc, I know I've asked you this several times, but really, how well do you know Mrs. Longfellow?"

Josh sighed. "Haven't we've gone through all this *ad nauseam*?"

"Relax, just checking." He turned his back on Josh and walked toward the door. Then he stopped as if he'd thought of something. "Wonder how much insurance there was on Longfellow's life, and who was the beneficiary."

"I'd think you'd know that already." Josh didn't bother to hide his anger at Mannheim's sly ploy.

The man ignored the comment. "Coroner estimates the time of death between midnight and two in the morning. Mrs. Longfellow claims she heard nothing after she went to bed around ten."

"So?"

Mannheim licked his index finger, then turned the page of his notebook. "That land of yours in Rancho Mirage, how much would you say it's worth?"

The man bounced conversation points like a yo-yo. Josh snapped his mouth shut, stopping his heated response of *None of your damned business*. Instead he answered politely, "I haven't got a clue. Considering the homes surrounding it, several million, I suppose."

Mannheim whistled low. "You're the sole owner?"

"Yeah, it seems so. That is, Maggie and I are. A title search has to be made. Why do you ask?"

Mannheim leaned forward and slid his notepad into his back pocket. "Can you figure any connection between Longfellow's death and your ownership of that land?"

"No, I can't. How does my owning Effingwell's land relate to the murder?"

Mannheim's head lifted, and he seemed to stare into space as though Josh's response had submerged into his unconsciousness, then slowly returned to a conscious level. "Huh? It just occurred to me that someone else might be interested in that property."

"I don't follow you."

"Doc, some crazy might want that land of yours. Some sociopath, some joker who's irrational, destructive, unremorseful . . ."

"Thanks for the definition of a psychopath," Josh said dryly. "Still, what in the hell does Longfellow's murder have to do with my property ownership?"

"I know of a case where a prospective land developer was gunned down."

Josh blinked, then realized the answer had come from Detective Todd. Not Mannheim. He turned and looked at the other officer. "Really? And at this point, am I supposed to ask, why?"

"I'll tell you why," Mannheim interjected, "because ownership of the land was not clear, and some nutcase thought it should be his."

"Mannheim, I just recently obtained the land. It was given to me in a quitclaim. You know that. As far as I know, the land has nothing to do with Longfellow or anyone else."

"Actually that's not quite true. The land, as you say, 'in question' was owned by *two* people according to the deed registered in the County Records Office—your patient who died . . ." Mannheim paused as if he was trying to remember. "What's his name?"

"Chesley Upton Effingwell," Josh offered resignedly.

"And there was another guy involved whose name is also Effingwell."

"You're referring to Chester Uriah Effingwell, the other name on the deed? They were brothers."

Mannheim, eyes partially closed, nodded slowly and sneered. "Two guys with similar wacky names. What in the hell were their parents thinking of?"

"How did you know about Chesley's brother?" Josh knew damn well he'd never spoken to anyone about Chester.

"We took the trouble to call the Riverside County Administrative Office." Suddenly Mannheim raised his hand. "Gotta run, Doc."

Todd was up out of the chair and right on the detective's heels.

When Mannheim reached the door, he stopped and turned, nearly bumping into Todd. He gave the man a dirty look and turned to face Josh. "Remember what I said, Doc. There may be a maniac out there who thinks you and the Missus aren't entitled to that land."

"Okay. So?"

"Watch your backside."

NINE

The following morning, Josh placed a cup of coffee on Maggie's night-stand, then leaned over and kissed her sleeping, angelic face. Her eyes fluttered, her lips puckered, and he kissed them gently. Immediately she kicked away the covers and pulled him closer. "Mm-m-m. Don't leave, lover."

"Didn't I satisfy you last night?" he asked, lowering his body onto the bed beside her.

She cooed, "Oh, my yes, it was wonderful, just won-der-ful." Her gown strap had slipped off her shoulder, exposing the upper part of her full breast.

Seeing it, Josh lowered his head and kissed the lovely mound.

She sighed. "Josh, what am I going to do with you? You're like an oversexed teenager." Before he could respond, she urged him over her and added, "Don't ever change."

* * *

At the breakfast table, Maggie refilled Josh's coffee cup, then studied his face. "Darling, you're so quiet. What's wrong?"

"I was thinking about something Mannheim said yesterday."

"About what?"

"He asked whether I thought Longfellow's murder was in any way connected with our parcel of land. Initially, the question seemed far-fetched; now, I'm not so sure."

Maggie buttered her toast. "Tell me what you're thinking."

"Suppose someone thought Longfellow was about to enter into a partnership with me . . ."

Maggie set her toast down and leaned toward Josh. "Are you suggesting that Prissy conspired with a third party to get rid of her husband so she could run the company herself and maybe purchase our land?" Maggie's eyes danced as she formulated her plot.

"Whoa, Maggie, slow down. Prissy has no partnership agreement with us. We've made no commitment with her or anyone else. In fact, I'd be inclined to get rid of that land without going through the hassle of development."

"That's it, precisely. Don't you see? Prissy's already figured that out. She's going to make us an offer to buy our property outright and develop it herself. But in my mind, she's tainted by the murder of her husband. I don't want to become involved with her. Let's find someone else who'll buy that land."

"Let me play devil's advocate: suppose Prissy were to offer us more than anyone else . . . by a sizable sum, say, several million dollars or so?"

Maggie placed her cup on the saucer."Why must you test my convictions?"

"All right, let's determine the value of that property. Do we know anyone else who's interested in it? There must be others. We haven't even put the word out yet. As a matter of fact, the day after I left the Riverside County offices, I got a call from a Ms. Sherri Aviloh in the Records Department telling me someone had phoned to say he was interested in our property and wanted to talk with me."

"And?"

"The number has a New York City prefix. I wrote it down on a piece of paper but can't remember where I put it."

"Did you check your wallet?"

"Yes, but it wasn't there."

"That's weird." Maggie looked at him. "Why would someone in New York call you? How could they have known about that land?"

Josh shrugged. "I have no idea." He pushed his chair from the table and stood. "Maggie, I really don't want to be involved in the development of that land. I have enough to do with my practice, and I don't want to give that up. All I ask is that you remember my pledge to Effingwell. The adobe house will not be sold. It's not negotiable under any circumstances."

"Josh, I understand your position. If you don't mind, I'll take full responsibility for handling and developing that property." Maggie was obviously excited about her new position as developer of prime property. "Of course, before any major decisions are made I'll confer with you. Actually, the thought of doing this thrills me." She grinned. "Besides, it'll give us a nice nest egg for our retirement." She threw her arms around him and peppered his face with kisses.

"Enough," he laughed.

She backed off, tilted her head, and smiled broadly. "Now find that paper and make that call to New York."

"I will."

Maggie left the kitchen while Josh went to the den and searched through his desk drawer.

Maggie approached him in the den waving two slips of paper. "Here's a message written in your hand. It reads 'Call Q at this number . . . .'"

"Where did you find that?"

"In your blazer pocket, along with another slip of paper, written in a woman's hand." She looked down at it. "It reads, 'P.L. 023-1492.'" Maggie inhaled with a hiss. "P.L.? Who, my dear, has left her phone number with you?"

Josh didn't correct her. He could have said P.L. stood for Peter Longfellow, but it wasn't the truth, and the lie would have made him uncomfortable. Besides, since she said "her," Maggie most likely guessed that P.L. stood for Prissy Longfellow. He added quickly, "Don't get upset! When she handed it to me, I couldn't very well discard it in front of her."

Maggie folded the paper and tore it to shreds. "Now call this Mr. Q." She glanced at the clock. "It's eight fifteen here, eleven fifteen in New York." She dialed, handed the phone to Josh, and pushed the speaker button.

Almost immediately a woman's voice could be heard. "CUE Enterprises. How may I direct your call?"

He leaned closer to the phone. "Is Mr. Cue in? This is Dr. Josh Harrington calling. I'm returning his call inquiring about my property in Rancho Mirage, California."

"Oh yes, Dr. Harrington. Please wait while I—"

"Miss . . ." Josh stopped her. "While I'm waiting for him, can you tell me what kind of business you're in?"

The woman's distinct Brooklynese accent answered, "We do impawting and expawting."

"Importing and exporting what?"

A male voice intervened, "Hello? Cue, here."

"Mr. Cue? This is Dr. Harrington from California. You inquired of the Riverside County Administrative Offices about my property in Rancho Mirage. Forgive me for asking, but what does CUE mean?"

"It's an eponym of Chester Uriah Effingwell, the second."

"Were you related to my patient, Chesley U. Effingwell?"

"I was his nephew—that is, in a manner of speaking."

Before Josh could comment, Cue added quickly, "I'm prepared to offer you a stock transfer in CUE Enterprises valued at twice the appraised value of the land."

Josh's heart stuttered and he swallowed before responding. "That's certainly a generous offer, but you'll have to forgive me if I sound reticent. I know nothing about you or your company. Can you give me some information?"

Cue spoke in a polished baritone without hesitation. "Certainly. My company deals in Russian imports such as oil, gems, and certain classified materials."

Classified materials? Did that include radioactive isotopes? No point in asking; the man would probably deny it anyway.

"Before I even consider your offer, Mr. Cue, I'd like information on your business valuation and a personal financial statement from your accounting firm. Also, I'd like to see a six-month history of the company's share values."

"I'll be happy to provide all that," Cue said. "Come to New York as my guest. I would be more than happy to arrange for airline tickets and suggest we spend a day or two taking in the bright spots. Get to know each other better."

"I appreciate the offer, but I need time to decide. I hope you don't mind my asking, but why do you want that property?"

"Not at all. My father and I developed several businesses in your area, years ago. Although I can get daily computer reports on occupancy levels at our hotels and returns from our theater showings, I do enjoy your salubrious climate in the winter and at the same time can check up on our holdings in person. Quite frankly, and this comes as a confession, I am addicted to your casinos. Unfortunately, I usually lose much more than I win."

"Would I be familiar with your businesses here?" Josh asked.

"Perhaps. We have a substantial ownership in a gated community, two movie houses, and a type of emporium for mature entertainment." Cue went on, "The adobe house holds many memories for me, and I'd like to restore it—"

Josh cut him off. "Mr. Cue, the adobe house is not for sale. It simply is not a negotiable item."

A brief silence followed before Cue responded. "I see. Well, that casts an entirely different light on the situation." He hesitated momentarily, then said, "But perhaps we can discuss that later." The conversation ended abruptly when Cue said he had a call waiting. He promised to get in touch again soon.

Josh looked at Maggie. "You heard the conversation. It seemed to raise as many questions as it answered."

"I don't understand. If this man is the nephew of our patient and his father's name appeared on the original deed, why would he not be an heir to that property?"

"My dear, you are as keenly astute as you are beautiful. I asked myself that very question and was about to ask Cue when he ended the conversation. Did you hear him say he was a nephew of Chesley Effingwell, 'in a manner of speaking'? So we don't know what his precise relationship was to our patient, or for that matter, to the other name on that deed."

Maggie's expression turned pensive. "Would you really consider going to New York? You would take me along, wouldn't you?"

"Of course, but before we think about that, let's do some research on this guy and his business. I'll call our legal beagle, Roscoe Farquhaar. See what information he can give us."

"Josh, aren't you concerned about doing business with the Russians?"

"Russians? We wouldn't be dealing with Russians. We'd be dealing with someone who deals with them. If we go to New York, we'll go with open minds, although frankly, I too am a bit leery about his offer."

"I wonder how Cue heard about your ownership of the Rancho Mirage land."

"That's another good question. One I was about to ask when he cut me off."

• • •

Later that day Josh told Maggie that Farquhaar had called to say CUE Enterprises was a privately owned company, so it wasn't registered with any of the brokerage firms. Getting accurate information on it wouldn't be easy, and he doubted that they would open their books.

"Well," Maggie said. "I hope Farquhaar is savvy enough to find out if any questionable deals or scams are involved with CUE Enterprises."

"Good point. If he doesn't, perhaps one of his cronies will." Josh grabbed the phone and punched in Roscoe's number.

The familiar Falstaffian bombast created an actual vibration in the phone. "Josh, my boy, how is my favorite corn-fed orthopod from the sovereign state of Illinois? . . . Yes sir, the sovereign state of Illinois, land of Lincoln, Obama, several jailed ex-governors, and Cook County political hijinks. Good to hear from you, my boy. How can this derelict officer of the court be of service?"

Maggie made a face at Josh, letting him know she did not enjoy listening to the lawyer. She mouthed the words, "I'm out of here. Have fun," and hurried out of the room.

Josh quickly explained that a patient of his had died and left him a quitclaim for property in Rancho Mirage.

Before he could take a quick breath, he was interrupted by Farquhaar. "Oh, you're speaking of Effingwell's property, the one who was killed by radioactive poison?"

Stunned, Josh sat heavily in his chair. "How in the hell did *you* know that?"

"Josh, my boy, such juicy calamities can never be fully secretive. One of my trusty informants advised me within minutes after the diagnosis was confirmed. In addition to that bit of startling horror, I was equally appalled to learn about Longfellow's murder-slash-hanging. I had known that good man for about twenty-five years. Such ghoulish occurrences hardly become our civilized community."

Josh frowned. "Mighty small world, if you ask me."

"At times." Farquhaar chuckled. "As for Effingwell's gift to you, I believe your professional life would have been infinitely simpler if you had merely accepted the munificent Medicare fee for his treatment and gone on your provincial and ethical way. However, since you accepted the largesse of your deceased benefactor, you are now burdened with the problems of land ownership and development." The attorney puffed. "And with that, dear boy, comes the exposure to avaricious souls. My advice to you is—"

By now Roscoe's preachy prattle had begun to irritate. Josh stopped him. "Don't forget I received that offer from a New Yorker named Chester U. Effingwell the second."

"I haven't forgotten. In fact, I know the family and their business holdings in the Coachella Valley."

"If that's the case, can Cue possibly be an heir to the property I've inherited? I'm a bit worried. The man has made a sizable offer on the land. Is there any way to find out about Cue's legitimacy?"

"Look, my boy, the Effingwells have had various businesses in our valley for as long as I can recall. However, I have not had the dubious distinction of representing them. All their primary legal affiliations are located in New York. If Chester Uriah Effingwell the second is at all unwholesome or is part of a bogus operation, we can learn of his nefarious ways soon enough . . ." Farquhaar paused then repeated, "Yes, soon enough."

Farquhaar paused again as if thinking, then resumed his train of thought. "There is an international network of thieving Russian entrepreneurs with operatives in the leading cities of the Western world. Most have assumed positions of ostensibly reputable businessmen but function as hoodlums . . . yes . . . detestable hoodlums."

The word *hoodlums* didn't sit well with Josh. "Uh-huh. Go on."

"There comes to mind one of my clients, a woman of Russian origin, from Minsk, I believe. She operates a most successful escort service here in the morally righteous and exceedingly respectable community of Rancho Mirage."

Josh's unease surged. "You mean she's a madame?"

"How delightfully perceptive you are, dear boy. This madame is a veritable charter member of the displaced Russian demimonde, and she possesses knowledge of illegal or quasi-legal activities of the Russian mafia operating in Southern California."

"What's her name, and how can I get in touch with her?"

Farquhaar seemed to find it difficult to answer questions simply and directly. Josh sighed and half listened to the lawyer as he embellished, obfuscated, and provided background verbiage that seemed inexhaustible.

Farquhaar also emphasized the importance of pursuing a certain protocol when approaching this madam. "She has a distinctive sobriquet in the trade. She is known among her patrons and the local constabulary as Big Tits Tatiana. But I should not call her Big Tits if I were you." With that, Roscoe roared with laughter that he could not suppress.

Josh lifted the phone a bit from his ear and waited until the man finished laughing.

Still chuckling, Farquaahr added, "Be sure you call her Tatiana, preferably Madame Tatiana."

"Thanks for the warning. Now where can I meet her?"

"She operates from her rather Byzantine establishment on Saddle Back Road off Clancy Lane in Rancho Mirage. I could phone and explain your needs, but you may wish to confront her personally." The lawyer paused again. "Besides, she may proffer a sampling of carnal delights from one of her nymphs."

Josh was nearly at the end of his patience. "Farquhaar, how is it that you can be helpful in one instance and so damned crass the next?"

"My boy, that type of juxtapositioning comes after years of practice. As for Madame Tatiana, she herself can engage your genitals in orgiastic gymnastics that only the most depraved could hope for."

TEN

Roscoe Farquhaar had made arrangements for Josh to visit Madame Tatiana that afternoon during a lull in her schedule. Josh was thankful that Maggie hadn't stayed around for the entire conversation with the lawyer; otherwise she would have let her objections to his visit to a madame's place of business be known. Instead, he simply told her he was going to visit a Russian woman by the name of Madame Tatiana. Maggie lifted her eyebrows but said nothing.

* * *

The two-story, sand-colored house perched on an elevated corner lot was an architectural mélange of Southwestern Indian, stark modern, and Russian Renaissance. Josh wondered how any architectural committee could have approved such a bizarre design. Perhaps every committee member had been royally seduced. He pulled into a circular driveway and parked near the entrance guarded by a tall ornamental iron gate.

Two gardeners, trimming bushes on either side of the entrance, stopped and watched as he emerged from his car. They did not have the short, swarthy stature or appearance of south-of-the-border itinerants but looked more like oversized Slavs. Both men, carrying loppers, headed toward him with menacing lumbering gaits.

Josh thought of making a hasty retreat to the car but, that option faded as he contemplated too long. Just as he anticipated resigning his body to the whims of those goliaths, a loud female command erupted from an open upstairs window.

The brutes stopped immediately, glanced up at the window, grumbled, then resumed gardening. Though relieved that they'd backed away, Josh remained wary and watched them out of the corner of his eye as he pushed a button to the side of the iron gate. Following a buzzing sound that signaled the release of the lock, he pushed the gate open and walked into an enclosed entryway to face a shiny lacquered door with bold brass hardware. An Eastern Orthodox cross was carved into the middle panel. Glass-covered alcoves on either side of the entryway protected paintings of ancient haloed icons that stared without expression. For some, he supposed, entering that house might have been akin to a religious experience.

Mounted in the corner above the door was a closed-circuit TV camera. Seeing it, Josh reminded himself to stand straight and appear businesslike. He squared his shoulders, turned his face toward the camera, and forced a smile. "I'm here to see Madame Tatiana."

When the door opened slowly, his eyes feasted upon an extraordinary vision, a curvaceous woman, approximately five foot eight, with an unusually pale complexion, a face with Siberian-Tatar features, including prominent cheekbones; large, dark, almond-shaped eyes enhanced by mascara; lips full, moist, and sensuous; a neck delicate and elongated; and a crown of braided jet-black hair flecked with sparkles and braided like a jeweled tiara.

Josh swallowed uncomfortably. Her pink sheer blouse with a neckline that plunged toward a broad jeweled belt revealed a bosom of the most extraordinary proportions, separated by a canyon-like cleavage.

It didn't help that her bulging breasts were made more conspicuous by a garment that lifted and gathered them inward. Diaphanous pantaloons belted below a ruby in her navel revealed a minuscule thong that barely concealed the perineum. She held an elongated, pearly cigarette holder with a king-sized cigarette in one hand. She extended the back of her other hand to Josh.

"Doktor."

Josh reached up and shook it gently.

Despite his intrigue of her, he couldn't help but mix the diagnosing doctor in him with his masculine approval. The hand, like a physiological calling card, revealed her state of health and, more significantly, her age. The loss of fatty tissue below the skin and the intrinsic muscle atrophy could no longer conceal the prominent bony joints or tendons. Blue, tortuous veins shimmered below the parchment-like skin speckled with so-called liver spots. Such was the welcoming hand of Madame Tatiana.

Brightly colored fingernails and rings of exquisite diamonds and gemstones in settings of gold and platinum adorned all of her fingers. According to his estimation, the madame had long reached the age of eligibility for Social Security benefits.

"Come with me." She guided him into an elaborate guest room scented delicately with a lilac fragrance and furnished in the excesses of both baroque and rococo styling, a room that might have been featured in a decorator's magazine at the turn of the last century. In the center on an ornately carved oval table, a burnished brass samovar was encircled by an old Russian tea set.

As Madame Tatiana spoke in general, social niceties, Josh paid more attention to her smoky voice suggesting chronic cigarette irritation. Her accent reflected an archetypical, unrefined Russian dialect. Josh watched her lips in fascination as she formed her words. When she referred to Roscoe Farquhaar as 'Roosco Fartquart' he chuckled, then realized his rudeness.

"I'm sorry, Madame, I shouldn't have laughed."

"*Nyet*, it is I who should apologize. I do have difficulty with American vords and names, but my vords are quite adequate when it comes to business matters . . ." She smiled. "Particularly my escort service."

She directed him to an oversized, soft leather easy chair that whooshed and engulfed him as he slumped into it. Josh looked upward and marveled at the enormous room with its high ceiling and elaborate crystal chandelier. The exposed upper floor was set off by a curvilinear wooden balustrade bordering rooms arranged in a large horseshoe pattern. Two arched stairways, one at either side of the guest rooms, formed graceful curves for ascending and descending the second floor. Josh imagined a guy in good physical shape negotiating the stairs in a sprint going up but barely having the stamina to crawl down.

Tatiana sat opposite him. "Vhat you think?" She pointed around to the large, revealing photographs framed in heavy gilt mounted on the walls, portraits of her beautiful escorts, which were meant to titillate and arouse. She leaned forward, placed a hand on his knee, and with a twinkle in her eye, said, "Pareheps, Doktor, you vould like a leetle divorsion vith von of my gorjous yung vomen?"

"Thank you, Madame Tatiana, but I'm a married man." As soon as he'd said that, he realized that had to be the most vapid non-sequitur of the day.

She leaned back and smiled. "Oh, my! Most clients are married men who enjoy change of scenery and change of, vhat you call, technik?" She motioned with her head toward the second floor. "Come, I show you."

"Uh, no . . ." Josh shook his head. "Thank you, but no." He explained in detail why he'd come to see her. When he finished, he sat back, a bit exhausted.

Tatiana crossed her long, shapely legs with measured slowness, leaned forward, and supported her chin with one hand, her elbow resting on her thigh. The pose had to be rehearsed for its anticipated effect. Her formidable bosom and cleavage became a focal point in her loose-fitting blouse. He made an effort to concentrate on her eyes, which were almost as seductive.

"Vhat is the name of this company?"

Had he forgotten to mention it? Josh adjusted his weight in the easy chair. "CUE Enterprises, located in Manhattan."

"Yes?"

"The name of the man in charge is Chester Effingwell the second. Do you know him?"

Her eyes glittered. She repeated the name softly, then smiled. "Yes, of course, my dear doktor, I know him very well." She stood and inhaled her cigarette deeply, then blew a series of smoke rings. The scene was reminiscent of a 1930s pre–Legion of Decency movie.

Tatiana removed the cigarette from its holder, stubbed it in an ornate ashtray, then set the holder aside. "Thees Effingwell character, he ees not a januwine payrson. How you say? He ees a frowd."

"A fraud?" Josh was beginning to see that Tatiana could switch from perfect English to flawed English whenever the opportunity called for it.

This time her English was nearly perfect. Tatiana began a lengthy reminiscence in telling the chronology of events. She had known the man in question from the time he was a twelve-year-old runaway from abusive and alcoholic parents. He found shelter with the help of stevedores around the docks on the Lower East Side of New York. They aided him in successfully dodging the authorities, while he subsisted on handouts, goods stolen from invaded cargo, then sold. That was almost fifty years ago.

One day, the wealthy and elegant Mr. Effingwell, dressed in a chesterfield coat and homburg hat, walked along the dock with his characteristic limp, a limp that somehow seemed to enhance his debonair carriage. He had been inspecting a recently arrived shipment. His gloved hand held a cane with a heavy crafted silver handle. He was accosted by the runaway, who threatened him with a knife and demanded money. Effingwell, angered by the insolence of the ragamuffin, struck him across the face with the handle of the cane. The boy fell and put his hand across his reddened and abraded cheek as a security officer ran to the scene and held the boy down.

When he realized how severely he had struck the boy, Chester Effingwell waved the officer aside. Overcome by remorse, he helped the frail youngster to a standing position, then questioned him and offered to feed him at a local diner. The boy ate voraciously and despite his wound was grateful to Effingwell for his subsequent mercy and generosity. Something about the boy's eagerness to please and his stoicism after the inflicted trauma appealed to Effingwell, who had no children. He told the boy he could live with him if he promised to behave and do as he was told. Effingwell was eager for the boy's companionship and the prospect of developing his character.

"Effingwell made from heem a pig million."

Josh blinked, realizing she had gone back to her fractured English. "You mean Pygmalion?"

"Vhatever."

"Madame Tatiana, how do *you* know all this?"

She sat once again and seemed to revel in the opportunity to evoke incidents of the past. She spoke of herself as a beautiful, wild teenager who was orphaned when her immigrant parents died in an auto accident. Being alone, she had joined a gang of kids who grew up by their conniving wits, stealing, pickpocketing, engaging in prostitution—any means of surviving on Manhattan's Lower East Side. She was a senior member of the gang when the ragamuffin was taken in. Eventually, she met Old Man Effingwell.

For some reason, she did not elaborate on those circumstances, and Josh did not press her.

She went on to say that Old Man Effingwell rescued her from gang existence and helped her get started in a modeling career, in which she became successful.

"He lent you money?"

"Oh . . . no. He gave me money—for what I gave him."

Josh thought it best, once again, not to explore that phase of personal history. "What business was Old Man Effingwell in?"

"The family was in shipping, importing and exporting. He was a partner."

"Whatever happened to the orphaned boy he took in?"

Tatiana raised her index finger to signify patience. She launched into a detailed account of how Old Man Effingwell became his role model, who trained him to live in a completely different world, one resulting from hard work and the rewards it brought. Effingwell grew quite fond of the boy and called him Cue, from the initials of his own name. He had him tutored, even to the extent of learning the manners and customs of a proper gentleman. With his initial intelligence, the boy became an apt and eager student. He grew tall and strong, and Effingwell had him work on weekends and during summers on the docks; he ran errands, charted and labeled freight; he became a stevedore, then a dock foreman, learning every phase of the importing and exporting trade. He participated in union meetings and brawls and became privy to the dock workers' chicanery. With his position of increasing authority, he became intolerant of those who disagreed with him and carried a concealed weapon with which he threatened disgruntled workers.

At age twenty, he enrolled at Columbia University, Effingwell's alma mater. He majored in business and economics, and as a graduation present was made a full business partner in CUE Enterprises.

Tatiana grew more animated. "Then he became a big shot! But one thing . . ." She hesitated as though searching for the proper words. "He was smart, but never well-liked. He stepped on people. He smashed heads."

She grimaced and squeezed her palms to demonstrate and went on to explain that he was eager to replace the old man. He suggested the old man retire many times.

"Did the old man ever legally adopt him?"

"*Nyet!*"

She explained that the old man had been separated from his wife for many years. His wife, a staunch Catholic, would not grant him a divorce. They lived separate lives. In summer she lived in the Hamptons, and in winter, Palm Beach, while Effingwell maintained an apartment in a Manhattan high-rise. She would not agree to adopt the boy, for whatever reasons. She never really liked him—not to her dying day.

Josh asked when she had last seen Effingwell. She said the old man and Cue visited together about ten years ago, when they came to look after their business interests and to visit with Chesley Effingwell, Mr. Chester Effingwell's younger brother. Although Cue was introduced as Chester's son to many, she knew that he was never legally adopted.

Soon after that visit, the old man disappeared she said like a puff of smoke. From then on, Cue came to the desert two or three times a year. He visited Tatiana and indulged his sexual needs with her escorts. Cue had been married three times, but his philandering resulted in nasty and expensive divorces.

Tatiana's original escort service was conducted out of a former movie actress's home in the affluent Las Palmas section of old Palm

Springs. The area was the playground for many Hollywood characters during the late 1930s through the 1960s. She personally entertained clients of glamour: movie stars, athletes, business tycoons, politicians, and religious leaders. More escorts joined as her service flourished. During one of his visits, Old Man Effingwell complained that the house was too déclassé and the neighborhood no longer attracted high rollers. After determining the shifting patterns of affluence toward the east end of the valley, he provided finances for building a larger, more elegant house in the developing tony Clancy Lane section of Rancho Mirage.

"He gave you money to build this fancy—er—pleasure palace?"

She nodded.

"That was quite generous."

She looked askance. "Quite generous? *Nyet!* For years in New York he have no wife. I was like wife: I cook, I clean, I feed, and I fuck him anytime he want. I better than wife. In California I pay him ten percent of my profits. He call it 'teething.'"

"Tithing?"

"You always correct me, Docktor."

"Sorry. I'm trying to make sure I understand completely. What happened to him? Did he pass away?"

"Who could know?"

"What do you mean?"

"After his association with Cue, he disappeared. Poof!" She snapped her fingers. "No one knows anything. He here one day and gone next day. Police, sheriff, FBI look for him. Old man nowhere, no one find him. Mister big shot, Cue, he say he cannot believe old man gone. He cry and say he have broken heart."

Tatiana stopped, leaned forward, and whispered, "But I no trust him."

"A fascinating story, Madame Tatiana." Josh braced against the massive arms of the chair and pushed himself upright. "But I am still at a loss as to what to do. Now if you can advise me, I'd appreciate your help."

"I give you any help I can."

"Should I consider selling my property to Cue? He's made a generous offer."

Tatiana looked to either side, bent her head forward, and in a half whisper said, "Listen to me, Comrade Doktor: That man is no good, he is bad payrson. He deals in, how you say? Contraband? He sell anything—stolen diamonds, guns, illegal brides, maybe even atomic bomb . . ."

The hairs on the back of Josh's arms rose. "And radioactive isotopes?" He watched her closely, to observe her response.

Tatiana gave him a questioning look. "I don't know from such things. But I tell you, you make deal with him, you make business with devil. You make business with me instead. I give you good honest dollars and maybe throw a girl in for one week."

Josh forced a smile. "That's kind of you, but I have serious doubts about my wife being amenable to that suggestion, especially the last part. I'm curious, Madame Tatiana. While Chester Effingwell was alive, did he trade exclusively with the Russians?"

"I think so." She went on to explain that many years ago Effingwell's wife was a Russian ballerina, a daughter of the royal Romanov family. She came to New York to perform and when Effingwell saw her dance, he lost his heart. "Mama and Papa Romanov very unhappy but finally say okay to marriage. Romanovs have good connections in Moscow and New York and put new son-in-law in import business," which was exceedingly profitable during the war years. Tatiana looked at her watch as a sign to end to the conversation.

Josh got the hint. "Thank you, Madame Tatiana, you've been very helpful."

"Anytime, sweetheart." She put her arms around his neck and brought her face close to his. Her exotic perfume failed to conceal her cigarette and vodka breath. He backed away and headed toward the exit.

As he closed the outer door, a vehicle pulled up; two plainclothesmen passed without glancing at him. Surprisingly, the burly gardeners merely looked up, then continued working.

ELEVEN

Returning to the office, Josh welcomed the astringent odor of antiseptic solution and rubbing alcohol.

Nearby, sorting through some records, Maggie in her white starched uniform looked wholesome, almost saintly, in contrast to the madame.

"The Federal Radiation Protection Agency's Mr. Sangamon called," Maggie said when she saw him enter. "He said to tell you they believe they've discovered the source of the polonium-210 found in Chesley's body. Shall I call him back?"

Clearly, Maggie was as eager to learn as he was. "Sure, go to it, sweetheart."

Ten minutes later, Josh learned from Sangamon that the source of the isotope was a lab outside of Moscow. Josh repeated phrases for Maggie, who stood so close she could have heard them herself.

"Normally," Sangamon said, "polonium-210 is used as a neutron trigger for nuclear weapons and as an atomic heat source for thermoelectric generators."

Josh whistled. "That's got to be rare and costly. How could a person get hold of that stuff?"

"Not sure," replied Sangamon. "One thing I do know: the isotope was estimated to be five million times more toxic than cyanide. The emitted alpha particles damage tissue severely on contact."

"Thanks. Appreciate you letting me know. If you hear anything else, don't hesitate to call." He replaced the phone on the cradle, then frowned. "Someone obviously had stolen a small amount and smuggled it into the country."

Maggie's expression turned grave. "Can it even be handled safely?"

"With impervious containers, I suppose. Once I heard that some lab techs were accidentally exposed to an isotope for an extended period of time. All of them developed cancers and died. It happened in Israel in the late 'fifties. Hush-hush type of thing. We were told of it later, to emphasize how dangerous polonium-210 can be."

Maggie's face drained of color. "How awful! What's being done about finding the perpetrators?"

"Sangamon seems to think they'll be found eventually. A Washington bureau is in touch with London authorities who investigated the death of a former KGB agent, Litvinenko, who took refuge in London."

"You're talking about the man where Russian agents got to him and slipped polonium-210 in his food?"

"Yes. From what I've heard, the Russkies have a history of being vindictive and using bizarre methods for seeking revenge on their enemies, sometimes years after the so-called act of betrayal to the Mother Land." Josh rubbed a hand over his face. "I'm willing to bet the trail of involvement goes right up to Putin. At that point, you can be sure all further investigative procedures will stop. There will be denials and counter-accusations. Meanwhile, our own foreign affairs department will wail against tipping delicate balances and nothing of consequence will be accomplished."

"So much intrigue!" Maggie followed Josh into his consultation room. "But what does this have to do with Chesley?"

Josh shook his head and shrugged.

As if sensing they needed to lighten the mood a little, Maggie tugged playfully on Josh's ear. "You didn't tell me about your visit with Madame Tatiana. Did she proposition you?"

"How did you—?" He stopped again, realizing he never could put anything over on his wife. Josh smiled and decided to play it safe.

"Not quite, but I did get an invitation to have pleasure with one of her escorts." He held up a hand. "Before you ask, I'll tell you—I refused."

"She could have whetted your appetite."

He wagged his eyebrows.

She laughed. "Now tell me all about it."

Maggie listened intently as Josh detailed his meeting. By the time he'd finished, Maggie no longer wanted to consider dealing with Cue. As far as she was concerned, the man sounded much too unsavory. After a moment, she said softly, "What about the disappearance of Chesley's brother? Did Tatiana have an answer for that?"

"No."

"Did she think Cue may have had a hand in it?"

"Tatiana had no explanation for any of it. It's still a mystery."

"Yeah," Maggie whispered. "And it's a mystery that may well be better off remaining one."

* * *

By the end of the day, Josh and Maggie had seen twenty-one patients and were heading toward the parking lot. Maggie climbed into the driver's seat. "Buckle up, dearie." Her command was automatic.

As soon as Josh sat in the Mercury Mountaineer passenger seat, he reached over and placed his hand on her right thigh. Maggie gave him a cursory glance.

"Just because," she said with a hint of breathlessness, "you're the boss hardly entitles you to take liberties with this employee's anatomy."

"But this employee has such lovely anatomy." He rubbed his palm up and down her leg.

"Thank you, love." Maggie put her right hand on Josh's left thigh. "My boss has a pretty good body himself. If he plays his cards right, he might be able to entertain a notion or two after dinner, providing he doesn't fall asleep." She glanced at him and pretended to pout. "You wouldn't have fallen asleep before we married. Why, I remember . . ."

Her voice became distant and muffled. Exhaustion pulled at him and caused his eyes to close.

Suddenly, he was awakened as his head snapped back, then forward, when the SUV came to a sudden halt in the garage.

Beside him he heard his wife laugh.

"Sorry to spoil your reverie, dearie, but we're home. Would you be good enough to get the mail?"

Josh yawned and climbed out of the vehicle. He walked across the street to the community mailbox and pulled out several envelopes and a handful of junk mail. By the light of the street lamp, he saw that one of the envelopes was from the Office of the Riverside County Assessor.

"Anything good in the mail, Josh?" Maggie's voice reached him from the garage door.

He shook his head and walked into the house. "Something's come from the county assessor in Riverside. Nothing good ever comes from the county assessor's office." He slid a finger under the sealed flap and opened the envelope. With one quick flick of the wrist he opened the letter, read it, then inhaled sharply.

"What is it? What's wrong?" Maggie rushed to him.

"Are they crazy?" Josh shook his head in disbelief and showed her the bill. "There's no way we can afford the tax on that property. That's it. We're getting rid of it now."

"Calm down, Josh. We have several weeks before making a decision." She took the paper and read it again. "We haven't even walked across that land, or for that matter, inspected the house. We really don't know what we've got. This may be much more profitable than you realize."

Josh snatched the assessment back and rattled the pages. "I'll tell you what we *won't* have—we won't have a damn financial albatross on our backs. That property, less the adobe, goes to the highest bidder, pronto."

TWELVE

Over thirty-five years ago, the good citizens of Rancho Mirage paid tribute to one of their favorite residents, the iconic Francis Albert Sinatra. They renamed Wonder Palms Drive, one of the main arteries of the valley, for him. A number of prestigious country clubs and private estates lined either side of the broad drive, separated by several miles of a median planted with seasonal flowers and native foliage. The location of Josh and Maggie's inherited property was in the newer section of the drive, which extended on an incline for a half mile south of Highway 111. The road had been disrupted by construction machinery, work crews, and trucks that made traveling the curved path hazardous.

Josh reached the summit after dodging orange pylons and yellow tape, then veered off cautiously to the left in an easterly direction. The vehicle bounced savagely on ill-defined rutted tracks. Boulders, jagged rocks, and potholes made the driving slow and the incline in places became perilous. Josh reached over and braced Maggie with his right arm as the SUV careened and lurched. Maggie cinched her shoulder and waist harness tighter and held on to the grab-bar above the window.

"Josh, avoid these bumps, will ya? My stomach feels queasy. Those damn breakfast burritos are about to get their revenge. Why did you let me eat them?"

Josh looked at her. "Should we abort this trip?"

Maggie remained noncommittal for a moment, then thrust out her clenched jaw. "No. We've come this far. As rotten as I feel, I want to see that adobe now and the land around it. By God, I'm going to develop that land or sell it at a good price. I've got strong feelings for this project. You just leave the business details to me."

After bouncing along for about two hundred yards of gutted terrain and desert scrub, they came upon a dirty, grayish-white structure, its lower part obscured by tall weeds. It was set back about twenty feet from the primitive road. As the derelict adobe came into full view, they saw its windows boarded up with lumber darkened by years of weathering.

Josh got out of the SUV and went to Maggie's side to assist her. "Come, Princess, let's explore our mighty castle, our royal domain." As he extended his hand and guided her, he remained concerned about her discomfort. "Are you feeling any better?"

Maggie's complexion was pasty and her eyes tired and lifeless. "My stomach is a bit queasy, but I'll make it." Maggie took his hand, and they walked to the front of the house. The cracks in the cement steps leading to the door allowed weeds to find refuge. A single wooden handrail had collapsed and lay on the ground, covered by overgrowth. On the weather-beaten lintel, splintered and fissured over the door, were the barely visible scripted words *Santa Nydia,* encircled by faded red roses on a green vine. A dirt-encrusted Yale door lock mounted above a corroded and pitted iron door handle appeared to defy entrance.

Josh reached into his pocket and pulled out the blackened key he had been given along with the quitclaim by the dying Effingwell.

As he slipped the key into the lock, he was unable to turn it. Sand and dust had accumulated in triangles formed at the lower corners of the door and jamb. Cobwebs laced the upper corners with snared insects. The varnish on the door was crazed and discolored by years of exposure.

After two attempts at opening it, Josh said, "Dammit! I should have known this key wouldn't fit the slot." Maggie unceremoniously took the key out of his hand, spat on it, wiped it with Kleenex, and reinserted it. The tumblers engaged and the door opened slowly, rupturing the cobwebs with an elastic pull. To his ears, the hinges creaked like those in an old film noir thriller. Only the eerie crescendo of an organ was missing.

At the threshold, they stopped and looked into the darkness, waiting for their eyes to adjust. Josh automatically felt for a light switch along the wall next to the door; there was none. They stepped inside cautiously. The air was heavy with mustiness and an unhealthy organic smell.

"Oh, ugh . . . it's awful." Maggie took a handkerchief from her purse and covered her mouth and nose. With limited light coming through the open door, some objects were becoming discernible. Do we have a flashlight in the car?"

"No."

Two hurricane lamps blackened with dust and carbon deposits sat on a rough-hewn mantel above a stone fireplace. A closer look by Josh revealed two partially burned candles in the lamps. A box of phosphor-tip matches also lay next to them. "How lucky do you think we'll be getting these candles lit?"

He picked up one of the hurricane lamps, removed its chimney, and held it while Maggie struck a match against the abrasive strip on the side of the box.

The wick sputtered a few times, then began to burn. A flash of light provided a glimpse into the room before the candle wick came to full light. Josh replaced the glass chimney and held the lamp above his head. Maggie lit the second lamp and replaced it on the mantel, then returned the handkerchief to her face.

"This place smells really, really awful."

"Dust and erosion, I would guess." Josh took a few steps more into the dark interior.

"More like decomposing carcasses—maybe mice, bats, cats, dogs, or even a coyote."

Josh almost laughed. "How would they get into this boarded-up place? These adobe walls are about eighteen inches thick."

"They'd burrow under the foundation, or bats and birds could come down the chimney. Who knows?"

"How would a big-city gal know about such things?" Josh challenged her humorously, not really expecting a serious reply.

Maggie sniffed, loud enough to be heard through her handkerchief. "I got around. Long before I met you, one of my beaus was a cattle rancher from eastern Washington. I spent four weeks on a working vacation with him, learning about critters and ranch living, among other things. I learned to shoot scampering vermin—even put a buck down at a hundred yards. I embarrassed him by shooting more targets than he did. Generally I handled guns pretty well."

"Oh, really? Have you had any recent target practice, Miss Annie Oakley?" Josh thought the question moot, since Maggie didn't have a weapon.

Reaching deep into her purse, Maggie brought up a small pistol less than five inches long with a polished chrome barrel and a grip of simulated ivory.

When she handed the piece to him, his jaw dropped. He first looked at her, then examined it closely.

"Where did you get this?"

"I've had it for several years."

"You have? How come I've never seen it?"

"I thought I showed it to you, but I guess I just didn't, that's all. Didn't think it was important."

He smiled when he noted the grip, adorned with bust portraits of Gibson-type gals on both sides.

"A Lady Derringer! What a sweet little weapon. But you can't be serious about its protective capabilities. This is nothing more than a decorative piece."

Maggie snatched the pistol back. She wiped the barrel and hand grip with her hankie and replaced it in her purse. "Darling, just don't provoke me to use it."

Josh held up one hand in mock surrender. "I promise to be ever-faithful and loving."

Suddenly she frowned and placed her hands over her abdomen.

"Stomach still bothering you?"

"A bit. What do you suggest we do with this place? Apply for a state or national historical landmark charter?"

Josh shrugged. "Haven't got a clue. Let's take a look around. Maybe we can open the rear door or knock some of the boards off the windows." They continued slowly toward the rear of the house. A dead bolt secured the heavy back door, which balked at Josh's effort at opening it. Finally, after tugging and swearing, it yielded, and a shaft of sunlight, almost too bright, flooded the room. Worn red brick-patterned linoleum with underlying board lines covered the floor. A dusty, white, chipped enameled electric stove on four tall legs stood next to a sink with an exposed drain-pipe below and a pump handle above. A wooden table with four straight-back chairs in various stages of disrepair occupied the center of the room.

Josh shielded his eyes from the westerly sun and stepped to the doorway to survey the remnants of a wooden patio. The outside flooring, made up of two-by-fours, had warped, rotted, and collapsed in places under someone's weight long ago.

Both stepped back inside and walked toward what was probably the living room. The floor creaked beneath them. Two serape-like blankets thick with dust lay on the floor in the middle of the room. That seemed odd in a room that was otherwise barren.

Josh placed a foot onto the blanketed area and felt a yielding sensation in the flooring and an increase in the creaking. He pulled the blankets aside; the floor beneath was clean in contrast to the dust around it. The blankets had concealed a trapdoor that measured approximately two by six feet. A recessed handle and hinges indicated skilled carpentry. He looked up at his wife. "Well, well, my dear, what have we here? Buried treasure? A wine cellar?"

"Maybe a corpse?"

Josh laughed. "Bring the lamp over here." He set the lamp on the floor and pulled on the recessed handle, straining to open the heavy door. After several attempts, he succeeded in lifting it. A draft of cool, foul air filled his nostrils.

"Oh, ugh! Now it's even worse." Maggie pressed the handkerchief against her nose and brought the lamp closer.

Josh picked up the lamp, bent over, and lowered it into the black hole. The sudden movement of scurrying and squeaking of small animals exploded from the hole.

Josh jumped away, nearly dropping the lantern.

Maggie screamed and jumped back, her hand and handkerchief still over her mouth.

Josh smiled sheepishly, then opened the trapdoor completely. He peered into the subflooring space to discover a mound of earth about six feet long and two feet wide. He kneeled over the opening and brought the lamp below floor level.

"Josh, be careful! I don't want you getting bitten by one of those things and getting infected by the hantavirus or rabies." Maggie leaned over the opening, removed the handkerchief from her nose, sniffed the air, then turned her head. "Ooh, what a vile stench!" She looked at Josh with troubled eyes. "You're really not going down there, are you?" It was more than a question; it was an implied command. She walked carefully to the mantel to pick up the hurricane lamp she had placed there.

In spite of Maggie's warning, he lowered himself into the dark crawl space, then reached for the hurricane lamp at the edge of the opening and placed it close to the mound.

"What do you think you're doing, for pity's sake?" Maggie's voice trembled.

"Be with you in just a moment." Josh pushed his pen into the soft, dry earth. The mound resisted prodding. Using his hand as a scoop, he brushed the loose earth to either side to discover a smooth surface—a thick, clear polyvinyl bag with a full-length zipper. With faster movements, he cleared more of the overlying dirt, from head to toe.

Suddenly his hand froze. *From head to toe?* Christ, that was it! He backed off and brushed his sleeve over his sweaty brow. He moved his upper body back and away to view a complete skeleton, sparsely covered with remnants of cloth.

He unzipped the bag to examine the remains more closely. A shattered, explosive-type hole in the frontal bone—probably an exit wound. Josh's thoughts whirled. Was this a male or female skeleton? He noted the prominent bony protuberances of the brows—probably male—and the absorption due to aging around the square-type mandible—older male. The teeth showed wear and extensive repair. The disarticulated rib cage with its increased depth and calcified cartilage also indicated advanced age. In addition, there was generalized arthritic spurring and age-related vertebral deformities. Josh removed a fragment of clothing that obscured the pelvis, which was definitely android.

The left hip joint caught his attention. An old disease had caused deformation of the left femoral head, which resulted in shortening of the leg.

He picked up the skull, turned it around, and discovered a symmetrical hole in the mid-occipito-parietal area—an entry wound made at close range. Carefully he returned the skull to its original position. The entry and exit wounds were on a horizontal plane. Someone had fired at point-blank range, creating a level trajectory. The ocular orbits were black and staring, the jaws typically set in a sardonic smile. The eerie silence accompanying Josh's examination was shattered by the high-pitched sound of breaking glass, followed by a low-pitched thud.

Josh froze, then yelled, "Maggie, are you all right?"

Hearing no answer, he leaped out of the hole.

He saw her instantly sprawled on the floor, unconscious. Next to her, the broken hurricane lamp, its candle drippings starting to burn the wood floor.

"Maggie!" Hurriedly, he pulled her away from the flames, then grabbed the old serapes and threw them on the fire, stomping rapidly to smother the flames. Even with his quick response, smoke soon filled the confined space. Josh lifted his wife into his arms and carried her through the front door.

The fresh air worked wonders. She coughed, gasped, and shook her head in confusion. Then she bent over and gagged. "Oh my God! I think I'm going to be sick."

"That's it. Come on, baby, let's get the hell out of here." Josh put his arm around her waist and placed her arm around his neck as he led her away from the front door. "What happened, sweetheart?"

Maggie, breathless said, "I watched you uncover the bag, then saw the skull, and everything went black."

With a cry, she spun sideways, leaned over some bushes, gagged and vomited.

Concerned, Josh held tight to his wife as her body muscles fought the spasms. Soon, undigested fragments of the breakfast burritos appeared, foul and sour smelling. When she could no longer vomit, she sagged against Josh and wiped her mouth with her handkerchief.

Tremulously, she said, "I'm fine now."

Like the woman Josh knew his wife to be, she straightened and said in a determined voice, "We should contact the police."

THIRTEEN

On his cell, Josh gave the police dispatcher his findings and location. Having helped Maggie into the SUV, he adjusted her shoulder/lap harness and hand-brushed her hair.

"Josh, stop being so solicitous; I'm all right now. It was really that awful food and the sight of those mice, that stinky smell, and that horrible skeleton. Yuck!" Maggie, still wan, shook her head and started to shiver. He placed her sweater around her shoulders, although the ambient temperature was in the upper 70s.

Walking around to the driver's side, he stopped at the sight of the left front tire and felt greater despair. It was absolutely flat, impinged on a rock. "*Damn*," he said, "now I've got to wait for the police and triple-A and hope to hell they can find their way up here."

Maggie, hearing him complain, moaned, "Oh, no! Can't *you* change the tire?"

"Who, me? The spare is hidden underneath the car and the back end has to be jacked up in this loose soil. No, thank you. I'm not that brave. We'll wait for the tow truck," he said as he got on his cell.

Within fifteen minutes, two vehicles came bouncing along the uneven terrain toward them, a Rancho Mirage police car and a blue Crown Victoria. From the police car two young, uniformed officers approached, followed by two plainclothesmen from the vehicle behind. At about twenty yards, Josh recognized Sergeant Mannheim, followed by Detective Todd.

Mannheim stepped past the officers and approached Josh standing in his soiled shirt and trousers. Mannheim glanced at him quickly. "Where's the rest of your rock band?" With little facial expression, he looked to either side. "Lose your guitar, too?"

Peering into the SUV, he said, "Ma'am, did you know your husband takes up more of our time than any ten thousand residents in this community?"

Maggie responded with a weak smile.

Mannheim then returned his attention to Josh. "Doc, I swear, no one is involved in more murders or dead bodies than you are." If he meant to be humorous, no one laughed.

Mannheim and Todd entered the adobe. When Josh started to follow, Mannheim said, "Doc, why don't you stay out here with the Missus? If we need you, we'll call you. As of now, this is a crime scene."

After ten minutes, Mannheim and Todd emerged from the adobe. On his cell, Mannheim requested a body hauler and dismissed the two uniformed officers. Twenty minutes later, a black unmarked panel truck from the coroner's office arrived. Two men removed a collapsible gurney and a black plastic, zippered bag. After a quick exchange with Mannheim, the men entered the house.

Fifteen minutes later, the coroner's men appeared outside, rolling the gurney with the black body bag. They peeled off their vinyl gloves, shoved them into a paper sack, and pushed the gurney into the back end of the van.

Watching the men work, Maggie flopped her head back against the seat rest.

Officer Todd must have noticed her movement. The policeman went to the passenger's-side window and bent down.

"Mrs. Harrington, would you like to be driven home?"

Maggie slowly shook her head. "No, thank you, I'm feeling better." Despite her attempt to sound normal, nothing about her ashen complexion suggested improvement.

Josh leaned across the seat and ran his hand gently over Maggie's head. "Honey, why don't you let the detectives drive you home? I'll feel better if you do. I don't know how long it will be before the tow truck arrives."

"I don't want—"

"Please, Maggie."

"Oh, all right."

Detective Todd immediately helped her out of the SUV and escorted her to the unmarked police vehicle.

To Josh's surprise, when Todd started the vehicle, Mannheim remained rooted beside the driver's door of the SUV. "Aren't you going with them?" he asked.

"Nope. I plan to stay here till the tow truck comes. I know the boys who work those rigs. One of them will give me a lift to the station."

"That's very considerate of you, but I'm perfectly able to wait by myself."

"Being considerate has nothing to do with it. It's just that I don't want you falling into another tub of shit."

Josh would have laughed if Mannheim hadn't said that with a serious tone. "What are you trying to say?"

Mannheim looked around, then said, "Your flat tire was no accident."

A chill raced down Josh's back. "No accident?"

"I'll show you. Come here." Josh followed Mannheim to the front of the vehicle. When the detective got down on his haunches, Josh did the same. "See the slash on the inner side of that tire? While you were in the house, someone was playing Mack the Knife."

"Why, for God's sake?" Like Mannheim, he looked around the grounds.

"Dunno." Mannheim straightened and dusted off his pants. "Lot of workers around here," he said and nodded across the road.

Josh stood as well. A construction site was directly across the road from the adobe house.

Heading toward them, a dirt motorcycle bounced over the uneven terrain.

Josh watched it approach. The driver wore a construction-type helmet and a short-sleeved western-type shirt, Levis, and a pair of soiled leather gloves.

At a distance of ten feet, he braked to a stop, dismounted, and rested the bike against its kickstand. As he walked toward them,

Josh noticed the man's gait had a quirky lurch. The imbalance Josh attributed to a shortened leg, possibly an old injury or childhood polio. His shoulders were broad with well-developed musculature, a condition seen frequently in those who compensate for weakness in the lower extremities. His orange safety helmet bore the name *Dan* in black block letters.

"I saw the police car." The man's voice, in an even, mild tone, asked, "Any trouble here?"

"Maybe," Mannheim answered. He scrutinized the stranger. "You see anyone besides the police come over here in the last hour or so?"

"Can't say I did." He pulled off his glove and stuck out his hand. "I'm Dan Aviloh." He tilted his head backward and jerked his thumb over his shoulder toward the construction site. "I'm the boss. That's my construction crew over there."

Mannheim nodded. "Those gotta be pretty costly digs. Who in hell can afford 'em?"

"In this area? You gotta be kiddin'! There's more moola here than you can imagine. Every house I put up is sold for over a mill before I dig the foundation. I just wish I owned more land like this." He waved his hand around Josh's property.

"Be careful what you wish for."

Mannheim's cryptic statement bewildered Aviloh.

"What d'ya mean?"

Before Mannheim could respond, Josh stepped forward. "I'm the owner; Harrington's my name."

"Harrington?" Aviloh smiled broadly. "So, you're Doc Harrington? Well, I'll be damned! My wife told me about you."

"Your wife?"

"Yeah, Sherri Aviloh. She works at the Riverside County Administration Building. Pulled records for you some weeks ago."

Josh smiled. "Yes, I remember now. She was very helpful."

"Doc, have you thought about what you're gonna do with this damned old eyesore adobe and the land around it?"

Josh wasn't in the mood to talk about the disposition of his property. "No, I haven't thought it all out, just yet."

Aviloh reached into the back pocket of his soiled jeans, pulled out his wallet, and handed Josh a card. "If you decide to sell, let me know. I'm interested. I'll meet or beat anyone's offer, and that's a fact."

Mannheim interrupted, "Aviloh, did you know Peter Longfellow?"

"Huh? Are you kidding? Hell, yes, I did. We were like brothers growin' up out here. We did everything together from day one . . . until I was stricken. Not even that kept us apart for long."

"Stricken?" Josh asked.

"Yeah, polio." He pointed to his left leg but gave no inclination that he wanted to talk about it. "Petey and I probably built half the houses around here. We worked together before splitting up to form our own companies."

"Split up?" Mannheim's right eyebrow lifted. "That must have made you two strong competitors."

Aviloh hesitated. "Don't exactly know what you mean by *strong* competitors. Sure, we fought over the same contracts sometimes, but, hey, that's business. When it came to personal matters, we'd knock ourselves out for each other." The man's face darkened. "If I ever catch the fucker who killed him . . ."

Mannheim cut him off. "Save yourself jail time, buddy; let the police handle that."

"Yeah, I suppose you're right. Anyway, if there's anything I can do to help, just call." He threw a casual salute, then mounted his Kawasaki and rode to the construction site on the other side of the road.

When Aviloh was out of hearing range, Mannheim said, "He didn't say anything about seeing the black panel truck or the gurney going in or coming out of the house."

"Maybe he was elsewhere at the time," Josh said.

"Sure, or maybe he didn't want to see 'em." Mannheim's cryptic remarks baffled Josh. "Let's sit in your SUV, Doc, and rest our weary asses." Mannheim crawled into the passenger seat, slumped down, and folded his arms, his right hand resting over his concealed holster.

When Josh pulled his driver's door shut, Mannheim closed his eyes partially and moved his tongue around his inner cheeks. In his deep but barely audible monotone, he said, "The creep who slashed that tire could be anywhere around here, just waiting."

Again Josh got that chill. "Waiting for what?"

"Could be someone who doesn't want you around here."

"For God's sake, why?" Josh was beginning to think he sounded like a broken record. *Why? What? How?*

Mannheim raised his brows and shrugged.

Not exactly the answer he wanted. Josh slid his seat back a bit from the steering wheel. "Listen, Mannheim, I appreciate the fact that you're here with me. Doesn't your wife object when you put in long hours?"

Mannheim continued to look through the windshield, his eyes at half-mast. "Got no wife. The only gal I ever loved died eighteen years ago, in childbirth."

Josh made a consoling comment and asked about the circumstances.

Speaking deliberately, Mannheim told of a botched-up home delivery by an inexperienced midwife who didn't know her elbow from her asshole. His wife bled to death, and the baby was stillborn. Mannheim continued, "Never should have happened. That bitch had no right practicing on my wife. I'll tell you this: from that time my attitude changed about a lot of things. On my watch every murder, every innocent loss of life, has to be accounted for." He exhibited more emotion than Josh had ever seen from him before. It was the kind of soulful, unburdening talk a man has when he's painfully lonely.

Mannheim's eyes shifted slowly from side to side with little head movement. He spoke in a sort of free association. "Tell ya the truth, gang- and drug-related murders don't do much for me. Of course, you understand, that's just between you and me. Those bastards could kill each other off as far as I'm concerned. It's the innocents caught in the crossfire or senseless, drive-by shooting, shit like that, that fries my liver."

When Josh thought Mannheim had vented his spleen, he asked, "Any progress on the Longfellow murder?"

Mannheim again shrugged, but this time he shook his head as well. "CSU has a hair or two, some smudgy fingerprints, shoe prints in a flower bed, maybe a tire tread." He brushed his nose with his thumb, then studied his thumb. "Frankly, I don't know how much any of that helps. It'll take snoop-dog detective work unless we get a lucky break. It isn't as though CSU doesn't do a damn good job, mind you, but all that crap on TV showing how crimes are solved in the laboratory . . . well, it usually ain't that way. Those brilliant crime analyses are strictly for viewer consumption. I don't buy that shit."

"You mentioned shoe prints in a flower bed outside the Longfellow home—wouldn't they be helpful?"

"Sure, but do you realize how many pairs of size-ten Nikes are sold, and in how many stores? I'm not saying we couldn't get better information if we had a hell of a lot more time and money, but we don't."

"What about the tire tread?"

"Yeah, what about it? Look, a plaster impression is fine, but what do you do with the damn thing? They're great when you can match 'em up to something. And as for the skeleton, it'll take some forensic nerds with a lot of luck to identify those remains. They may even come up with a clue or two from the decomposed rags, but I wouldn't count on that either."

"What about dental records?"

Mannheim sighed impatiently. "If they can be matched, fine. But where do they start? Speaking of starting . . ." He leaned forward, took a handkerchief from his back pocket, and unfolded it, displaying an old car key with an attached coin-sized logo. "This little gem was lying on the ground under the bagged skeleton. We might be able to trace the make and model of the car to a dealership or rental agency. Either should be able to give us a name."

Josh studied the attached logo. "Looks like a Lincoln ignition key. Two dealers in the valley sell those cars, new."

"Good, that'll limit our search, unless the car was brought in from another area." Mannheim put on his half-glasses and brought the plastic disc close to his squinting eyes. "Coachella U-Drive Enterprises," he read aloud, then replaced the items in his handkerchief and pocketed them. He cleared his throat and swallowed, his Adam's apple bobbing in his scrawny neck. "If I remember correctly, the U-Drive operates out of Cathedral City. We'll pay them a visit."

Mannheim looked at Josh sideways. "You got any ideas who that skeleton belongs to?"

Before Josh could answer, Mannheim asked,

"What about the other name on that deed of yours?"

"You mean Chester Uriah Effingwell?"

"Yeah, that's it. What the hell do we know about him? He continued, "Jeezus, will ya listen to those names: Chester Uriah Effingwell and Chesley Upton Effingwell. Now there's a pair of monikers that could make a couple guys hate their parents for a lifetime."

Josh smiled briefly, then changed the subject. "I got some information from Madame Tatiana."

"What the . . ." Mannheim reared his head, and with a smile that could be mistaken for a sneer, said, "Doc, don't tell me *you* fired off a few rounds at Big Tits' place, too."

"No, no—"

Mannheim interrupted. "Your secret's safe with me."

"Dammit," Josh tamped down on his irritation. "Let me explain: I went to Madame Tatiana for the sole purpose of gathering information on Chester Effingwell—in fact, she knew him well."

"Did you learn anything new?

"Maybe—"

A rumbling from behind interrupted the conversation. Mannheim looked in the rearview mirror.

"Tow truck's here."

He stepped out of the SUV. When the truck slid to a stop, he waved at the driver and yelled, "Pedro, what the hell took you so long?"

"Sorry, Sarge, this place ain't easy to find."

"That it ain't. When you're through here, I'll need you to take me to the station."

Pedro looked down from the cab. "No problema."

Mannheim turned to Josh. "Doc, do me a favor: as soon as that tire is changed, get the hell outta here. Follow us out. I don't want you targeted by the crazy sonofabitch who slashed your tire." He looked at his watch, then glanced at the nearby construction site. At 3:45, the laborers had gone for the day, leaving an almost eerie silence after the roar of the earth movers, front and back loaders, and air-splitting nail guns. The late sun cast long shadows on the motionless mechanical behemoths.

A sudden movement in the brush brought an instantaneous response from Mannheim. He whipped out his gun and squatted behind the SUV. He signaled Pedro and Josh to get behind him. When both men were safe, he steadied his gun with both hands and yelled, "Come out with your hands up!"

No response. No movement.

Mannheim's nostrils flared with intensity.

Josh held his breath. Motionless and tense, all three of them stared at the brush.

Suddenly the tall weeds moved again, and this time out hopped a medium-sized rabbit that scampered off.

"Shit!" Mannheim dropped his arms and relaxed. "A goddamn rabbit." He replaced the gun in his shoulder holster and walked angrily away.

Neither Pedro nor Josh said a word.

When the spare tire was in place, Josh insisted Pedro and Mannheim leave before him, since it was easier to back the truck out on that single rough lane. Josh would follow them.

On Sinatra Drive, the tow truck left Josh behind and was soon out of sight. Josh drove slowly down the road with its 10-degree grade. Near the bottom, an ominous rumble sounded, and grew louder with each passing second.

Looking in the rearview mirror, Josh caught a glimpse of a white, mud-spattered truck bearing down on him. The truck looked like the one that almost ran him down several weeks ago.

Josh stepped down on the accelerator. "Where did that sonofabitch come from?" He focused on the road and intermittently the rearview mirror. The driver's features were indistinct, but a ruddy face was framed by long black hair. Within seconds, the massive truck's grill began to fill his entire mirror. Josh had no doubt the bastard intended to push him into the heavy traffic of Highway 111 below, or . . .

Glancing to the right, Josh took in the narrow ledge of pampas grass bordering a steep dropoff. Was it possible the driver intended to send him over the edge? Reflexively, Josh yanked the SUV's wheel to the left and immediately bounced onto the low-lying median. With all his might, he slammed on the brakes, bringing the car to a squiggling stop. The truck roared past, spewing dust and debris.

Seconds later, screeching brakes and blaring horns sounded at the intersection of Frank Sinatra Drive and Highway 111 below. Josh released his grip on the wheel and got out of the SUV. Slowly, he surveyed the tires—no flats and no wheel damage. Without a doubt, he knew it was that same dirty white dump truck, or one like it, on the I-10 that had struck the rear end of his vehicle before. And, like before, he hadn't seen any identifying company names or license plates. He got back into the SUV and wondered who was trying to frighten or kill him. He had misgivings about having torn up the turf and probably the irrigation system on the median, but he'd had to get away from that sonofabitch. He would notify the city clerk about the damage in the morning.

He wouldn't tell Maggie about this incident; she would worry terribly. Maybe he was overreacting to something that was not intended to be malicious. He was ambivalent about Maggie assuming sole responsibility for developing the land. Suddenly the land and prospective building sites were becoming less attractive. He knew Maggie could hold her own against most adversity and even welcomed a challenge, but he had to be sure of her safety. He pledged his moral support, for whatever that was worth, but made his position clear; he could not give his time and effort to the project and handle his practice concurrently. Now his main concern was keeping Maggie safe from the crazies.

* * *

Maggie lay on the sofa with a damp compress on her forehead, her eyes closed, when Josh entered. Seeing her, he backed away quietly, but as he did, her eyes fluttered. "Josh?"

"How're you feeling, sweetheart?" He came back and sat on the sofa, near her knees.

"Better, now that you're here." Still pale, she removed the compress and smiled wearily. "Sorry I caused such inconvenience. Did everything go well after I left?"

"Yes, fine. How was your ride home with Detective Todd?"

She sat up and told him Todd's story: his family background and the travail of his great-grandparents, who came across the desert in the late 1800s. They acquired land from the railroads eager to have agricultural products to ship. That land is now Rancho Mirage. Maggie thought the detective wanted to keep her interested in something other than her nausea. He was probably afraid she might upchuck in the police car.

"What happened to his grandparents' land?" Josh asked.

"They were swindled by a fruit-packing company whose management made life intolerable."

"How?"

"At night they circled the house on horses, yelling obscenities, firing rifles, setting fires, cutting off the water supply—just terribly frightening and nasty things. Then they offered the owners a pittance for their property."

"So they were forced to sell?" Josh asked.

"We arrived here before I could ask any more questions, but from our conversation, I got a good insight into how some of the valuable land was obtained by so-called land barons."

Leaning over, Josh kissed Maggie on her head, then walked toward the bedroom to change into his sweats.

She called out, "Josh, there's a letter from the hospital administrator's office. It's on your dresser."

The letter read like a text quoting information from the hospital nuclear and radiation department: ". . .measurement of the toxic substance was made by alpha-particle spectroscopy; the intensity of alpha energy was determined to be the direct cause of death in the case of Mr. Chesley U. Effingwell. The alpha particles of polonium-210 were most probably introduced in solids or liquids given the patient sometime before he was admitted to the hospital."

Josh reread that last line and noted the underlined word *before*. Yamamoto wanted to emphasize that the hospital could not be held accountable for any wrongdoing. That point would be important in any contentious litigation. In addition, Yamamoto apologized for any offensive comments he might have made to Josh in his office.

In an offhand manner he once again alluded to the Rancho Mirage property, stating that if Josh were interested in selling the whole or any part, he knew investors who would make serious bids, but if Josh should be disposed to making a charitable donation of the land to the hospital foundation it would be most graciously received. Established in a will, that property would create considerable tax savings to Josh's estate.

How considerate of those financial experts to render unsolicited opinions on other people's property, Josh thought. He handed the letter to Maggie, who'd followed him into the bedroom. "What do you think?"

She quickly read the contents. "That's interesting. Do you think Yamamoto included himself among the investors?"

"Maybe." Josh went back to changing his clothes.

"Well, if he did, do you think he'd be capable of killing for that property?"

"Maggie." Josh stopped unbuttoning his shirt. "Your imagination is running wild."

She made a face at him. "There's a good chance that Yamamoto knew Longfellow. After all, Longfellow was one of the major building contractors in the valley. It wouldn't surprise me at all if he had bid on the new hospital wing."

"Okay, what's your point?"

"Don't you see? Yamamoto and Longfellow knew about the land long before Effingwell gave it to you, and between them they might have conspired to . . ." Maggie's voice trailed away.

"To what?" Josh prompted. "I'm not sure I follow your convoluted thinking. Frankly, I don't see Yamamoto as a murderer."

FOURTEEN

Maggie gave the clothing in her closet a cursory review and without enthusiasm asked, "Josh, should I wear a black dress or a light-colored pants suit for the memorial service?"

"Wear whatever you'd be comfortable in. The clothes aren't important; it's the fact that you're paying your respects." Josh slid the knot of his tie into place.

"Do you think Prissy's a mournful or a merry widow?" Maggie asked as she headed toward the bathroom.

"How should I know? Prissy confided in me that she and Peter had not been intimate for many months. I really don't know how she feels."

Maggie, in a dark slip, stood in front of the washroom mirror with a curling iron, putting the finishing touches on her hairdo. "Who do you think will be there?"

"I don't know. Peter Longfellow was a well-established contractor, dealing with big bucks. I'm sure some valley big shots will show up."

"Good. That's what I think."

Josh looked at his wife as if she'd lost her mind. "Why is that so important?"

She gave him a kiss on the cheek as she returned to her closet. "You'll see."

* * *

Valets, college-age men, dressed in white shirts, black trousers, and black bow ties, ran to the SUV; one opened the driver's door and greeted Josh with a broad smile as he handed him a parking stub. The other opened the door for Maggie and assisted her. The broad circular driveway at the Longfellow estate provided spaces for about ten cars. The others had to be parked on nearby streets. A caterer's truck near the service entrance had Josh thinking this could be more like a celebratory Irish wake than a sedate memorial service.

Parked along the driveway, a late-model, chrome-yellow Ferrari convertible displayed a vanity plate reading *PRISSY L*. Behind it, for sheer contrast, was Farquhaar's tired Saab sedan with dents, grimy windows of near-opacity, and a mud-spattered plate reading *RUF-1*. On the rear window a finger message read, "Wash me."

In the foyer on a console under a mirror, a guest registry lay open. Maggie scanned the names, then looked at Josh. "I don't know anyone here except Roscoe Farquhaar." She signed their names, paused in front of the mirror to make some quick adjustments to her hair, then took Josh's arm and walked into the great room. Soft rock background music was barely audible above the chatter punctuated by laughter. A group of would-be mourners turned merrymakers hovered around the long bar.

A voice called out, "Joshua, my boy, Maggie! Over here. Over here." There was no mistaking the timbre, the tonality of the Bostonian's cry. Turning, Josh saw the rotund form, the jowly, red-faced Farquhaar, as he elbowed his way through the crowd holding a glass of wine in one hand and a canapé in the other, his pudgy pinky extended delicately upward.

Josh watched him approach, fearing the man was going to either spill the wine or catapult the canapé down some unsuspecting woman's front or back.

Eventually, Farquhaar reached them—refreshments intact.

"So glad to see you. You both look absolutely smashing. Maggie, my dear, you are ravishing, and you, Joshua, would put Beau Brummel to shame." He smiled, pleased with his clever bon mots. "Have you seen our hostess, Prissy?" He whispered in Josh's ear, "If my sexual orientation were otherwise constituted, I'm sure I could be quite interested in her. Yes, quite interested."

Looking about, he continued, "Don't know why Peter couldn't have loved her. Maybe if he had found a way to muzzle her incessant chatter . . ." Farquhaar blinked rapidly. "Do you think either found sexual gratification elsewhere?" Stopping long enough, he plunged the black caviar canapé into his mouth, then licked his thumb and index finger.

"Roscoe, how well did you know Peter Longfellow?" Maggie asked.

Roscoe gulped his half glass of wine, smacked his tongue against his palate, and smiled. "Wonderful chardonnay. Smoky and yet fruity. Wonderful, yes, yes. What?" He looked at Maggie as if trying to recall her question. When it surfaced, he blurted, "Ah, yes, how well did I know Peter? He, my dear, was one of my first clients in the Valley—lovely man, lovely man. Quite successful, you know."

"Did he have enemies in the business world?"

"Maggie, my fair blossom, there hardly walks a mortal who has not incurred the wrath of some misbegotten soul."

Josh intervened. "Excuse me for disrupting the conversation. Did Longfellow have enemies who hated him sufficiently to kill him?"

Farquhaar turned and raised his brow. "Joshua, you hardly give me room to negotiate. Aren't you aware that the lawyer's forte is to talk and obfuscate and meander until the answer becomes almost meaningless?"

Josh sighed. "Just tell me, to your knowledge, did he have any serious enemies?"

"Well, perhaps one or two who thought he was guilty of financial chicanery. But I can assure you . . ." Farquhaar's attention turned to something over Josh's shoulder, and he let his words fade away.

Josh turned. Prissy approached, wearing a black satin gown with a plunging neckline that converged with a star-studded diamond brooch. A long slit on one side of the gown revealed her shapely well-tanned leg in a gown that might have been designed for one of the candidates at the Hollywood Oscar awards. She smiled at Josh, embraced him, kissed him on the lips, then backed off.

Slowly, she faced Maggie, surveying her from her hairdo to her dress shoes. "This must be the lovely wife of my old lover." She extended her hand. "In case you haven't heard, I'm Penelope Longfellow. People call me 'Prissy,' and I suspect a few other things as well. Did your handsome husband tell you how crazy I was about him in college, and that we shared fun times?"

Maggie maintained a quiet dignity and smiled pleasantly, in a way that would have made the *Mona Lisa* envious.

Actually, Maggie was left speechless by Prissy's appearance. Was this the unattractive home economics major whose picture she had discovered in Josh's yearbook? Unbelievable! She could have been the undisputed winner of the International Complete Makeover Contest.

Heat rose at the back of Josh's neck and over his ears. He had never been intimate with Prissy, and she damned well knew it. He hoped Maggie wouldn't be taken in by Prissy's lies.

He looked at his wife, marveling at her calm composure.

"Thank you for coming," Prissy said. She kept her attention locked on Maggie. She took hold of Maggie's hands and held them. "I'm sure you know I'm quite interested in purchasing your Rancho Mirage property. If you'd rather form a partnership, I'm amenable to that idea. The thought of working with Josh—I mean, both of you— would be wonderful."

"I'm sure it would be." Maggie politely withdrew her hands from Prissy's. She reached for Josh's arm and smiled. "If you'll excuse us, there are some people we would like to say hello to." With the ease of a woman of class, she led Josh away. Under her breath, however, she whispered, "If that horny bitch thinks for one minute we're going to do business with her—"

"Hello, Doc." A hand shot forward, stopping Maggie from finishing.

Josh looked at the owner's hand, then upward to the speaker.

"It's Dan Aviloh. Remember me? I'm the contractor working next to your land in Rancho Mirage." As if in an afterthought, he turned to introduce his wife. "This is my wife, Sherri."

"Yes, of course." Josh smiled. "I remember both of you. This is my wife, Maggie."

Both women acknowledged each other with a smile. Josh noticed that Sherri seemed a bit subdued and red-eyed. As if she'd been crying.

Dan, with his hail-fellow-well-met approach, would have been at ease in any company. Without apology for his brashness, he asked, "Have you decided what you're going to do with your property and that adobe shack?"

Josh shook his head. "No, we haven't, not yet."

"Doc, as I said before, I'll make you a damn good offer." He looked around, then stepped closer so he wouldn't be overheard. "Prissy would kill me if she knew I was trying to horn in on her. She'd do anything to get her hands on that property. She talked to me about developing home sites there, homes ranging from two to five mill, easy." He nudged Josh and winked. "Give me a call, Doc. I'm sure we can do business, and I'll show you how to make some *real* money."

Sherri remained quiet, holding a tissue to dab her reddened eyes and nose. She excused herself and walked away, a bit unsteadily.

Maggie turned toward Sherri's husband. "Is she all right? Perhaps I should go with her."

"No, no, she'll be fine." He waved his hand to dismiss Maggie's concern. "She feels bad about Petey's death, and all this stirs up memories. She might have had a drink too many to forget. We were a pretty close foursome, for a lot of years." In spite of Dan's assurances, Maggie hurried after Sherri, placed her arm around her waist, and accompanied her out of the room.

Josh said, "Dan, you knew Peter better than most. Did he have any enemies, anyone who would have wanted to kill him? Was he in debt?" Aviloh shook his head after each query. "I hope you don't mind my asking, but was it possible he was having an affair? Was there a jilted woman, an angry boyfriend or spouse?"

Drawing his head back, Dan smiled. "Hey, Doc, that's about five big questions." He laughed. "You got a deputy's badge?" Dan shook his head. "Nah, Petey was liked by everyone. Everyone except maybe his—"

He stopped abruptly when Roscoe, bleary-eyed, approached with another glass of wine. His seersucker jacket appeared tighter and more disheveled. With a flourish, he said to the two men, "What have we here? A morbid convention for the dearly departed? You'll not convince St. Peter to open those pearly gates for *our* beloved Peter unless you show some mirth. Come now, a bit of Rabelaisian merriment. Drink up, you morbid mortals, and convince the winged saint that he's chosen wisely to admit our dearly departed to cavort among the angels in the Celestial Kingdom. Yes, sir, a wise choice for the Celestial Kingdom." Roscoe held his glass high, brought his head back, and gulped the rest of his wine.

Aviloh had little tolerance for Farquhaar's verbal theatrics and hurried off with a transparent excuse. Despite Roscoe's ebullient comments, Josh thought the occasion should have been more somber.

Some time later, Maggie and Sherri returned. Sherri left the steadying support of Maggie's arm to look for her husband.

Maggie whispered to Josh, "Poor thing had more than she could handle. She upchucked and soiled her dress. I had the maid help me clean her and that mess; then we had her lie down in one of the bedrooms. We forced two cups of black coffee down her, and I did nursing for the past twenty-five minutes."

Josh kissed his wife on the nose. "You'll be rewarded in heaven."

"With all this talk, I haven't had a chance to tell you what Sherri told me in the restroom." Maggie elbowed her way through the great room and led Josh out the front door to the lawn, where she inhaled deeply. "Ah, this air smells good. That vomitus lingered in my nostrils. Yuck!" She took another deep breath and exhaled slowly, then looked about to be sure she could not be overheard. "Sherri begged me not to say anything to anyone and swore me to secrecy. If I tell you, you must promise not to say anything to anyone."

"If you tell me, you'll have violated your promise."

"Josh, don't be difficult."

He raised his right hand. "Okay, tell me. Scout's honor."

"You simply won't believe what she told me." Maggie held Josh's arm firmly, demanding his complete attention. Her bright eyes locked onto his. "Can you believe Sherri was in love with Peter Longfellow?"

"Why doesn't that surprise me? The way she carried on in there, all that sobbing and drinking to forget—"

"No." Maggie tugged impatiently on his arm. "I mean really, really in love."

"Okay, really in love—idyllic, emotional, physical?"

"All of the above with all the trimmings. Don't laugh. She described their love as an exquisite and intense affair."

"All right, I believe you. How long had that been going on? Two weeks, a month, a year?"

"Try over three years."

"Over three years, and she thought no one else knew? That's a secret for the most naïve."

"She swore I was the only one privy to their secret."

"That's quite a burden she unloaded on you. Why do you think she chose you as her mother confessor?"

"Because she was somewhat potted and probably found it easier to pour out her pent-up grief—a grief that no one except another sympathetic woman could possibly understand."

"So, Mother Teresa, what did you deduce from that?"

"Don't you see? That gives us another suspect in Peter's murder."

"Really? How do you figure?"

At that moment, Dan and Sherri Aviloh emerged through the front door and walked toward Josh and Maggie. Dan's left drop-foot gait, although evident to Josh's clinical eye, did not seem to be much of an impediment. Sherri held onto his arm for her own balance.

"Well, Doc and Mrs. Harrington, it was good seeing you both, even though the occasion wasn't meant to be cheerful. Let's get together for dinner sometime up at our place." Dan offered his hand and Josh shook it.

Sherri gave Maggie a shy smile. "I do hope you'll come."

"We will," Maggie answered and returned her smile.

Josh and Maggie watched as the couple walked toward one of the parking valets. Sherri's backside outlined in a black suit was youthful, and her figure had escaped the matronly spread of many women her age. Her calves, shapely in high heels, made Josh realize she could have been quite appealing to Peter. Prissy, on the other hand, although physically attractive, was coarse, competitive, and self-absorbed, unlike the soft-spoken, reticent friendly Sherri.

She reminded Josh of some of the girls from rural southern Illinois whom he had known while a student Downstate, those with a homespun demeanor, the type who projected an aura of wholesomeness and sincerity. One of them came to mind: a minister's daughter, Bunny Hasenpfeffer, a plump, blond, blue-eyed, outwardly shy freshman. Being away from home for the first time, she had shed the repressions of her rigid upbringing and found glorious joy and freedom copulating like a feral rabbit. In their clandestine frenzied meetings, she would hurriedly disrobe, and if Josh was too slow, she'd tear into his shirt, unzip his pants, and pull them off. During intercourse she would bite, scratch, and yell in the throes of orgasm. Although the sessions had been exquisitely exhilarating, Josh always left in a state of near exhaustion. Years later, he learned that Bunny had married a minister, raised a family of four, and become a pillar of the community and church.

He had never judged the morality of those girls who must have experienced the same ravenous, hormone-driven urges as he, the same primal need for physical and emotional contact. In time, the overwhelming, raging sex drive had simmered for him, and the frequent need for carnal communication subsided. Fortunately, it had never completely disappeared but recurred at a more manageable rate.

Maggie studied his face. "Josh, you're deep in thought. What are you thinking?"

"What's that?" Josh rubbed his chin. "Nothing important. However, there is something that bothers me. What you said about Peter and Sherri—I was wondering about their relationship, and what you meant when you said that gives us another suspect in Longfellow's murder."

Maggie's blue eyes nearly sparkled. "Supposing, just supposing, Prissy learned about her husband Peter's relationship with Sherri?"

"Are you suggesting that Prissy, at about one hundred and twenty-five pounds, bashed in the skull of her two-hundred-pound husband, put a rope around his neck, hoisted him up, and then hanged him from the chandelier?"

"She could have had an accomplice, you know."

Josh frowned. "Hadn't thought of that."

"Oh dear." Maggie sighed and directed Josh's attention toward the house. "Here comes trouble."

Walking toward them, Roscoe Farquhaar emerged from the house weaving, barely able to steady the glass of wine he held. Just as he reached the driveway, a dark sedan turned in and narrowly missed him. Swearing, Farquhaar made a rapid but clumsy side-step and spilled wine onto his jacket. He glowered at the driver, who had parked next to him.

The moment the driver rolled down his window, Farquhaar let loose a rapid slur of abusive language. When he finished venting his spleen, he stumbled to the car and bent over to see inside. "Well, well, if it isn't my old nemesis, the pride of Thousand Palm's Homicide Division, Officer Timothy Mannheim, the harbinger of sorrowful news and malevolent happenings, and his sidekick, the quiescent Detective Todd. What do the infamous grave diggers want with these poor souls who came to mourn the loss of a noble spirit? Yes, a noble spirit."

Mannheim frowned. "Sorry we missed your fat ass, counselor. One less ambulance chaser would hardly be missed."

At the receiving end of a string of malcontent verbiage, Farquhaar was annoyed; his moon face darkened to a deep red. "See here, you, you foul-mouthed, ill-mannered, contemptible scarecrow. I'll have your badge and make you wish you never—"

"Easy, Farquhaar," Mannheim held up a hand. "You'll blow a gasket. All that goddamned hot air will escape and you'll end up a grease spot on the pavement."

"Why you . . . you . . ."

When Roscoe began to sputter, Josh decided it was time to intervene. He quickly crossed the grass, with Maggie hot on his heels. He put a hand on the lawyer's arm. "Let Detective Mannheim get out of his car, Roscoe."

He nudged Farquhaar away from the police sedan. Mannheim emerged from his side of the vehicle and cast a baleful eye at the beleaguered attorney. Todd left the driver's side and approached the two verbal combatants.

Josh said, "What brings you fellas here, Sergeant?"

Mannheim grunted, "Can't resist a party given by an attractive, wealthy widow."

Farquhaar must have found his voice again. "You abomination, your presence can only cast a dismal pall wherever you go. Yes, a dismal, dreary, decadent pall." Content that he'd cast enough aspersions on the detective, he started to stumble away. Suddenly he turned as if he'd changed his mind and delivered more shot. "You, Sergeant Mannheim, are nothing but a putrid mass of decomposing carrion."

"Careful, counselor," Mannheim said in his cold monotone. "You want to be sure we don't mistake you for a drunk and disorderly vagrant and lock your fat carcass in the tank until you sober up."

Farquhaar drew his glass back in a threatening gesture, spilling what was left of the wine on himself.

Seeing that the lawyer was about to fling the glass at him, Mannheim remained unflappable. "Go ahead, throw it. Let me charge you with assault and battery—then you can spend some real time in the slammer. Even as drunk as you are, you can't be that stupid."

The officer's threat must have hit a mark, for Farquhaar straightened his shoulders and fumbled unsuccessfully to button his jacket. "I believe I hear someone calling me." With a sniff, he spun on his heel and walked unsteadily away from them to engage someone else in conversation.

Once the man disappeared into the house, Mannheim turned to face Josh. "Glad I caught you, Doc. I think we found the murder weapon."

Josh looked at him, puzzled. "Murder weapon? Whose?"

"Longfellow's." Mannheim opened the back door of his car and retrieved a weighty toweled object. "It was partially buried in the bushes on your property."

"*Our* property?" Maggie stared down at the wrapped object with horror. "What was it doing there?"

"Good question. That's what I was asking myself."

"What is it?" Maggie seemed fixated on the murder weapon.

"Let's get to some better light and I'll show you."

He headed for the light shining from a lawn lamp post. Carefully he uncovered the olive-drab towel to expose the object, wrapped protectively by a heavy plastic bag.

"It's an andiron. One that was missing from Longfellow's fireplace; couldn't find the damn thing anywhere in the house, but suspected it was probably used to bash in Longfellow's skull."

"I see." Josh's mind whirled with all he'd learned. "What prompted you to look for it on our property?"

"That's just it. We weren't looking for it there. CSI was on the case. They were combing the subflooring where the skeleton was found and also the area around the adobe. In fact, every inch within thirty feet of the adobe was combed at my request."

"And this . . . ," Josh pointed at the weapon, "is what they found?"

"For sure, I didn't expect them to find a different murder weapon—that was a goddamned unexpected bonus. Like I told you, Doc, it takes snoop-dog detective work, and in my case, twenty-eight years of intuition, doubt, suspicion, and groping to uncover a few clues—if I'm lucky."

"Okay . . . that I understand. But did CSI find anything pertaining to the victim I found?"

"Nothing yet." Mannheim rubbed the back of his neck as if it pained him. "I was also hoping maybe whoever slashed your tire might have been in too much of a hurry. Maybe he became careless and dropped something, anything—a knife, gum, a candy wrapper. If we're lucky, he might have left a shoe print. CSI inspects every goddamn rock and blade of grass while they're there." The sergeant sighed. "It's paid off so far. They found the andiron in the bushes, not twenty feet from the adobe."

"Why in the hell would anyone drop the murder weapon that killed Longfellow there?" Josh was beginning to think his life had spun totally out of control.

"Dunno, but I have a few ideas. For one thing, when I'm through with this andiron, I'm sending it to the lab for bloodstains, fingerprints, and anything else they can find." He brought the andiron closer to Josh. "Take a look at this thing: the top is a bust of Satan with his goddamn horns, shitty grin, pointed ears, goatee, and long nose."

Maggie hissed. "It's revolting. But what I'd like to know is why was it found on our property?"

"It's just a guess, but I'm thinking that some sonofabitch, probably the same one who slashed your tire, might have been planning to whack you, also."

Maggie inched closer to Josh. "Why him? How did the murderer know that we would be out there?" She looked at her husband. "And why with the same murder weapon?"

"Maybe some kind of weird symbolism, someone trying to send a message that only his own fucked-up mind could understand." He glanced at Maggie, "Sorry, ma'am."

Maggie clutched Josh's arm. "Why us? How are we involved in all of this?"

"You're the new owners. That's all I can think of. Bad luck." Mannheim shrugged. "Besides, there's a helluva lot more questions I can't answer yet."

Josh pointed toward the andiron. "I assume you're here now with that because you want to know if it's a match to the one inside."

"Yep. You got it, Doc."

Maggie said, "That ought to create a sobering jolt among that bunch of drunks and freeloaders."

"Wouldn't it be better if you found another time to verify this?" Josh asked.

"Yeah, Doc, I suppose I could, but . . ." Mannheim sneered. "I figured it might not hurt to show this thing for shock purposes. You know . . . catch the reactions, the facial expressions that might suggest involvement."

Again, Josh thought of the number of people inside. "You'll have to be quick about it, Mannheim. There have to be over forty or fifty people in there."

Maggie looked at the house. "Do you actually think someone in there might be the murderer?"

"That's always a possibility, little lady. He, she, or they might want to mingle with the mourners to cast off suspicion. It's happened before."

"That's really perverse—how disgusting!" she said.

Mannheim nodded. "Who the hell can figure out the screwed-up mind of a murderer?"

FIFTEEN

The young car valets stopped to watch as Maggie, Josh, and Detective Todd followed behind Mannheim in a funereal-like procession through the front entrance. As Josh had anticipated, Mannheim's foreboding appearance brought an immediate halt to the mourners' festivities. A path like the parting of the Red Sea was created for the detective, who moved deliberately and held the clear plastic–protected andiron in his gloved hands. Prissy, seeing their approach and the effect it had, came from the opposite end of the room to confront the officers.

"What the hell's going on here?"

Mannheim glanced at the andiron in his hands, then at Prissy. She stared at the object, then turned ashen and walked unsteadily to a nearby chair. Her reaction heightened the drama and created a deeper quietude among the revelers.

Mannheim walked toward the seated Prissy. "Sorry, ma'am, I didn't mean to cause a fuss. Just wanted to know if this andiron was taken from your home."

Prissy turned her head aside and said nothing. Slowly she turned back to look at Mannheim. "It's been missing since Peter was murdered. It's one of a pair from the fireplace in his den." Still unsteady, she stood and held the arm of the chair.

Todd hurried to her side and placed his arm around her waist. "Are you all right, ma'am?"

"I'm quite all right." She removed his arm from her waist disdainfully.

Maggie whispered in Josh's ear, "You stay with the officers and Prissy; I'm going to use the upstairs restroom and look around. I want to see how the rest of this mansion is furnished."

Prissy led the detectives and Josh to the den off the great room. She stopped momentarily at the open French doors and surveyed the room that functioned as a small theater, library, and trophy room. She explained that the room was Peter's domain, and she seldom invaded his privacy.

Mannheim and Todd walked toward a restored fireplace mantel, one that might have graced a *casa grande* in old California. On a raised hearth inlaid with Mexican tiles stood an andiron, a mirror image of the one Mannheim held. He bent over to study it but did not touch it. He turned toward Prissy. "Is this old? Do you know if it has a stamp of origin?"

Prissy, resuming her customary impatience and superior attitude, said, "I have no idea. If you're curious, pick it up and look for yourself."

With his customary deadpan expression, he said, "I prefer not to, ma'am."

"Oh, for heaven's sake." With a huff and some difficulty, she picked up the weighty andiron and examined it for identifying marks. It says right here, *Hecho en Mexico.* She pointed behind the brass devil's head and showed it to Mannheim before replacing it. "Now, is there anything else you want? If not, I'll get back to my guests." She looked at Josh. "Darling, all this has left me very upset. Are you coming back to the great room?"

"If you don't mind, I'll look around here with the detectives."

That apparently wasn't the answer she wanted. "Suit yourself." Prissy walked toward the door.

Mannheim called after her, "Mrs. Longfellow, do you mind if I take this andiron to the lab?"

With her back toward him she raised her hand dismissively. "Take whatever you want, but *please* leave. You've already managed to spoil the memorial celebration."

Mannheim avoided touching the decorative end of the and-iron. He held it by its base and placed it in a plastic sack that Todd held open.

Josh watched the procedure and asked, "Why do you need this andiron? It's obviously a twin to the other."

"I need Mrs. Longfellow's fingerprints on it, Doc."

"Why not just ask her to give you a set of her fingerprints?"

"She's not obligated to do that, and besides, I don't want her to think she's under suspicion—not yet. Better let her think she's not a suspect. Maybe she'll do something stupid to incriminate herself."

"And if you do find her fingerprints on the suspected murder weapon?" Josh asked.

"We'll put her name high in the *possible to probable* column—that's no real proof but enough to make the cheese more binding."

"Other prints also may show up on that."

"Doc, I can see you're right on top of things. If you ever get tired of sawing bones, join us." Mannheim looked around and sniffed upward. "Smell that? That's the stink I smelled before, kind of like candles and something else." He and Todd left the room carrying both andirons.

After the men left, Josh opted to stay and look around. The room held a treasure trove of memorabilia—maybe a thousand clues to Longfellow's past that led to his murder. A part of one wall served as a gallery for black-and-white photographs dating back forty or more years. A youthful Peter Longfellow in a baseball uniform posed with his middle-school teammates. The players' names were listed below the pictures. Seated next to Longfellow was a youngster named Daniel David Aviloh. A banner above the group proclaimed the Indio Scouts of the Coachella Valley as the Junior League Baseball Champions of 1967. The black/white photo was aging into brownish discoloration.

Josh looked at progressive photos of the boys as they participated in football, baseball, and basketball. He compared pictures where Peter Longfellow and Daniel Aviloh shared front and center positions for several seasons; then something had changed. In a photo of the seventh-grade football team, Peter as captain sat in the center while Aviloh stood off to the side in a white shirt and dark pants; he apparently had not participated as an active team member. Was it about then that Daniel had contracted polio?

In a later photo, both Peter and Daniel stood in athletic tights and T-shirts at either end of a barbell stand, hands on hips, flexing biceps and hunched forward in a weightlifter's pose to exaggerate neck, chest, and abdominal muscles. Daniel's left lower extremity indicated a definite loss of girth. A slight body tilt to the left suggested shortness in that leg. Josh nodded to himself. The picture confirmed his suspicions.

On another wall, a number of shelves held volumes of leather-bound and hardcover books, such as the western sagas of Louis L'Amour and Zane Grey, and fantasy tales by Edgar Rice Burroughs. Books on another shelf were devoted to the occult: *Demonology Through the Ages, Devilry in Ancient and Modern Times,* and *Mystics, Warlocks and Witches.* A theater-sized TV screen was flush-mounted on another wall facing twelve leather club chairs in two rows, the chairs separated by small tables for holding drinks and ashtrays.

From behind him, someone stepped into the room.

Josh turned and was relieved to find Maggie standing in the doorway.

She hurried over to him. "Wow, this is some kind of place! Upstairs is like something out of Dante's *Inferno* or Poe's *Murders in the Rue Morgue.*"

At that same moment, Prissy and Dan Aviloh entered the den as well. Josh placed his hand on his wife's arm as a warning.

Prissy spoke first. "Hey, you two, how about joining the rest of us? The good times are rolling at the bar."

Dan Aviloh reached for Prissy's hand. With the other, he pointed to the photos on the wall. "See the pictures of big, handsome Pete and the gimpy shrimp next to him?"

Prissy yanked her hand out of his and looked at him reproachfully. "How many times do I have to tell you, I don't want to hear that crap?" She turned abruptly and walked out of the room. Her request that Maggie and Josh join them had obviously been forgotten.

Dan looked at them, shrugged, and followed after her.

"What was that all about?" Maggie made an exaggerated face. "Talk about drama."

"And how. You were about to tell me what you found upstairs."

Maggie leaned toward Josh and began to describe Prissy's enormous bedroom. "She has a massive and eerie dark carved wooden four-poster bed with swagged maroon velvet drapes. I thought the room looked like an unholy shrine; it was awesome, spooky, and smelled of incense."

Josh looking at her widened eyes filled with excitement said, "This is beginning to sound interesting. What else did you find?"

"The walls were painted a deep red, almost black. One wall had a curtained alcove like an altar, with a half circle of candles on the floor in front of it. There were painted symbols on the wall—an upside-down cross, a five-pointed star, and a goat's head. I was afraid to spend any time there, but I couldn't tear myself away. It was all so mesmerizing. I tiptoed into an enormous clothes closet; I swear it had to be the size of a four-car garage. One rack held exquisite formal wear, hand-sewn beaded dresses of silk and fine woolens."

Maggie, still excited, went into further detail. "What really caught my eye was a shelf with long leather boots, and wait till you hear this: mounted on a wall was an arrangement of whips and cat-o'-nine-tails, handcuffs, spurs, leather thongs and straps, spiked gauntlets, and the most grotesque masks with horns and spiked teeth. Just thinking about them makes my skin crawl."

"Slow down, baby, you're talking too fast."

"Oh, it was fascinating, but so frightening." She looked into Josh's eyes. "What do you make of all that?"

"It sounds like a warehouse for sadomasochistic events."

"Josh, do you think Peter Longfellow suffered a ritual murder?"

"I'm beginning to wonder."

She fingered her purse nervously, "I feel kind of guilty about this. When I left the closet I took one last look around that creepy room. In the corner was a stand of DVDs. I picked one up, couldn't read the label in that poor light, and brought it toward a lamp at the opposite corner, when I thought I heard footsteps. My heart just about leaped out of my chest. I jammed the DVD into my purse, ran to the door, and peeked down the hall. Thank God no one was there. I tried looking nonchalant coming down the stairs. When I didn't see you with the others, I came looking for you here."

Josh looked around. "Let's get the hell out of this godforsaken place with its devil worship."

"I agree. This place gives me the creeps."

SIXTEEN

The next day, Maggie entered Josh's consultation room holding a chart. "Your four forty-five appointment has arrived. It's Dan Aviloh."

Josh's brow furrowed. "Dan Aviloh? What's he doing here? He said nothing to me about a health problem last night." He took the new-patient chart and flipped it open. "What's his complaint?"

"Progressive weakness in his left leg, worse in the last few months."

Josh glanced at Maggie's notes. "Ask one of the girls to bring me a cup of coffee, and ask Dan if he'd like one, then bring him in. I'd like to talk to him before we put him in an examining room."

"No problem." Maggie gave him a quick kiss on the cheek and walked out.

With a five o'clock shadow and a smile that belied his painful limp, Aviloh immediately extended his hand when he entered Josh's office. The man's firm handshake revealed thick, callused skin resulting from years of hard labor. For some strange reason, Josh thought of Sherlock Holmes, the fabled detective, who claimed he could determine a man's occupation by merely inspecting his hands. Josh might have guessed this patient's line of work, if he hadn't already known. Dan's thickened fingernails, like his palms and fingers, harbored dirt and grime that resisted ordinary washing. Some early arthritic knobbiness at the finger joints caused a permanent cupping of the hand as in a grasping configuration.

"Doc, I have to apologize for the way I look, and if I don't smell fresh, it's because I just came off the job."

"No apology necessary. Why don't you sit down?"

The door opened and Carmenita, the receptionist, arrived with two mugs of coffee and set them on the desk. She smiled and asked if there was anything else she could do. Aviloh watched her backside as she left the room. He arched his brows and snarled. "Man-oh-man, Doc, that's real eatin' stuff."

Josh ignored the comment. He came around his desk and sat on the edge of the corner. "So, what's the problem?"

Aviloh rolled up his left pant leg and began to remove the leg brace attached to the heel of the shoe that provided one inch of elevation. "I hate to complain, but this fuckin' leg's slowing me down. By the end of the day, I'm really fighting it, and the goddamn brace is biting into my ankle." He wore thickened socks and moleskin pads over the bony, atrophic ankle, where the skin was reddened from irritation.

Josh bent down and removed the pads slowly. Even so, Aviloh winced.

"Sorry, Dan. Tell me about your leg; start from the beginning."

Aviloh slumped in his chair and launched into a history taking him back to his eleventh birthday, celebrated with six of his buddies in the backyard of his home in Indio. Pete Longfellow, of course, his closest pal, was there. The kids horsed around in a plastic pool for hours, even after sundown. He remembered feeling tired, then chilly. That night, in bed, he developed a fever and thought he was going to burn up. In the morning, he was unable to move his legs and had difficulty breathing. His neck became rigid as a board, and he ached like crazy all over. The doctor was summoned, took one look at him, and told his mother he had polio. She just about collapsed when she heard that.

"Didn't you receive polio vaccine?"

Aviloh shook his head. His folks were leery, since there had been publicity about a bad batch of vaccine that actually caused polio. He remembered being bundled and brought to the Desert Hospital in Palm Springs, where he was placed on the critical list in a ward with several other polio victims. His parents were told that if he survived, he might be a basket case. He remembered vaguely the terms *bulbar* and *spinal*, and his mother was told that he had both types. He was trapped in an iron lung and said he would never, ever forget his fear of dying in that giant tube, and he would never forget the hours of the whooshing sound of the bellows.

After several weeks the doctor gave his parents the good news that he had improved, and that in itself was a miracle. Painful weeks followed while he received the Sister Kenny treatment: hot packs, massages, and limb movements. Only the left drop-foot persisted.

When he returned to school six months later, he came roaring back, even though he wore a cumbersome brace. "I didn't run as fast as I did before, but in our small school I played most of the sports. The only guy who could beat me was Petey Longfellow. But hell, he was always better'n me in everything. He was a sort of hero to me."

He hesitated before he spoke again. "Tell ya the truth, I guess I always kinda envied him. I never said this to anyone else, Doc, but the illness left me sort of insecure. I guess I became what some might call an overachiever. I wanted what everyone else had. If I couldn't buy it, I stole it. I paid my debt to society and turned out straight. But I'm still damn competitive and there is a lot that I want. Jeez, Doc, here I am mouthin' off, and none of this has anything to do with my leg."

"You did remarkably well," Josh said as he made notes in the patient's chart.

"Yeah, I guess I did. In our school, the competition wasn't too swift."

"So, you and Peter Longfellow remained friends for many years."

"Hell! We were like brothers. If some guy made the mistake of calling me 'gimpy' or 'crip,' Pete would haul off and whack the shit out of him—not that I couldn't do it myself, mind you, but Pete was faster on his feet." Dan remained quiet for a moment and looked at his leg. "So, Doc, what about this bum peg?" He studied Josh's face. "Is it gonna get worse?"

Josh cupped his chin in his hand. "That's a distinct possibility. You're probably suffering from what we call post-polio syndrome. We know that years after the initial attack there is a progressive deterioration of the spinal tract neurones that normally stimulate the—"

"Whoa, hold it, Doc, you're losing me. In other words, nothing can be done, right?"

"Not entirely."

"Okay, what can be done? I can't stop working."

"Several things—none of which will restore function, of course, but may slow the rate of disability and improve your motion. Before we go into that, does anything else bother you?"

"Yeah." Aviloh looked around and spoke in a hushed tone, "Doc, I'm hung pretty good, but my pecker ain't responding. I almost never get a hard-on with my wife. I don't think I can satisfy her anymore. And to tell the truth, I don't think she gives a damn and at this point I'm not sure I do. At least not with her."

"Does that imply that you're able to satisfy someone else?"

"Well—" A knock at the door disrupted the conversation.

Maggie leaned in from around the door. "Doctor Harrington, the girls will be leaving soon." She must have noticed Aviloh's pant leg rolled up and his bare foot. "Should I get the patient ready for the examining room?"

"Yes, that'll be fine." Josh stood and motioned for Dan to follow his wife. "I'll be in shortly."

When Josh entered, Dan had disrobed except for his undershorts. Through the open part of the examining gown in back, Josh could clearly see the shorter left leg with smaller girth. As he began the examination, he immediately detected a motor loss in several muscle groups below the left knee that affected foot function. He wrote a prescription for an improved brace, then cleansed the area from the mid-leg to the foot and applied fresh moleskin pads to the irritated prominences of the ankle. He asked Aviloh to stand on graph paper, then with a pen outlined both feet; a distinct size discrepancy existed.

Dan stepped off the graph paper. "Doc, as you can see, I have to wear two different-sized shoes. Of course, I have to pay for two pairs every time I'm fitted."

He looked down the front of the gown at his groin. "Now what about lazy willie here? Got any magic pills to bring him back to life? Christ, Doc, there was a time when just thinking about getting laid made this pecker stand at attention. Later, it took a little coaxing, a little feel here and there, a little tit squeezing, all that used to work quick, like that . . ." He snapped his fingers. "Hell, if I get laid once every two weeks, I'm doing good."

Josh knew the man was developing a critical walking problem, but he was obsessed with his erectile dysfunction. He went to his Rolodex, then wrote the names of several urologists who might be able to help him. When he handed Dan the sheet of paper, he asked, "Anything else on your mind, Dan?"

"Yeah, Doc, there is. I want to talk to you about your property. You know I'll enter into any kind of arrangement you'd like. I could do a lot with that land." He extended his arm in a broad sweep. "I can see Mediterranean-style homes. Big homes with red-tiled roofs, porticos with large arches, kidney-shaped pools and tennis courts on those hillside properties overlooking the valley—"

Josh cut him off. "Dan, Maggie and I haven't decided on its disposition yet."

"Doc, I'd just about kill to get my hands on that property."

* * *

After Aviloh left, Josh was sitting on the swivel stool completing his notes when Maggie came in and stood behind him.

"Let me guess. Aside from his leg problem, he made another offer to buy our land?"

Josh told her about their conversation, then closed Aviloh's folder and turned around to look up at her. Maggie leaned forward and ran her hands through his hair. "Salt and pepper, my favorite colors." She kissed the top of his head. "Have I told you lately how much I love you?"

"Yes, but don't let that deter you from telling me again." He stood and put his arms around her waist. "You sure know how to make a guy feel romantic."

The jarring ring of the phone shattered the moment of precious intimacy.

"Let it ring, the service will pick it up," Josh said.

Maggie embraced Josh more firmly, then in a predictable move released her hold on him and picked up the phone. She listened for a while, then covered the mouthpiece with her hand. "It's the ER operator at the hospital. Said Mrs. Sylvia Horowitz fell and broke her left humerus, just below the shoulder. The nurse wanted to know if she should temporize and give her a sling and pain medication and send her to our office tomorrow."

Josh swore softly and tossed his lab coat on a chair. "What in the hell has the practice of medicine come to? Why should anyone with a fracture go without immediate treatment? Tell the nurse I'll be there in twenty-five minutes."

"Josh, you're so conscientious. No wonder patients love you."

SEVENTEEN

As they headed toward the hospital, Maggie said out of the blue, "I'd like to know more about Prissy."

Josh caught the tone of his wife's dislike. To keep the atmosphere amicable, he decided he'd be better off telling all he knew. "When I think back to our university days, and the way she appeared and acted back then, some of her current interests and attitudes are more understandable. At least I think I can better comprehend the psychodynamics, but hell, I'm no psychiatrist."

"What are you talking about?"

"The reason she might have turned to devil worship."

"Oh, that."

"I doubt that her beliefs are those of Gothic satanism, the kind maligned by organized religion since the Middle Ages. I'd bet hers is modern satanism, only fifty or so years old, promoted by a former carnival barker in San Francisco. Satan, to them, is symbolic of power, energy, and sexuality. You know, all the feel-good hedonistic traits that are largely tolerated in a permissive and affluent society."

Maggie appeared impressed. "Since when did you become an expert on Satan worship?"

"A couple of years back, I became curious when I treated the gunshot wounds of two teenagers who called themselves satanists. They made the almost fatal mistake of canvassing the home of an avowed member of the National Rifle Association."

"Ah, and of course he would have a formidable collection of guns. Go on."

"The boys, one night, sneaked around the man's property, wearing their odd-looking dark baggy clothes and long coats." Josh turned the corner and headed down the last street going toward the hospital. "They foolishly thought they could break into the man's house and help themselves to his cache of guns. Instead they got peppered with buckshot." Josh smiled. "I spent hours in the OR plucking pellets out of their behinds and their legs. The shots that penetrated bone remained buried, as a permanent souvenir of a stupid misadventure."

Maggie sighed. "Some kids never learn."

"True. However, I did. That's why when you told me about Prissy's bedroom altar, I remembered some of what I learned back then. Modern satanists are rebels who forfeit any allegiance they might have had to established religious orders and their . . ." Josh lifted one hand off the steering wheel and formed a quotation mark with his fingers . . . "hypocritical doctrines."

"Are they also involved with those horrendous episodes of high school mayhem and ritual animal murders?"

"Not sure. The new satanic bible makes no mention or even suggests such unlawful or antisocial behavior. It does encourage members to rethink old prejudices and misconceptions. According to what I read, members are encouraged to think more liberally about morality but are advised not to violate the law."

Maggie twisted on the seat and grinned at her husband. "If my parents, God rest their sainted souls, knew that I married a man who spoke kindly about Satanists, they'd—"

Josh stopped her. "Hold on, that's simply not true. I don't speak kindly or unkindly of those people. And, they're certainly not my cup of tea. But let me remind you: the church your parents attend, like most others, at some time fostered its share of murder, intolerance, plunder, sexual abuse, and hypocrisy—all in the name of the Lord Almighty. Some of those wonderful practices are alive and flourishing today, thank you."

Maggie appeared uncomfortable. She turned in her seat and stared straight ahead. "Oh really? And what about hope, faith, charity, and the conscience of mankind?"

Josh waved a hand, signaling a truce. "We can argue nonstop and settle nothing. It's just that I refuse to accept the wholesale condemnation of any group because it's the popular thing to do. I'll mention just one incident, and then I'll say no more about the matter. You may recall about twenty years ago, a wave of child molestation hysteria swept the country. Pre-kindergarten teachers were involved. They were accused of hideous crimes by rabid fundamentalists who were aided and abetted by unscrupulous attorneys who falsely accused them. I knew two of those teachers who lost their homes, their savings, and their reputations trying to defend their innocence."

"I do recall that vaguely. So, what? Your point is that you're speaking in defense of Prissy?" Maggie asked.

"Let's just say I think we shouldn't cast stones based on suspicion."

"Well, you have to admit, the crazy stuff in her bedroom is pretty weird."

Before Josh could reply, Maggie took a different tack. "I place Prissy at the top of my list of murder suspects."

Josh gave up trying to follow her train of thought. "All right, what was her motive for killing Longfellow?"

"The usual reasons, I suppose. Maybe Peter was an abusive husband. Maybe she wanted his fat insurance policy, or maybe she wanted to take over the construction firm and all its assets."

Josh thought for a moment and shook his head. "I doubt all of that. Number one, Prissy's dominant personality wouldn't tolerate any spousal abuse. Number two, Mannheim said the insurance policy on Longfellow amounted to 150,000 dollars. That's hardly worth the risk of jail time. Number three, taking over the day-to-day operations of the construction firm is not exactly the kind of job a self-centered prima donna wants in spite of her desire for money. Somehow those things just don't add up."

"Okay then. What if Prissy has another man and wanted Peter out of the way?"

Josh mulled that over, then shrugged. "If she's guilty of murder, why did she choose such a god-awful way of getting rid of him, and why in her own home?"

The hospital came into view, and Josh pulled into the doctors' parking lot. Together they headed for the ER. A tall, attractive woman wearing a concierge badge greeted them. "Dr. Harrington, your patient, Mrs. Horowitz, is waiting in room two."

They were interrupted by a thin, bug-eyed, unkempt man in his late twenties or early thirties, gesticulating wildly and arguing loudly with one of the attendants. A security officer alerted to the commotion stood at his desk, hiked his trousers, and started toward the disruptive man. As he passed them, the officer mumbled, "Another methamphetamine jerk wanting narcotics. Happens every day. This place is becoming a collecting station for all kinds of wackos."

X-rays were handed to Josh, who took them to a viewing room off the reception area. The views of Mrs. Horowitz's left shoulder revealed an undisplaced fracture with minimal swelling of the soft tissue. He demonstrated the findings to Maggie and Mrs. Horowitz, informing them the fracture could be treated without surgery. Learning of the diagnosis and proposed treatment, Mrs. Horowitz reached for Josh's hand and held it tenderly to thank him. She apologized for any inconvenience she might have caused. For the umpteenth time in his career, Josh had been rewarded by a patient's profound gratitude. How fortunate to be in this profession, he thought.

In the parking lot, his sense of satisfaction faded abruptly when the specter of darkness loomed before him.

Gaunt, hawk-nosed, stoop-shouldered, Mannheim mumbled, "Evenin', Doc, Ma'am." His dour expression, filled with his usual cynicism, reminded Josh of the unrelenting Javert of *Les Misérables*.

Josh stopped in his tracks to study the haggard expression on Mannheim's face. "What are you doing here? Don't tell me you're following me."

"Don't flatter yourself, Doc, you're hardly my only interest in life. I'm checking up on a possible homicide brought to the ER. However, now that you've mentioned it . . . we reexamined the site where the skeleton was found at your adobe, and we found work gloves and fabric remnants."

"And?" Josh thought how for all the guy's cynicism, he didn't give up easily and he was damned thorough.

"The fabric with the store's label was identified as an expensive Italian import. A silk/wool weave from a suit sold at Desmond's in Palm Springs."

"Desmond's? They went belly-up five years ago. How will that help us?"

Mannheim went on to explain that the store's retired general manager was contacted and said that all sales records for the fifteen years prior to closure were placed in a public storage facility. Mannheim had gone through those records and had come up with a short list of customers who'd purchased that suit, which was sold for only one season, ten years ago. "Doc, you're a pretty good amateur sleuth. Whose name do you think we found on that list?"

Before Josh or Maggie could guess, Mannheim's cell phone rang; he took the call and stepped beyond their hearing range.

Josh said in a subdued tone to Maggie, "I don't know why the skeletal remains couldn't be identified. They have teeth for dental records, they know the height of the man from his bony structure, and the forensic anthropologist could probably estimate his age within five years. With all that plus the records from the Missing Persons Bureau of ten years ago, they should have strong clues as to the identity."

Mannheim returned. "Now where was I?"

"You were going to tell us who purchased that suit of clothes," Maggie said.

"So I was. Do you care to guess?" He directed his question to Josh, but Maggie volunteered.

"I'd say Chester Effingwell," Maggie replied.

Mannheim pushed his tongue around his inner cheek and tried unsuccessfully to suppress a smile. "Anytime you want a job in forensics, little lady, you be sure to give my name as a reference. I like the way you think."

Mannheim's deliberate and laconic manner made Josh impatient.

"What else have you got for us, Mannheim? We'd like to chat, but we'd also like to get home for dinner."

"Just before you leave, maybe you'd like to know we got information on that car key I found near the skeleton."

"All right, our dinner can wait. What about the key?" Josh asked.

Mannheim referred to his small spiral notebook. "The car, a 1997 Lincoln Mark VIII, was rented from an agency in Palm Springs on February 24, 1997. Records show the key was replaced at a cost of ninety-five dollars to the renter."

"So, who rented the car?"

"Dunno yet." Mannheim turned and began walking toward the ER.

Josh called after him. "Don't you know? Everyone knows you can't rent a car without a driver's license. There's got to be a name."

Mannheim stopped and turned slowly. "That's right, Doc, but with a little moola to grease a palm, that information can disappear—no trouble." He looked at his watch. "Call tomorrow; we'll meet at the sheriff's office. We'll compare notes on Big Tits—uh, that is, Tatiana—and a few others." He glanced sheepishly at Maggie and walked away.

"Josh, how would he know about Madame Tatiana?"

"Did I tell you as I was leaving Tatiana's place, a Crown Vic was in the driveway and two plainclothesmen passed me as they went inside?"

"How did you know they were plainclothesmen?"

"I'll wager that the most elegant whorehouse in the Coachella Valley and its notorious madam is known to every cop in or out of uniform within a radius of twenty-five miles—no, make that a hundred miles. Those were two unsmiling guys with bulges under their jackets, coming out of a sedan that can be identified by any ten-year-old at a distance of a hundred yards . . . really, how difficult can that be?"

"I just don't understand why these places are not shut down. Certainly they shouldn't be patronized, and especially by police."

"When was the last time you read about a whorehouse bust in the Coachella Valley? Now, a Hollywood or a Beverly Hills venue with big-named clientele—that's different."

Maggie was concerned about the girls' health problems arising from venereal diseases. She remembered seeing the sad results of untreated cases during her career as a nurse. "Don't the girls have to be examined periodically by a health officer? If that's true, their existence has to be acknowledged. Do you think there's payola involved?"

Josh smiled, "Does the sun shine in the desert?"

"Did it bother you that those detectives were going into Tatiana's?"

"I really didn't think much about it then."

"Weren't you curious enough to want to talk with them? You know the whorehouse is an illegal place." Maggie's questions were taking on a type of edginess.

"That's the last thing I would want to do. I'm grateful *they* didn't stop *me*. They probably thought I was just another john who'd unloaded his rocks."

EIGHTEEN

Maggie went directly to the computer in the den while Josh went to the wine cooler in the kitchen to get Maggie's favorite chardonnay. As he began filling two goblets, Maggie yelled from the den.

"Josh, come here! Look at this: a message from Carlos Grandee."

"Who?"

"Carlos, Suzanne's husband. Suzanne from Kenilworth, Illinois. Suzanne whose grandfather left us a million dollars. Oh, don't tell me you've forgotten?"

"Sorry, love. Hope he isn't planning to renege."

Josh set the glasses of wine down on the desk next to the computer. While he looked over Maggie's shoulder, he removed his tie, stretched his neck, and unbuttoned his collar.

"I'm not exactly sure. Listen to this: he's planning to be in Indian Wells next Friday for a business meeting. His commercial acquisition department is proposing the purchase of property on El Paseo Drive. He says he's eager to see me again and meet you. If we're free, he'd like us to reserve a table for dinner at seven o'clock. He has his own transportation from the airport. He'll call us when he arrives. Suzanne and the children send love."

Maggie clasped her hands over her chest. "Isn't that exciting? You'll love Carlos. He's such a gentleman, just like you. I'll make reservations at Shame on the Moon and e-mail him. Now, if *he* wanted to buy our adobe and the acreage around it, he would be more than welcome to it."

Josh instantly remembered his promise to Effingwell. He shook his head. "Not the house. I told you, Maggie, only the land is for sale. Incidentally, how did he learn about our land anyway?"

"I told him about it when I visited Suzanne and her family in Chicago, remember? He was well acquainted with the area since his company owns a number of properties on Rodeo Drive in Beverly Hills and in Palm Beach, Florida. At the time, he seemed quite interested. He also mentioned something about wanting to build a winter home here."

"Really? I thought you told me he had a winter home in Naples, Florida."

"He does, along with another one in the Bahamas and one on the French Riviera." Maggie looked at Josh. "Why are you shaking your head?"

"I can't imagine the kind of wealth that could support that many estates. Who does the windows?"

Hearing the droll tone in his question, Maggie laughed. "With that kind of money, dearie, one can afford to hire an army of domestics."

NINETEEN

Maggie's anticipation and excitement about seeing Carlos again was transparent. "Josh, wouldn't it be wonderful if Carlos were interested in our property? He could build a lovely home for Suzanne and the girls and be close to his construction project on El Paseo. I'm so eager to know what he's thinking."

At the restaurant the hostess, Ginger, greeted Josh and Maggie with her usual warmth, giving them both an embrace and a kiss. Even with the population nearing a half million in the Coachella Valley, friendliness still existed in cozy enclaves reminiscent of small communities. The restaurant was an oasis, hidden from the constant traffic on Highway 111 and the intersection of Frank Sinatra Drive. In a world often catering to the senseless cacophony of the big city, with its digitally enhanced background noise that interfered with conversation and digestion, it was an isolated pocket of civility.

Ginger assured them that their guest would be directed to their favorite table in the Garden Room, a relatively secluded section.

Ten minutes after being seated, Maggie waved excitedly as their guest was ushered to the table. Josh stood to meet him. Carlos, at about six feet, with an athletic posture, smiled easily. He made a slight bow toward Maggie and was about to kiss her hand when she wrapped her arms around him. Formalities quickly disappeared, and he kissed both her cheeks.

Josh smiled and extended his hand. "Señor Carlos—"

"Please, just plain Carlos. Carlos happens to be a name given to me by a Spanish uncle years ago. He thought it sounded more cosmopolitan than Pyotr Gregorovitch and more mature than my family's nickname, which I fortunately outgrew—Boychik." They all laughed.

The dark-haired man grasped Josh's hand warmly with both of his.

"I can't begin to tell you how pleased I am that you were able to meet with me." He looked around the room and smiled. "This seems to be an ideal place for an intimate dinner. Would you mind if I selected the wine?"

The sommelier approached and handed the wine list to Carlos, who selected a fine cabernet sauvignon. The usual small talk about families and weather ensued until the waiter returned with the wine bottle for Carlos's approval. Carlos swirled the wine in his glass, breathed its bouquet, noted its legs, then tested it against his palate. He nodded for the waiter to pour all around, then proposed a toast in French to good health and good friends.

He smiled easily. "I love the casual lifestyle you enjoy in Southern California, and I'd like to be your neighbor, at least for part of the year." His dark, animated eyes glanced at Josh and then at Maggie. "Have you thought about selling that acreage in Rancho Mirage? I'd be delighted to take it off your hands—at a fair price, of course." His self-assuredness was neither offensive nor overbearing.

Maggie leaned forward. "Carlos, forgive me for asking, but what is there about our parcel that appeals to you?"

He hunched forward. "Several things: firstly, I have tracked the growth rate in this area for the last ten years. The growth is constant and with the influx of wealthy retirees, high-end shops should do quite well on El Paseo Drive. First-rate retail stores will rival the exclusive shops on Rodeo Drive in Beverly Hills. I would like to be around at certain phases of the construction. Secondly, I want to be reasonably close to one of our manufacturing plants in El Segundo. Thirdly, Suzanne loves the desert, and as you know, she and the children adore you, Maggie." Carlos reached across the table to take Maggie's hands in his.

Maggie smiled. "And I love them too, but as a practical matter, wouldn't you be wiser to consider a residence at the Big Horn Estates or Magnificent Mesa Estates? Those properties are lovely, and they're practically next door to our acreage. Have you seen them?"

"Yes, my dear, I have and they are, as you say, quite lovely. However, your property is much more desirable. Our needs for housing call for adequate acreage removed somewhat from nearby housing developments where we might disturb the residents."

"Are you planning to have rock concerts with lots of amps?" Josh asked facetiously.

Maggie looked at him and rolled her eyes. "Josh, please."

Carlos smiled. "My business demands that I attend meetings in several principal cities, often at a day's notice. We require quick access to our private jet. When I'm visiting here, our jet plane is in a hangar at LAX. We need a heliport here, a pad for our helicopter, which can take us to and from our jet quickly."

Josh stared at Carlos and leaned into the table. "Are you sure you can operate a helicopter in a residential area? There must be ordinances that forbid—"

Carlos held up a hand. "Forgive me for interrupting; I'm aware of city, state, and federal ordinances. One of our corporate branches is engaged in the research and development of a super helicopter for the armed services, one that is whisper-quiet and super fast. That project has been given top priority and supersedes all restrictions."

"I see." Josh nodded, knowing that Carlos must have been aware of air space restrictions in an urban area. His importance to the Pentagon and national security gave him top priority.

Carlos explained that when he gets a call from the Office of the President or the Secretary of Defense or the Joint Chiefs of Staff, he must suspend all other activities and appear in D.C., ASAP. Suzanne had pleaded for him to slow down or delegate more authority, but he found that too difficult. He acknowledged that he was driven by his A-type personality, his need to be in on everything and oversee all transactions. He cited an example: in three days he was scheduled to meet with the board of directors of an aeronautics engineering corporation in Stratford, Connecticut, to negotiate a contract for the sale of helicopter parts involving millions of dollars. He could not and would not risk assigning that job to anyone else. He pushed himself back into his chair, took a deep breath, and released it slowly. "Forgive me for monopolizing the conversation. Let me hear from you two."

Josh thought this might be a good time to discuss Cue and his interest in the Rancho Mirage property.

"Carlos, we've had a bid from a New Yorker whose company is CUE Enterprises. Are you familiar at all with that name?"

Carlos knitted his brows, pursed his lips, and responded with deliberation. "The organization, as I recall, is reputed to have what one might call an odious taint. Are you saying he is my principal competitor for your land?" Carlos hunched forward and fingered the stem of his wine goblet. "Please understand, I fully appreciate the fact that you are free agents, and I would not impose my friendship on your decision; however, I would be grateful if you allowed me to bid on the property." He sipped his wine and waited for their comments.

"As a matter of fact," Josh said, "there are several people interested in that land."

"Hold on, please; let me get their names on my iPhone."

Josh started to enumerate the names while Carlos jabbed at the minute keyboard with his closed pen. "There is Penelope Longfellow, a widow of a murdered contractor; she is now head of her husband's construction company. There's Dan Aviloh, another contractor who is building costly homes next to our property. There's Gerrick Yamamoto, the administrator of the Eisenhower Hospital—"

"Hold on, please spell that name." When Josh did, Carlos punched the name in.

"Lastly, there's a purveyor of adult entertainment, a Madame Tatiana."

Carlos closed his iPhone and slipped it into his jacket pocket. "If any of those people come in with a bid higher than mine, you have the option of selling to them. I understand that, but I am obligated to explain my proposal to my board of directors, who will approve or disapprove. While I am usually not forced into a position of exercising extreme frugality, I am compelled to present proposals of bona fide value."

Maggie held out her hand to touch Carlos's forearm. "There's something else you should know. The adobe house is under police investigation, and in any case, it is not for sale. Josh promised his dying patient that it would never be sold."

Carlos looked questioningly at Maggie, then at Josh. Maggie continued to outline the events leading to the findings of the skeleton in the subflooring of the adobe.

Carlos said, "I can't imagine such a thing. Why would anyone want to bury a body beneath a house?"

"Good question," Josh said. "Perhaps the murder took place in the house, and the killer didn't want to risk disposing of the corpse outside."

"A reasonable assumption." Carlos nodded. "I'm curious—not that it makes a great difference, but do you think the murder was premeditated?"

"Possibly. A well-crafted, flush-mounted door in the floor with concealed hinges and a handle suggests premeditation to me," Josh said. "Although a crawl space was probably in the original construction plans, since electrical conduit and plumbing pipes had to be laid down in advance of the adobe walls. I think the preexisting crawl space provided a convenient grave site for the murderer."

"You may be right. That certainly wouldn't deter me from building around the adobe." Carlos studied their faces. "You say Mrs. Longfellow is interested in obtaining that property? Is she a strong competitor in the bidding?"

Maggie shot a glance at Josh. "Not if I have any say in the matter."

Carlos looked at Josh with an arched eyebrow.

Josh shrugged and said, "She who must be obeyed."

Carlos smiled. "Then am I correct in assuming that the most serious competitors are Mr. Effingwell, also know as Cue, and Mr. . . . ? I'm sorry, I've forgotten his name."

"Aviloh, Dan A-V-I-L-O-H," Josh repeated slowly.

Carlos looked at the name on his iPhone. "I find this interesting, D. Aviloh—Daviloh. With a little imagination, that could be construed as *devil*, at least in Spanish, French, or Italian." He waved his hand. "No matter, that's coincidental and unimportant, a point of interest only to a language buff. I can understand Aviloh wanting your property;

he's already building homes next door. Has Cue Effingwell told you why he was interested?"

"No, although I had planned to ask him," Josh said.

"What about this Madame Tatiana?"

Maggie interrupted. "She's the other woman I won't deal with, so there's no point in discussing her."

"I seem to be missing something here," Carlos said.

Josh looked at Maggie, then at Carlos. "Carlos is entitled to some background here. Let me try to fill you in. Years ago Madame Tatiana, who now runs a highly successful escort service, had been intimate with Cue's father, the man whose name appeared on the deed along with our deceased patient, whose name was also Effingwell, Chesley Effingwell, a brother. Mr. Chester Effingwell from the East Coast sort of guided the destiny of this Madame Tatiana and helped her establish a rather successful career."

"Where is this Chester Effingwell whose name is on the deed?"

"He disappeared about ten years ago and was declared legally dead some years later. A title search revealed that his will did not specify an heir. The property was to be granted to the survivor at the time of death—that is, the remaining brother, who was our patient," Josh said.

"I would think the court would award his son half the property," Carlos said.

"The so-called son, Cue, who is now head of CUE Enterprises, was never legally adopted," Josh said.

"His lawyers might make counterclaims since he was a *de facto* son," Carlos rebutted.

"So far, there has been no demand for a legal contest, and our lawyer, Mr. Farquhaar, has advised us to exercise our rights of ownership. In fact, in his own words, he said he would be delighted to joust with any Wall Street law firm no matter how prestigious. The thought of matching skills with one of those high-powered legal beagles thrills him to his very core."

Carlos seemed neither impressed nor amused by their lawyer's braggadocio. He reached into his jacket and pulled out a pocket secretary, and wrote numbers on a slip of paper. He tore the top sheet off, turned it over, and pushed it across the table. "No need to seriously consider the dollar amount now. Put it aside, then compare it with your other bids. Talk to your tax advisor; determine whether an incremental distribution would be more advantageous than a lump-sum payoff. All I ask is that you inform me of your decision within a month. Furthermore, would either of you object if I were to personally interview each of the persons who are interested in your property?"

Josh looked at Maggie and shrugged. "I have no objections, but why would you want to talk with them face-to-face?"

"If any one of them is offering more than I, they might know something I don't. In other words, I would like to know what makes your property so attractive to them. You see, my offer is based on established land values, that is, what comparable acreage in the area sold for in the past two years—figures compiled from local realty offices. To that amount, I added ten percent for expected appreciation in the next four years. You know how desirable the land is to me, and yet, there are limits . . ."

Maggie toyed with the remaining ounce of wine in her goblet, swirling it in small circles on the table. Josh reached over and gently held her wrist. She stopped, looked up, and said, "Oh, sorry, I was just thinking." She looked at Carlos. "Would calling those people to our home be more convenient for you? You could interview them separately in our den—but not Madame Tatiana or Mrs. Longfellow, of course."

Carlos smiled. "Thank you, Maggie, that is most considerate." He sat back, tented his fingers, and said contemplatively, "These people may not want to discuss their plans with me. I understand that. If they want to form some type of partnership or coalition among themselves for a portion of that parcel, that would be fine. However, they must be told by me that I am capable of outbidding them. Furthermore, they must be informed that I intend to build a heliport, which may make their anticipated development less desirable. For those reasons, I would like to talk with them personally."

Josh said, "There are two incidents I will mention that may or may not influence your decision about purchasing the property. For that matter, we don't even know if they were associated with our ownership of the land, but we feel obligated to make a complete disclosure. The first was finding our front tire slashed while we were in the adobe discovering the skeletal remains. The second was an attempted ramming of my vehicle by a construction truck on Sinatra Drive, the road leading away from the adobe."

Carlos sat back and furrowed his brow, his lower lip thrust forward. "These acts are really small events in our industries. We have efficient ways of handling such nuisance problems."

Maggie appeared relieved by Carlos's response.

Josh mentioned that visiting Cue might be inconvenient. "You'll have to travel to New York to interview Cue."

"New York is practically my provenance, Josh. I am as much at home there as I am in my Chicago suburb. As for Madame Tatiana, we should get along famously. Forgive my vulgarity, but in the business world, people are forever trying to screw you, and I can assure you that is not at all pleasurable, whereas Madame Tatiana's talent might be much more agreeable." He suddenly laughed. "Of course, I am only joking. Myself, I am a very happily married man and have no desire to lose what I have."

Josh leaned toward Maggie, took the back of her hand, and kissed it. "My sentiments exactly."

TWENTY

Maggie walked into Josh's consultation room and pointed to his desk phone. "It's Sergeant Mannheim; he'd like a word with you."

Josh, standing, took the phone almost reluctantly. A call from the Prince of Darkness always created some apprehension.

"Yes, Sergeant. Of course I know him. Maggie and I had dinner with him the night before last—" Josh suddenly stopped. "He's where?"

The color in Josh's face faded to an ashen gray. He gripped the edge of the desk and felt a weakness in his legs as he replaced the phone. He shook his head, trying to compute what he had just been told.

"Josh, you look as though you've seen a ghost! What's the matter?"

"Have the girls tell the patients we'll be detained at the hospital with an emergency."

"For heaven's sake, tell me what's going on!"

He grabbed Maggie's hand and said gruffly, "Carlos was almost fatally injured in a freeway accident. He's at the Trauma Center in ICU."

"Oh, my God! What happened?"

Josh crossed the room to the closet where he kept his jacket, and Maggie ran for her purse. They leaped into the SUV, fastened their belts, then with tires squealing sped out of the parking lot.

While Josh weaved through the traffic, Maggie leaned toward him. "What else did Mannheim tell you?"

"Not a lot. Just bits and pieces. According to the hospital, the chauffeur was killed on impact when Carlos's vehicle struck an abutment at an overpass on I-10 last night at about seven twenty-five—Jaws of Life were used to extricate him from the rear compartment. A witness reported seeing a dump truck sideswipe them, pushing Carlos's vehicle into the abutment and then speeding off."

"Who was driving the truck?"

"Nobody seems to know, and no one got a license number. Someone said the truck had a construction company name, but they couldn't read it."

"Has Suzanne been notified?" Maggie asked.

"They've had trouble getting in touch with her. Apparently she's been out of town. Carlos had a lucid moment this morning and managed to mumble my name. Homicide detectives were in the room at the time and heard his request. That's when the call came in from Mannheim."

He looked in the rearview mirror. A motorcycle with a red light was bearing down on them. "Damn! Of all times for a cop to nail me!" Josh pulled to the side of the road.

The officer dismounted and stood next to Josh's open window. He unbuckled his helmet strap and pushed the tip of his helmet back. "Your driver's license, please."

Josh removed his license and handed it to the officer.

"I see you're a doctor. Dr. Harrington, you were traveling twenty miles over the speed limit, sir."

Josh perhaps skewed the truth just a bit when he said that he had a seriously injured patient and was responding to an emergent call. He was sure the officer had heard such excuses before and had to exercise on-the-spot judgment for believability.

The officer assessed Josh's sincerity and said, "Doc, you want to be careful you don't become a victim of excessive speed. Why don't you follow me?" He moved his motorcycle to the front of the SUV, looked over his shoulder, and signaled Josh to follow. They scattered traffic as the motorcycle siren wailed and its lights flashed. They reached the hospital in minutes.

Josh waved his thanks as the officer turned his Honda around and sped off.

Josh held Maggie's arm and rushed to the ICU. He stopped at the nurses' station, conferred with the nurse supervisor, then went to Carlos's room, where privacy curtains had been drawn. Josh could discern three shadowed figures. He opened the curtains and went to the foot of the bed, where two techs were adjusting a pelvic traction apparatus. The third figure, a nurse, was checking one of two IVs, a saline/lactose solution with antibiotics. With a quick glance, Josh noted a urinary catheter collecting several hundred ccs of blood-tinged urine in a plastic bag attached to the bed frame. A heart monitor traced the EKG on an overhead screen, and an unattached breathing apparatus remained at the head of the bed.

After the techs left, Josh talked quietly with the nurse for several minutes to get her assessment before she left the room. After she left, Josh spoke to Maggie and described Carlos's condition, adding, "Poor guy can't hear us. He's unconscious, and he looks bloody awful."

Josh studied the distortion of Carlos's face. His handsome face, grotesquely disfigured, was hardly recognizable. The blue-black eyelids were swollen shut. Lacerations on his face, neck, and chest had congealed blood. His nose was a blob, displaced to the left side of his face. The nostrils were stuffed with pledgets of bloodied cotton around plastic inhalation tubing. A nasogastric tube from his mouth led to a collecting bottle with bloodied mucus. His open mouth was bordered by swollen, purple lips punctured by small lacerations and bruises. The upper central incisors were missing, creating crater-like hollows in the jagged gums. His dark hair was disheveled and matted with clotted blood. A temporary aluminum splint on his deformed right wrist indicated a fracture awaiting definitive treatment.

Maggie, seeing Carlos's face, had been filled with sympathetic revulsion. She took a step back and was startled when she bumped into Dr. Dick Williams, head of the Trauma Section. "Oh, I'm so sorry," she said.

"Not at all," Dr. Williams said. He turned toward Josh and gave him a firm handshake. "Glad to see you, Josh."

Josh introduced Dick to Maggie and said, "Dick, this is my wife, Maggie. She's a nurse from Cook County Hospital, our old stompin' grounds."

Dick Williams nodded toward the comatose Carlos and said, "We've got one helluva traumatized patient there. I saw him in the ER just after the ambulance brought him in last night. If he makes it, he's going to require tons of treatment—pelvic fractures, multiple facial fractures, right forearm fracture, chest and abdominal contusions, and God only knows what's going on in his belly."

Maggie, wide-eyed, followed Dr. Williams's every word.

"Christ, I hope he makes it," Josh said quietly. He had an urge to get into a scrub suit and start doing something, anything. "Did someone order more blood? How many units has he had, what's his crit and hemoglobin now?"

Dr. Williams patted Josh's shoulder. "Take it easy, Josh. Everything that can be done is being done. The kids in the ER did what they had to do last night, and these folks in ICU handle trauma cases every day. You remember such cases at the Cook County? Most of those patients survived." He tugged at Josh's arm and signaled for Maggie to follow. "Come, let's review his X-rays and discuss treatment."

At age sixty-nine, Dick Williams an avuncular figure remained unflappable, the consummate surgeon who seemed to rise effortlessly above the chaos typically depicted in TV emergency-room dramas. His movements were purposeful without creating a flurry of attention; he gave orders without sounding demanding; he encouraged and complimented without being patronizing. A fringe of white hair surrounded a bald, pink shiny pate like a low-lying halo on an aged angelic figure. His starched white lab coat failed to conceal a modest pot belly.

With Dr. Williams in the lead, the three walked into the darkened X-ray viewing room. The bluish light from the viewing boxes cast an eerie glow. The doctors reviewed each X-ray, pointed to areas of trauma, and discussed treatment. They agreed that open reduction and fixation of the displaced pelvic fractures would be necessary, as well as surgery on the forearm fracture.

"Any chance Mr. Grandee can be shipped to a hospital near his home?" Maggie asked.

"Only if the attending doctor is willing to sign the death certificate. I'm hoping, but I'm not altogether sure, he'll even be with us tomorrow." Dr. Williams collected the X-rays and replaced them in a brown paper jacket. "There may also be soft-tissue injuries of the chest and belly." He glanced at Josh and Maggie. "Too bad about the other two in the vehicle."

Josh looked at him. "What other two? I heard of only one—the driver. Who else was there?"

"The woman, of course."

"What woman?" Maggie took a step closer and stared at Dr. Williams.

"I thought you knew. Didn't the police or hospital inform you? According to our phone conversation with Mr. Grandee's wife in Illinois this morning, the driver accompanied him on all his trips; he was a sort of valet, chauffeur, and personal guard."

"What about the woman?" Maggie persisted.

"Apparently, she was a local resident. According to an ID found in her purse, she had a Russian-sounding name."

"Tatiana?" Josh asked.

Dr. Williams shrugged. "Perhaps, I'm not sure. It sounds vaguely familiar. I was called into the ER to examine the body. She was DOA . . . too many severe injuries . . . probably died right after the accident." Williams shook his head. "An interesting finding was the extent of her plastic surgery. She was the epitome of the plastic surgeon's skill— silicone breast implants, abdominal tucks, buttocks enhancement; what teeth remained were implants. Even her hair, a fancy wig, was carried in by the ambulance attendant."

Certainly sounds like Tatiana, Josh thought.

"What in the world were Carlos and Tatiana doing in that limo?" Josh asked.

The silence in the darkened room was shattered by a deep voice emanating from the doorway. "What the hell do you think they were doing, Doc?"

All three turned to look at the tall, thin figure whose facial features were obscured by the backlighting, but there was no mistaking its identity; it belonged to the macabre Detective Sergeant Timothy Mannheim. "If Dr. Williams won't tell you, I will." Dick Williams said nothing as Mannheim approached, looking at the X-rays as though he had diagnostic capability.

"Our overripe Barbie Doll was blowing Daddy Warbucks."

Maggie turned away as though it would help to avoid further calumny from the outspoken detective.

"Mannheim, don't be ridiculous. What the hell are you talking about?" Josh asked the question in a kind of denial, principally for Maggie's benefit. He didn't care to hear any more of Mannheim's tactlessness and hoped the detective had the decency to keep quiet.

Mannheim ignored him. "Go ahead, Dr. Williams, tell Doc and Mrs. Harrington what you know about this case. What's the polite term, *fellatio*?"

"Now is not the time and place to discuss this." Again, Josh hoped Mannheim would get the point and stop.

Mannheim pulled his head back, raised his shoulders, and opened his palms on outstretched arms. "Hey, the question was asked, Doc. You wanted to know what those two were doing in the backseat. Well, I'm telling you what the police report will show. And for your information, I don't really give a good goddamn what they were doing. All I want to know is who in the hell caused those to people to die."

Maggie must have found her voice. "Do all these details really have to appear on the police report?"

Dick Williams looked at Mannheim. "Would the world come to an end if the report omitted that finding?"

"Like I said, I don't give a damn. We already know what happened in the backseat of that limo. We don't need a statement saying that Mr. Carlos Grandee's penis was almost bitten off." He stopped, hiked his pants and said, "Of course, our photographer has pictures of a pretty disgusting gnarly old cock, and—"

"Stop it, Mannheim!" Josh barked his anger. "Just what are you trying to prove here?"

"Don't get your dander up, Doc. I'm here to investigate the homicides. A preliminary investigation at the accident site showed that another vehicle was involved, a hit-and-run. We found paint residue and pieces of a truck headlight assembly. We'll be checking truck repair garages in Indio, Coachella, and Cathedral City and maybe, just maybe, we can catch the sonofabitch who caused this."

TWENTY-ONE

Walking to their vehicle in the doctors' parking area, Maggie looked at her watch to remind Josh that Suzanne's plane would be arriving from O'Hare in an hour.

"Remember to keep those lurid details about Carlos and that woman from her," she said.

Josh shook his head. "Be realistic—there's no way we can hide the fact that two people were killed in that car, and one happened to be a woman; that's been in all the papers and on TV."

"I know that, Josh, but Suzanne doesn't have to know about Carlos having his, uh, his member practically bitten off."

"How long do you think that will remain secret?"

Maggie sighed but did not respond. "I'm so terribly disillusioned by all this. I saw Carlos much differently. I thought of him as a gentleman, a family man—"

"Don't judge him too harshly. We simply don't have all the facts."

"What are you talking about? There's no point speaking in his defense. The man is simply guilty of the basest kind of behavior. I am so ashamed for Suzanne and the children, I could cry."

Josh attempted an explanation. "Think of Carlos as having a night out, feeling the need for companionship, maybe the sort of gratification he doesn't get at home." As soon as he said that he wished he hadn't.

"Stop it, Josh! Don't try to justify that."

"Sweetheart, you're working yourself into a lather. People do stupid things, even brilliant people."

Maggie turned her head, no longer wanting to participate in the conversation. Josh, on the other hand, had a compulsion to continue, hoping it might rationalize his point. "Look at our *esteemed* presidents, from George Washington to Barack Obama, forty-four in all. How many do you think had extramarital affairs?" When Maggie did not reply, he said, "According to my reading, all of them were culpable, with the possible exception of five or six, and historians can't be sure about them. And one was decidedly homosexual."

"What's the point of all this? And why are you dwelling on it?"

"Didn't mean to upset you, darling. It's just that I don't want you to dislike Carlos because he failed to live up to your vaunted expectations. He's a high-achiever, a guy who probably lives an otherwise exemplary life. For all his contributions to the national defense and the economy of the country, we should be grateful he escaped death."

Maggie pouted and remained quiet.

Carmenita, Josh's receptionist, called Josh on his cell to tell him she'd rescheduled the waiting patients. When she'd finished with the names, she continued, "You also have a message from Sergeant Mannheim. He asked that you stop at the Rancho Mirage sheriff's office tomorrow when you have a moment."

Once he'd hung up, Josh repeated the message to Maggie, then joked, "Wonder what our favorite macabre sleuth wants, other than seeing your pretty face?"

"Don't be ridiculous, Josh. I think of him as most unappealing, a sort of nonsexual being who is not attracted to women. Frankly, I can't imagine women being attracted to him, either."

Josh sobered. "I'd venture to guess that you're mistaken on both accounts."

"Why do you say that? Do you know something about him that I don't?"

"He told me about his sweet love twenty years ago. She and the child died in childbirth."

"How sad! Just like Chesley Effingwell." Maggie turned in her seat to look at Josh. "I'm sorry to have misjudged him."

"To respond to your second comment: some women find a tall, mysterious-looking guy attractive. Frankly, I doubt that he'd discourage a sexy come-hither look."

"Well, I hope he's not expecting one from me."

• • •

The small anteroom of the Rancho Mirage sheriff's office must have been built at a time of stringent contract budgeting. Its interior block-wall construction and meager dimensions might have come in at lower-than-projected costs. Behind the glass panel at the information desk, a short, busty female officer in a neatly starched olive-drab shirt with permanent creases wore a badge that sloped on her bosom. She jotted down Josh and Maggie's names before buzzing Mannheim's office.

In an office of minuscule dimensions, Mannheim sat at a small desk with several folders, a phone, and a computer, which were his only visible properties. He stood as Josh and Maggie walked in. His lanky frame was covered by a loose-fitting, white short-sleeved shirt with a stringy dark tie, a style in vogue when he was at the police academy at least three decades ago. His black pants, in dire need of tailoring and pressing, were too long and rumpled above his shoes. When he sat gripping the arms of his chair, his long, spidery fingers reminded Josh of those on Lincoln's statue in Washington.

Mannheim pointed toward two chairs. "Have a seat."

As Josh sat, he noticed that Mannheim had studied Maggie's face and bosom with more than casual interest. He wondered if Maggie was aware.

Mannheim flipped pages in a spiral notebook. "We ran a check on several truck repair shops and found nothing that even vaguely matched the description of the truck that rammed Carlos Grandee's limo."

"Does that mean you've finished the hunt? You didn't call me in just to tell me this, did you?"

Mannheim glanced at him from the corners of his eyes but did not respond. He moistened his index finger on his lower lip, then turned another page. "Results of Riverside Lab's spectroscopy says the paint chip taken off the smashed-up Cadillac showed a white truck color compatible with a late-model International; a headlamp housing fragment was also identified. We haven't located the truck yet, but we will."

"Wonderful, what now?"

"Hold on to your britches, Doc; I thought you might want to know that the wrecked Cadillac was registered to a local owner."

"I don't understand," Maggie said. "I assumed Mr. Grandee was chauffeured by his own driver in a car he maintained here."

"The car was registered to Rancho Mirage Escort Services."

"Wait a minute. That's Tatiana's place," Josh said.

Mannheim shuffled a few more papers, then looked at each of them from under his bushy brows. "That's right. Funny, I should have noticed that earlier." He frowned and tapped his notebook against his other hand. "We discovered another item of interest." He paused, perhaps for dramatic effect. "Can you possibly guess what else we found in that wreckage pile?"

Josh could almost come to hate the man. He shook his head. "Since when did we start playing twenty questions?"

Mannheim's smile, an almost unnatural event, challenged his usual craggy, narrow face. He waved Josh forward and spread several photos on his desk. "Look at these." He pointed to enlargements of some of the photos, then poked at one photo three times. "That, my friends, is a camera we found concealed in the vehicle's headliner. The lens, we figured, was directed right where the action in the backseat took place. At about sixty frames per minute, this high-pixel-image producer gave a pretty good action series of what was going on."

"But why?" Maggie asked.

"Extortion, little lady, blackmail, illicit exposure, a rose by any other name . . ." Mannheim trailed off, yet the gleam in his eyes spoke volumes.

"So, that was her game," Josh said.

Maggie looked at Josh and tilted her head, assuming the quizzical expression that usually preceded a pithy question. It wasn't long in coming. "Josh, suppose Carlos was unaware, suppose he was drugged and didn't know what was going on. Is that a possibility?"

"Yeah, it's a possibility, but that would be a stretch. An erection can be sustained through a semiconscious state."

"Wouldn't blood analysis show whether he had been drugged?" she asked.

"Maybe. Unless he was given a short-acting, quickly excreted drug. I could get in touch with the lab and ask if any foreign substances were found in the blood sample."

"We'll take care of that," Mannheim said.

"It *is* possible that Carlos was completely innocent all along. I just knew it." Maggie's tone was declarative and final.

"That, ma'am, is a conjecture only the most naïve could entertain." Mannheim, with his fingers intertwined behind his head and leaning back in his chair, poked the concavity of his inner cheek with his tongue. He seemed reluctant to allow any challenge to his notion of Carlos's role in the prostitution-for-hire event. "You've got to admit that it's hard to imagine any scenario other than one of procurement by a rich guy who's found in a car driven by his chauffeur while a whore is giving him a—whatever."

Maggie said, "Detective, you have no right to make that assumption without much more evidence than you have." She turned her gaze to the papers on Mannheim's desk and focused on one item. "I couldn't help but notice that you have a memo that says, 'results on prints from AFIS on Cue II.' What does that refer to?"

Mannheim had to think for a moment. "Oh, that? It's a report from the Army Fingerprint Identification System. You'll remember we found the ignition key to a ten-year-old Lincoln Continental under the skeleton in the subflooring of your adobe house."

"Whose prints did you find?" Maggie asked.

"No one's. Unfortunately, there were too many indistinct and degenerated markings on it for a positive ID."

"So the key's another blind alley?" Josh sighed. He was beginning to think the whole damn thing was a circle heading into infinity.

"'Fraid so. Another aggravating problem we ran into—" Mannheim picked up a piece of paper and waved it. "We couldn't recover all the records from the rental car agency on that 1997 Continental. The fact that the agency no longer exists didn't help, either. What records we did find in storage gave no return date on that vehicle. It's just as though it vanished with the lessee."

Mannheim tossed the paper back onto his desk, but something jumped out at Josh while he watched the paper land. "Let me see that." Mannheim gave it to him. Josh studied it closely, trying to see what he failed to notice before. Then it suddenly hit him. "Look at the initials of that company name." He held the paper in front of Mannheim, then in front of Maggie. "Here's a *C* as in *Coachella*, a *U* as in *U-Drive*, and an *E* as in *Enterprises*. Do you think that's just coincidental with the name CUE?"

Mannheim took the sheet and studied it. "Well, I'll be goddamned! Now, why didn't Harry Todd see that and bring it to my attention?"

"I guess that could explain why the records on that rented car were expunged," Josh hazarded. "When you own the company, you can do whatever you damn well please with records, including making them disappear."

"Someone wanted to give the impression that Old Man Effingwell drove off into the sunset and just disappeared. Both him and the car vanished without a goddamn trace, just like that." Mannheim snapped his fingers.

"Undoubtedly someone collected insurance on the old man and the car," Josh said.

"Why?" Maggie looked at Josh, then at Mannheim.

Mannheim returned her look disdainfully. "Because the old man was snuffed, that's why, and the murderer didn't want to leave any clues." His voice became progressively strident.

"Who killed who?" Maggie asked.

"Ma'am, who the hell do you think killed who? Cue killed his old man—that's who!"

TWENTY-TWO

On that cool March evening, American Air Lines flight #410 from Chicago's O'Hare arrived on time at 7:05. Maggie and Josh waited in the lobby of the Palm Springs Airport with others who milled about the passenger exit, waiting for deplaning passengers.

Maggie recognized the smartly dressed Suzanne in her designer suit and cape and rushed passed the *Do Not Enter* sign. The women, emotionally charged, collided, then alternately laughed and sobbed in each other's arms. Suzanne buried her head in Maggie's shoulder as some passersby stared. Maggie introduced Josh to the tearful Suzanne.

Josh extended his hand and said, "Suzanne, please accept my concern for Carlos. Everything that can be done is being done. He's going to require quite a bit of care, but I'm certain that if all goes as planned, he'll function reasonably well in a few months."

Suzanne's eyes searched Josh's for a more optimistic prognosis. Knowing her need for the truth, he said, "Unfortunately, his injuries were severe, and rehabilitation will be long."

The three of them walked to the baggage claim; Suzanne, in the middle, spoke gratefully as she held on to Maggie and Josh. "Thank you both for coming."

At the baggage carousel Suzanne dabbed her teary eyes. "I can't believe this awful thing happened to my darling Carlos." She searched Josh's eyes again, pleading reassurance. "He is going to make it, isn't he?"

Josh took her hand in both of his and said, "We'll do everything humanly possible to see that."

People waited on either side of the baggage conveyer as the motors started to whirr and the belt began its snakelike motion. Standing near the opening where the luggage emerged, a tall man in a dark suit doffed his black leather cap when he saw Suzanne. She responded with an abbreviated wave and a slight smile.

"Someone you know, Suzanne?" Maggie asked.

"Yes, that's Horace, don't you recognize him? He's Carlos's chauffeur. He picked you up at O'Hare and drove you to our home. I phoned to tell him to meet me here at the baggage claim."

Josh turned quickly to look at Suzanne. "Wait a minute. I thought Carlos's chauffeur was killed in that accident."

"That's what I thought," Maggie chimed in. "Suzanne, what's going on?"

Now it was Suzanne who appeared bewildered. "No, no; I assumed that the chauffeur who was killed was the driver for the person meeting Carlos."

Horace, in his early sixties, at about six foot two with broad shoulders, a straight back, and a serious demeanor, gave the impression of a rock-solid pillar of strength. He alternated glances between the emerging luggage and Suzanne until he yanked two large bags off the line and rolled them toward the three. As he approached Suzanne, he removed his hat, lowered his head, and murmured, "I'm very sorry about Mr. Grandee, Ma'am."

"Thank you, Horace," she said, then introduced Josh. "You remember Mrs. Harrington, who visited with us in Kenilworth four months ago."

With a controlled smile, he nodded. "Yes, Ma'am."

He pulled the suitcases beyond the automatic exit doors that opened with a whoosh and headed across the street toward a curbside parking area marked *Reserved for Official Vehicles*. Then he walked toward the trunk of an elongated dark-gray Jaguar Vanden Plas.

Suzanne said, "I have a big favor to ask. Would you two please ride with me to the hotel? There's so much I need to talk about. Horace is staying in a motel near the airport. He'll return you here to your car."

Horace placed the suitcases at the rear of the vehicle, then hurried to open the rear door and stood sentinel-like as the three clambered in with Suzanne sitting in the middle. Cushy, soft leather seats, thick-pile carpeting, and oversized armrests created the sensation of being in a cozy cocoon. Horace put the suitcases in the trunk, then slipped into the driver's seat. The quiet, silky-smooth acceleration and the closed partition between the driver and rear passengers made conversation easy in the luxury of that highway Pullman.

"Suzanne, what did Carlos tell you just before his accident?" Josh asked. "Did he mention the name of the person he was going to meet?"

"He left a brief itinerary on the e-mail and listed the names of several people he planned to interview regarding the parcel of land he hoped to acquire from you."

"Did he mention a meeting with a Madame Tatiana that night?" Maggie asked.

Suzanne's brows knitted. "Yes, yes, now that you mention it. Just two days ago I talked with him and teased him about doing anything risqué. A person called *Madame* might mean trouble. He laughed and assured me there was nothing to be concerned about." As if to allay her own doubts, she added, "Carlos, as you know, is a man with extremely high moral and ethical standards."

Maggie glanced at Josh and shook her head almost imperceptibly to warn him against saying anything to the contrary.

"Did you determine why Horace didn't chauffeur him?" Josh asked.

"He made no mention of that. Of course, we can ask Horace now." Suzanne pushed a button on the side armrest. A small red light appeared on the headliner before she spoke in conversational tones: "Horace, why didn't you drive on the night of the accident?"

He pushed a button on the dash that turned red and without turning his head, spoke into an overhead mike pickup. "Mr. Grandee phoned to tell me he was going to be driven to a meeting and didn't need my services that night, Ma'am." After a pause, he added, "I'm sorry I didn't drive; that accident never would have happened."

Suzanne pushed the button to turn off the intercom. "Now we know what occurred. Did either of you know this Madame?"

Josh looked at Maggie. If he denied knowing Tatiana there would be questions later; it was best to be circumspect.

"Yes, I have met her. She was interested in bidding on our parcel. Carlos wanted to meet with each of the bidders and propose a type of partial sell-off." He turned and held Suzanne's hand. "Because of what happened, I'm sorry he proposed that meeting."

Suzanne nodded and dabbed her teary eyes. "Carlos had interested his corporate directors in developing a group of retail stores on El Paseo Drive. He has an astute sense for business development, and as for me, I'd love to be near you for a month or two in the year."

Maggie squeezed her hand and said, "That would be a lovely treat."

Suzanne continued, "What gives me some concern is Carlos's plan to have a heliport near an affluent residential area. I was thinking about the noise, but Carlos assured me that would not be a problem. I hope I'm not divulging any top-level secrets, but with new technologies, the helicopter, which is still under wraps, would be capable of taking off and landing almost silently. The government is sponsoring that research and development."

Josh leaned toward Suzanne and lowered his voice, even though the chauffeur probably could not hear. "Do you think the Russians are interested in getting that information? Do you think they'd be engaged in industrial espionage?"

"Are you thinking they're behind that accident?" Maggie looked at her husband to question his thought of espionage.

"Even if they were," Suzanne replied before Josh could, "what could they hope to gain by killing Carlos? The research and development would go on without him."

Horace directed the car on Ramon Road toward the I-10. At 7:45 p.m. there was little traffic, and thanks to a full moon, visibility was good even though there were no streetlights. Suddenly, a large dark vehicle with off-road lights and a menacing grill like the bared teeth on a snarling predator crossed the midline at about one hundred yards and barreled straight at them. With split-second maneuvering, Horace veered the Jaguar onto the right shoulder. Tires screeched in a cloud of sand and dust that enveloped the vehicle. The three passengers careened forward, then violently backward, tugging at the shoulder/lap restraints. The car did a complete turn as the big vehicle roared by. After lurching to a halt, Horace stomped on the accelerator to give chase. Suzanne quickly reached across Maggie, pressed the button on the armrest, and commanded, "No, Horace. No, don't follow him." Horace decelerated and made a cautious U-turn to resume the intended route.

"Are you women all right?" Josh asked.

Maggie, breathless, cried, "Oh, my God! I thought we were dead there for a moment."

Suzanne, remarkably composed for having barely escaped a dreadful collision, leaned forward and pressed the intercom button. "Thank you, Horace." Without turning, he raised his right hand and waved to acknowledge her gratitude. Suzanne sat back and looked at Josh and Maggie. "He's had defensive driver's training and knows what to do in these situations. It's not the first time he's avoided certain disaster. Kidnapping attempts were made when he drove Carlos in the Far East and Europe."

"I think that maniac was trying to kill us." Maggie said.

"When is this craziness going to stop?" The realization dawned on Suzanne how close they'd come to dying. Her face became pinched, and her lips trembled. "They tried to kill Carlos, and now us. Why?" She leaned forward and held her face in her hands.

"I think the police should be notified right now," Maggie said.

Suzanne nodded, sat up, and pointed to a green light above the chauffer to indicate that he had already called on a cell phone mounted in the headliner above. "It's already been done."

TWENTY-THREE

The valet approached the Jaguar as soon as it had stopped under the porte cochere. Horace moved out of the driver's seat and walked briskly around the back of the vehicle, then to the right rear door to assist Maggie and Suzanne. With a remote, he opened the trunk and pointed to the luggage for the valet.

Maggie insisted on accompanying Suzanne to the registration desk, then to her room, while Josh waited in the car. Horace drove the car to a limited-time parking zone near the entrance. Once parked, he lowered the privacy window and turned to talk with Josh.

"Mrs. Grandee will call when she's settled in to give me instructions for the morning. If you'd like, sir, you're welcome to join me in the front seat."

Sitting in the front passenger seat, Josh allowed his senses to absorb the luxury around him, the inviting aroma of new leather, the gold-plated instrument bezels, and the liberal use of exotic wood accents. "Surely, this isn't a regular company car."

"It's a company car, all right, but it's a lot different than any Jag off the showroom floor. Mr. Grandee went to Coventry, England, to order this baby." He pointed to the wood-trimmed dashboard and console. "This is genuine Circassian walnut, but that's only what you see; what you don't see is the missile-resistant glass, the bomb-proof undercarriage, and the self-inflating tires. But here's the real zinger:

there's an Aston-Martin engine under the bonnet that'll do zero to sixty in three and a half seconds flat. This baby is anything but ordinary."

Horace sat back, removed his cap, loosened his tie, took a deep breath, and exhaled through blown-out cheeks. With closed eyes, he began to ruminate. "The damned accident that almost killed my boss never should have happened, and it wouldn't have if I was driving. No sir, and I would have killed the sonofabitch who caused it."

Without changing his position, he raised the driver's right arm-rest, reached into a deeply recessed compartment, and pulled out an object wrapped in a soft, yellow chamois-like cloth. He uncovered it to reveal a gleaming, chrome-plated .357 Colt Python, which he held below window level. He wiped the barrel and handle with a delicate, almost sensuous touch, then recovered and replaced the gun in the armrest.

"Horace, do you remember anything else that was unusual the night your boss was almost killed? Did he sound different on the phone? Was there anything in the way he spoke that concerned you?"

"It's like I said, Mr. Grandee phoned early that evening. His voice sounded normal; there was no excitement or change in it. He was going to be driven to a casino about thirty-five miles west of here, sounded like Morgoney or Maronie . . ."

"Morongo?"

"Yeah, something like that. I asked if he wanted me to tail him, and he said no. Now, I'm sorry I didn't."

"Did he say who was going to pick him up?"

"Some woman . . . he didn't give me her name, like it wasn't important."

Josh was convinced of Horace's fealty to his boss. Horace also probably knew many of Carlos's habits when the two of them were away on business. "Horace, normally I would say this is none of my business, but was Mr. Grandee the sort of guy who would seek out the company of another woman when traveling?"

Horace shifted his eyes toward Josh. "If I didn't respect you, Doc, I'd tell you it's none of your damn business. But just for the record, let me set you straight. Mr. Carlos Grandee is one of the most honorable and most decent men who ever walked the face of this earth, bar none. He's a saint, that's what that man is."

"I appreciate your sense of loyalty; however, you haven't answered my question."

Horace turned toward Josh, obviously annoyed. "Mr. Grandee would no more cheat on his wife than, than she would cheat on him. Why the questions?"

Josh knew he had irritated Horace, so he decided to be straight forward. "There was a woman in the backseat of that limousine with your boss."

Horace interjected with hostility, "So what? Mr. Grandee often entertains female clients and employees. He respects women and treats them the same way."

"According to the police, it appears as if there was a sexual encounter between Carlos and the woman."

"No way!" Horace's voice rose and his complexion darkened. "Mr. Grandee would never do that to Mrs. Grandee. I know the man. Mr. Grandee had to have been drugged or unconscious to allow some woman to fuck him or blow him or whatever the hell she was supposed to be doing. He's too goddamn decent and too goddamn smart to allow anyone to take advantage of him. I'd stake my life on that. I've been his chauffeur, bodyguard, and what do you call it—his *confidant—for* twenty-nine years. I've been with him since the day of his confirmation when I was hired by his daddy, another great guy. No one knows Mr. Grandee better than me." He jabbed a thumb into his chest twice for emphasis. "Me! You hear? Believe me, once I see that Mrs. Grandee is settled, I'm going to the police and give them a piece of my mind. There's no damn way I'm going to let them go around implying any bullshit about his character."

TWENTY-FOUR

As soon as he opened the rear door to the office off the parking lot, Josh saw Carmenita waiting outside his consultation room. She caught his eye and tilted her head toward his door, then gave the hitchhiker's sign in its direction. Silently, he formed the word, "Who?"

She mouthed back, "The police."

He closed his eyes and shook his head in resignation, then opened the door. Sitting in two chairs facing his desk were Mannheim and Todd.

"Well, gentlemen? To what do I owe this pleasure? Don't bother to get up."

Mannheim popped the gum he'd been chewing and looked at Josh sideways. "We're here regarding the vehicle that ran Mrs. Grandee's limo off the road last night, the one the chauffeur . . ." Mannheim frowned. "He told us—among other things—he couldn't get a complete make on the vehicle trying to force him into an accident. But he did think it could have been a Hummer. We figure they might have had you or Mrs. Grandee in their sights from the time her limo left the airport."

"How did they manage to get ahead of us and on the other side of the road?"

"Dunno, but we'll find out. On a hunch, I thought about Dan Aviloh. I've already talked with him. Of course, he denied any knowledge of the incident. Claimed several people in his outfit have access to a Hummer, his chief foreman and his purchasing agent, among others. He provided an alibi for his own time last night, which we'll check out."

"I appreciate your telling me," Josh said. "Is there something else?"

Detective Todd pushed back in his chair and said nothing but smiled his enigmatic smile.

Mannheim made no effort to leave. "Truth is, Doc, I wanted some information from you. Tell me about Dan Aviloh, his medical problems. He told me he saw you here several weeks ago."

"Mannheim, you know there's doctor/patient confidentiality that must be respected."

Mannheim waved his right hand. "Save the holier-than-thou crap for the Sunday church social, Doc. We're talking attempted murder here, for Chrissake. You could've lost your life, along with your wife's and two others'. You know we can subpoena your records and tie up your office, so don't act like a schmuck."

Josh hesitated, having been influenced by years of rigid ethics and burdened by a sense of immutable righteousness. However, Mannheim was right about one thing. They'd almost been killed last night, and it hadn't been the first time his and Maggie's lives had been threatened.

Despite the fact that he resented Mannheim's demanding and crude mannerisms, he decided to provide as much information as he could and still stay within the realm of doctor/patient confidentiality. "What do you want to know?"

Mannheim chewed his gum deliberately. "Is the guy all there? Maybe . . . a little wacko?"

That caught Josh off guard. It was nothing at all like what he'd expected Mannheim to ask. "I thought his responses were reasonably normal, but I'm no psychiatrist."

"Did he confide in you about anything that would make you believe he's a suspect in Longfellow's murder?"

"Excuse me?"

"Let me put it another way, did you think he acted at all peculiar-like?"

"No, not really."

"Hm-mm. Tell me about his gimpy leg."

Now the detective was entering dangerous waters. Josh was not about to defy the request and have Mannheim berate him again. He buzzed the front desk and asked Carmenita to bring the folder on Dan Aviloh.

After she brought it, he opened the chart to the section on physical findings: leg measurements, muscle functioning, vascular and neurological evaluations. He was about to set the chart on his desk when Mannheim reached over and grabbed it.

"You don't mind if I look at this, do you, Doc?"

"As a matter of fact, I do." His objection didn't faze the detective.

Mannheim studied the sketched outline of both feet and asked, "What reason did you have for doing this?" He held the chart up for Josh to see.

"The custom shoe builder needs an outline of the feet, that and an impression of his soles made with the patient standing in a Styrofoam layer."

"Uh-huh." Mannheim studied the foot outlines. "Remember those shoe prints I talked about in the flower bed outside the Longfellow home found the morning after the murder?"

"The ones you thought might be useless as clues?"

"That's right." Mannheim snapped his gum. "Thanks for reminding me that on occasion I'm a jerk. I'll admit I make mistakes, but not too often. Have your girl make a copy of this foot pattern, would you?" He leafed through the rest of the history and physical exam without looking at Josh. "Did you notice that tattoo on his left forearm?"

"Of course I did," Josh said.

"Attach any significance to it?"

"No. Should I have?"

Without looking up from the chart, Mannheim said, "Aviloh said it was some kind of mystic good-luck symbol, some sort of crap like that. I knew it was put on during his reform school days."

"I didn't know about that."

"We ask a different set of questions than you do."

* * *

Two weeks after the accident, Carlos Grandee had made significant progress. His pelvic, facial, and upper-extremity fractures, immobilized with metallic plates, screws, and wires, showed the first X-ray evidence of healing. Josh collected the X-rays off the view boxes in the X-ray room and replaced them in their brown envelopes. He took the elevator to Carlos's floor and hurried into his room to greet him with a cheerful smile. He noted much of the swelling, discoloration, and deformity of his face had subsided, and Carlos was again recognizable if hardly handsome. "Life's a lot better without that nasogastric tube, isn't it?"

Carlos salivated, but he was able to converse with difficulty through his wired jaws. The initial period of amnesia and confusion had disappeared. A neurological evaluation had shown his cranial nerves to be grossly intact and cerebration was judged to be borderline normal. IVs had been discontinued and liquid feedings were being given through flexible straws. The urinary catheter continued to collect fluid that was no longer blood-tinged.

When Suzanne and Maggie returned from the coffee shop and walked into his room, Carlos's eyes welcomed them with a tight sardonic-looking smile because of the wires.

"Are you feeling better, sweetheart?" Suzanne leaned over to kiss his forehead. He blinked and managed a short nod and a guttural, slurred, "Yes."

After a limited conversation, he fell asleep while Suzanne and Maggie sat in chairs next to his bed and whispered to each other.

Seeing the women occupied, Josh excused himself and went to the doctors'/nurses' station to confer with Dick Williams, who was making chart notes.

The physician looked up as Josh joined him. "How's our battered patient today, Josh?"

"Good."

"Wonderful. According to his chart, it looks as though he's definitely on the mend. Have you consulted with a plastic surgeon about reconstructing his mangled penis?" Williams didn't wait for an answer. He seemed to direct his question to the page on which he was writing. When finished, he tapped his pen against the paper and looked up. "Mr. Grandee will be lucky if he can pee without a catheter."

"The plastic surgeon is considering what to do now."

"Excellent. Damn, it looked like a Braunschweiger caught in a lawn mower." He shook his head with judgmental piety. "Fellatio really shouldn't be attempted in a fast-moving vehicle, too many chances for calamity. I remember one night when I was an intern, when three of us dated three first-year nurse trainees—"

"Dr. Harrington?" The ward clerk approached with a mobile phone in her hand. "Dr. Kochsiek, from pathology. It's for you."

Josh took the phone and listened. He thanked Dr. Kochsiek then smiled and signed off. Dick Williams was about to resume the story of his ancient peccadillo when Josh touched his shoulder and said, "Forgive me for interrupting, but I just learned that our patient was drugged at the time of impact."

Williams blinked several times. He placed his pen on the lined sheet and became serious. "Drugged?"

"A fast-acting drug, like Brevitol, before the crash. I've got to be sure the police know."

TWENTY-FIVE

The phone rang.

Maggie sighed and rolled over in bed to see the dresser clock. "Oh, I hope it's not an emergency. It's five after eleven; you'll never get any sleep."

She handed Josh the phone and turned on the nightstand lamp. "It's Mannheim."

"Mannheim?" He took the phone and listened. Finally he spoke: "Yeah, that's a real kick in the pants. I'll talk to you tomorrow."

"What was that all about?" Maggie asked, leaning on one elbow.

"Mannheim got my message that pathology confirmed Carlos had been drugged. He figured with that information and the fact that the camera in the limo was filming the oral sex act—"

Maggie slapped her thigh. "Of all the rotten tricks! I knew all along that man was innocent. What about Tatiana's role in all this?"

"What about her?"

"Well, what's going to happen to her body? Hasn't anyone come to claim her yet?"

"Not that I know of." Josh plumped his pillow and set it against the headboard. "I should talk with Farquhaar about her, God rest her tormented soul. Old Roscoe's the one who recommended her to me initially when I inquired about Cue. Maybe he knows someone who can see to the burial arrangements." Josh leaned back against the pillow. He was too charged up to want to sleep. Maggie lay with her back toward him. "Maggie, this whole thing bothers me. Ever since Chesley gave me that property, our lives have been screwed up. I think it's time we review everything that's happened and everyone concerned."

"At this hour? Get to sleep, for pity's sake." Maggie pulled the cover over her head.

Josh studied the lump of covers next to him. If she refused to look at him, he could still talk to the covers. "Fact number one: Six months ago, Chesley Effingwell dies after being poisoned and leaves us an adobe and acreage in Rancho Mirage."

A mumbled voice floated up from under the covers. "Tell me something I don't know."

"Bear with me. I only mentioned these facts so I can keep them straight in my own head. Fact number two: Prissy Longfellow, a woman I haven't seen in years, suddenly shows up, telling me her husband would like to buy the land."

"I refuse to talk about her royal harlotry."

Josh nearly laughed at the disgruntlement in Maggie's voice. "Fact number three: Before I have time to actually meet Peter Longfellow, he suddenly dies."

"You mean murdered, don't you?"

"Okay, murdered. Fact number four: Soon after that, we get a call from Cue in New York, who claims to be a nephew of Chesley and is adamant about purchasing the property."

Josh held up four fingers. "Since I know nothing about the guy, I ask Farquhaar to seek information on him. He refers me to Madame Tatiana, who tells me Cue is an unsavory guy to deal with. Number five—"

"Please shut the light when you're through recounting all this delightful information."

"Fact number five," he repeated. "Madame Tatiana, herself, shows interest in obtaining the land. Fact number six: Two other people want to acquire the land: Mr. Yamamoto, the administrator of the hospital, and contractor Dan Aviloh, a lifelong, devoted friend of Peter Longfellow, now deceased. So, how many people does that make?"

Maggie pulled the cover off her head. "You're not going to take the hint and go to sleep, are you?" She sat up and propped her pillow against the headboard as well. "Okay, well, there's Carlos Grandee, he's number six. And . . ." She raised seven fingers. "Seven if you want to include Officer Harry Todd, whose great-grandparents were cheated out of—"

"No." Josh stopped her. "We've listed all the possible suspects without reaching for the least likely. There's only one other someone I'd like to zero in on."

He eyed his wife's tousled hair and sleepy, sexy look. He leaned over and drew her into his arms.

Maggie giggled and snuggled closer to him. "So, what's stopping you?"

"Nothing." He pulled her farther down onto the bed and covered her body with his. "Nothing at all."

＊ ＊ ＊

Palm Desert's El Paseo Drive, like Beverly Hills' Rodeo Drive, boasted of stores that catered to the carriage trade, prestigious merchants: Saks Fifth Avenue, Burburry, Gucci, Ralph Lauren, and Tiffany were but a few. Actually, El Paseo was more attractive than Rodeo Drive, its medians resplendent in the colors of seasonal flowers and adorned with contemporary statuary, some pieces oddly pixilated, others starkly geometric. The mile-long avenue was elegant, and the traffic moved at a leisurely pace. The area had risen like the phoenix in an arid desert in just the past decade and catered to the valley's affluent residents, as well as camera-toting tourists.

However, not all buildings were new, or elegant. Some predated the influx of modern architecture by forty or more years and had escaped rigid construction standards. They had been assembled in cost-constraining boxlike configurations with banal stucco finishes in the pink and beige popular in the 'forties through the 'sixties. Roscoe U. Farquhaar, Esq., Attorney at Law, had an office on the second floor of such a building. Actually, the building did not front El Paseo, but rather behind it, along a well-maintained parking strip that was virtually an alley.

His office was approached by a stairwell at either end of the building or a central elevator of questionable reliability. Maggie recalled an experience when the elevator moved jerkily, then stalled between floors; her reaction had been claustrophobia bordering on panic. After five minutes that seemed like an eternity, the elevator moved.

Rather than run the risk of similar unpleasantness, Maggie said, "Josh, we're using the stairs. I don't trust that old elevator."

Roscoe's office door had an opaque glass pane bearing his name and title in gold-leaf block letters outlined in black, a sign-painting technique long out of vogue.

His small outer office with its low-lying ceiling of discolored acoustic panels was dominated by the receptionist seated at her commercial-type gray-green steel desk, an enormous woman whose obesity took refuge in a wild flower-patterned muumuu. A name plate on the desk read *M. Haioliani.*

The moment Josh and Maggie entered, they were greeted with a smile above a gelatinous triple chin. "Dr. and Mrs. Harrington . . . how nice to see you again. Mr. Farquhaar will see you now."

Josh was grateful, because the only other chairs in that anteroom were stacked with irregular towers of manila folders bulging with poorly contained contents.

Maggie was first through Roscoe's door. The moment he saw them, Farquhaar stood from behind his desk and waved.

"Come in. Come in, my dear, dear friends."

Roscoe skirted the desk laden with more stacks of folders, some bound with thick rubber bands that failed to keep all their contents tidy. "Allow me to make room for you." He hurried around his desk to remove the folders from two chairs.

The late-morning sun had begun to create a penetrating heat, and Farquhaar's open-collared shirt revealed beads of perspiration on his foreshortened neck as well as areas of moisture under his armpits. "I'd turn the window air-conditioner on, but it makes a horrible racket, just horrible, and blows papers around. With ice water and a floor fan strategically placed, I think we'll get by."

He clicked on the ancient wood-box intercom and bent over the speaker. "Millicent, my Hawaiian flower, *agua frio, por favor.*"

"What?" came the reply from the intercom's speaker. "You mean water?"

"Yes, yes, that's right, cold water, please." He turned off the intercom and shook his head. "She's been in California over twenty years and still doesn't understand a word of Spanish."

Josh decided not to waste time. "Roscoe, what can you tell us about that horrendous accident that killed Madame Tatiana, her chauffeur, and almost killed Mr. Grandee?"

Farquhaar picked up a manila folder and started to fan himself, his reddened face appearing like a balloon compressed from above and below when he began to smile.

"I'm not sure I have the information you lovely people seek. In the beginning, I, too, could not fathom the events of that evening and had wondered why the accident occurred." He looked at both of them, then continued in a hushed, metered cadence matching the speed with which he fanned himself. "It was staged, you know, absolutely staged, a rehearsed conspiracy, a premeditated calculation with the most evil of intent. The work of some malevolent spirit, yes, a malevolent spirit."

"What in the hell do you mean, 'staged'?" Josh interrupted, his anger building. "There's a man lying in the hospital who was near death. His condition is damned real. That certainly wasn't staged. Not to mention two other people died."

"Josh, honey." Maggie put a hand on Josh's arm. "I don't think that's what Roscoe is saying."

"Yes, yes, my darling girl. You're right as constitutional law and quite perspicacious. For your husband, I should have been more specific; forgive my maladroit phraseology."

The lawyer scooted several folders away from the corner of his desk. He awkwardly hefted his beefy hip and sat. "'Tell me not in mournful numbers . . . and things are not what they seem,' a bit of Henry Wadsworth Longfellow, my dears, no relative of Peter's, heh-heh."

Josh hadn't the foggiest notion of what Farquhaar was trying to convey. He glanced over at Maggie, then at the ceiling, hoping for divine explanation.

"Let me confound you further." Farquaahr stopped, then bent over his desk and flipped the intercom's toggle switch. "Millicent, my lithesome Polynesian *wahine*, have our visitors come in yet?"

"Yes, they just arrived. Should I send them in?"

"Yes, my pearl of the sea."

Farquhaar lifted his heavy thigh off the desk and stood facing the door. He folded his hands and rested them on his protruding abdomen. His florid, jowly face melded into his chest without the intervention of an observable neck. Even his smile, accompanied by slitlike eyes, reminded Josh of those ubiquitous plastic or chalk Buddhas sitting benevolently on counters in Chinese restaurants and Thai beauty shops.

The door opened slowly.

Maggie and Josh turned to focus on the door.

In the doorway, like a Khrushchevian clone, complete with ill-fitting clothes, stood an unsmiling gnome. He stomped into the room and surveyed it silently. As if satisfied, he nodded.

Josh studied the man. He knew him, but couldn't remember from where.

At that same instant, in strolled a tall, veiled, exquisitely dressed woman whose delicate fragrance preceded her. Her slow, exaggerated movements could belong to only one person.

Josh bolted to his feet. "Madame Tatiana?"

Beside him, Maggie stood as well. She stared at the Russian woman with wide eyes.

Farquhaar rushed across the room to meet her, but was halted by the Slavic character.

Instantly, a hailstorm of Russian invective left the woman. The coarseness of her tone was startlingly incompatible with her fairy godmother–like appearance. The bodyguard snapped to attention, then bowed submissively. He walked backwards to the door, stopping only when his backside hit the door frame.

Farquhaar bent forward and kissed the back of Tatiana's hand, then held it and guided her forward. "Madame, you know Dr. Harrington, and this is Mrs. Harrington."

Tatiana took her hand out of Roscoe's and lifted her gossamer veil. She studied Maggie closely. "You haf goot taste, Doktor." Gracefully, she crossed over to Maggie and caressed her face lightly, then turned to Josh and cupped her hand to whisper in his ear, "She make you goot fuck, no?"

Heat shot up Josh's neck and blossomed onto his face. He hoped Maggie and Roscoe had not heard her actual words.

Gathering his composure, Josh took her hands into his and said softly, "I thought you were dead."

TWENTY-SIX

"On the contrary, Doktor. I am very much alive." She removed her hands from Josh's and gave Maggie a smile. "Your husband is very sweet, is he not?"

Maggie nodded but remained silent. From the moment the woman had entered the room, Maggie sensed something about the Russian that the men had not. Madame Tatiana demanded total attention, yet beneath all her sexual wiles, there was a vulnerability about her.

That intrigued Maggie. She watch with rapt attention as Roscoe offered Tatiana his desk chair, then swept a large pile of papers and folders off a chair sitting in the corner. Once he had the chair situated near Tatiana, he leaned toward her and whispered something only she could hear.

She nodded and turned to look at her bodyguard standing near the door. With a spate of Russian, she pointed a finger toward the door.

Though the man appeared unhappy with the command, he exited the room.

"Good. Now we can talk." Roscoe rubbed his hands. "Madame Tatiana, our good friend Dr. Josh has had the terrible misunderstanding you were killed in the limousine along with a chauffeur when it crashed and almost mortally wounded Mr. Carlos Grandee."

Tatiana watched as Josh returned to his own chair next to Maggie. "I am sorry to have put you through such sorrow, Doktor."

Sitting opposite the woman, Maggie caught an instant of remorse. Tatiana was telling the truth. She decided to watch the woman closer.

Josh started to speak, but Roscoe beat him to it.

"Tell us, did you ever meet with Mr. Grandee?"

Tatiana shook her head. *"Nyet."*

"Where were you when the accident occurred?" Roscoe asked his questions in rapid order.

Tatiana sat upright, touched her hair lightly, and spoke slowly, occasionally misusing a word or phrase that could have been construed as vulgar or inappropriate. Her failure to understand the nuances of American idiomatic expressions led to pronouncements that might have startled or amused the unsuspecting.

Maggie remained fascinated by her conversation punctuated with earthy expressions. She glanced toward her husband. He, too, seemed captivated.

"You're sure you never met Mr. Grandee?" Roscoe seemed to want to hammer in that point.

"I did not. Only spoke with him over the phone. I requested a time and place for us to meet. I said I vanted us to meet at the Morongo Casino."

"Why there?"

"Because I did not vant to meet at my own establishment." She paused as if to heighten the dramatic effect. "I have . . . what do you say? Privacy leaks?"

Tatiana reached into her jeweled handbag and produced a small device. "This was removed from my personal phone."

"May I see it?" Roscoe held out his hand.

With slender, graceful fingers, Tatiana placed it in the palm of his hand.

Adjusting his half glasses lower on his nose, he brought the device closer to his face. "You are so correct. This, my dear lady, is a *bug*, a pick-up, a listening device."

Maggie almost laughed when Roscoe struck a Churchillian jaw-thrusting pose.

"So, Madame? Who in heaven's name had the temerity to invade the sanctity of your sacred privilege?"

Tatiana seemed to preen at Roscoe's expressive verbiage. "I have good idea. I will tell you." Tatiana took the bug from Roscoe and returned it to her handbag. She stood and ran her hand down her backside, hip, and thigh to draw attention to her svelte figure. Taking several steps away from the desk, she cradled her chin with her right hand in a dramatic pause made more suspenseful by extended silence.

Again, Maggie marveled at Tatiana's command performance technique. Though a part of her wanted to hate the woman for being who she was, another part almost admired her. Why . . . she wasn't completely certain.

Roscoe *tsk*ed several times. "Come, come, my dear, who is this villainous character who would spy on one of our most genteel, refined, and trustworthy citizens? Reveal the culprit's name, and I shall encumber his freedom for invading your civil rights under Federal Code number—"

Tatiana whirled around. "Mister Lawyer, close your mouth. Don't make foolish talk." The woman was clearly annoyed by Roscoe's bombast and the interruption of her center-stage performance.

Maggie almost giggled. She turned her head toward Josh and noticed that he, too, appeared to be struggling to suppress a smile. When he noticed her eyeing him, he gave her a wink, then went back to watching the performance between the silver-tongued lawyer and the haughty Russian queen.

Roscoe appeared to have shrunk in size. "I'm sorry, my dear. Please, please continue."

Tatiana's deprecating expression expanded. She chose to remain silent even longer to punish him for his discourtesy.

That sat well with Roscoe for only a few minutes. He looked at his watch and drummed his fingers on the desk. Two seconds later, he blurted out, "For the love of Aristophanes, tell us what you know!"

Tatiana cast a baleful eye on Roscoe, then turned her back on him. She raised her head. "The woman who died in the crash, pretending to be me, was one of my own escorts." Tatiana sniffed. "How one could become disloyal to me, it shatters my heart." She placed a hand on her bosom. "Marianna had been lured with promises of big cash rewards." Tatiana's chin lifted. "My girls earn fabulous money just for ordinary *tricks,* as much as a thousand to three thousand dollars a night. Of course, that does not include house calls and all-nighters."

Tears filled Tatiana's lovely eyes. "How could any one of them become disloyal and betray me for money?"

"A sacrilege, I agree," Roscoe murmured sympathetically. "Shall we move on? Did you know the driver of the limo?"

Tatiana waved an impatient hand. "He was an inexperienced *muzhik,* a former co-worker of the one who accompanied me today. He, too, had been promised big money. The *muzhik* talked to others. They tell me the driver boasted he was ordered to turn the camera on while the escort disrobed and prepared the pigeon for slow and repetitive sexual activities. All Marianna had to do was make sure camera would show explicit body parts, movements. Make victim's identity unmistakably clear."

"Madame Tatiana, how do you know all this?" Josh asked. "After all, the woman is dead and the only survivor, Mr. Grandee, claims he was unable to tell us anything about the sex act."

"My dear Doktor," she said, slinking toward him, "the little tricks what these girls do, I did myself before I became a lady. But I never use drugs for what you call performance enhancement, and I never want to make my john to sleep. I want him alive and hungry for pussy cat. My girls talk among themselves and then they tell me. I am like their mama when they are in my gorgeous home. I already discuss these things with Detective Sergeant Mannheim. He's no dummy, you know. He can put long things in round holes."

"What is Marianna's last name?" Maggie decided she'd had enough of staying out of the conversation. "It will be wanted, I'm sure."

"Cherenkoff. Marianna Cherenkoff, a girl with a little too much ambition."

"Of course." Josh snapped his fingers. Now I remember. When I asked Dr. Williams if the dead woman's name was Tatiana, he thought it was something like that. Now I can see how he could have confused the name *Marianna* with *Tatiana.*"

Maggie turned to Madame Tatiana. "One thing I'm curious about: how did Marianna substitute herself for you?"

Tatiana sighed and returned to her chair. "I too have been wondering that. My calls must have been intercepted. After that it would be easy for someone to intervene and pretend to be me."

Roscoe shifted his bulky weight uncomfortably. Obviously he wasn't used to sitting on such a narrow chair for long periods of time. "Undoubtedly, someone—whoever the evil miscreant may be—is determined to have Carlos Grandee back away from pursuing the land deal."

"I think you're right." Josh glanced at Maggie. "I bet the plan was to blackmail Carlos with lurid photos and have him bow out."

"If that's the case," Maggie said, "why the accident? Granted, having the chauffeur and Marianna die might save the killer money. But why try and kill Carlos if the plan was to blackmail him?"

"Good point." Josh thought for a moment. "Maybe it wasn't part of the original plan. Maybe it was just an accident."

Maggie shook her head. "No, I believe the limo was deliberately run off the road."

Josh's expression hardened. "If you're right, that means it's possible we have two killers out there."

Maggie suddenly realized that Roscoe and Tatiana hadn't said a word while she and Josh talked. She glanced at Roscoe. "There is more than one prospective buyer wanting our property. Their lives may be in jeopardy as well." She frowned. "But which ones?"

A scratchy, staccato voice on the old intercom interrupted before Roscoe could respond. "Mr. Farquhaar . . . *squawk* . . . *ee—ow—ee*—has arrived."

Roscoe struggled to rise from the chair. "Send him in, my delicate Polynesian pearl."

Maggie chuckled inwardly. There was something amusing yet irritating in Roscoe's puerile manner of communicating with his secretary.

She, along with the others, faced the door as it opened.

Silence pervaded the room. Maggie once again saw the chilling aspect of the prince of darkness framed by the open door; the bearer of unwanted news, the cynic with a distrust of anyone even remotely connected to the murder.

It was the chief of the local homicide division, Detective Sergeant Timothy Aloysius Mannheim.

He sauntered deeper into the room. In his croaking monotone, he began, "Well, I see we have a formidable collection of professionals here."

He turned toward Farquhaar. "Stop your money-making clock, Mr. Attorney-at-Law. Don't charge your clients for the next ten minutes of my time."

Next he zeroed in on Josh and Maggie. "Here we have two professionals from the big-money health industry."

Like a pro who loved attention, he pivoted and faced Tatiana. "And here we have a member of the world's oldest profession, the one who is probably the wealthiest of all."

He tilted his head back and to one side. "And her hired goon, Ivan the Terrible, standing guard outside. What a lovely group."

Roscoe raised his nose in his usual imperious way. "Mannheim, we tolerate your tasteless sarcasm and abusive insults only because we have little choice. We're given no options in the selection of our law enforcement officers, none at all, no, none at all." He reached out and flicked an imaginary object off his desk. "We are made to accept whatever dross is cast upon us."

Mannheim ignored him. He took a step toward Madame Tatiana. "Since you, Madame, showed us some cooperation in our investigation, I'll let you in on a secret."

Mannheim glanced at the others. "I don't know how much she's told you, but we have a pretty good idea who ordered the bug to be placed in her personal phone." He walked toward the upright electric fan, put his back to it, and lifted his jacket to get the full breeze. "Madame, the bug was installed by a local electronics maven, not to mention a computer hacker who's done time in a federal pen."

"Ahh, I see." Tatiana appeared pleased. "Where is this man now?"

"In jail, awaiting trial."

"May I ask how your inept department managed to nab him?" Roscoe Farquhaar seemed a bit put out at being ignored.

"That's none of your damn business, Counselor." Mannheim hesitated, then recanted. "Actually, we used a snitch, and that's more than you need to know."

"Sergeant." Maggie kept her voice polite. "I hope you don't take offense, but what *are* you doing here?"

He looked at her. "Little lady, I've had occasion to ask myself that same question several times in the last half hour. As a matter of fact it may surprise you to know, Madame Tatiana and her esteemed attorney asked me here today. Madame is gun-shy now about using her personal phone and is reluctant to walk into the sheriff's office."

Mannheim pointed at the intercom. "Farquhaar, buzz Hilo Hattie. Have her bring in a chair for me, will ya?"

Surprisingly, the lawyer did what the detective ordered without a protest.

Once Mannheim was slumped in a folding chair, with his spindly legs stretched outward, everyone was given the privilege of staring at a pair of white rumpled socks beneath black, crease-less trousers.

Mannheim folded his arms over his chest, his eyes shielded by bushy brows. "Thanks to Madame, here, she gave us reason to pursue our highway felony hit-and-run suspect with renewed interest. The special-bodied Fleetwood limousine, smashed to hell, was a rented vehicle."

Roscoe sniffed. "That, detective, is not a surprise."

"Well, it should be. Do you know any rental agency that will rent or lease an expensive limousine to anyone who is not a licensed chauffeur?" Mannheim eyed the lawyer with amusement.

"What is your point, dear fellow?" Farquhaar must have known he'd been one-upped.

"Simply stated, the limo rental service allowed an unlicensed alien to drive their vehicle, proving that they were most probably in cahoots with the plan to blackmail." Mannheim zeroed his deep-set eyes on Farquhaar. "The vehicle was also outfitted with costly camera equipment." The officer drew in his legs and sat upright. "Trick is . . . who owned, do you suppose, the limousine rental service?"

Tatiana jumped to her feet. "I know. Mister Big Shot Cue, that dirty, lying, cheating pig. I told you before, he is no good."

"Madame, you're so right!" Farquhaar must have thought he was about to lose his client. He banged his fist onto his desk. "He's got to be one pompous ass thinking he could pull off that caper. Yes, a bloody pompous ass."

"Excuse me," Maggie asked. "What is so terribly important about the property to make Cue take such extreme measures for disgracing Carlos?"

Josh answered first. "My guess is that Cue figured he would be unable to bid successfully against Carlos. If he could involve Carlos in a sex scandal then his board of directors would deny him the means to purchase that property."

"Yes, of course, I understand. But it doesn't explain why Cue so desperately needs to own that land and the adobe."

Mannheim must have read her mind, he grinned, then abruptly looked down at his worn, unpolished shoes. "I've got a theory about that too, Ma'am."

"Theory, shmeory." Tatiana sat upright and threw back her shoulders, giving everyone a clear view of her enormous bosom. "Cue, he want adobe house too much."

Mannheim gazed at her, "And why is that?"

"Because I say so." Tatiana folded her arms across her chest. "You go arrest him now. Make him talk. You will see. I am right."

While Tatiana and Mannheim talked, Roscoe's head turned back and forth as if he were a spectator at a tennis match. He must have heard enough. "Madame, the police will need evidence before they can arrest him—yes, indeed, strong evidence."

That obviously didn't please Tatiana. She glared at him. "In Russia, police make arrest. They make own evidence."

"We operate differently here," Mannheim said flatly.

"So what you do? You just make talk?" Tatiana threw up her hands. "You need confession from Mister Big Shot? My *muzhik* get confession from him, like that." She snapped her fingers.

Mannheim shut his eyes and sighed. "I didn't hear that." He slapped his hands on his thighs and stood. "I think I'm through here." When he reached the door, he turned back. "We'll need more findings before our prosecutor can initiate extradition proceedings from New York."

As he opened the door, Tatiana called out, "Mister Detective, two of my workers were killed in that accident. Despite their disloyalty to me, something must be done. What will you do?"

Mannheim hesitated. Finally he looked at her. "Like I said. Until we have more proof, nothing." With that said, he walked out the door.

TWENTY-SEVEN

A one-story beige stucco building in the heart of the Palm Desert commercial district was almost obscured by the fruitless pear trees on its lawn. A polished brass plate to the right of its recessed door read *Acme Forensic Services of Southern California, Inc. Est. 1979.*

Josh handed an envelope with the official seal of Riverside County to the receptionist. The envelope was addressed to Dr. Sheldon Collis. The woman accepted it with a smile. "Who shall I say is calling, sir?"

Josh gave her his card and waited in the small anteroom, where he surveyed the framed documents on the wall attesting to the achievements of the laboratory and its staff. One large framed newspaper article declared, "DNA proves man killed wife five years ago. Local laboratory helps convict man."

"Dr. Harrington, Dr. Collis will see you now."

The receptionist instructed Josh to open the waiting-room door when a buzzer sounded. A second later, he was led down a long hall to a small office.

Seated before a white binocular microscope with an attached square-foot-sized upright screen, Collis turned to greet Josh when he entered.

Collis, in his early sixties, of medium build, and wearing a white starched lab coat, shook Josh's hand. "Sergeant Mannheim told me you were coming. You're interested in that Peter Longfellow murder case. Well, let me show you what we've got."

Josh accompanied him to a room with a solid wooden door. Collis removed a set of keys from his pocket, inserted one into the door lock, and turned it until it clicked. On a panel next to the door, he punched in a coded sequence.

Turning the knob, he announced, "Voilà!"

They walked into a room that lit up instantaneously.

"Seems like a lot of security you have here." Josh looked around.

"Have to." Collis frowned. "After two episodes of evidentiary findings being stolen, we started taking greater precautions."

Josh studied the laboratory. The windowless room measured about twenty feet square and contained a bank of gray-green steel cabinets five feet high and three feet deep on three walls. On the fourth wall, an open-shelf library held books on such topics as chemical analyses, biological determinants, and histopathology. The center of the room was occupied by a wooden desk with four chairs, a reviewing screen for microfiche, and two computers.

"When was the last time you saw a speck of dust in this room?" Josh asked jokingly.

Collis laughed. "Nothing that doesn't belong gets into this room." Pointing to cameras in opposite corners, he said, "Smile, you're being watched and filmed." He went to one of the desk computers and punched a number of keys. Once finished, he walked over to one of the cabinets and pulled out a drawer. He removed a thick manila folder and placed it on the wood desk. "Here are our results." When the contents were spread, Josh noted the many printed pages, photographs, DNA patterns, chromatograms, and other seemingly cryptic materials.

Collis selected two items. "These may be of interest to you."

Josh recognized the copies of the tracings of Dan Aviloh's footprints that Mannheim had taken from his office. Then he picked up a transparent copy of the right shoe print found in the newly planted flower bed outside the Longfellow den.

Collis had superimposed the shoe print over a footprint. He looked at Josh. "Does that suggest something to you?"

"Yes, but the shoe size is a common one. If I were a defense lawyer, I'd say this doesn't necessarily identify my client as the man."

Collis must have anticipated Josh's response. He removed the second or left foot print, which was smaller than the first, and super-imposed a shoe transparency over it. He placed both prints and transparencies side-by-side. "Now look: two imprints taken at the same time at the same place. Is that convincing?"

Josh studied both. "The imprints match Dan Aviloh's feet and shoes."

"Exactly. What are the odds that someone else might have feet of different sizes and had worn different-sized shoes to match those feet?"

"I have no idea."

"Guessing in round numbers, I'd say about a hundred million to one."

"That certainly places Aviloh at the location. Unfortunately, it doesn't reference the time."

"Good point, but not entirely valid."

Collis adjusted the report and pulled out a second page. "We know from the depth and clear cut of the shoe impressions that the marks were fresh, only hours old at the most before degradation from sprinklers, wind, and garden tools might have obliterated them."

"Interesting. Hadn't thought about that. See anything else?"

Collis picked up a photograph of a plaster cast made from a tire impression near the flower bed. "These tire treads are compatible with tire sizes from a number of large vehicles: a Ford Excursion, Chevrolet Avalanche, Cadillac Escalade."

Josh had another vehicle in mind. "How about a Hummer?"

"Depending on the model. Probably."

"What would it take to make an iron-clad case against Aviloh? If it is him." Josh's mind whirled with possibilities.

"I'd say, find Longfellow's blood on Aviloh's clothes or shoes, or his prints on a murder weapon, like that andiron."

"The police had to look at Aviloh's clothes and shoes, didn't they? And what about the andiron?"

"They went to Aviloh's home and asked to see his clothes. They'd been washed with bleach. No RBC's could be found. He said he took a pair of old shoes to the Angel View Charity along with some old clothes—maybe coincidental, maybe not—anyway, the shoes are gone and the clothes show nothing."

"What about the andiron?"

"Wiped clean, no prints; some grease smudges, but that's all."

"So, what you're saying is all Mannheim has is a set of shoe prints and a lot of suspicion and probabilities."

"Exactly."

TWENTY-EIGHT

Suzanne was seated at Carlos's side. She had been encouraging him to take liquid protein through a flexible straw and alternated that with an infant-sized spoon containing a pabulum mash.

When Josh entered the room, the man's eyes brightened. Gently, he pushed Suzanne's feeding hand away, swallowed whatever remained in his mouth, then said in a guttural voice, "Hello, Josh."

"Carlos, I've just looked at your latest X-rays. They look terrific." Josh smiled at him. "Better prepare yourself for a move to a convalescent facility."

Suzanne also smiled. "That's wonderful news."

Josh leaned over and kissed her cheek. "How are you holding up, Suzanne?"

"Good," she said. "Once Carlos is able, we've made plans to stay with one of our friends at their home at Big Horn Country Club. You will come by to visit us, won't you?"

"I have too much time, effort, and worry invested in this guy not to visit."

Suzanne , weary, looked up at Josh while feeding Carlos. Josh relieved her of the spoon. "You look as if you need a break. Why don't you treat yourself to a cup of coffee and a croissant in the cafeteria?"

"Well, I would like something to drink. Will you be here?"

"Sure. I'll stay until you get back." Josh patted her arm. "It'll give us guys a moment or two to commiserate."

As soon as she left, Josh sat in the chair Suzanne had vacated. "Now that you're doing better, can you recall exactly what happened on the night of the accident?"

Carlos's knitted brows and side-to-side eye movements indicated his frustration.

Josh knew Carlos wasn't frustrated just with his memory fading in and out, but from his inability to speak as well. "That's okay, Carlos. Do what you can. I'll try and keep my questions simple. Nod to say 'yes' and shake your head to indicate 'no.' Did you plan to meet with Tatiana that night?"

Carlos closed his eyes and nodded.

"Had you ever seen Tatiana prior to that evening?"

He shook his head, but also managed to utter a throaty, "Never," through his wired jaws.

"Did you stop to have a bite or a drink with a woman before you left your hotel?"

Carlos nodded, then mumbled incoherently.

Josh reached in his jacket for a notepad and gave it to Carlos, along with a pen.

With a shaking hand, Carlos wrote and held out the pad: *wine, hotel bar.*

"Ahh . . . what happened once you got into the limo?"

He wrote: *Tired, passed out.*

"I see. Then you weren't aware of anything after that?" Josh paused. "Like being sexually stimulated?"

An expression of bewilderment crossed Carlos's features.

Clearly the man had no memory of what happened after the hotel.

Josh pointed to Carlos's pelvis. "Are you able to urinate more normally now?"

Carlos rocked his hand, indicating "more or less."

"How about pain?"

Carlos nodded, lifting his thumb and index finger with a two-inch space between them.

Josh smiled. "A small amount, huh. That's good."

* * *

Since all the doctors' parking spaces were taken, Josh parked his SUV in the area designated for hospital employees. The lack of parking spaces for doctors was a source of chronic frustration that seemed to be continuously ignored by the administration. Although Josh's vehicle was higher than sedans or sport coupes, it was dwarfed by a four-wheeled pickup to his right and an armored-like vehicle to his left. Squeezing around the oversized rearview side mirror of the pickup, he had difficulty opening his door and climbing into the driver's seat.

Carefully, he inched the SUV backward, then headed through the parking lot that led to the exit that dumped out onto Country Club Drive. Just as he reached the exit, a thought hit him. Normally, large trucks were not allowed in the special parking area. They had been assigned to another lot.

Another thought came on the heels of his first one. The vehicle parked on the right of him was like an army personnel carrier. *A Hummer!*

It had to have been. He remembered now noticing the road lights mounted on the cab, like those used in a rally.

The coincidence was too much. Josh made a quick U-turn and headed back through the large parking lot. Was it possible it was the same one that had sped toward them the night he, Maggie, and Suzanne left the airport? When he reached the row he'd parked in, he drove slowly past the space he had occupied.

It remained empty, but so was the space next to his. Whoever owned the Hummer had driven away. But where?

"Damn!" Josh slapped the palms of his hands on the steering wheel and looked around. Surely the driver hadn't gotten too far.

Nothing moved. Not one single vehicle. Josh gave up his search and headed again for the Country Club Drive exit. At least there was one thing in his favor. Security would have a record of which employees owned Hummers.

TWENTY-NINE

"Thanks for coming in on your lunch break, Aviloh." Mannheim pointed to a chair on the other side of his desk.

Aviloh looked around the confining office. "I don't mind telling you I get a little antsy being around the cops' hangout. I'm not going to need a lawyer for this, am I?"

"Not unless you've got something to hide." Mannheim had given the retort so many times, it left his mouth without thinking. Fortunately for him, it placed a perp, any perp, at a psychological disadvantage.

He opened his spiral notebook. "I've got a few questions for you to answer."

Aviloh looked at him suspiciously, then folded his arms across his chest and with bravado said, "Start askin'. I got nothin' to hide."

"Why were your footprints found outside the Longfellow home the day after Peter Longfellow's murder?" He walked slowly behind Aviloh's chair, so Aviloh would have to turn in his seat to watch him.

"I don't know what you're talking about."

Mannheim stopped abruptly.

Seeing him, Aviloh swallowed and corrected himself. "Yeah, I remember now, Petey asked me to help him install some new windows, some with an extra R rating. You know, the sun-blocking shield kind?"

"Really? Now why would he ask you to help him when he's got his own window installers?"

The skin around Aviloh's eyes twitched. He cleared his throat. "As best as I recall, he was between jobs and gave his crew time off—not unusual in the building trades. Besides, I had time to spare, and I was always happy to help ol' Petey."

"You wouldn't mind if I called Mrs. Longfellow to confirm that, would you?"

"Hell . . . no. Be my guest. She's probably in Riverside working with my wife, Sherri, at the County Administration Building. Here's the phone number." Aviloh almost seemed relieved. He pulled a worn slip of paper from his wallet and handed it to Mannheim.

Mannheim took the piece of paper and headed for the door. "Let me make this call. Stay put. I'll get right back to you."

Once he'd made the call, he smiled and headed back to where Aviloh waited. To help with his next step, he carried two mugs of coffee with him. He placed one on the desk in front of Aviloh. "Mrs. Longfellow must have had a lot on her mind. When I asked about having windows installed the day before her husband's murder, she told me she had no idea what I was talking about."

Aviloh paled, then put his coffee mug down slowly.

Mannheim walked around the desk, sat and studied Aviloh. "Then when I mentioned what you said, she suddenly remembered you had—lucky for you."

"What d'ya mean, lucky?" Aviloh flashed him a sneer of confidence. "Look, I've got nothing to hide, I told you. Ask me anything."

Mannheim took a long, slow sip of his coffee. Once he'd swallowed the semi-hot liquid, he pointed his cup toward Aviloh's. "Would you like a doughnut with that?"

Aviloh shook his head. "No."

"A couple things bother me, Dan. You don't mind me calling you Dan, do you?

Again, Aviloh shook his head.

"Dr. Harrington said he was rear-ended by a large truck on I-10, which sped off. It happened about two months ago while on his way home from Riverside." Mannheim took another sip of his coffee.

Aviloh shrugged. "Don't know anything about that."

Mannheim lowered his cup. "I see. Funny thing, though—just about three weeks ago, on upper Sinatra Drive, another one of those trucks came barreling down behind the Doc's SUV. Doc said it scared the crap out of him."

Aviloh prepared to speak. Mannheim held up a hand. "As a matter of fact, it was that same day you came over from your construction site to ask about all the police activity, remember?"

This time Aviloh returned Mannheim's gaze and nodded slowly.

"Since your equipment was the only machinery around, I kinda figured the truck belonged to you. That's a reasonable assumption, right?"

Aviloh cleared his throat, stretched his neck, and began fidgeting with his keys. "Look, Mannheim, I don't know a damn thing about any of that shit, I swear it. I'm hearing alla this for the first time."

"Hearing what?"

"About Dr. Harrington being almost run over."

"Would you be willing to take a lie detector test to prove that?"

Aviloh's eyes made rapid side-to-side movements. "Yeah. I guess so. Sure, why not?" He hesitated. "Only, I'd better talk to my lawyer first."

"Of course, Danny boy. Where's your cell?"

When Aviloh pulled his cell phone from his pocket, Mannheim asked, "By the way, any of your drivers have long black hair?"

The question startled Aviloh. Mannheim watched the man try and gather some sort of bravado again. "Yeah, sure, like I got a macho wannabe Indian brave on the payroll. Why ya askin'?"

"One of the truck drivers who tried to run Doc Harrington down had long hair."

Aviloh was about to speak but decided not to.

"Okay, Dan, never mind calling your lawyer now. You can do it later. However, I do appreciate your time. I figure this information will save us time in court."

Aviloh nearly dropped his cell phone when he tried to slip it back into his pocket. "Court? What the hell ya talkin' about?"

"Relax, Dan. If this case goes to court, and I for one hope it doesn't, it'll be months away before it starts."

"Can I go now?"

"Not just yet. I have another question or two. What kind of trouble did you get into as a kid?"

Again, Aviloh demonstrated that nervous eye twitch. "Like a lotta kids, I was a little crazy at times."

"How crazy?" Mannheim deliberately kept his tone light.

"One night after a few brews, two of my buddies and me hot-wired a car, spun it out of control, and totaled it—that's about all."

"Uh-huh? What else?"

Aviloh turned pale.

"It really isn't all, is it? As a matter of fact, you were a repeat offender. I heard something about a case of grand theft auto. You've also faced rape charges, which were dropped when the girl withdrew her complaint."

"She made a mistake."

"Maybe, but you had enough time to get some jailhouse tattooing while waiting for her to change her mind."

Mannheim leaned forward and pointed his closed pen at a tattoo on Aviloh's left forearm. "What's this oddball figure? This half man, half whatever-the-hell-it-is, with a yard-long pecker?"

Aviloh covered the tattoo with his other hand. "C'mon, I was a kid then. What difference does it make now?"

Mannheim said nothing. Just kept pointing his pen at the tattoo.

The action unnerved Aviloh. "All right. If you gotta know, it's an incubus."

"A what?"

"An incubus, a sort of free spirit that fucks women at night. Look, like I said, I was a crazy kid, that's all."

"Do you believe in satanism?"

"Do I what? What kind of question is that?" Aviloh sighed, "Look, for Chrissake, I've got twelve men waiting on me for work orders. D'ya mind if we bring this shit to a halt?"

"Sure. Just one more thing: do you have a set of rally lights on your Hummer?"

"Hell no!"

THIRTY

After office hours, Maggie and Josh headed home in their SUV. Josh inserted one of his favorite CDs and smiled when the soft music filled the vehicle.

Maggie snapped her fingers. "That reminds me. We've never looked at that CD I took from Prissy's room. Do you have any objections to watching it tonight?"

"No, but if it's one of those family get-togethers with someone's Uncle Joe mugging at the barbeque with a two-foot-high chef's hat and a cutesy apron holding a hot dog on a long fork, I'm gone."

"I don't think it will be. This disc has one of those strange signs on it like a devil-worship symbol."

"After dinner tonight, we'll look at it, but if I fall asleep during it, and if you find something of interest, let me know. If you don't, don't bother to wake me."

. . .

While they were filling the dishwasher, the phone rang. Maggie wiped her hands and took the call. She placed her hand over the speaker and whispered, "It's our favorite detective, Sourpuss."

Josh made a face at her and took the receiver. "Yeah, Mannheim, what is it?"

After four minutes of a one-sided conversation, Josh hung up.

"What did he want?"

"He took my suggestion and asked hospital security to go through its list of personnel with parking permits to determine who owned that Hummer."

"And?"

"You'll never guess whose name is on that vehicle."

"Josh!" Maggie stomped her foot.

"G. Yamamoto."

"The hospital administrator? What did he say when Mannheim talked with him?"

"He didn't. Yamamoto's out of town for a few days."

Maggie shook her head. "I'm telling you, this case gets stranger and stranger every day."

"You're telling me."

Later, while Maggie put the disc in the CD player, Josh went to his den to make them both a drink. No sooner had he started to pour when she dashed in.

"Josh, come here, you've got to see this."

When she'd pulled him into the living room, she shoved him onto the sofa. "Watch." She clicked the CD player's remote and joined him.

Josh whistled. "Looks like nothing but a screen full of pink flesh."

"I can't believe what I'm seeing." Maggie put her hands to her face with enough space between her fingers to catch most, if not all, the action.

Josh cleared his throat, a bit uncomfortable. It was an unprofessional porno flick with panning and jerking movements, the kind shown at stag parties and smokers. The movie left nothing out. Every bodily orifice was violated and genitalia had the starring roles.

Josh was too tired or too preoccupied to react as Maggie might have expected: his eyelids grew heavy and he began to nod.

Maggie poked him. "Josh, look, I've been there!"

"Eh?" His foggy realm dissipated in an instant. "You're in that flick?"

"No, no! Silly, that room, I've been in that room. That's Prissy's room. See that huge bed? Look. Someone's tied down and her legs and arms are spread."

"Who's starring in this Oscar-winning epic?" he asked, straightening on the sofa. A Bach oratorio with organ accompaniment served as musical background to lend greater distinction to the cinematic masterpiece. The sound track was interjected by a series of grunts and groans and skilled dialogue such as, "Oh, baby" was repeated constantly.

Maggie squinted and bent toward the TV. "I can't tell who they are. The quality of the film is so bad. Besides, the lighting is too uneven. Do you think the gal could be Prissy? With that exaggerated makeup and that wig, it's hard to tell."

Josh got off the sofa and walked toward the TV to peer into the picture, but the details became even less distinct. He could discern a male cracking a whip on either side of a prostrated female, who exhibited mock terror. She tossed her head to either side to avoid the lashes and pulled alternately on the tethers.

The camera panned the room to show the altar-like recesses and the arc of votive candles around a bier-like structure in the center. Smoke from the candles added to the eerie ambience.

Josh returned to the sofa, next to Maggie, who continued to stare in open-mouthed disbelief. Despite the unprofessional quality of the film, sexual maneuvers in every conceivable mode had been demonstrated and repeated *ad nauseam* for twenty-five minutes.

When the film ended abruptly, Josh gave an uncomfortable cough. "No credits. No cast of characters. A cinematic triumph."

Josh thought for a moment. "Can you show the last five minutes of that disc again?"

"Why? Is there a method you want to add to your repertoire?" Maggie asked with just a twinge of sarcasm.

"Don't be ridiculous. Look closely at the male."

Maggie reversed the disc and watched the male in the missionary position move in a steady, undulating copulatory rhythm.

"Look at the back of his head," Josh said. "His hair is tied in a ponytail."

"What's so unusual about that? Many guys have ponytails: old Hells' Angels, artists, musicians, those with little or no hair in front."

"Yeah, but the driver who tried running me off Sinatra Drive had a ponytail."

"Oh, you never mentioned that to me—what happened?"

"Not much; some guy in a truck was crowding me from behind and ran me onto the median. He had a ponytail. Maybe just coincidental."

Maggie removed the disc. "What should I do with this? I can't return it to Prissy. Should I give it to Mannheim?"

"Would you care to tell him how you just happened to remove it from her bedroom?"

"Well, no, but I thought if he knew about it . . ."

"Suppose we mail it back to her from a distant post office? You know, without a return address, and let her worry about where it's been."

Maggie clapped her hands and laughed, "Oh, Josh, that's deliciously devilish." She came to him and wrapped her arms around his neck. "Are you sure you're not into that satanic stuff?"   "Why?" He bent his head and nibbled on her earlobe. "Are my horns showing?"

THIRTY-ONE

Mannheim sat alone in the hospital administrator's anteroom. While he waited he looked at his notes, then at his wristwatch.

Seeing him, the secretary smiled weakly. "He should be ready to see you soon, I'm sure."

The woman's veiled apology failed to appease Mannheim. Twenty-five minutes was more than he had planned to wait.

His wave of resentment reached a crescendo. Uncrossing his lanky legs, he stood, stretched, scratched his backside, then headed for the administrator's door. He had waited long enough. Just as his hand reached the doorknob, the door opened.

"Come in, Detective. I do apologize for the long wait." Mr. Yamamoto appeared flushed. "I was having a three-way phone conversation with building contractors and didn't want to subject you to a shouting match. I find that a woman contractor is no easier to deal with than a man. Maybe worse."

Yamamoto escorted Mannheim into his office. He walked to his desk and pointed to a chair on the other side for Mannheim. "Now, how can I help you?"

Mannheim's irritation at the wait was not mollified by Yamamoto's ingratiating smile or his explanation for the delay. In an unfriendly monotone, he asked, "Sir, do you drive a Hummer with a rally package?"

Yamamoto cocked his head. "I beg your pardon? Why do you ask?"

"A simple 'yes' or 'no' will suffice, sir."

"No, I don't drive one."

Mannheim read from his notebook, "Hospital security records indicate that a 2009 Hummer with California plates, number . . ."

Yamamoto nodded and waved his hand to stop the recitation. "Yes, I own it, but I don't drive it. That gas-guzzler was bought for my son, Gordon, when he started college at Riverside."

"Is it usually parked in the staff parking lot?"

"Only when he comes around to ask his old man for a handout." Yamamoto smiled. "You know how that is."

"No, sir, I don't. Can you tell me where he can be reached? We'd like to ask him a few questions."

Yamamoto's complacency turned to deep concern. "Is he in trouble?" The administrator leaned forward. "Detective, he's a good boy; he's never been in trouble. Look, if he's done anything wrong, I'll be happy to—"

"That's not necessary. Just give me his phone number and address, please; we'd like to talk to him."

* * *

Detective Harry Todd was on his way to the Riverside campus. An hour earlier, he had phoned young Gordon Yamamoto to advise him that he was coming to ask a few questions. The fifty-five-mile ride to the college was a welcome respite, since it provided an opportunity to do some investigating without the smothering presence of Mannheim.

After dodging a number of highway construction hazards, Todd finally located the orderly layout of the university campus. He parked in the No Parking zone at the residence hall and lowered the sun visor with the sheriff's logo. Two students wearing worn, faded Levis and reversed baseball caps eyed him as he stepped into the elevator. He looked at them and thought of his own sons at college. He was proud of his boys, both of them.

The door to room 310 was partially open. Harry knocked gently.

"Come in." A young man wearing a T-shirt over cutoff jeans turned to face him when he entered.

"I'm Harry Todd. Are you Gordon?"

"Yes, sir." The young man inadvertently took a step backward to lean against his desk. At about five foot ten and lean, with dark hair cut short, he appeared diffident and respectful.

The room had a small desk, two wooden chairs, a dresser with a mirror, a single bed, and a closet. A computer occupied the center of the desk, along with an open calculus text with selected passages underlined in transparent yellow.

Harry selected one of the two chairs in the room and glanced around. The walls were decorated by an eclectic assortment of photos: baseball players, Broadway musical and theater posters, and an enlarged portrait of Albert Einstein with his compassionate, weary eyes and wild, frizzy hair.

Young Yamamoto sat rigidly near the edge of his chair watching Harry as the detective referred to the notebook he'd taken from his jacket pocket.

"Tell me what happened on the night of March nineteenth at about ten p.m. on North Ramon Road. We have an eyewitness account that claims you were driving your Hummer on the wrong side of the road at a speed that could have killed two carloads of people."

The anxious twenty-year-old cleared his throat, gripped the seat of his chair, and looked at the ceiling, then down at his hands. "Detective Todd, sir, I swear I never intended to harm anyone." He stammered, "I had a date with this girl, Michelle—well, she really wasn't my girl, just someone I met at a sorority dance two weeks before. We sort of hit it off, you know?"

Gordon shifted on the chair. "Actually, she came on to me kind of strong. We dated a few times after that. She wanted to spend an evening with me alone. I figured that was okay, but I didn't want anyone to see us at a local motel." He wiped his sweaty palms on his pants and with the bottom of his T-shirt wiped his brow.

Harry understood the trials of youngsters. Young Yamamoto's nervousness reminded him of another time when he'd grilled one of his own boys for a misdemeanor. "Go on."

"We decided to go to a hotel in Palm Springs. I figured fifty miles off campus should have been a safe distance. I turned off the I-10 at Ramon. I guess Michelle hit the bottle . . ."

"Whoa." The hairs on the back of Harry's neck bristled. "Back up. Are you saying you'd been drinking?"

Young Yamamoto's eyes widened. "No, no, sir. I swear it. I don't touch the stuff if I'm going to drive. Please believe me. My father made sure I'd never do that. He showed me photos of kids who'd been driving drunk and were brought to the hospital."

Harry nodded, relieved the boy had some good sense. "Tell me what else happened."

"Well, Michelle was feeling kind of frisky, I guess. She took off her seat belt, scooted over, and got real friendly—kinda touchy-feely." Gordon's face reddened. He glanced around the room. "Gosh, I don't know how to say this."

"Take your time, son. I've heard it all before."

"It's just that I don't want my dad or mom to know." His eyes implored Todd. "You won't have to tell them, will you?"

"No promises, but I'll try to be discreet if I have to say something."

Gordon swallowed with difficulty. "Michelle started fiddling with my zipper." He hesitated, looked at Einstein's picture, then turned away quickly. "She had trouble getting the zipper down at first. All the while I was getting kinda excited. Finally she put her hand on it, and before I knew it, she started massaging and squeezing it. I came all over—er—I mean I ejaculated and when that happened, it shot to the other side of the road—the car, that is, and headed right for that oncoming car.

"Oh God, I thought it was the end for all of us. It was a miracle that the other car swerved at the very last second." He looked at Todd, hoping for understanding. "The people in the other car—are they all right? Are they?"

"Yes, no thanks to you or your Michelle."

Barely audible, Gordon Yamamoto sighed in relief. "I'm awfully sorry; please tell them I'm really, really sorry. I'll never let anything like that happen again, I swear."

Todd nodded, then rose to leave. Seeing that the boy was still upset, he asked nonchalantly, "Incidentally, what about Michelle? Did you two have an adventurous evening?"

Gordon grimaced. "Not exactly. Truth is, I couldn't keep up with her."

"So, you're no longer seeing her, I take it?"

"No, sir. She hooked up with a phys-ed major."

THIRTY-TWO

Tatiana sat in the back of her Grosser Mercedes limousine at the Saks Fifth Avenue parking facility in Palm Desert. She removed a cell phone from her jeweled bag and punched in numbers.

The moment the party answered, she purred. "Doktor Harrington, do you know how much I am lonesome for you?"

"Hello, Tatiana. How are you?"

"So sad. How about you come and make an old *Matushka* happy?" She laughed. "That is if your darling, sweet wife is not there."

"She is."

"Then don't tell her I flirt with you, all right?"

"I won't have to. She said to tell you, she already knows you flirt."

Tatiana laughed even louder. She liked the doctor's wife even more. "This is my loss."

"What do you want, Tatiana?"

"I call to tell you, Mr. Big Shot, Cue, is flying into Palm Springs, this afternoon. Maybe, he comes to make a good deal for you."

"Did you notify Detective Mannheim?"

"I am three steps in front of you, darling. Detective Todd is already at airport."

* * *

Harry Todd parked the Chevy Impala in front of the baggage claim exit. After turning down the sun visor with the sheriff's emblem, he ordered the uniformed policeman with him to stay with the car. Five minutes later, he hurried to the deplaning area and walked beyond the *Do Not Enter* sign. He flashed his ID at the TSA officers and proceeded to the American Airlines gate. The overhead monitor displayed the arrival time of flight #1143 from Chicago as 1:25 p.m. Todd checked his wristwatch: 1:22. He patted the bulge under his jacket and out of habit, jiggled some pocketed coins.

He stood in front of the flight exit gate and studied each male walking from the plane. Young men and those in sloppy casuals he ignored. When about half the passengers had deplaned, he grew anxious. Had he missed his quarry? Assuming a more aggressive stance, he studied every emerging male more closely.

As the line of passengers dwindled, he felt a quiver of anxiety.

Todd waited as the last two stragglers emerged. A handsome man, probably in his fifties, with a trim build, carried an attaché case and pulled a wheeled suitcase. At his side, an attractive airline attendant also pulling wheeled luggage smiled coquettishly; both appeared to have established a relationship with promise for greater intimacy.

Todd stepped in front of the man. "Mr. Cue Effingwell?"

"Yes." With a haughty glance, Effingwell looked him up and down. "Do I know you?"

"No, sir. You don't. I'm with—"

"Just a moment." The man leaned toward the attendant and said in an avuncular tone, "My dear, why don't you run on ahead? I'll call you at the hotel after I've finished with this fellow."

For a brief moment, the woman's smile faltered. Then she nodded and walked away.

When the flight attendant was beyond hearing range, Effingwell's smile vanished. He turned to Todd. "Now, who in the hell are you and what do you want?"

Todd flashed his badge and maintained his enigmatic smile. "I'd like you to accompany me, sir, to the sheriff's office."

"Sheriff's office? Why?" Anger glittered in the man's eyes. "Why should I go anywhere with you?"

"Are you resisting arrest, sir? Would you prefer that I put cuffs on you here?" He made a move to reach into his back pocket.

"No. Put those goddamn manacles away. Why are you here?"

"You're a suspect in the murder of Chester U. Effingwell."

"What?" Effingwell's jaw sagged. "You're suspecting me in the murder of my own father? And who said he was murdered? He disappeared ten years ago. Murder was never established."

"It's been established now."

"Don't be ridiculous." Effingwell's upper lip curled into a sneer. "You hicks have more goddamn nerve than sense."

"If you'll come with me without fuss, things will go much smoother."

"And what if I don't? Will there be a posse coming after me?"

"No sir. We prefer not to have a lot of uniformed men around the airport unless absolutely necessary. No reason to create passenger concern. However . . ."

He pointed to a number of airport security guards who had been alerted and were stationed at regular intervals. "Shall we go?"

Without a word, Effingwell headed for the exit. Once there, Todd directed him to his waiting car. Before getting in, Effingwell said over his shoulder, "This better be good, or I'll sue your cockamamie, two-horse town for every last nickel it steals from the Indian casinos."

At the car, the uniformed officer who Todd had ordered to stay placed cuffs on Effingwell and with his hand on Effingwell's head, guided him into the rear seat. The luggage was placed in the trunk.

*　*　*

Once Todd had removed Effingwell's cuffs, the suspect rubbed his irritated wrists and glanced around the interrogation room. Then he focused on Todd and Mannheim. "All right, let's get this over with."

Mannheim took an instant dislike to the New Yorker. "Thank you for agreeing to come to headquarters," he said, opting to keep his tone flat.

"Save the goddamn phony politeness. I can assure you, I'm not here of my own accord, and you'd better have a damn good reason for my inconvenience. I know a few influential people who will have your sorry asses in a sling. I want my attorney here and now."

"From New York? That'll take awhile," Todd said.

"That's stupid! I can get their local representatives."

"Of course." Mannheim straddled a wooden chair backwards and leaned forward. "While we're waiting, why don't you get comfortable?"

Effingwell looked at him suspiciously.

"I'd like to go over a few charges we're making against you." Mannheim intended to be nonconfrontational but with this pompous ass, he thought that might be difficult. "Would you like a glass of water or a cup of coffee?"

"Water."

Todd left the room and brought a glass of water, which he placed on the desk in front of Effingwell.

"Now tell me what this is all about."

"Something that happened ten years ago," Mannheim answered. "You and your father came to Rancho Mirage to visit Madame Tatiana."

"Madame Tatiana?" Effingwell laughed. "She was hardly the primary reason we came here. We had other business interests."

"Uh-huh." Mannheim wasn't impressed. "You rented a Lincoln Mark VIII at the airport. In fact, the car was delivered by your own rental agency, Coachella U-Drive Enterprises." Mannheim's bushy brows dipped, forming a V. "How am I doing so far?"

Effingwell shrugged, took a sip of water, and shook his head. "I don't remember. Christ, that was ten years ago."

"Maybe I can refresh your memory." Mannheim referred to his spiral notebook. "Surprising what we can find. We located a ledger sheet of that defunct car rental agency. Found it in a storage shed. Funny thing, though, a return entry was missing from that ledger. Actually, it wasn't removed, it was whited out."

Effingwell shrugged. "So what? Are you going somewhere with this?"

"Oh, yeah. Our lab techs were able to reconstitute the original writing, which revealed names, vehicle ID, driver's license, temporary address, and credit card number. Would you like to see the data?"

Cue hesitated, then folded his arms across his chest. "All right, we rented a car, so what?"

"Wonder why there was an attempt to delete the return date on that vehicle?" Mannheim asked his question with deliberate slowness.

"I wouldn't know." Effingwell remained defiant. The corners of his mouth turned into a sneer. "The old man must have had his reasons."

"Such as?"

"How in the hell would I know? Remember, ten years ago? Maybe he wanted the accountant to show expenses for a longer business trip, or maybe he didn't want his wife to know."

Mannheim stood and walked slowly behind Effingwell, then bent over and said into his ear, "I'll tell you what I think. I think *you* had the car records altered. You wanted to create the impression that your father had an accident, drove off a road into a canyon or something like that. Right?"

Cue jerked his head to the side. "Don't be ridiculous."

"Am I?" Mannheim returned to his chair. "His body was never recovered; neither was the car. You collected insurance on the old man as well as the car. Insurance records indicated a half million on the old man and eighteen grand on the car."

For once, the New Yorker sat stony-faced and mute.

Mannheim knew he'd touched a nerve. "We found the ten-year-old car key, by the way."

Again no response from Cue.

Mannheim upped the stakes by increasing the volume of his voice. "You know where we found it? At your uncle's adobe house. Evidence points to you, Effingwell. *You* shot and killed your father by putting a bullet in the back of his head."

Cue leapt to his feet. "Christ, what a goddamn rich imagination you cops have! I suppose you've got the murder weapon to go along with it."

Mannheim didn't blink an eye. "No, we don't have the weapon, but we do have the shell, a .38 caliber. We also learned from the New York State Weapons Registry that you bought an S&W .38 revolver two months prior to the killing."

Effingwell sank back into his chair. "So? I bought a gun back then. Big fucking deal. People buy guns all the time. It doesn't mean they buy them to kill someone. There is such a thing as needing 'em for protection, you know?"

"Maybe."

"You've got nothing but speculation and innuendo. Incidentally, where did you find the body?" He took another sip of water, maintaining an air of detachment.

Mannheim turned slowly to face Todd. "I don't remember saying we found a body, do you?"

Harry Todd smiled his enigmatic smile and shook his head.

Mannheim went on the offensive. "What did you do with your gun, Effingwell?"

"It was stolen from my apartment," Cue answered without hesitation.

"Sure it was. Well, here's a bit of news I've left out. The skeletal remains of your father were found. Dr. Harrington found them in a heavy plastic bag in the subflooring of the adobe house. But then you wouldn't know anything about that, would you?"

Cue went suddenly stiff. A minute later, he glanced at his watch, then pulled at his French cuffs. "If you have nothing further, I've had enough." He stood and buttoned his jacket. "I'm leaving. Have someone call a cab for me."

"No, I don't think so." Mannheim stood as well. "We're holding you on a murder charge."

"Really? On what evidence?" Effingwell sneered at him. "So far, from what I've heard, you have nothing. Not a damn thing that will convince a jury I'm guilty."

"Ahh, but we have. We found a pair of latex gloves next to the skeletal remains. A bad oversight on the part of the killer, wouldn't you agree? Our lab with its advanced technology took the perspiration and dead skin cells from the inside of those gloves and compared that DNA with your DNA."

"My DNA? You don't have my DNA, you four-flusher."

Silently, Harry Todd removed a latex glove from his pocket, put it on his hand, and reached for the base of the glass of water. Todd said, "We do now."

Effingwell blanched. Slowly, he brought the back of his hand across his mouth, deforming his lips.

Once Todd had passed the glass on to a waiting policeman, Effingwell snarled, "What in the hell do you smart asses think you're doing? This is entrapment. Wait until my lawyer hears what you've done. He'll sue you and your department for fraudulent practices."

"Big deal. I'm sure it'll go nowhere. So . . . sit down."

"You . . . you . . ." Effingwell began to stutter. "You're acting like the damn KGB. Well, I'm not going to be railroaded like some ignorant Russian peasant."

"Sit down!"

Effingwell jumped at Mannheim's roar and scurried back to the chair.

Seeing the man shrink in size while he sat, Mannheim came to stand in front of him. He slipped his hands into his rear pants pockets and leaned forward. "Russian peasant, huh? How prophetic that you should say that, Mr. High and Mighty."

"Don't call me that."

"Why not? Something tells me you're gonna be charged with an act of espionage and terrorism and spend your life in a federal pen."

"For what?" Effingwell attempted to rise again, but Mannheim whipped his hands out of his back pockets and pushed him down.

"For poisoning your uncle, Chesley Effingwell, with a highly toxic, radioactive isotope, polonium-210, which came from a lab in Moscow."

"What? You're making no sense at all."

"No? Your uncle was poisoned just before or during the time he was hospitalized four months ago."

"I still don't know what in the hell you're talking about." Cue's chin shot out as if he'd regained his confidence. "I've had enough. I'm calling my lawyer now."

"Fine, go head. He's in New York. It'll take him five hours to fly out here. Meanwhile, you're gonna have a nice little visit with a cell."

While Cue placed his call, Harry Todd tilted his head toward the door. Mannheim nodded and followed him out.

"Mannheim, we don't have enough evidence to charge him with murder."

"Maybe not, but it won't hurt to have him sweat a bit." Mannheim sighed. "The games we have to play, huh?"

Todd glanced at the closed door. "What's all this DNA nonsense from perspiration and dead skin cells? That's the first I've heard about it."

"He doesn't know that."

"It wouldn't hold up in court."

Mannheim shrugged. "So, I'm guilty of a little creative evidence. Let him sweat and think we have enough to hang him."

"His attorney will make mincemeat out of us."

"It won't be the first time a shyster's had my balls in a vise. Once Effingwell gets out, I want a tail put on him. Make sure he doesn't make a run for it. And get a court order to keep him from leaving the country."

"On what charges?"

"Tell the judge he's a damn flight risk, and we *do* have enough evidence to say he's a probable murderer."

Todd shook his head. "Flimsy evidence, if you ask me."

"I didn't ask you." Mannheim started walking. "It's time to notify the Preacher."

"Preacher?" Todd quick-stepped behind Mannheim's loping stride.

"Our illustrious, anointed, saintly State's Attorney General, Jim Bennett. I'm going to call his office, in Sacramento. He'll know what to do with this pretentious asshole."

"Why not just get the DA out of the Riverside office?"

"Because . . . ten years ago Bennett was the DA on the case when Old Man Chester Effingwell disappeared. Back then, he told me, he'd never forgive himself for not being able to bring Cue to trial since he was the prime murder suspect even then."

Todd whistled. "Whew, this is starting to sound interesting."

"Ain't it though? Jim had a ton of circumstantial evidence but not enough to convince a waffling judge to bring him to trial. The chance to get at Cue again is going to make Jim come in his shorts.

Back then, everyone in the department knew the sonofabitch was guilty. Cue's not going to walk this time. The Preacher would never forgive me if I didn't call him. Besides, he needs this publicity for the upcoming election."

"How can you be sure that will be enough to bring him here?"

"I know Jim. He'll come, all right, like a tomcat who smells pussy in heat."

Todd, almost apologetically and reluctantly, asked, "Suppose the skeleton isn't Cue's old man?"

"Don't worry. It's the old man, all right. Listen, if we can't nail him for the murder of his father, we'll get him for his uncle's murder by radioactive poisoning. If those charges fail, we'll get him for espionage, terrorist activities, and plotting with a foreign nation. There's a federal law that provides for the death penalty in a case where murder was committed by an imported toxic substance."

Todd pulled on Mannheim's arm to slow him down. "You're making a hell of a lot of assumptions, and how do you know about murder by a toxic substance?"

"I got it on the Internet."

THIRTY-THREE

State Attorney General Jim Bennett, at five foot seven, 175 pounds, ramrod straight with a jutting jaw, piercing eyes, and a bulldog demeanor, paused on the air steps of the Lear jet, his eyes searching the landscape. As a Vietnam marine paratrooper, he probably never emerged from a plane or chopper without expecting enemy fire.

Mannheim smiled at the sight of the man. Always on guard. He jabbed Harry Todd's side. "Come on. Let's go." He started walking and waved as Bennett descended to the tarmac followed by his minions, two somber men dressed like the Blues Brothers but without fedoras.

When they came face to face, Bennett looked Mannheim up and down. "Still the same old slept-in look." He grasped Mannheim's hand firmly and shook it. "You old scarecrow, you'll never get a job modeling for Brooks Brothers, but hey, what the hell, who cares whether you wear off-the-rack or custom-tailored? Right? As long as you get three squares a day, an occasional piece and don't get caught taking a bribe."

Bennett was the only one who laughed.

"Yes sir. You got that right." Mannheim released Bennett's hand and stepped to the side. "This is my partner, Harry Todd. Good man. He has a healthy suspicion of all lawyers."

Bennett nodded and shook Harry's hand hard. "When you shake an attorney's hand, you want to be sure you know where his other hand is."

They all laughed politely.

"So . . ." Bennett turned back to Mannheim. "Tell me what you've got on this sonofabitch. God, I can't believe it. My old nemesis, Mis-ter Cue Effingwell, is back in town. I can't wait to get at that fraudulent, murdering bastard. I've been waiting a long time for this."

Bennett turned and quickly introduced the Blues Brothers. In unison, the three lawyers faced the jet as a fourth member of the state's prime legal team appeared, a thirty-something, exotic brunette with olive skin, sloe eyes, and a sensuous mouth, wearing a smartly tailored, snug-fitting suit. She descended the steps in a deliberate, hip-shifting movement that emphasized her supple curves.

Mannheim heard Todd inhale sharply. He glanced at his partner and nearly laughed. Todd's jaw dropped as the enchantress of his wildest erotic dreams headed his way. She was his Greek goddess of love, Aphrodite, or more possibly the Semitic goddess of love, Astarte.

Her jacket and open-collared silk shirt revealed cleavage that would have taunted the most celibate. With broad-rimmed glasses and an upswept hairdo, she must have piqued Todd's recall of the clichéd movie secretary who whips off her glasses, removes a hairpin, and shakes luxuriant tresses that cascade over bare pearly-white shoulders, then smiles a killer smile.

Mannheim teasingly poked Todd. "Close your mouth."

The officer snapped his mouth shut and turned his gaze downward so as not to stare at the magnificent assemblage of femininity.

Bennett introduced her. "Tim and Harry, this lady is another of our legal experts, Ms. Heidi Schprintz, a woman of enormous talent."

She smiled politely and shook both men's hands. "How do you do?"

"Well . . ." Bennett poked an index finger into Mannheim's chest. "Down to business, hey? We don't want to charge Effingwell with murder just yet. No reason to screw up our case before we even get started. No sir, I want to get right to this bastard. Have him think we know all about what he's done before his attorneys emasculate us or the fancy boys at the FBI get to him."

"FBI?" That surprised Mannheim.

"Affirmative. They'll go after him with some trumped-up charges of kidnapping and murder, anything they can get their manicured pinkies on."

Bennett's trio picked up several suitcases from the plane's baggage compartment and headed for a shiny black Suburban waiting at the terminal curbside.

Before Bennett slid inside the Suburban, he pulled Mannheim aside. "How much time do we have before Effingwell's gooks get here?"

"They're due in sometime this evening."

"Good. Pick Effingwell up from the police station and bring him to the Larson Center in Indio."

"Will do."

Once the State Attorney General and his entourage drove away, Mannheim and Todd hurried to their dusty, stodgy vehicle and rode off, Todd at the wheel.

"Mannheim, I still don't know why you call him Preacher."

"It's a moniker he got years ago from the boys in Riverside. For one thing, he's got religion up the kazoo. He can recite the Good Book chapter and verse, prays before meals, never uses the Lord's name in vain. He's an amateur biblical scholar who'll hit you over the head with the Good Book—a real pain in the ass, sometimes. Years ago he had to make a decision between becoming a priest or a lawyer, figured he'd get you for your sins one way or the other—he's scrupulously honest, can't stand offenders of the law or the Holy Scriptures."

"So, with all that piety, what's his downside?"

Mannheim shifted his deep-set eyes toward Harry. "Loves women, but he is discreet and always, always makes sure they're of legal age."

"Doesn't he have a wife?"

"He's between wives, at the moment."

* * *

Jim Bennett burst into the interrogation room, followed by his minions.

"Well, well, if it isn't my old friend, Cue Eff-ing-well. You remember me, don't you? Jim Bennett—I was the District Attorney, now I'm the State's Attorney General. These are my associates."

With rapid fire, he introduced his subordinates to Cue, who acknowledged their presence with less enthusiasm, except for Heidi Schprintz, who captured his prolonged stare.

Bennett put his foot on the seat of the chair opposite Cue, leaned forward on his knee, and pointed his finger at him. "I'll tell you right now, we've got your scrotum in a nut cracker. No doubt about it. The sooner you confess, the easier it will go for you. So don't engage in any evasive bullshit and don't waste our time. Understand?"

Effingwell defiantly started to rise from his chair.

"Just sit where you are; no need to stand," Bennett said.

Cue looked at each unsmiling face and slid deeper into his chair. "Look, I've made it quite clear; I'm not answering any questions until my attorney gets here."

"That's fine, Effingwell, but my staff and I want to advise you, give you fair warning, we've gathered hard evidence, so you'll know what you're up against. That way you'll be better prepared to make decisions and perhaps accept a deal that could spare you the death penalty or life in prison."

"Life?" Effingwell's voice leaped an octave. "You've got nothing—"

Bennett cut him off. "The sooner you face up to a few facts, the sooner we deal. No jury is going to be lenient in a patricide case where the killer got away the first time around."

Bennett straightened from the chair he'd leaned on and started preaching as he walked slowly around the room, looking alternately at the ceiling, then the floor. "We know what happened. We have a trail of clues that are irrefutable. You stood to inherit a fortune, and you wanted it then and there. You could have waited. The old man probably didn't have many more years left, anyway." Bennett's rapid-fire condemnation had become almost unbearable, and Cue wasn't given the remote opportunity for rebuttal.

Effingwell's shoulders sagged. The haughty demeanor he wore like a suit of armor in the beginning began to crumble under Bennett's unrelenting accusations, which were punctuated with biblical references. Cue loosened his tie and unbuttoned his collar. Signs of stress appeared as he blinked rapidly and wiped his brow. Finally he managed to regain some bluster. He lashed out verbally,

"Bennett, stop this stupid, fucking grilling. I'm going to leave this shit hole right now."

Bennett raised two fingers as in pious benediction and quoted, "'This is none other but the house of God, and this is the gate of heaven.'"

That confused Cue even more. He looked up at Bennett. "What the hell is that supposed to mean?"

Bennett ignored his question, and signaled Heidi to remain with Cue while he and the Blues Brothers left the room.

Heidi sat close to Cue, her smooth, rounded knees all but touching his, and when she hiked her skirt to cross her legs, more of her comely thighs were revealed.

Cue's disposition did a 180-degree flip-flop at Heidi's nearness and the fragrance of her perfume was intoxicating. She held a steno pad in her lap and inched her skirt even higher.

He focused on her shapely extremities: the soft, inviting, Rubenesque contours of her legs, arms, and bosom had inflamed his orgasmic senses.

Heidi moistened her lips with the tip of her tongue, an act that further stimulated him. She saw Cue's bizarre behavior as an opportunity to have him divulge incriminating information. With remarkable chutzpah, she read her fabricated notes as though she had just taken his dictation.

"You admitted to having shot and killed your father, Chester Effingwell, then burying him in February 1999?" She glanced at him and asked, "Didn't you think you'd be caught? Did you think your life would be spared?"

Cue ignored her comments. Either he had not heard them or they failed to register.

With a smarmy smile, he bent over in front of her and held the arms of her chair, bringing his face close to hers. "Baby, you're the reason my life was spared." He summoned an antiquated charming manner, one that had served him well for many years. "In the grand scheme of things, this chance meeting wasn't by chance at all, my dear. We were destined to meet; now don't deny it. Tell me, what I must do to make love to you?"

His talkativeness was what Heidi had hoped for, but there was something terribly disturbing and irrational about the guy. She suspected he might have been tippling but was unable to detect alcohol on his breath. His eyes danced with anticipation.

She brought her head back as he brought his forward. "Tell me what you know about your uncle Chesley Effingwell's death."

The moment she said his uncle's name, Cue appeared flustered. He blinked several times, then shook his head rapidly trying to clear his befogged mind. His expression sobered and he stood. Squaring his shoulders, he pulled his jacket sleeves over his shirt cuffs.

"Where the hell am I?"

His bearing and expression suggested a push/pull switch in personality, like that of an epileptic recovering from a fit, then having no recall of the immediate past. He stared at Heidi. "Who the hell are you, and what's going on here?"

Heidi, frightened by his chameleon-like change, fought to remain calm as she returned to reading the fictitious notes from her pad. "You were about to tell me of your Uncle Chesley's death."

He nodded absently. "I was? Where was I?" In an effort to appear cogent and responsive, Cue looked at Heidi as he would his own secretary. "Read me that last line."

Heidi flipped back the page and continued the charade of reading the nonexistent notes. "In the matter of Chesley Effingwell's death, which occurred at the Eisenhower Hospital . . ." She trailed away, indicating that was where he'd stopped dictating.

Cue, walking in a circle, his hands behind his back, looking at the ceiling, then at the floor, said, "Yes, I recall quite well now, thank you." His eyes focused on some distant point. "The Kremlin never accepted the reports of my father's disappearance and the later reports of his assumed death. Somehow they confused Chester U. with Chesley U. Effingwell or more likely refused to believe they could actually be two different people." He stopped walking and looked at her. "The two names had often been confused over the years. In the Kremlin's collective paranoia, they figured they had been duped after paying millions for space-war blueprints that were never delivered by my father. The Russians were determined to exterminate him, and they waited and plotted for all those years. The director, the choreographer of their vengeance squad, was that strutting peacock—what's his name? Putin—yes, that's it, Putin."

Heidi suppressed her excitement, hoping Cue would continue his stream of consciousness. She sat upright, pretending to stop writing, her pencil poised over the steno pad to begin again. She wore a wire, so everything would be recorded in Effingwell's own voice. "Go ahead, sir. I'm ready."

He nodded. "Father entered into a deal with the U.S.S.R. in the 'seventies to supply data for their intercontinental and interplanetary ballistic missile defense systems. They had their own version of a Star Wars campaign and knew my father could deliver top-secret, highly classified documents—for a handsome price, of course. Chester insisted on prepayments, which wasn't the usual policy for the Russians, but they were desperate to win or at least catch up to the U.S. in the space-wars race. They put millions into my father's numbered Swiss bank accounts. My father moved that money around like pieces on a chessboard: to other banks and investment firms around the world. It would have taken a team of financial wizards years to track that laundered money. My father knew where every dollar, every pound, every franc, and every deutschmark was."

Heidi scribbled several words on the blank page she'd flipped to. She looked up at Cue. "You said the Russians wanted to exterminate him and that they probably confused your hospitalized Uncle Chesley for your father. Can you explain why they wanted to kill your father?"

"Excellent point. Of course." Cue started pacing again. "In the end, Chester could not deliver the goods after he accepted payment. The simple fact was there never had been an effective program for U.S. missile deterrence. President Reagan's program was an exercise in deception. It was a sham, a false premise designed to make the Russians think their ICBMs were of no value if they ever deployed them against the U.S. The gigantic hoax was perpetrated by the Pentagon. The Russians were furious over my father's failure to deliver the goods. The frequency of their threats tapered off, but the harsh reality was they never, ever forgot."

"Would your father have considered returning the money to the Russians?"

Cue stopped in front of Heidi and placed his hand on her head as though delivering beneficence. "Little lady, you can't possibly begin to comprehend the world of conniving thieves, the betrayers of civilization, the architects of genocide, the despoilers of humanity . . ."

It took every bit of her willpower not to shudder under his hand.

As if an unseen question had been asked, Cue began pacing again, mumbling unintelligibly.

The door at the far end of the room opened slightly. Heidi turned toward it.

Jim Bennett poked his head in. Seeing that Cue's back was to him, he gave Heidi a questioning glance. She motioned him to close the door and surreptitiously put her finger to her lips.

"Mr. Effingwell?" She paused in her note-taking and looked at Cue when he stopped. "I'm a bit confused here. Your father dealt with the enemy even though he knew he could lose his life for committing treason. Why would he do that?"

"For him the risk was worth it. After all, he did it for millions of dollars. Money was all that mattered to him. He had no friends to speak of; he never gave me his complete love or trust, nor would he ever turn the business over to me. His relationship with his wife was practically nonexistent. She referred to him as a whoremonger, a slimy snake, and a decadent thief, among other things. Sadly, her assessment wasn't completely wrong. They communicated only in shouting matches. He was alienated from his only living relative—his brother, Chesley—whom he wrote off as a ne'er-do-well years ago."

Heidi couldn't believe how much the man talked and how much he was willing to reveal. "How would you characterize *your* relationship with your father?"

"What was that?" Cue jerked visibly. He glanced, wide-eyed, around the room as though he had just arrived. He stared at Heidi with suspicion. "Who the hell are you? What're you doing?" His expression darkened and he walked menacingly toward her.

Heidi scrambled to her feet. She stood and held the steno pad like a shield between them. "I . . . ah . . . was writing what you told me to."

"Told you? I told you nothing. Let me see that, bitch." Cue lunged forward and made a grab for her steno pad.

Heidi stumbled backward. "No. You can't."

"Oh can't I?" Cue grabbed her neck and drew her to him. She let out a piercing scream. He grappled for the pad, which she held out at arm's length.

The door to the conference room flew open. Jim Bennett and the Blues Brothers surged toward them and pulled Cue off Heidi. One man locked an arm around Cue's neck; the other ensnared Cue's arms.

It did little good. With the strength of an animal gone berserk, Cue threw off his attackers, then faced them like a cornered beast. He bent forward and brought his arms into a broad arc like a challenged gorilla.

The Blues Brothers quickly regained equilibrium and charged head-on. They slammed rib-cracking body blocks to his midsection, then delivered a stunning chop to his neck and a swift kick to his groin. Cue grabbed his crotch, bobbled like a grazed bowling pin, spun around, fell on his back to the floor, then looked up in wild-eyed bewilderment.

One of the Blues Brothers leaned over to assist him. As he did, his jacket opened to reveal a holstered pistol. Cue reached up to take the proffered arm, then in a stunning movement, snatched the pistol, pointed it nervously, and yelled, "Put your hands up. All of you! Stand against the wall. Put your guns on the floor. Now, don't move. I'll kill the first sonofabitch who moves. I swear it." He leaped up from the floor and pointed the gun at Heidi. "You, come here. Now! Stand next to me."

Heidi stood at his side, trembling. He grabbed her around the waist and with his other hand placed the gun to her temple.

"I'm walking out of here with her. Try anything dumb and I'll blow her fucking head off. Put the car keys on the table—slowly."

One of the Blues Brothers brought his right hand down and reached into his pocket. "Slowly, I said. Don't do anything stupid."

When the man did as he was told, Cue nudged Heidi forward. "Get the keys."

She did.

"Put them in my pocket."

Together, Cue and Heidi moved crablike toward the door.

"Hold it, Effingwell." Jim Bennett kept his hands in the air. "Think about what you're doing. You're going to have a dozen cops on your tail as soon as you try to leave. There's nowhere to hide. Let the girl go. You don't need a kidnapping rap added to your conviction. Give yourself up, and you'll probably live. We'll forget this little episode."

"Shut your goddamn mouth and keep your hands up." With Heidi at his side, he released his hold on her to place his hand on the doorknob.

"There's a cop on the other side of that door who'll shoot to kill," Bennett said.

Cue pulled Heidi in closer to him. "Don't try to shit me, Mr. Big Shot Attorney." Cue opened the door slightly and saw a uniformed cop, then quickly closed the door and in doing so, took his pistol off Heidi. In that split second, she jabbed him in the solar plexus and flung herself away.

Seeing her go, one of the Blues Brothers whipped out a concealed gun and pointed it at Cue. "Effingwell, I've got this gun pointed between your eyeballs. You want to challenge me?"

With his hostage gone, Cue's eyes darted from his challenger to the door. His few seconds of indecision were like an eternity. Slowly, he bent over as if to put his gun on the floor.

Heidi released a sob of relief and clutched her neck.

Then, in a lightning countermovement, Cue lifted the gun upward, placed it to his temple, and fired.

The explosion was deafening.

Horrified, Heidi watched as her abductor swayed with eyes glazed, took a step toward her, then fell face first to the floor.

"Oh my God!" Heidi covered her face in both hands. Jim Bennett hurried over and embraced her. "It's okay. It's all over now. I've got you."

The smell of gunpowder was redolent, and blood spattered the nearby wall like a pointillist painting. Brain matter oozed from the exit wound in Cue's head. A pool of blood bathed his head; his nonseeing eyes stared.

The door to the hall flung open and two uniformed cops burst in. "What the hell's going on here?" Hard on their heels, security agents and onlookers followed.

Mannheim, who had been in the hall, ran through the open door. He pushed aside the uniformed men and looked at the corpse, then at Bennett. He scowled. "Goddammit, Jim. I wanted help on this case, not an execution-style solution—not before we got some answers from this guy."

Bennett still held Heidi in his arms. "We got answers. It's all on tape. Ms. Schprintz was wearing a wire."

When Mannheim gaped, Bennett added, "For the record, the guy shot and killed himself. Wasn't about to face a long prison term. That's it, *finis*, over and out. The crazy sonofabitch got exactly what he deserved and saved the state a bundle of cash. We'll write this up nice, neat, and airtight so that no bleeding-heart liberal can blame us for denying him due process."

"Did you find out *why* he killed his father?" Mannheim asked, still not sure it was all over.

Bennett put up his hand. "How many times do I have to tell you? We got it all on tape. Thanks to Ms. Schprintz. He killed the old man to take over his investments, his position of power; he wanted to be the big boss."

Bennett turned toward the Blues Brothers. "Let the reporters and photographers in. Be sure we get a front-page spread."

Both men nodded.

Before leaving the room, Bennett stopped. "I'm sorry, Tim, for sounding so abrupt. You're a good cop, I know that , and I'm going to talk to the chief about promoting you."

Mannheim turned his back and stepped away before Bennett finished.

Todd walked into the room and glanced once at the corpse, then at Mannheim. "What the hell? You okay?"

"Yeah, sure." Mannheim pulled out a pair of gloves from his coat pocket. "Let's go through his personal effects before the boys from the coroner's come in."

Mannheim slipped on the gloves and reached into Cue's inner jacket pocket. Inside was a thick ostrich-skin wallet. Carefully he thumbed through a number of cards and pulled out cash. "This guy carried 'C' notes like I carry one-dollar bills." He pulled out a folded note that read "call Dr. Jordan at CDC about tests." Mannheim showed the note to Todd.

"CDC? What's that?" Todd asked.

"The Centers for Disease Control, I suspect. Check it out. The number has a four-oh-four area code. I don't know what the guy had, but whatever it was, he doesn't have to worry about a cure."

"Suppose he had a deadly, transmissible disease and we're already contaminated." Todd jotted the number in his notepad.

"You've been watching too many stupid medical horror shows." Mannheim replaced the note into the billfold and slipped it inside a plastic evidence bag.

"Oh yeah?" Todd put away his notepad. "What about the airplane passenger with the incurable TB who spread his germs as nicely as you please?"

There was no humor in Mannheim's voice when he said, "Just make the goddamn call, will you?"

THIRTY-FOUR

Dr. Bruce Chisholm, plastic surgeon, whose reconstructive efforts on Carlos's face were no less than magnificent, was removing his latex gloves as Josh walked into the room.

Carlos had been moved to a spacious bedroom converted into convalescent quarters in a Big Horn estate. In his usual ebullient manner, Chisholm gave Josh a firm handshake and announced, loud enough for Carlos to hear, "Your patient's got a penis that's going to be the envy of every guy in the locker room and the topic of conversation at the ladies' bridge club."

Despite his wired jaws, Carlos managed to speak. "I may just change my profession and become a porno star."

"You should be so lucky," Josh said.

The two doctors chuckled while Chisholm uncovered Carlos's pelvic area. He motioned with his head for Josh to look. "How do you like this masterpiece?" The elongated skin tube representing the reconstructed penile shaft was at least one and a half times the size of an average penis in the flaccid stage. "Isn't that a charmer?" Chisholm admired the newly grafted site, then looked at Josh, who nodded soberly.

Josh had seen many shapes and sizes when he conducted what G.I.s called short arm examinations. Most appendages were ordinary except for those ravaged by venereal diseases: syphilis, gonorrhea, and mixed bacterial infections. With the duty, he had become an unwitting expert on the penis in health and disease.

"What do you think of Dr. Chisholm's work?" Carlos asked with a slight slur.

"Beautiful job, but don't get complacent. You know you're going to lose an inch of that after circumcision, so don't go bragging just yet, and don't recommend the procedure to friends."

"I'll be grateful just to pee and hope sensation returns soon."

"You'll be a tiger on the prowl in no time." Chisholm returned the covers and waved as he left.

Josh pulled up a chair and sat next to Carlos. "Maggie and I decided if you're still interested in that parcel of land, you're welcome to it. But please do us a favor and don't interview the others who are interested. The last time you attempted that, you almost lost your friend down there. God alone knows what other parts you could lose next time."

Carlos smiled, then patted the side of his buttocks. "I suppose this could be next."

Josh admired how the man never once lost his optimistic humor. "You'll be leaving this place soon. Your pelvic fractures are healing well, and your facial wounds look like the romantic scars of a Prussian duelist. With your rugged good looks and your oversized wank, you're going to be much in demand."

"Not in too much demand. My wife is all I care about." Carlos smiled weakly. "Josh, there are still questions that trouble me about the accident."

"For instance?"

"Who sent that chauffeured limousine to the hotel to pick me up, and who was the woman who posed as Madame Tatiana?"

"According to Madame Tatiana, the gal was one of her own employee escorts who was bribed. Whoever lured her into playing Tatiana's part also paid off the chauffeur and requisitioned the limousine."

Carlos's eyes moved from side to side, mirroring his analytical thinking. "How did a third party learn that I was to meet with Madame Tatiana?"

"Tatiana's telephone was tapped."

"Ahh . . . I see now."

"One person had a keen interest in listening in on her conversations."

"For God's sake, why?"

"She told me that about twenty years ago, Old Man Effingwell, Cue's father, had set her up in business. According to their arrangements, he was to receive ten percent of her gross receipts, that included not only the take on prostitution, but drinks sold from a concealed bar and illegal gambling conducted in a side room."

"Okay, that I can understand."

"Well, after the old man disappeared ten year ago, I guess, Cue, his son, continued to collect the monies, but with his paranoia, he believed Tatiana was skimming."

"So he had her bugged."

"It seems so. Bugging devices were found in every room. We might have got more information if he hadn't killed himself. The police were fortunate to locate the installer, an ex-con identified by his M.O. He posed as a telephone repairman, a two-time loser eager to tell the cops everything he knew in exchange for less prison time."

Josh's cell phone rang. He pulled it off his belt and looked at it. "It's my office." Josh pressed the talk button and brought the phone to his ear. "Yes, Carmenita? Oh, I see. All right. Tell Sergeant Mannheim I'll be there in twenty minutes."

• • •

"Thanks for dropping by, Doc. I wanted you to see this fax from Dr. Jordan at the Centers for Disease Control regarding Cue Effingwell. Maybe you can interpret his medical jargon. I'd have the department doctor tell me but he's on vacation. Thank God, too. Whenever I talk with him it's as though he's speaking in tongues. He fumfits. Usually I don't understand a friggin' thing he says."

Josh took the report and put on his glasses. Raising his eyebrows, he reread several statements. "According to this, the coroner in Indio had examined Cue's corpse, including the brain, and found macroscopic lesions that he could not identify. He prepared slides of the tissue for microscopic examination and wired the enlarged electron images to CDC in Atlanta."

"Uh-huh. That I know. But what does this Dr. Jordan say?"

"There are areas of the hippocampus and horn of the fornix revealing spirochete invasion."

"Whoa. Doc, don't start playing department doctor on me. Use plain English. What the hell's the importance of all of that and what is it?"

. . .

Josh felt a physical and emotional release after leaving the close confines of Mannheim's cubicle-like office. Cruising along Eldorado Drive, he took in the glorious array of springtime plants and flowers. The magnificent colors and forms of the blooming verbena, cacti, jacaranda trees, azaleas, and hibiscus were everywhere. Much of the Valley had been planned in the last two decades with wide streets separated by planted medians that rewarded residents for their higher taxes. The glitz and glamour of some Hollywood luminaries and politicos who made their homes in the desert were honored to have their names selected for streets, avenues, drives, and public schools.

Frank Sinatra, who had long been a part-time desert resident since the 1940s, was honored when his name was chosen for the drive on which his own home and those of other affluent residents were located. A number of exclusive country clubs had already existed there. His contributions to the development of the area and his philanthropies were well known.

Perhaps less well known was his intolerance to the hostile policies of the established waspy enclaves that limited or barred minorities from membership. With his cronies, he established a country club and golf course that welcomed the unwelcomed.

As Josh approached his clinic's parking lot, he saw more cars than usual. That indicated either he was tardy or some unscheduled patients had arrived. He looked at his watch: twenty minutes late, which meant he would be one patient behind in his scheduling all afternoon unless he short-changed someone's time, and he was reluctant to do that.

"Josh, if you hurry, you'll still be late," Maggie said as she helped him into his white coat. "What held you up?"

"I'll tell you between patients."

Maggie handed him the first patient's chart. "Can't you start now?"

He quickly thumbed through it and headed for the examination room. "Several years ago there was an outbreak of syphilis in a New York City suburb."

That took Maggie by surprise. "I beg your pardon?"

"Cue Effingwell had evidence of tertiary syphilis, which affected his brain and obviously his thought processes. The pathologist at the Centers for Disease Control found spirochetes, the organism of syphilis, embedded in his brain tissue."

"Really? But what has that to do with an outbreak of syphilis in a New York City suburb?"

"That's where Cue lived. Apparently, he infected a number of women—housewives, waitresses, and even teachers—with a penicillin-resistant strain. The increase in the number of cases came to the attention of the CDC after local doctors and clinics reported the unusual number to the state health department."

"What a horrible man!"

"Agreed. Cue's diseased brain would explain his diminished capacity for good judgment and his strange emotional outbursts. When he had blood tests some months ago for a routine physical examination, his serology was positive, and he was advised by his doctor to start treatment, but he refused or delayed it."

"I'd think treatment would be mandatory."

"Well, let's say it should have been. In Effingwell's case, it's an academic issue now."

"What about all his contacts?"

Josh hesitated at the door. "Aha, therein lies the problem."

* * *

Maggie and Josh were met by Suzanne at the front entrance to the estate at Big Horn. It had been a full month since Carlos's accident. Suzanne walked between them arm-in-arm down the long foyer toward Carlos's room. She stopped at the door of a hallway closet.

"I really shouldn't burden you with this, but there's something I must show you. This came in the mail yesterday." She opened the closet door and removed a shoe-box-sized package wrapped in brown paper from an overhead shelf. "I kept this from Carlos. He doesn't need any more stress." She handed the box to Josh, who shook it gently.

"Is it okay to open it?" he asked.

"Yes, of course. I'd much rather have you open it than Carlos."

Wrapped in tissue lay a primitive doll made of muslin with painted facial features. The mouth had a broad evil grin, the eyes were wide and staring, the chin was painted with a pointed goatee, and the exaggerated ears pointed upward. It was clothed in a red costume with two hatpins stuck into the area of the chest.

Maggie gasped, "A voodoo doll!" She put her hands over her mouth.

"I don't suppose this came with a return address?" Josh looked at Suzanne.

Suzanne shook her head. "The postmark was Palm Springs." She reached into the pocket of her slacks and handed Josh the folded note that had come with the doll. He took the note, composed of letters and words cut out of newspapers and magazines, and read aloud, "It would be smart for Senior Grandee if he did not buy any real estate around here. If he does he will have a bad fate. Signed, Satan."

"How horrible! What a terrible message," Maggie's said with obvious disgust.

"It's too damned ridiculous to be taken seriously." Josh lowered the doll back into the box.

"About as ridiculous as satanism?" Maggie asked.

Josh did not respond. He held the note at its edges and brought the paper to the sunlight coming through a window. The uneven lettering was glued to an eggshell-colored, bonded linen stationery. The upper border of the sheet had been cut off, suggesting the removal of an embossed, engraved, or printed heading. "Someone unfamiliar with Carlos's background believed he's of Latino origin and misspelled *señor*; the note itself lacks proper composition."

Maggie looked up and read the note. "Mannheim would love to get his hands on this, I bet."

"You got that right." He handed Maggie the box and pulled out his cell phone. "Let's give him a call."

THIRTY-FIVE

"Come in. Come in, my dear. You look absolutely ravishing, yes, absolutely ravishing. And if you don't mind my saying so, so much better than when you wore that dreary black mourning attire." Farquhaar's smile expanded his pink cheeks and displayed his too-even, overly white dentures. At eleven thirty, his office appeared as disorganized as usual.

Prissy, burdened with a leather briefcase and a Burberry shopping bag, did not return the cordial greeting but glanced around the cluttered room with a deprecating sneer.

"Why can't you find a more presentable suite? Or at least have someone clean up this pig sty?" She looked at the carpeting. "You haven't even replaced this miserable, threadbare floor covering. Aren't you ashamed? It looked bad enough last year; now it's deplorable, just disgusting." She took a tissue from her purse to wipe the seat of a chair he had hurriedly pulled out for her opposite his desk.

"My dear, your judgment of my wretched and untidy office is quite accurate, yes, quite accurate. I offer my humblest apologies."

"I really don't know why Peter continued to have you do his legal work."

Prissy had just crossed the line of fairness and reason. The appearance of his office should not have been a measure of his knowledge of the law. In Farquhaar's assessment, she had no right to impugn his legal capability.

His usual amiable demeanor, which might have been miscon-strued by Prissy as that of a namby-pamby, was about to reverse itself as he prepared to fire off a salvo or two.

He sat back in his seat and straightened his wrinkled tie as it lay on his rotund belly. "My dear Mrs. Longfellow . . ." His words were delivered deliberately and soberly. "Peter, your husband, was my very good friend. He sought my services for the first time twenty-five years ago, not because I was the only Harvard law graduate in this profes-sionally barren desert, where many charlatans hold law degrees from diploma mills and foisted their smarmy faces on billboards, telephone books, and newspapers to openly solicit personal injury, divorce, and D.U.I. cases." It might have been one of the longest sentences he'd ever uttered, but it proved his point. He could hold his own with anyone.

"No, my dear lady," he offered grandly. "Your husband came to me because he found me to be knowledgeable, honest, and sincere. And what is more, my fees were commensurate with my endeavors. Being a New Englander with a penchant for fiscal responsibility, I could account for every nickel, dime, and dollar on my billings."

"That's nice." Prissy sounded bored.

Roscoe ignored her. "Your husband and I," he added, "shared a relationship based on mutual trust and respect—yes, mutual trust and respect. On that one occasion, three years ago, when he felt adventur-ous—foolishly adventurous, I might add—and sought the advice of a large corporate law firm based in L.A., he lost not only *his* investment but the monies of participants who put their trust in him. Before he embarked on that folly, he showed me a prospectus, and I pleaded with him to walk away from it. As you know, he did not and eventually was forced to declare bankruptcy, an unfortunate development indeed. I was able to bring him through that most difficult time, although his investors remained inconsolably hostile. Yes, I brought him through, and he was grateful. Of course, you know who made money on that deal?"

Prissy nodded. "The L.A. attorneys."

"Quite so." Farquhaar glanced about. "If my office isn't as tony as those of the more flamboyant members of my profession, perhaps it's because my fees are modest, as are my personal needs." Again he fingered his wrinkled tie, then leaned forward on his elbows. "Although

I appreciate your continued patronage of this office, I should like you to know that you are free to seek legal advice elsewhere. I shall make all records available, post-haste, without acrimony or recrimination."

Prissy clearly hadn't expected that. However, being the woman she was, she was not about to apologize, because it might be construed as a sign of weakness.

She sniffed and pretended to still be obsessed with his office. "At least you could ask your landlord to make even the most modest improvements—a fresh coat of paint, new carpeting, or modern light fixtures."

Roscoe smiled. "I would, my dear, but he is a parsimonious lout, tight as a tick, stingier than Scrooge."

"Who is this delightful character?"

He leaned back and with his Cheshire cat grin explained, "It is I, my dear. It is I."

"You?" Prissy shook her head, looked up, and rolled her eyes.

Clearing his throat, Roscoe proceeded as though the foregoing discussion had never occurred. "You're not working at the Riverside County Administration today, my dear?"

"Not today or ever again. I gave my notice two weeks ago. I have too much to do now that Peter's gone."

He studied her quietly, taking in her expression and body language. Finally he asked, "Doing what?"

"Running my husband's business."

Roscoe smiled, tented his hands under his chin, and said, "Capital idea, my dear, just capital. How may I be of service?"

Prissy lifted her black Prada case and dropped it on his already cluttered desk. "Look over these contractor/owner proposals and make sure I'm not getting screwed." She removed a number of documents from the case and placed them directly in front of him.

Roscoe gathered them and placed a heavy rubber band around them. "Yes, yes, I shall take care of them, anon."

"One more thing." She reached into her shopping bag, picked up a black box, and placed it next to her papers on his desk. "Check this out. It came in the mail three days ago."

"Why give it to me?"

"Because I want your opinion."

Surprised, Roscoe looked at Prissy, then looked at the box. "What surprise awaits me here?"

"Go ahead, open it."

He lifted the lid partially, peeking under it before removing it completely. Cautiously, he separated tissue to expose a primitive muslin doll in a black dress. Two hatpins penetrated the chest area.

His hands flew upward and his eyes widened. "What in the—a voodoo doll?"

This time Roscoe couldn't keep his voice from scaling up two octaves. "A presentation from the Gullahs? What sordid nonsense is this?"

"That's not all." Prissy handed him a folded note. "This came with it."

Roscoe's pince-nez glasses dangled from a cord around his neck. He picked them up and read the words that had been cut out of newspapers and magazines and glued onto the stationery. "'Forget about buying more land in Rancho Mirage if you want to stay alive.'"

Roscoe pushed back in his chair and pointed to the lettering. "This, my dear, constitutes a threat to your life. Your civil liberties have been breached. This is a violation of federal law number—"

Prissy stopped him. "Spare me the dramatics. What's your advice? Should I forget about it? This isn't the first time I've been threatened."

"I'd take this matter directly to the police and—"

Again she cut him off. "You know damn well the cops are going to say they can't do a thing. Illegal use of the mails is outside their jurisdiction, and I don't need the FBI snooping into my affairs."

"This is much too serious to ignore. A psychopath may have you in his gun sight. I beseech you to allow me to contact the police."

Prissy waved her hand in resignation. "Suit yourself. But you do it. I don't have time for such nonsense." She straightened her skirt and walked toward the door with her briefcase and shopping bag. "Call me when you've finished those papers, and don't worry about anyone sticking pins in me. I've been pricked before."

Roscoe peered over his glasses and nodded. "Yes, my dear, I dare say you probably have."

THIRTY-SIX

At 5:10 p.m., Maggie walked into Josh's consultation room with a chart she held behind her. "I bet you can't possibly guess who your last patient is for today?"

He looked at his watch. "You want to play games at this hour? Forgive me if I don't try," he said as he prepared to dictate a report.

She became kittenish. "If you guess correctly, within six names, I'll do something nice for you—tonight."

"Such as?"

"You've got to guess first."

He lunged for the chart behind her but she held her ground, forcing him to lean against her. With a giggle, she brought her hands around his neck and pulled his head toward her for a kiss.

When she pulled away, with the chart remaining in her right hand, he looked into her mischievous eyes. "I think the nice thing you promised for tonight might have already started."

"Oh, no you don't. You've got to play my game first. C'mon, guess who your last patient is."

"I give up, who?" he asked in mock defeat.

"Detective Sergeant Timothy Aloysius Mannheim, that's who."

Josh slapped her backside playfully. "You sure know how to deflate an eager sex drive. What's his complaint?" Before she could open her mouth, he waggled a finger at her. "Don't think for one minute I won't exact payment tonight."

"My dearest, you're confused—you *lost* the bet. You'll do *my* bidding tonight; you'll be my love slave."

"That sounds like a win-win situation. I'm looking forward to enslavement or bondage, or whatever."

"Don't let your imagination run wild. I'm just an old-fashioned girl with modest demands. Now put Casanova on hold and we'll get on with examining our patient. Mannheim is really here as a patient, believe it or not."

She read her notes from the chart: "Right shoulder pain of one week's duration following brisk movement with heavy object . . . no swelling, no discoloration or crepitation. Pain on all movements of shoulder. Some relief with aspirin and warm moist applications. Patient is right-handed."

Josh arched his eyebrows in surprise. "That's a mouthful. Okay, let's get some X-rays, and put him in an examining room."

• • •

Three views of the shoulder revealed no fractures, dislocations, or obvious osseous pathology. Mannheim sat forlornly on the examining table with a surgical gown covering his bare upper body. Maggie moved to tie the strings on the back of the loosely hung gown so Josh could study the man's sharply defined rib cage and shoulder blades. His usual hang-dog expression was exaggerated by his obvious discomfort.

He studied Josh's expression as he looked over the X-rays. "What is it, Doc? Did I chip a bone or pull a muscle?"

"You probably overexerted your biceps tendon, causing an irritation known as tendonitis. We can relieve your pain with an injection. How did you injure your shoulder?"

Mannheim placed his left hand over the right shoulder as though to protect it. "Do you remember that missing andiron from Peter Longfellow's home? The one we found on your property? The one we figured someone used to bash in his skull?"

"Yes, of course."

"The damn thing weighed about twenty-five to thirty pounds and had to be raised high enough to make a hole in his skull."

"And you know that for a fact, how?" Josh asked.

"Well, let's say, I had a hunch, so I called Dr. Elaine Walsh, the forensic anthropologist at the L.A. coroner's office. She told me she had access to a number of unclaimed corpses and invited me to try to reproduce the kind of trauma shown on Longfellow's skull. So I hopped on over and gave one a whack."

"What was the verdict?"

"You gotta be kinda strong. Enough to lift that much weight over your head and bash in a skull. That's when I hurt my shoulder."

"Oh my." Maggie appeared to be impressed with the officer's attention to detail. "Were you able to reproduce the trauma?"

"What do you think?" Mannheim dug his bony fingers into his right shoulder, where the outlines of the deltoid muscle could be seen through his thin skin. He rubbed the shoulder; then, as he attempted to flex his arm, he suddenly bent forward and cringed with pain. He bit his lower lip and murmured, "Jee-zus," then remained silent for a few seconds, holding his breath, until the acute pain subsided and color returned to his pale face. He looked at Maggie and grimaced. "Now you know."

"I know you hurt yourself, but did you succeed in duplicating the blow to a skull?"

"Barely." Mannheim watched uneasily as Josh tore open the paper sack containing a sterile syringe. "Is it gonna hurt, Doc?"

"Not much." Josh picked up a small bottle and shook it. "Why are you sharing all this with us now? Every other time we talked, I kind of got the impression you suspected us."

"Doc, I never considered you seriously as the killer. Was just following protocol." His eyes followed Josh as he put two ccs of fluid into the syringe. "You must have known that Mrs. Longfellow was my prime suspect. It's just that I had trouble figuring out the logistics of her husband's death. The gal is obviously smaller and weaker than her husband was. If she's involved, she would've had to have an accomplice. Killing a man as large as Peter Longfellow, not to mention hanging him by that rope to the chandelier by herself, would be impossible. Naw, she had to have help."

Maggie looked at Mannheim's holster and harness hanging on the chair. Typical of the way her train of thought ran, she came up with a question Josh would have never considered. "How did you intend to reach your weapon when you could hardly move your shoulder?" she asked.

"Who the hell said I could?" he asked tersely.

Josh smiled. He located the point of greatest tenderness by probing the shoulder, then injected the lidocaine to anesthetize the skin. Mannheim pulled his head back, gripped the edge of the examining table, and grimaced as the needle was introduced. A second injection, consisting of a steroid suspension, was given through the anesthetized skin. Within a minute, Mannheim looked around with an unbelieving sense of relief. With one of his rare smiles, revealing irregular and yellowed teeth, he cautiously moved his shoulder in small circles. "Goddamn, Doc! That's a hundred percent better. You're okay."

Once Maggie had placed a Band-Aid over the injection site, Mannheim slipped his arms into his shirtsleeves and started to button his shirt. Perhaps the anxiety of the moment, the perspiration resulting from activity, and the heat of the day created body odor that embarrassed him. "Excuse me if I don't smell fresh. I'm going to shower as soon as I get home."

He started to tuck in the bottom of his shirt, then snapped his fingers. "Which reminds me, Doc. Speaking of odor . . . there was an odor, I guess the polite term would be fragrance, the night I brought that andiron to Mrs. Longfellow's memorial service for her husband. I smelled that same smell another time, and I can't recall where."

"Why is that important?" Josh asked.

"'Cause it seemed unusual at the time. Kinda strong. I thought it was a woman's perfume, in combination with something else." He shook his head. "Damned if I can think of it, though."

"Detective Mannheim?" Maggie gave the officer a frustrated look. "Are you really any closer to knowing who killed Peter Longfellow? It's been three months since his murder. Do you have any clues—any strong suspects?"

Mannheim's sunken eyes, like narrow windows protected by the overhanging eaves of his bushy brows, looked over at Maggie. "No, Ma'am, but that case is still on our front burner. I do have my suspicions, but I can't tell you everything we know." He replaced his holstered gun on his left side and cinched up the harness, then slipped into his jacket. Once ready, he squared his shoulders and pulled at his shirt cuffs. "Jeez, that feels better."

He headed toward the door, then turned to look at Josh. "One thing more, could you give me a list of all persons who were interested in buying your property? I mean everyone."

* * *

Maggie flipped off the office lights, turned on the security system, then locked the door. She and Josh headed toward their SUV.

"What do you make of everything Mannheim said?" Maggie asked. What's he going to do with that list of names? Do you think he still considers Prissy a prime suspect in her husband's murder?"

"One question at a time, love. Firstly, he's going to do what every good detective does: list all suspects, then rule them in or out. Secondly, we know after his experience at the forensic anthropologist's lab, he figured it took a strong man to lift that heavy andiron and create enough momentum to penetrate that skull."

"I still think Prissy is the one. But who would her accomplice be?"

"Someone Prissy trusts, I suspect."

"She could have hired someone, paid him off, then sent him on his way."

"Possible, but doubtful. I believe a premeditated murder would have been neater than that bloody mess. Why would Prissy want it in her home, where she becomes an immediate suspect? No, this is different; there's an element of the unforeseen. The unexpected. There's the circumstance of opportunity."

"What if it was a ritualistic murder?"

Josh shook his head. "Are you thinking about the voodoo doll and that eerie collection of satanic paraphernalia in her bedroom? All that hocus-pocus crap doesn't impress me one goddamn bit."

"Honey, your language is becoming quite coarse. It's not like you."

"Sorry, but I don't see devil worship fitting into this equation. Those types of nut-heads use satanism to justify their hedonism, all the feel-good, self-indulgent orgies—alcohol, drugs, nudity, sex, flagellation, and porn flicks. I would think murder would be at the opposite end of their euphoria scale." He hesitated to mull over his words, "Of course, I could be mistaken."

"What about ritualistic murder as the ultimate thrill?"

She had a point. He hadn't thought of that. Josh shrugged. "Perhaps to the singular perverted mind—okay, maybe two perverted minds—but getting a whole group of satanists to agree to murder, especially in a community of wealthy, privileged high-achievers, that's too weird to contemplate."

Maggie's eyebrows arched. "Really? What about Charles Manson and his followers? They were a small group capable of murder."

"That's a whole different psycho-sociopathic group . . ."

Maggie cut him off. "And what about the group who participated in the *Murder on the Orient Express*?"

Josh smiled. "Agatha Christie probably never had a course in abnormal psychology. Anyway, my dear, I'm only suggesting that whoever, satanists or others, did not set out to murder Peter Longfellow. And, as I've already said, I could be wrong. Dead wrong. Allow me to change the subject. Let's get back to my punishment for failing to guess our last patient's name."

Maggie tilted her head, put her index finger to her lips, and said, "I'm leaning toward tying you up in bed, spread-eagle, nude, and start kissing you and flicking my tongue lightly from your lips down to your you-know-what. Would you consider me a deranged pervert? Or a satanist?"

"Neither. I would think of you as my uninhibited, unrestrained, and fully committed lover who could make me ecstatic. And if that constitutes my bondage, my servitude, my punishment, I shall forever be indebted to Detective Mannheim—and you, of course."

"You need not concern yourself with that sort of punishment or with being indebted to Detective Mannheim. What I have in mind for you is quite different."

"I can hardly wait." He smiled.

"That's good. Tomorrow is trash pickup. You can take the barrels out tonight and when you're done with that, you can help me fold the laundry."

THIRTY-SEVEN

Mannheim sat at his desk and studied the list of names Doc Harrington had given him. As though timed by a metronome, he slid his thumb and two fingers down his pencil, reversed it, and repeated the movement over and over.

Someone tapped his shoulder. He jerked and spun around. "Jeez-uzz, Harry! Don't go sneaking around like that."

"Sorry, Tim, didn't realize you were deep in thought."

Mannheim leaned back in his chair and threw his pencil onto his desk. "It's this goddamn Longfellow murder. What are we overlooking? Why haven't we had a break?" He poked the two voodoo dolls on his desk. "And these cockamamie dolls."

"Did forensics come up with anything on those dolls or shoe-box notes?"

"Nothing—*nada*—zip. Someone must have worn gloves. A regional distributor for stationery said that paper was sold in three stores in the valley: Macy's, Robinsons-May, and Office Depot. We'll run down individual sales for the past year until we come across a familiar name."

"That's a big order. Then what?" Todd asked.

"What do you mean, 'Then what?' You take every damn detail and build on it. That's basic police work. Remember?"

Harry Todd sighed. "I haven't heard that since my introductory course in criminology, at the Academy, twenty-six years ago."

Mannheim picked up his pencil and looked at the list again. When he came to Peter Longfellow's name, he stabbed the pencil down. "Poor bastard, brutally murdered with an andiron, then hanged." He stood and scratched his behind. "I'd say his bitchy wife and some bozo gotta be prime suspects."

"Even though she got one of these voodoo dolls herself? Not to mention a threatening note?" Harry asked.

"She's a clever broad. Hell, for all we know she could have sent that goddamn thing to herself just to throw off suspicion."

Todd looked down at the list. "What about this guy?" He pointed at a name. "Yamamoto, the hospital administrator? He seems like the least likely suspect to me."

Mannheim shook his head in resignation. "Why would anyone want to kill for a goddamn piece of land?"

Todd knew it was a rhetorical question, but he answered anyway. "In the hope of developing it and making a few million simoleons, that's why."

Mannheim flopped back into his chair. "Okay, let's start again. Let's concentrate on the land developers."

"That takes us back to Mrs. Longfellow," Todd said pragmatically.

"Exactly, her and maybe Dan Aviloh. But let's not dismiss Yamamoto and Tatiana, just yet."

Mannheim tilted his chair backward and cradled the back of his head with interlocked fingers. His brooding eyes focused absently on a far wall. "I want to interview each one on this list and grill the shit out of him or her until we get a confession. One of them has got to be the killer or knows who the killer or killers are." He took a deep breath and exhaled audibly. "Let's pay a visit to everyone on this list and ask questions, maybe put the fear of God in them, or maybe the devil."

"Should I notify these people we're coming to see them?" Todd asked.

"Hell, no! A little surprise visit oughta shake 'em up. That way they can't prepare answers or have their fuckin' lawyers tell them what they *can* and *can't* answer."

"How much time are you allowing for these inquiries?"

"How much time? As long as necessary. That's another lesson you were supposed to have learned in your class on 'The Art of Interrogation.'" Mannheim handed Todd some printed sheets. "Here are FBI reports on some of these people. Familiarize yourself with the information; it could be helpful."

• • •

Maggie sorted the office mail, placing envelopes containing payments and bills into two piles and advertisements and nonessentials into another. She picked up an announcement-sized envelope with Josh's name neatly scripted in calligraphy. She handed Josh the envelope and looked over his shoulder as he pulled out the announcement and read:

"Dear Dr. Harrington:

The firm of P.S. Longfellow, builder of estates of extraordinary quality, cordially invites you to attend a meeting of great urgency."

"Really?" Maggie continued to read over his shoulder.

Josh read on: "A highly vocal group called STOP OVERDEVELOPMENT OF COACHELLA or SOC has undertaken a campaign to halt further development in subdivision A-197, under the pretext of preserving the natural environment."

Josh stopped reading and glanced at his wife. "Now this sounds interesting."

"I'll say. Keep going."

"We need your support to address these misinformed adversaries who would impede our much-needed eco-friendly construction progress in the Coachella Valley. As a landowner you are strongly urged to attend. A buffet with libations will be served. Saturday, April fifth, at four thirty. Your immediate response will be greatly appreciated. Phone or e-mail at the following . . ."

Maggie said, "Josh, that's less than a week away."

Josh held the invitation to the light. He felt the texture, smelled it, and looked for a watermark. "Expensive." Looking at Maggie, he asked, "You'll come with me, won't you?"

Maggie shook her head and smiled. "Not on your life, my dear. Firstly, the invitation was sent to you. It did not include me. Secondly, Suzanne and I have been planning a shopping spree on El Paseo for weeks and decided on that very same day. Horace, her chauffeur, will be picking me up and we intend to have a girls'-day-out party which will be strictly first class, including luncheon at a chic French restaurant." Maggie whirled about. "Ooh-la-la."

"Thanks. You're sticking me with that landowners' meeting all alone, where I'll have to listen to self-righteous contractors defending their rights to make enormous profits."

Maggie wiggled up to him, and in her best sympathy-evoking plea, placed her arms around his neck. "Darling, go as my envoy. Find out how serious the opposition is to the development of our land, and for my sake offer a rebuttal. I'll ask Suzanne to have the chauffeur swing us by Prissy's at about five forty-five to six o'clock. Your meeting should be coming to an end at about that time. If you finish earlier, call me on your cell. If I don't hear from you, we'll come over anyway and rescue you. By then you should be ready for a reprieve. Beside, you won't be there long enough for Prissy to get her hands on you, although I'm sure she'll try."

* * *

Harry Todd started the engine, then looked at his watch. "It's four thirty. May be a bit late to call on the hospital administrator, especially on his day off. Besides, he could be gone for the day, and, well . . . I'd like to have dinner with the family tonight."

As soon as the words slipped from his mouth, Harry knew he was in trouble with his boss.

"Listen, Todd, if you wanted a nine-to-five job you should have gone with Wal-Mart or Burger King. I don't ask you to bust your ass often. After we put a lid on this murder you can take a long weekend and go on a second honeymoon for all I care. Go visit Los Angeles, hit the Barrio, have some refried beans and fart your way down Olvera Street."

Mannheim stopped, thought a while, and gave Todd a tight smile. "But for now you're on this job, so drive the damn car and quit bitching. We're going to call on everyone on Doc's list at our convenience, not theirs. It's almost four fuckin' months since Longfellow's murder, and Sacramento keeps reminding the chief that we have an unsolved, high-profile homicide. He wants to know why we're sitting with our thumbs up our asses."

"Does that worry you?"

"It doesn't make me feel good, and it sure as hell doesn't give you much to brag about, either. Someone is playing us for goddamn fools. That pisses me off. I don't care who the hell we inconvenience; we've got to get some leads."

• • •

Yamamoto, wearing a tank top and sweatpants, stood at the door and stared at the two detectives before him. He clenched a cigar between his teeth and grumbled, "What can I do for you fellas?"

A basketball game appeared on the TV screen behind him.

"We'd like to ask you some questions." Mannheim kept his explanation short and to the point.

"About what?"

"Doctor Harrington's land."

A puzzled expression crossed Yamamoto's face. "I see. Come in. The place is a little messy. Wife's out playing Bingo with the girls." Yamamoto cleared several sections of newspaper off the sofa. "Can I get you something to drink?—a Coke?—a cup of coffee?"

"No, sir. We're fine."

Mannheim selected one of the upholstered chairs opposite to Yamamoto, who sat on the sofa. Harry took the other chair.

"We'd like to ask you if you know anything about Peter Longfellow's death."

Surprised, Yamamoto looked at Mannheim, then at Todd, and back at Mannheim. "I thought this was about the land I wanted to purchase. How would I know anything about Longfellow's death?"

Mannheim referred to his spiral notebook. "Mr. Yamamoto, at the onset, I want you to know we're aware of certain facts about your background."

Yamamoto broke into a broad, self-assured grin . "Really? Well, tell me what you know about my dull and prosaic existence." He leaned back and put his arms across the back of the sofa, extended his legs, and crossed them at the ankles.

"To begin, your life wasn't exactly dull and as you say, prosaic. Back in the 'sixties you spent a year in San Francisco with a group of hippies or flower children or whatever the hell they were called in the Haight/Ashbury district. You were part of a gang who burned draft cards, vandalized an army recruitment station, and set fire to the flag of the U.S. of A."

"Hey, wait a goddamn minute." Yamamoto's relaxed expression disappeared and he bolted upright. "We were just rebellious kids, that's all."

Harry removed several folded sheets from his jacket pocket. "According to an FBI report, they didn't see it that way. You and your pot-smoking buddies were fined five hundred dollars apiece and had to do community service for ninety days."

"All right. So what? What the hell does that have to do with Longfellow's murder?"

"Not much; we just want to impress on you the fact that we're aware of certain things and would appreciate straightforward answers." Mannheim referred to his notes again. "We know, for instance, that you led a group of American Japanese to Washington, D.C., to confront the president about getting reparations and an apology from the government for mistreatment of interned Japanese during World War Two."

"That's right, and I'd do it again." Yamamoto became defiant. "You're not holding *that* against me, are you? And again, what the hell does this have to do with Longfellow?"

Before Mannheim could respond, Yamamoto asked another question: "Do your records also show that I enlisted in the army and was awarded a purple heart and a silver star for 'Nam? That under heavy fire, I led a platoon to safety and got shot up in my left leg?" He pulled up his trouser leg to show a long, irregular retracted scar over his left shin. "Are you aware that I headed the district Red Cross drive, and that I'm on the mayor's advisory board?"

Mannheim nodded slowly. "Yes, sir. We are. Our records show you served your country with valor. We're also aware that you've made notable civic contributions."

"All right, then, tell me again what all this has to do with a murder. I seem to have lost the reason for this damned inquisition."

Mannheim's lips formed a thin line. "Three years ago, you and several others entered into a business arrangement with Peter Longfellow. You committed five hundred thousand dollars as your share in a commercial building venture. You took a deed of trust on your home to pay for that investment."

Yamamoto flushed. "So what? I still don't know what you're getting at."

"Allow me to refresh your memory." Mannheim looked at his notes. "Do you recall a lawsuit you initiated against Peter Longfellow, who was a general partner in a construction project that failed? You claimed malfeasance and mismanagement of funds."

"And you think I'd kill him for that?" He rose to his feet.

Mannheim blinked but remained impassive. "People have been known to kill for less."

"Yeah? Well, I'm not one of them."

"But you're still paying on that debt."

"So what?" Yamamoto repeated. "That's none of your goddamn business."

"Someone overheard you say in court, 'That sonofabitch should be shot!'"

"That's all hearsay, bullshit. And you know it." Yamamoto walked to the door and held it open. "It's time for both of you to leave. Good night."

"Well, that went well." Todd said, getting into the driver's side. "Do you think Yamamoto was capable of killing Longfellow?"

Mannheim shrugged. Placing his hands deep into his pockets and slumping in his seat, he groused, "I'd want to kill any sonofabitch who took my money and pissed it away."

THIRTY-EIGHT

The following afternoon, Harry Todd pulled into the circular driveway on Clancy Lane. Mannheim opened the passenger door, swiveled, and exited the car. He walked the inclined path toward the sheltered front door of the brothel with its carved Orthodox cross.

Todd followed closely, eyeing the gardeners suspiciously.

They, in turn, glowered at him.

Mannheim looked straight into the video camera in the upper right corner of the entryway and flashed his badge. "C'mon, Tatiana, old girl," he said and pushed the doorbell. "You've got two old cocks here who can't do anything but remember how good it used to be."

"Speak for yourself," Todd muttered.

Mannheim turned to look at him but ignored the comment.

The ornate door with leaded-glass panels opened slowly to reveal the notorious madam of the most celebrated sporting house in the Coachella Valley. She stood before them, an image of aging but remarkable beauty, a beauty enhanced by the efficacy of plastic surgery and cosmetics, clothing like gossamer that revealed more than it concealed, and jewelry that glittered from her ears, neck, wrists, and fingers. Even the meticulously coiffed hairpiece had sparkles and a small tiara with faux diamonds.

"Boys, you come here without telling Tatiana? All my girls are busy." She controlled her smile to guard against violating her makeup.

"Will little Tatiana do?" Placing her hands on her hips, she advanced her pelvis provocatively.

"Tatiana, ten minutes with you would probably kill me," Mannheim said with a tight smile.

"I'll take my chances," Todd said cheerfully, not really meaning it.

"You boys are so silly. I know you don't want pleasure from me. Come in, come in. What can I do for you?"

Whether it was Tatiana's voluptuous femininity and the aura she projected or the opulence of the surroundings, Harry Todd seemed to have been transported to a state of numbing rapture. He proceeded, open-mouthed, into the room and stared at the trappings dripping with sensuality. Tatiana motioned the detectives to sit in the engulfing leather club chairs while she sat in an upright chair that would reveal her enormous bosom more advantageously. She crossed her long, shapely legs slowly and allowed the folds of her gown to slip to either side.

"Boys, can I offer you a little something? A drink, maybe?"

Mannheim shook his head. "Madame Tatiana, a serious allegation has been made against you in the murder of Peter Longfellow."

Tatiana's composure changed. Her jaw visibly tightened and her eyes, heavy with mascara, narrowed. "What you say? What means 'allegation'? You make fun from Tatiana?"

"Not at all. Try to understand. We learned that you signed a note for a half million dollars to invest in a shopping center that was to be built three years ago by Peter Longfellow. When the project failed, you entered into a lawsuit with others. You went to court, then for some reason you refused to press charges. Why was that?"

Tatiana did not respond immediately. Mannheim watched her lips purse, her nostrils flare, and her eyes turn fiery.

"Those somabitch Los Angeles lawyers for Longfellow tell my lawyer, whole world going to know I make money from whorehouse, gambling, and whiskey. Los Angeles lawyers say government will put me in jail and take from me escort services to collect back taxes. My lawyer said you must drop charges."

"Before you withdrew your charges in court, you were held in contempt and fined two hundred dollars." Mannheim looked up from his notebook. "Tell me about that."

"Listen, Mister Detective, you already know everything, I not tell you more." With a defiant air she stood and turned her back to the two men.

Mannheim, in a louder voice, continued, "You were fined for yelling an obscenity and for making a death threat at Mr. Longfellow, isn't that right?"

Tatiana folded her arms over her chest and continued to ignore him.

"Do you know what I think?" Mannheim pointed his bony finger at her, even though he knew she couldn't see it. "I think you might have killed Longfellow with the help of those two goons out there." He pointed toward the garden area. "They could have smashed his skull, then hanged him as a warning to anyone else who might think of cheating you. That's a little Old World method of taking care of enemies. Isn't that right?"

Tatiana stomped to the phone, picked it up, and stabbed at the buttons while keeping her back toward the detectives. Without saying a word, she replaced the phone, and the two simian-like gardeners appeared inside the front door. They ambled menacingly toward the detectives.

Immediately, Mannheim and Todd reached for their guns. "Hold it right there," Mannheim said, "or we'll blow your fuckin' heads off!"

Together, he and Todd lifted their pistols and pointed the guns toward the men. The goons froze. Todd said nothing, but his eyes danced with excitement.

Mannheim tilted his head toward Tatiana without taking his eyes off the brutes. "Tatiana, you goddamn fool, tell these bastards to put their hands up and walk backwards to the wall or we'll haul your money-making ass to jail along with them!"

A hurried command from Tatiana sent the two gardeners backing toward the wall with their hands up, nodding submissively. Tatiana slumped in a chair and began sobbing. "I afraid you take Tatiana to jail and she never come out. Nobody will bail her out. Please, I beg you. You must believe Tatiana. I do not kill Mister Longfellow." She dabbed her tears as they streaked her mascara, creating a sorrowful clown-like mask.

Mannheim glanced between the pleading madam and her henchmen. "Well, what do ya say, Detective Todd? Should we run them all in?"

"It's your call, Detective Mannheim." Todd assumed a serious posture.

Mannheim started slowly for the door. He signaled with his pistol for the gardeners to leave, then turned around. "Tatiana, the next time you do something so goddamn stupid as to call your *muzhiks* to threaten us, we'll run all of you in, or maybe we'll just kill you and claim self-defense."

"No, no! No next time, I promise. I make you gift of any girl, even Tatiana herself."

Mannheim ignored her and continued to walk toward the door.

Todd held on to Mannheim's sleeve. "Wait, maybe we could work something out."

Mannheim tugged his arm away. "C'mon, lover boy, we have things to do." As he got closer to the door, Mannheim turned again to confront Tatiana. "Something else bothers me. You lost five hundred thousand dollars in a bad deal with Peter Longfellow, yet you made an offer to buy Doc Harrington's land in Rancho Mirage. That deal would have set you back millions of dollars. In fact, you told him you would beat any offer he got. Isn't that right? Maybe the IRS should take a closer look at your books."

Tatiana seemed to shrink; her shoulders drooped and her head and neck bowed. "I did not make offer with my own money," she said softly.

Mannheim walked toward her. "What did you say? You didn't offer your *own* money? Whose money did you offer?"

Her soulful eyes looked into his and in a barely audible voice she murmured, "Cue's."

"Cue's? What are you talking about?" Mannheim stood over her, waiting for an explanation.

"Cue wanted property very bad. He say he cannot offer more than appraised value without making suspicions."

"Suspicions about what?"

"He not say. He cancel my mortgage payment for one year if I make good deal with Dr. Harrington."

"So you had no personal interest in that property?" Mannheim asked.

"No! Of course not. What I'm going to do with more property I cannot afford? I already have biggest sporting house in valley."

Once in the car, Todd looked at Mannheim. "What she says makes sense now that we suspect that the corpse under the floorboards of the old adobe was Cue's father. Cue wanted to get that property before anyone else did. I wonder what took him so long to go after it?"

"Damned if I know."

THIRTY-NINE

Maggie walked across the bedroom and watched Josh slip into his corduroy jacket. It was the day of his meeting with Prissy Longfellow and the other business leaders.

"When you get to Prissy's, I expect you to be absolutely proper, and by all means standoffish. Don't you dare let that hussy get anywhere near you. If I hear she's been cozying up to you, I'll rip her apart."

Josh adjusted the coat, wondering if Maggie had made her pronouncement in jest. He decided she had. "You have my word, dearie. Who could possibly entice me after I've made love to you?"

"Uh-huh. I could name a few who would try." Maggie adjusted his tie and hand-brushed the shoulders of his jacket. "I wonder what Prissy's strategy will be for fighting this group of concerned citizens for a less-congested Rancho Mirage."

She suddenly stopped brushing. "I wonder if Roscoe Farquhaar is handling the legal end."

Before Josh could hazard a guess, Maggie added, "I suppose Yamamoto will be there too, and Dan Aviloh, and some of the business owners."

"I expect there'll be a few well-heeled entrepreneurs."

"My, oh my, won't you have fun."

* * *

As they drove on the valley's main street, Highway 111, Mannheim looked at his watch: 3:45.

"Here it is April fifth and this damn traffic is still heavy. Why don't the tourists leave already?" The congestion was aggravated by frequent stoppages caused by construction crews and equipment. "Let's make another call."

"Who?" Todd looked over at his boss.

"Dan Aviloh, at his building site off Frank Sinatra Drive."

The muscles in Todd's jaw tightened in annoyance; one day he was going to get enough nerve to tell this neurotic, compulsive sack of bones to back off. Why couldn't he be satisfied with an eight-hour workday like most normal human beings?

He decided to voice one of his rare objections. "Mannheim, let the next shift do that. I've had enough of this overtime crap without compensation." In truth, he would much rather be at home nursing a Bud and watching TV, or, if he really got lucky, making love with the wife since the boys were away at college.

"Hey, buddy boy, this is *our* case. No one else's, remember? You want to quit? Get a new partner. Go ahead. As for me, I've got more to do on this goddamn case."

Chagrined, Todd straightened in the driver's seat. He dreaded Mannheim's criticism and the loss of opportunity for advancement. Now was not the time to make his senior partner angry, but he had to let him know that he wasn't entirely happy. "What is it that bothers you about Aviloh that you have to talk with him right now?"

"There's something about that guy's loyalty to his dead pal, Peter Longfellow. It's always bothered me."

"You think he doth protest too much?"

"Yeah, something, like that."

Fifteen minutes later, as the vehicle bounced and lurched near the construction site, Mannheim's head struck the headliner. "Goddammit, Todd. Watch where the hell you're driving. You just went over a wood pallet."

"There's too much debris around here. I can't avoid it all," Todd snapped back.

D. Aviloh Construction. Fine Homes from Concept to Award Winning Estates read the sign on the dirty green mobile field office. The detectives walked up three steps to the closed door. Mannheim knocked twice, then opened the door without waiting for permission.

"What can I do for ya?" A gravelly voice emanated from under a yellow hard hat with the name *Bushwhacker* stenciled on it. The wearer, a bronze-hued, ponytailed, muscular male in his late thirties or early forties with cutaway sleeves and tattoos, looked up from blueprints spread on a makeshift table.

The mobile office, a boxlike room, reeked of stale cigars, cigarettes, and beer. A steel desk with two folding chairs occupied the far end of the room. In the center, a four-by-six-foot plywood board supported by two sawhorses held a number of flat blueprints. Rolled blueprints in pyramidal formations were stacked on top of two steel file cabinets. Irregularly tacked notes hung on a corkboard mounted behind the desk. An old white refrigerator with a soiled door hummed in a corner.

"Aviloh around?" Mannheim asked, chewing a toothpick.

"No, he ain't here." Bushwhacker turned his back and ignored the detectives.

Neither of them moved.

Bushwhacker grunted, "Look, I said he ain't here." He pointed to the door. "Feel free to leave."

Mannheim moved the toothpick from one side of his mouth to the other. "This isn't exactly a social visit, buddy-boy." He displayed his badge. "You expecting him soon?"

Bushwhacker had a sudden change in attitude. "Hey, guys, why didn't you tell me you were cops? I thought you were salesmen hawking some crap. Yeah, sure, he should be back here any time. Here's a coupla chairs. Can I get you a drink—a Coke, a beer?" He tipped his hard hat back on his head and moved toward the refrigerator.

"Don't bother." Mannheim gave the man a once-over. "Nice artwork." He pointed to the tattoo on his arm. "'Born to Kill.' You an ex-con?"

"So what if I am? I've kept my nose clean ever since I got out."

"Uh-huh." Mannheim glanced at the blueprints on the table. "Is this what you're working on?"

"Nah, that's a proposed layout for a whole new project on the acreage across the road, on that doctor's land—what's his name?"

"Harrington," Todd said.

"Yeah, that's it."

"I didn't know Aviloh was going to develop that land," Mannheim said.

"Maybe; Dan said he had plans for building on it. He's been talking a lot about it lately."

"That so?" Mannheim approached Bushwhacker. "You drive a truck for the company?"

Bushwhacker hesitated and looked at Mannheim suspiciously. "Yeah, sometimes, why?"

"Think back about four months ago. Do you remember driving a white dump truck and hitting the rear end of a car on the I-10 near the Monterey off-ramp?"

Bushwhacker stiffened. He studied Mannheim, then looked at Todd. His lower lip protruded as though he was trying to recall. Slowly, he shook his head. "No, I don't remember that."

Mannheim again moved the toothpick slowly from side to side. "Let me give you some advice, buddy-boy: don't bullshit me and don't cover up for some sonofabitch. If you do, we'll throw the book at you and your stupid lies will come back to bite your ass. Y'understand?"

"Uh—yeah, sure, I suppose I coulda tapped a car on the freeway and not known it. Those trucks are so damn big, and the cabs are so damn high, you know . . ." He trailed away and held up his hands as if that helped to explain.

"Yeah, yeah, I know. Now listen to this: three months ago, do you remember tailgating a car up here on Frank Sinatra Drive and making it run onto the median?"

This time Bushwhacker's face darkened.

"And," Mannheim pressed, "what about the crash when *your* truck hit that Cadillac limo on the I-10 four months ago, killing two people?"

Bushwhacker's eyes darted from side to side. "Killing?" He shook his head. "I don't know what you're talking about. I'm not saying nothin', nothin' more till I talk to a lawyer."

Mannheim detested that response and thought the law had been skewed to give more protection to the criminal than the victim. He made sure his position as a law enforcement agent was never completely negated by such defenses. "You're allowed. But . . ." He let the word trail out for effect. "You can make it a hell of a lot easier for yourself, here and now, by telling us who ordered you to do all that."

Bushwhacker was about to respond when the door suddenly opened.

An unsmiling Dan Aviloh stepped in. He hesitated momentarily as he looked at Bushwhacker, then at the detectives. Limping toward the table with the blueprints, he snapped, "What are you guys doing here?"

"Keep your shirt on, Aviloh. We're here to speak to you."

Aviloh quickly turned over several pages of the blueprints and scowled. "Jee-zus, are you still talking about Pete's murder?"

"That's right, and two vehicular homicides, plus aggravated assault on the Interstate."

Hearing that, Aviloh balanced himself against the table. "Come off it. You can't pin any of that shit on me or anyone else in this company, and you fuckin' well know it."

Mannheim pulled the toothpick out of his mouth and flicked it in a waste basket. "I know that a paint chip found on a Cadillac limo in which two people were killed came off a late-model, white International, the same kind of truck I see around here."

"You're blowin' smoke, Mannheim. Y'know how many of those trucks operate in this valley?"

Mannheim didn't respond to the question but pointed his finger at Bushwhacker. "Your boy here says you're planning to build on the Doc's property across the road. Is that so?"

"That's just a proposal I made to show Harrington what could be done with his land." Aviloh sat at his desk, pulled out a pen, and shuffled some papers. "Now, if you'll leave, I've got work to do."

"Not until we're finished." Mannheim walked to his desk. "Where were you the night Longfellow was murdered, January twelfth?"

Aviloh picked up a pencil and started writing. "You know where I was. I was at the Monterey Casino. I told you that before, and you can check with the pit boss."

"So you said. Guess the time's come to check that out. In the meantime, don't plan any long trips." Mannheim pointed at Bushwhacker. "That goes for you too."

FORTY

Harry Todd maneuvered the police sedan in the long line of traffic that inched along Highway 111. "Do you think Aviloh might have been responsible for that freeway disaster?"

"Cue was a more likely culprit for that backseat porno caper involving Carlos Grandee, but for the accident itself? I believe someone else pulled that off."

Todd thought about it. "Who besides Cue, and the guy intercepting phone calls, would have known that Grandee was meeting with the bitch pretending to be Tatiana?"

"If we knew that, we'd probably have our killer. That's why we're interviewing all these freakin' suspects." Mannheim looked ahead and scowled. "What the hell's holding up traffic? What're we doing on this goddamn road, in the first place? It's always crowded with tourists and old farts who don't know enough to take an alternate route. Flash your lights. Let's get this goddamn crate out of here. We've got an appointment to make."

Todd looked to either side. "Even if I did turn on the lights, we couldn't get anywhere; there's construction on both sides. People have nowhere to go."

The roar of motorcycles came up from behind. An instant later, two sped past them, weaving in and around the stationary cars.

Todd pointed at them. "Did you see those bikers? That's Aviloh and Bushwhacker. Those crazy sonsobitches are on dirt bikes. Where in the hell are they going in such a hurry?"

"Don't know, but wherever it is, they'll probably get there before we get out of this shitty traffic."

• • •

At 4:25 p.m., Josh used the heavy door clapper twice at the Longfellow estate, then waited a few seconds before knocking again. He pushed the backlighted doorbell, the one that played the "Beer Barrel Polka" theme, and still got no response.

He pushed the massive door handle. To his surprise, the door opened onto the darkened foyer. He walked slowly into the dimly lit great room. Without lights and without people milling about, the room took on a foreboding appearance. Its somber furnishings, dark drapes, and massive chandelier were more awesome than beautiful. Josh remembered that same chandelier was used to hang Longfellow, and he moved quickly away from under it.

"Hello—anyone home?"

No response.

Josh looked around—no food, no drinks; the place looked ghostly.

Concerned, he gazed at the circular stairways in the living room as they wound upward symmetrically to the second floor. The beauty of that art nouveau structure with its graceful turns and floral designs now seemed constricted and cold.

A faint quivery voice called, "Josh."

He stopped and strained to hear. "Prissy?"

He went to the curved stairway and looked up.

"Josh?"

This time he was certain the voice wafted from upstairs.

"Prissy?"

"Are you coming, Josh? We're waiting for you."

The faint melancholy strains of Saint-Saëns's *Danse Macabre* now floated down, along with the sweet, mawkish odor of marijuana.

Panic began to rise in his throat. He looked at his watch: 4:30. Where were the other landowners? They should have been there by now.

"Josh, we're still waiting for you." High-pitched laughter accompanied the music.

The urge to leave immediately took hold. His temporal arteries pounded, and a dreadful uneasiness gripped him. Whatever was being conducted upstairs was not for him.

Turning, Josh started for the front of the house. On the parquet floor, he heard the footsteps of two men. Around the corner came Dan Aviloh, and behind him a larger, swarthy, muscular man with a ponytail.

Aviloh squinted in the dim light and stopped several feet in front of Josh. "Well, well, hello, Doc." Extending his hand, he said, "You alone?" Dan's breath reeked of gin and his sclerae were bloodshot.

Josh had an even stronger urge to leave. "Yes, I'm alone."

"Good." Aviloh made a half turn to introduce his foreman. "Doc Harrington, this is Clarence Bushmill, better known to friends and enemies alike as Bushwhacker."

Josh thought this was hardly the time for social amenities as Aviloh went on to explain that Bushwhacker was a member of the Morongo tribe, pure southwestern Indian except for an Anglo grandfather who stirred the pot with his dick.

At that, Aviloh laughed. Bushwhacker didn't.

"It's time for me to leave. Doesn't look to me like there's going to be a business meeting." Josh attempted to sidestep the two.

"Wait a minute, wait one goddamn minute, Doc." Aviloh caught Josh's arm and brought his ruddy face next to his. "You can't leave now; the party hasn't even started."

"Party? I thought this was a meeting about community resistance to land development."

"Sure it is. Now let's go upstairs."

Every instinct of doubt and repugnance gripped Josh. "No."

Aviloh and Bushwhacker positioned themselves on either side of him, putting their arms around his waist and forcibly directing him up the spiral staircase.

"Hey, take your hands off me! I'm not going anywhere with you two."

Bushwhacker produced a hunting knife and held it against Josh's side.

Josh froze, but Bushwhacker increased his hold on Josh's waist and with his other hand, pushed the tip of the blade more firmly into his side.

"C'mon, Doc, don't fight us," Aviloh said. "We're asking you, nice-like, to join a discussion group on proper land usage. That's why you're here, right?" Aviloh smiled sardonically. "Either you're with us on this proposition or you're against us. If you're with us, there'll be no problem; if you're not, maybe we can convince you otherwise."

Josh broke out in a cold sweat and was practically carried up the stairs by his captors. The last time he'd felt this fear, he was slogging on the Mekong Delta in 'Nam.

Aviloh pushed the chamber door open and Josh became momentarily stunned by the scene before him.

In the dim, candlelit room among flickering shadows, the swelling, repetitive refrain from *Samson and Delilah* provided the background for the sensuous gyrations of the almost-nude female dancers whirling and moving their arms gracefully, like wings, in sheer, flowing costumes. Their identities were concealed by grotesque African tribal masks.

"I refuse to have anything to do with this."

"Too bad, but you do." Aviloh shoved him inside.

Votive candles burned in a broad oval pattern around a draped, elongated table.

It reminded Josh of a coffin.

Two masked females in flowing robes moved rhythmically to the increasing tempo of the music, then whirled their filmy costumes around him. Instinctively, he ducked to avoid their contact.

Muffled laughter behind the masks gave Josh no hint as to the identity of those voices. Again he made a futile attempt to wiggle free from the grasps of the two enforcers.

Aviloh put his mouth to Josh's ear. "Easy, Doc, we don't want to hurt ya. You're our most important guest, but ya gotta cooperate."

"Cooperate, for what?"

"We're gonna make an offer on your land that ya can't refuse." Dan laughed.

"That land is not for sale to you," Josh protested.

"We kinda figured that might be your attitude at first, so we prepared this little party for you to reconsider."

Josh stared at what he imagined might be a sacrificial altar and pushed furiously against his restrainers. "Go to hell!"

As he said it, one of the dancers stopped and moved deftly behind him. She lifted the lower end of his jacket and pulled his shirt out of his trousers. Before he could protest, he felt the sting of a syringe needle prick his buttocks.

"What was that?" Josh tried to turn around.

"Just a little shot, Doc. It's goin' to make ya a lot more cooperative," Aviloh said.

Almost immediately, Josh had difficulty focusing; the features of the room and the people blurred, then disappeared in blackness.

*　*　*

"He's out."

The masked dancer who'd injected him pointed toward the table. "Put him there."

Bushwhacker hefted Harrington and carried him to the draped table encircled by candles.

Two of the dancers quickly removed his clothing.

He lay nude on the draped table with an overhead light that beamed directly on his pelvic area. A second light was directed at his face.

"Get me soap and water," one of the women directed. "I want him nice and clean. Be sure light and camera are on his face and down here, so we get proper identification. I don't want to go through this again."

"Why all the goddamn sterility?" Bushwhacker laughed. "You gonna operate?"

"In my profession, to be clean is necessary. And in a manner of speaking, I am going to operate."

"Hell, none of them whores I ever saw asked me to clean up like that," Bushwhacker said.

"When you shop in cheap places, you get cheap treatment. Besides, Harrington is entitled to the very best, and I am the best."

FORTY-ONE

The dashboard clock read 4:27. Todd adhered to the posted twenty-mile-per-hour speed limit. Mannheim sat up and looked around, his deep-set eyes canvassing the enormous estates with their spacious lawns and stately royal palms. He shook his head. "Jeez-us, it's quiet around here, like Forest Lawn." He raised his shoulders and brought them back, opening his jacket to expose his holstered revolver.

Todd glanced sideways. "You expecting a little action?"

With a sarcastic side-mouthed comment, Mannheim said, "Every now and then I fantasize being 'Dirty Harry.'" He grew introspective looking at the community of multimillion-dollar homes, each one with more bedrooms and crappers than any six people could possibly use at one time. Often there was only one couple schlepping around, waiting for the grim reaper. It was like they were sitting in a giant funeral parlor waiting for their number to be called. "Look at these goddamn mausoleums, will ya?"

"I'm glad you're sounding like your own cheerful self."

"Just being observant. Shit happens in these places too. Think about the house we're coming to, the Longfellows', one goddamn monstrosity that has death and decadence stamped all over it. That crazy killing and hanging . . ." Mannheim pointed to the large edifice at the end of the block. "That's it, over there."

Todd nodded. "I see it. Do you think Prissy Longfellow is a black widow spider who eats her lovers after they finish?"

"If you ask me, it's probably before. Step on it. I've got a bad feeling."

* * *

The gothic grandfather clock in a corner of the great room bonged once at 4:45.

"Get those lights focused on the action!" Aviloh shouted at Bushwhacker. "And be sure that camera's recording."

Aviloh remained by the TV monitor, watching the action.

Bushwhacker seemed to disapprove. "We're going through a hell of a lot of trouble just to get this guy to sign over a piece of property. If you'd let me at him, I'd have that paper signed in three minutes."

"Listen, you muscle-bound dumbass, how many times do I have to remind you? You were supposed to run interference with that goddamn truck on the freeway, not ram that limo and fuck up the operation royally. We wouldn' hafta do this if ya'd followed instructions."

"Well, it wasn't my fault. That stupid limo driver veered toward me. Before I could get outta his way—wham! I had no choice. That's when that bullet-head lost control and smashed that baby into that overpass support."

"Yeah, yeah, just keep pointing that camera. I'll handle the lights." Aviloh's movements were not impaired by his limp as he adjusted the spotlights and placed a compact disc into an audio player. "This movie's gonna be one goddamn masterpiece, complete with classy background music." One of the three masked dancers remained seated in a darkened corner while the other two hovered over Josh's nude body.

FORTY-TWO

Maggie and Suzanne handed their shopping bags to Horace, who placed them in the trunk of the Jaguar parked along El Paseo Drive. "I think we should call on Josh and pull him away from that group of contractors meeting at Prissy's," Maggie said as she slipped into the backseat of the limo. "What do you think?"

"Sounds like a fine idea."

Suzanne read the address to Horace. He punched it into the GPS and headed toward the Rancho Mirage estate without a word.

Fifteen minutes later, Maggie sat forward in her seat and surveyed the impressive home as they drove toward the entryway. "It looks as if the meeting might be over. I see only Josh's car."

Uneasiness washed over her. The moment Horace pulled to a stop; she reached for the door handle. Even so, the chauffeur beat her to the door and opened it for her.

"Why don't you two stay here? I'll go to the house and see what's going on." Maggie clutched her purse and started for the estate entrance.

"Hold on, I'm going with you!" Suzanne called after her.

Before Maggie could dissuade her, Suzanne motioned for Horace to stay in the vehicle and ran after her.

. . .

Josh's eyelids began to flutter as he emerged from his unconscious state. Agitated, he bolted to a sitting position. A woman was at his lower abdomen. "Who are you? What are you doing?" Josh lashed out, striking an upright lamp that crashed to the floor. Despite his groggy state, his strength was uninhibited, he kicked the shoulders of the woman near his groin and she went sprawling on the floor.

Aviloh rushed toward Josh, only to be struck in the face with a roundhouse blow that sent him careening backward, his arms rotating like windmill blades.

Bushwhacker came at Josh from the opposite side and leaped at him. Not even in his state of hyperexcitability could Josh fend off the man's brutish strength. Bushwhacker pulled him off the table and pinned him to the floor.

Aviloh, still dazed, shook his head, then felt his bloodied nose and aching jaw. He attempted to stand but fell, then rose again to walk unsteadily toward Josh and Bushwhacker.

The smaller man bent over Josh, his nose dripping blood onto Josh's face. "You shouldn't have done that."

Josh attempted to turn his head aside but was stopped.

Aviloh gripped Josh's jaw between his fingers and pulled a folded form out of the back pocket of his pants. "Listen, Doc, enough fuckin' around. You're gonna sign this goddamn deed over to me, or else."

"Or else what?" Josh grunted through his clenched jaw.

"Or else we're going to show this blow job to every newspaper and TV station in the Coachella Valley. And the medical society. How does that grab you?"

"You can go to hell. I'm not signing anything."

Bushwhacker, with Aviloh's assistance, grappled with Josh to tie his wrists and ankles with nylon cord and lift him back onto the table.

Josh fought them all the way. The rope cut into his skin. Exhausted, he lay back, taking in deep breaths, but his anger flashed.

Aviloh held a handkerchief under his bloodied nose. "Sorry you feel this way, Doc."

While Bushwhacker made sure Josh wouldn't move again, Aviloh limped across the dim candlelit room to return with a weighty object. He brought it close to Josh's face. "Take a good look. That's right, it's an andiron, just like the one that smashed old Petey's skull. In one minute, you're gonna wish you'd been smarter."

"You'll never get away with killing me."

"Sez you. I've gotten away with it before." Aviloh sneered, "If you ain't gonna sign, I'll draw up more papers, complete with your forged signature showing that you deeded the property to us for an agreed price—our price."

"Go to hell, Aviloh."

"Maybe I will, but you're going first. We're gonna put your fuckin' body into your own car, then haul it out to the desert and torch it. It'll just be another derelict shell. Hell, they probably won't find your bones for ten years."

At that moment, Josh knew he was running out of time. He read the insanity in Aviloh's eyes. His only hope was to stall. Hope for a chance to escape. "I thought you and Pete were close friends."

Aviloh's eyes widened like those of a man on the verge of complete madness. He leaned close and spoke above a whisper in Josh's ear. "Oh, yeah, we were close all right. Until I found out he was fucking around with my wife. I threatened to kill her, but she only laughed in my face. Told me I didn't have the guts."

Aviloh held a handkerchief under his bloodied nose. "Hell, we hadn't fucked for so long, I figured I didn't need her. And I wasn't goin' to do time for killin' her, either." Again, he whispered into Josh's ear. "Well, I got back at both of them. I started playing around with Prissy, and ya know what? Prissy was more'n willn'. She talked about gettin' rid of Petey. Said she'd take over the company, and we'd be partners. I told her I'd think about it. That pissed her off, and I swear she started playing mind games with me."

Keep him talking. Josh swallowed against his dry throat. "Why didn't both of you just get divorces? It would have been easier."

"We talked about it, Prissy and me, but she said she'd lose too much in a settlement. Matter a fact, I would too."

"After you killed Peter, why did you hang him?"

"Shit. I didn't plan it that way. Believe me, now I wish to hell I didn't. I think about it all the time. The day it happened, Prissy and me had an early dinner at the casino. I was planning on a little party with her at the hotel afterward, but she said she had to hurry home because you were going to be at the house. She was gonna try to convince ya to sell your land to her. Once you did, the two of us could develop it.

"I took her home and headed back to the casino for a little more action. I happened to look at the passenger seat and saw Prissy's wallet. Christ, I knew she had her driver's license, insurance ID, and credit cards in it, and she had to take that long trip to Riverside in the morning. I headed back to her home. Petey's truck was in the driveway. I guess he had already talked with you. Anyway, I parked on the street facing Petey's den, which was lit up. When I got closer, I saw Petey and Prissy. They were arguin', yellin' and cussin' pretty good. Petey shoves her and she falls ass-over-teakettle across the room. She's bawlin', holdin' her face in her hands, and crawls to the sofa."

As long as Aviloh was on a talking jag, Josh was willing to listen. The longer the man talked, the longer he lived. Again, Josh swallowed. "Go on."

"I musta gone nuts when I seen that. I pushed the window up and jumped into the middle of that damn fracas. I threw a right hook into Petey's midsection. He doubled up. I smashed him in the face with my knee."

Aviloh's voice rose in pitch. "Petey staggered toward the fireplace. I ran after him. I was getting crazier by the second, I swear it, till I didn't know what the hell I was doin'. I picked up the andiron and smashed his head. Hell, I didn't want to kill him, but shit, after I hit him and I heard the crunch, I knew he was good as dead. Damn, he bled like a gored ox. I had his blood all over me."

Aviloh's lips thinned. "Then Prissy goes all bananas. I try to calm her down, but she yells at me not to touch her with my bloody paws. She gets the crazy notion to hang him, make it look like a devil-worship thing or some such shit to confuse the cops. I got the rope from the drapes, and the two of us string him up. I never seen anything that looked so God-awful bad; he's blue in the face and his eyes are poppin'out. The two of us scrubbed that damn place down with rags and towels and put them in the washer with a lot of bleach.

I took the andiron with me, and the next morning threw it on your adobe property before I went to work. I didn't expect anyone to find it in the bushes. Hell, even if they did, they wouldn't make the connection. That's the whole story. Now ya know too much, and ya can kiss your sorry ass goodbye."

● ● ●

Maggie was about to ring the doorbell when she noticed that the door was slightly ajar. She looked at Suzanne and shrugged. She pushed the door slowly, and both women tiptoed into the darkened foyer.

Maggie remembered signing the guest book on the console from her last visit at Peter Longfellow's memorial. There was no guest book. Why were there no lights? The women advanced cautiously into the great room, then looked to the top of the winding stairway, toward the room from which the sounds of laughter and music emanated. Maggie's heart thumped. She extended her arm behind to stop Suzanne and whispered, "Listen—voices and music—'Boléro'?"

Both advanced slowly up the stairwell. At the top of the landing they stopped. Maggie inched toward the door, which was opened just a crack. She pushed it slightly to hear the rhythmic, repetitive phrases becoming fortissimo. Maggie peeked into the room and jerked backward, bumping into Suzanne. Horrified, she reached into her purse.

● ● ●

Todd drove into the circular driveway and parked behind the Jaguar limo. "Well, I'll be damned, look who's here." Todd pointed through the windshield to the two motorcycles near the entry. "We may be interrupting a little cabal."

"Who's that?" Mannheim walked toward the Jag and knocked on the chauffeur's window, flashing his badge and signaling him to lower it. "Who're you waiting for?"

"Mrs. Grandee and Mrs. Harrington." The driver looked at his watch. "They went inside about five minutes ago." The chauffeur hesitated and looked at his side mirror. "Do you know your left front tire is almost flat? You can't ride on that."

Mannheim looked at the flattened tire, snorted, spat, and muttered, "Shit."

Todd, standing next to him, nodded. "I should have known. All those damn carpenter nails on that construction site. I'll call the tow service."

"Not now. Come on."

Mannheim led Todd to the entryway. When they noticed the door ajar, they stepped into the darkened foyer and pulled out their guns. In a half whisper, Mannheim said, "Something stinks here. Where the hell is everyone? And there's that goddamn smell again. What is it?"

Harry sniffed. "You're slipping, Mannheim. That's a combination of marijuana and scented candles. Do you hear that music coming from above?"

"Yeah, let's go."

Mannheim climbed carefully up the stairway, two steps at a time. Todd followed with his Glock at the ready.

* * *

Aviloh held the handkerchief against his nose and motioned at Bushwhacker. "At the count of three, bash in his skull."

Bushwhacker, his eyes bulging, took a deep breath, lifted the andiron slowly over his head, and waited.

"One—two—"

"Hold it!"

Standing in the open doorway, her legs spread for stability and her arms extended, Maggie held a Derringer.

"Stop!" a woman shouted from the back of the room.

Almost simultaneously, a second command came from behind Maggie.

"Put the gun down, missy!" Mannheim rushed past her, but as he did so, his shoulder collided with Maggie's arm. The forward motion set off her Derringer.

POP!

A chorus of screaming voices filled the room . . . mainly from the women behind their ugly masks.

But it was when the andiron fell out of Bushwhacker's hand, narrowly missing Josh's head, that Maggie realized where her shot had hit.

Bushwhacker dropped to his knees and grasped his right shoulder. Blood squirted between his fingers and ran down his arm.

"I'll take that peashooter now, Mrs. Harrington." Officer Todd walked up to her and held out his hand. "Best if you go downstairs now with your lady friend. Mannheim and I will see to this mess."

Maggie handed him her pistol but ignored his order to leave. She ran straight for Josh. "Oh, my poor darling, what have they done to you?"

Josh, shivering, covered his genitals with his bound hands. Maggie embraced him, then grabbed his clothes from a nearby chair. She untied his hands and ankles and helped him dress.

Suzanne had wisely retreated down the stairs when ordered.

With his revolver pointed at Aviloh's head, Mannheim said, "Stand up, prick. Raise your hands and walk over to the wall. " He motioned to the masked women. "Ladies, don't move. No one leaves this goddamn coven till I find out what's going on."

Over his shoulder, Mannheim said to Todd, "Call for backup. Have them send an ambulance for the bleeding asshole there." He looked at Bushwacker, who still remained on his knees. "Okay, buddy-boy, get up and walk to the wall beside your boss."

Once the man did as told, Mannheim looked back at the masked women. "You beauties, go sit in the chairs and don't move. Keep your hands at your sides where I can see them. Do as I say and don't interrupt me." He pointed his revolver at the figure on the left. "Take off your mask and put it on the floor—slowly." He maintained just enough tactile pressure on the trigger in case someone became aggressive.

Harry Todd, gripping his pistol with both hands, stood at Mannheim's side. The first female removed her mask and bent forward to place on the floor. Mannheim watched closely as she shook her head to fluff her hair.

"Well, well, if it isn't our hostess with the mostest, Mrs. Penelope Longfellow." Mannheim commanded, "Tell us, what the hell's goin' on here?"

"I have nothing to say to you. I want to talk to my lawyer."

"You'll get your chance, sweetheart; now sit back and keep your hands where I can see them. Any sudden movement and you're dead, understand?" He looked at the woman next to Prissy. "All right, number two, take off your mask and put it on the floor, slowly—I said slowly. Now let's see your charming face."

Mannheim and Todd watched expectantly as she lifted her mask.

"I'll be goddamned." Mannheim nodded, then shook his head. "You haven't learned a thing, have you? You're a pathological liar, and that's just for starters. You remember pleading and telling us you wouldn't get into any more trouble? And here you are, up to your perfumed ass in more shit. Tatiana, I hope to hell they throw the book at you. And don't tell me you just stumbled into this cesspool thinking it was a Russian tearoom."

Tatiana raised her arm as if preparing to speak in her defense when Mannheim shouted, "Put your arm down and don't say a goddamn thing!"

Aviloh, with his swollen and obstructed nose, yelled in a nasal voice, "Jesus, Mannheim, get me to a doc. I'm bleeding to death."

"You might be lucky if you do before a jury gets through with you."

"Now wait a goddamn minute. All I wanted was to scare the doc here. I got witnesses to prove it. What's more, we're going to sue *you* for breaking and entering and for shooting for no damn good reason."

"I haven't fired a shot."

"Then I'll sue Harrington."

"Try it." Mannheim turned toward the third female, who sat apart in the shadowy corner of the room. "Okay, number three, remove the mask and put it on the floor. Easy, now."

Mannheim turned to Aviloh. "Recognize this lady, hot shot?"

Aviloh squinted into the dark recess of the room. His eyes bulged with eventual recognition. *"Sherri?"*

She stood and shouted in defiance of Mannheim's order, "You contemptible bastard!" Her eyes blazed at the beleaguered Aviloh, whose bloodied face darkened in anguish and confusion. "I'd never consent to be a party to murder—unless it was yours—and to think you were crazy enough to want to kill the doctor for that land. How insane are you?" Before Aviloh could respond, she added, "You thought I didn't know you were whoring around with this vile hussy, this bitch." She pointed to Prissy, who looked away. "I saw a copy of the invitation you sent to Dr. Harrington and thought I'd better get here to see what you and your bitchy friend had planned."

"Jesus, baby, you know I love you and wouldn't do anything to hurt you."

"Shut up, you miserable bastard!" Sherri continued yelling, "I'll tell everyone what a creep you really are. I'll let them know that Peter Longfellow was my real lover, a man who made me feel like a woman, a man who was sweet and caring and treated me respectfully, like you never could."

She turned and glared at Prissy. "But Peter was married to this creature who refused to give him a divorce."

Prissy turned her head aside.

"And you," she glared at Aviloh again, "you murdered him!" Her fury reached a crescendo as she rushed toward Aviloh sitting on the floor, looking at her with pleading eyes. Before Mannheim could intervene, she kicked the side of Aviloh's bloodied face with such force that tears, blood, and mucus flew off. When he put up his hands to protect his face from further assault and attempted to stand, Sherri kicked him in the groin. After a loud "Oof," Aviloh bent over, grabbed his crotch with his bloody nose rag, and fell moaning to the floor.

When Mannheim ran to restrain Sherri, Todd walked toward Aviloh and ordered him to put his hands behind his back to be cuffed. Aviloh brought his left wrist back and Todd locked the ring on the left wrist. As Todd reached for his right wrist, Aviloh spun around to deliver a stunning blow with his right to Todd's jaw. Todd stumbled backward, slipping and sliding till he struck his head on the opposite wall, then fell in a heap. Aviloh ran to the dazed Todd, snatched his

Glock, and pointed it at Mannheim, whose back had been turned as he tended to the distraught Sherri.

Aware of the commotion, Mannheim raised his revolver and turned, then stopped when he realized Aviloh already had him in his sights.

In a loud staccato, Aviloh yelled, "Drop it, copper. Kick it over. Don't fuck with me, or I'll kill you. I swear it." His animal ferocity had pushed him beyond reasoning and Mannheim sensed it. He had been in similar situations and knew better than to challenge a maniacal outlaw. Besides, there were too many people in harm's way. Slowly, Mannheim placed his .45 on the floor in front of him and put his hands up, never taking his eyes off Aviloh. He pushed the gun with his toe toward Aviloh.

"I know you got a cap gun in your pocket. Take that out too and put it on the floor. Try using it, and I'll kill ya."

When Mannheim did as ordered, Aviloh reached down and picked up the guns, shoved the .45 in his belt, and put the Derringer in his pocket. He held Todd's pistol in his free right hand. The handcuffs dangled from his left wrist. "I'm gettin' the hell outta here and don't follow me."

He ran out of the room, then raced down the circular stairway and out the front door.

Mannheim followed, but not so close as to be an easy target. Josh, angered and humiliated by what he had been put through, followed Mannheim.

Maggie shouted, "Josh, stay here!" She started after him, hoping to stop him by grabbing his shirtsleeve as he ran past her.

Outside, Suzanne stepped in front of Maggie when she came running out. The impact nearly knocked both of them over. "Maggie, stop! Don't follow them."

Aviloh jammed Todd's gun in his belt and hopped on his dirt motorcycle. He tried to kickstart the engine.

Mannheim, a few steps behind Aviloh, yelled, "Aviloh, give it up, you can't get away!"

"Fuck you, copper. I'm not stickin' around to let 'em put a noose around my neck." He kicked the pedal several times until the engine roared to life, and he raced out at a 45-five degree angle as he left the circular driveway.

Horace, behind the wheel of the limo, watched the harried movements of the motorcyclist with the handcuffs dangling from his left wrist. Mannheim ran toward the limo, with Josh in pursuit.

"Did you see that sonofabitch run out of here?" Mannheim waved his hand at Horace.

"Yes, sir, he's probably heading for the I-10. You want to catch him?"

Mannheim dove into the passenger's side of the car. "Damn right I do. Damn, damn, damn, I don't have my piece, and besides, he's got a helluva head start."

Josh jumped into the back.

Mannheim looked over the seat. "Where the hell do you think you're going, Doc? Get out of here, you can't come along. My ass is in a sling as it is. I don't need a felony reckless endangerment charge thrown at me."

"I'm staying," Josh panted. "I want to be sure that bastard gets caught. He was ready to kill me up there."

Mannheim shook his head and looked at Horace. "You really think you can catch him?"

"I'll catch him. I'll make him look like he was going backwards. That dirt bike has a max speed of about eighty. This car can do twice that." Horace slipped the car into gear and spun out after the motorcycle. "By the way, there's a piece inside the armrest. You might need it."

Mannheim opened the armrest and pulled out the chamois-covered Python. He flipped the barrel, checked the chambers, opened the safety, then placed the gun on the seat between his legs. He yanked out his cell phone and started punching numbers. "I'll notify the highway patrol if we ever spot that sonofabitch."

"Sounds good." When Horace reached the end of the private drive, the rear tires squealed and the car catapulted toward the I-10.

In the rear, Josh rapped on the window that separated the chauffeur's compartment from the passenger side. He signaled Horace to lower the window to allow him to converse directly. Despite the high rate of speed, Horace hit the gear box selector and continued to put the Jag's alternate manual transmission through its paces, heading north on Bob Hope Drive toward the I-10. On a posted fifty-mile-per-hour drive, the Jag slipped eel-like around slower traffic. The purring of the 600-horsepower engine gave no hint of strain as the speedometer oscillated between ninety-five and one hundred miles per hour.

Mannheim looked from side to side, then forward, and slunk down in his seat. He pulled on the seat belt and snapped it into place. Out of the corner of his mouth he muttered, "You just went through a red light at Gerald Ford Drive." If he had expected a reaction from Horace, he didn't get one.

The green signs of the freeway on ramps came into view, indicating east and west approaches. "Are we going west toward L.A. or east toward Phoenix?" Horace asked.

Mannheim rubbed his jaw. "Police records gave an Indio address for Aviloh. Most of these assholes drive toward their home territory. They figure they'll ditch their vehicle, then run for cover to some sympathetic neighbor."

"Got it." Horace turned the Jag onto the eastbound ramp and shifted gear to put it into a low-flying mode. A subtle jerk from the power train resulted in squirt-like acceleration, accompanied by the low rumbling of the four mufflers and exhaust pipes. The speedometer read 110 miles per hour as the vehicle moved with precise lateral movement and no appreciable sway. The veil of darkness had obscured most other vehicles beyond two hundred yards. Only the red taillights were visible, and Aviloh's bike had none.

Josh craned his neck forward, then to either side, hoping to get a glimpse of the bike. He knew the lugs on Aviloh's tires made less surface contact and provided greater risk for spills. The injuries from high-speed motorcycle accidents often resulted in crippling injuries and even amputations, if not death. He recalled long hours in the OR when he attempted to repair mangled extremities from motorcycle crashes. Getting shattered bones aligned and fixed with hardware was tricky enough, but suturing nerve ends was tedious and often unsuccessful. At times the blood supply was compromised beyond tissue viability and gangrene ensued. To complicate matters, large patches of skin were often missing, or excessive swelling made skin closure impossible. Plastic repair with skin flaps or substitute materials was necessary.

He slid forward in his seat and blinked at the sight of a motorcycle about fifty yards ahead. "There it is!"

"I see it, sir." Horace turned on the high beams to target the motorcycle. The Jag had decelerated when another vehicle pulled in front of it.

With deft flicks of his wrists, he made the Jag leap to the right lane, then speed forward to pass the interloper. Like a crab, the Jag jumped back into the left lane and was less than thirty yards behind the motorcycle. Horace flashed his lights on and off, hoping Aviloh would have the good sense to pull over. Aviloh ignored the signal and maxed out his acceleration to eighty-five miles per hour.

Mannheim fingered the .357 Python in his lap and rolled down the passenger's window. He ordered Horace, "Get closer—maybe we can convince the sonofabitch to slow down and move to the side of the road."

Josh swallowed. "You plan on using that thing?"

"Only to give a warning shot—unless he shoots first."

The reassuring wail of sirens and the flashing of red and blue lights pierced the darkness from behind. "The cavalry's arrived," Mannheim said.

Aviloh, traveling at eighty miles per hour, looked over his left shoulder. His left hand was extended with the handcuffs dangling from his wrist. He fired a round. The bullet missed its intended mark but hit an unsuspecting car in the right lane. The vehicle jerked to the right shoulder and squealed to a stop. Mannheim's facial muscles pulsed with tension as he leaned out the window, pointing the gun at the motorcycle. "That crazy sonofabitch is looking to die."

Aviloh fired again. The bullet grazed the Jag's bulletproof windshield in the right upper corner, leaving a radiating web of fine cracks.

A police chopper had joined the chase; its spotlight targeted the motorcycle. Aviloh, ignoring the beam, turned his head and extended his left arm backward to fire again. Only this time the opened handcuff caught the edge of the rear fender, stopping him.

They watched as Aviloh tugged repeatedly and furiously to free it. Then it happened. He lost control of the bike. It careened wildly across the median, spewing dust and dirt, and slid into the westbound traffic.

Heading for him was a massive Peterbilt. Its air brakes hissed and screamed as the giant carrier shuddered and skidded, tires squealing, laying down a haze of blue smoke and thick rubber residue. As if in slow motion, parts of Aviloh and the motorcycle were crushed under the twin axle wheels of the semi. His remains splattered across the highway and the motorcycle squashed like an aluminum can, with parts scattered under the semi.

Horace slammed on his own brakes and expertly brought the Jag to a halt on the barren median a short distance from the truck.

"Jeez-zus, the sonofabitch caught it this time," Mannheim said. Horace nodded.

Josh forced back the bile that rose in his throat.

Several cars had already stopped and their occupants ran to the scene. The Jag was followed by the patrol cars, their warning lights adding to the heightened confusion. Immediately, flares were placed well behind and to the side of the accident.

The trucker, ashen and jittery, climbed down from his driver's perch and approached the police apprehensively. "Christ, I never saw him coming, honest-to-God. I didn't know what I hit. Where'd he come from?"

An officer led the trucker to the backseat of a patrol car, where he could regroup and answer some questions.

Mannheim, with a flashlight given to him by Horace, walked the length of the semi toward the rear with its tandem axles. The helicopter pilot trained his light on the carnage below, then flew off.

Josh walked up beside Mannheim. Despite his professionalism, he was visibly moved by the carnage. "What a grotesque hodge-podge of body parts!" He identified the mangled and crushed remains of the corpse with its flattened skull and exposed thoracic and abdominal viscera. The putrid smell of death was already identifiable. Aviloh's skin had been ripped off. His facial muscles were peppered with ground-in debris. His nose, lips, and brows had been torn away, and brain matter had been squashed to either side. His sinuses were laid bare, and remnants of his flattened mouth with its multi-fractured jaw and teeth presented a hideously wide sardonic smile.

"That crazy sonofabitch . . ." Mannheim's voice was flat, without emotion. "He won't be killing or threatening anyone anymore." He leaned over the mangled corpse, then picked up several metallic fragments . . . gun parts, a barrel and a chamber from his own piece. "Shit. There goes six hundred and fifty bucks down the toilet."

The detective straightened and looked at the remains once more. "This guy was vermin. He deserved to be squashed." He pushed past a group of onlookers, photographers with flashing lights, and EMTs who were going about bagging body parts.

As Josh turned to follow, he caught sight of Aviloh's left leg, twisted and obviously broken. The brace remained intact.

Eventually, Josh and Horace caught up with the detective.

Seeing them, Mannheim turned. "You guys might as well leave. When it comes time for you to testify, I'll get in touch."

"What about you?"

"Don't worry about me. Once I'm through here, I'll catch a lift back to the station with one of the CHPs."

Josh looked back at the accident. "As much as I disliked the man, it was a horrible way to die."

Mannheim sneered. "You think this sonofabitch would have expressed as much sentiment if Bushwhacker had dented *your* skull?"

FORTY-THREE

The bright lights of the Jaguar lit the circular driveway of the Longfellow mansion and stopped in front of the recessed entrance. Maggie and Suzanne waved eagerly from the front door. Detective Todd stood off to one side, holding a cloth to his head. He looked at his watch, obviously peeved at having been detained.

Josh opened the front passenger door and although emotionally and physically exhausted, ran to Maggie's welcoming arms.

"What happened?" Without releasing Josh, Maggie took a short step back and searched his eyes.

"I'll explain later." He moved her gently aside. "Right now I've got to find my wallet and a few other things upstairs in that damned den of iniquity."

"I'll go with you."

"No, I'll be gone only a moment or two. You keep Suzanne company." Josh was about to raise the yellow tape that cordoned off the front entrance and duck under it when Detective Todd stepped in front of him.

"Sorry, Doc, you can't go in there."

Impatient with protocol, Josh sidestepped Detective Todd and brushed past him. Todd reached for his gun, then realized it had been taken by Aviloh. He yelled, "You could face serious charges, Doc."

There was no response.

Todd called out again halfheartedly, "Don't touch anything, and watch where you step."

Josh ran through the foyer and the great room to the winding stairway. He bolted the stairs two at a time.

The sight of the bedroom/altar caused a visceral response . . . a revulsion that immobilized him momentarily He focused on a spot beneath the chair where his clothes had been thrown. Lying on the floor were his wallet, cell phone, a pocket knife, and loose change. He examined the wallet for contents and placed it in his pocket. Then he walked to the center of the room and gazed at the eerie paintings and symbols on the walls and tried to comprehend their arcane meaning. He saw things he had not or could not have noticed when he was forced into the room by Aviloh and Bushwhacker. While staring at the unholy artifacts he sniffed the lingering scent of burning tallow, incense, marijuana, and gunpowder. He walked carefully to avoid Aviloh's and Bushwhacker's bloody droppings.

The tribal masks lying on the floor looked even more sinister in the silence of the empty room. Shadows from the flickering candles seemed to exaggerate and even move the ugly features of the scowling mouths and the hollowed eye sockets.

Just as he was about to leave, he caught sight of a foreboding Victorian dark-mahogany antique armoire, a seven-foot-high piece set against the back wall. As a child he had been frightened by the very appearance of a similar one in his grandmother's home. He had been admonished by a maiden aunt never to go near it. As a child, he imagined it harbored some scary, evil things.

Now the piece of furniture beckoned him, drawing him to it. Josh hesitated, not exactly certain he wanted to see what was inside. His curiosity won out. He pulled on one of the scrolled door handles, then the other. Neither door opened. The need to see inside heightened. Pulling out his pocket knife, he selected a narrow blade and inserted it into the blackened keyhole with its ornamental escutcheon.

A click signaled the release and Josh pulled on the handles of the tall doors, which opened with predictable squeaking. A number of black caps and gowns with tented hoods and perforations for eyes like those worn by the Ku Klux Klan hung in a row from a high rod.

Josh leaned over and opened a drawer below the hanging clothes to find several stacked muslin dolls, voodoo dolls, like the one Suzanne had shown him—the one sent to Carlos with the cryptic message. He pulled open another drawer and found swatches of colored sackcloth used for making doll clothes. A third drawer held long hatpin needles and spools of colored thread. He guessed at the contents of the fourth drawer before opening it, and he was right—it contained several shoe boxes and tablets of writing paper, along with magazines and newspapers from which words had been scissored out. With a curse, he slammed the drawers and shut the long doors of the armoire.

Josh turned his back and walked out of the room, reluctant to turn around for one last look.

As he stepped out of the mansion to where Maggie, Suzanne, and Detective Todd waited, a CHP squad car arrived. Detective Mannheim and two uniformed officers stepped out.

Mannheim looked at Josh. "Well, Doc, I can't say it hasn't been interesting. You and the Missus are damned lucky to have survived this crazy caper." He approached closely and whispered in his ear, "You missed an opportunity to become a porn star."

Josh looked away in disgust and refused to comment.

Mannheim chuckled. "Hell, you probably couldn't handle the demands of the job anyway."

Maggie kissed Suzanne good night and watched as Horace escorted her to the Jag.

Josh took Maggie's hand and walked to their SUV. Seated in the vehicle, she reached for her bag and pulled out a boxed compact disc.

Josh watched with a note of suspicion and said, "Don't tell me you helped yourself to another one of those marathon porn flicks from the collection of garbage upstairs?"

"Oh, Josh, how could you accuse me of doing anything like that? This is something I picked up at Barnes and Noble. I thought you might enjoy it."

Josh took the CD, examined the cover, and smiled. He leaned over and kissed Maggie on the cheek. The CD was a Frank Sinatra album, *Bewitched, Bothered and Bewildered*.

"Now, that's more my style."

EPILOGUE

The source of the polonium-210 recovered from the body of Chesley U. Effingwell was traced to a nuclear laboratory outside of Moscow. The official hard line of the Kremlin was in absolute denial of involvement, a situation that taxed the credulity of the entire Western world and gave rise to diplomatic stresses. Vladimir Putin, then president of Russia, refused to discuss the matter with the media.

Cue's New York office is under investigation by the U.S. Attorney in New York and the FBI. The estate faces indictments for violation of the U.S. code for arms trading as well as sales of other contraband and military secrets to foreign agents.

Dan Aviloh was charged posthumously with aggravated second-degree murder in the case of Peter Longfellow and the attempted murder of Dr. Harrington.

Prissy Longfellow was charged as an accomplice to murder in the case of her husband, Peter Longfellow, and is awaiting trial. Her culpability in the attempted murder of Dr. Harrington by her deceased partner and lover, Dan Aviloh, is yet to be determined.

Madame Tatiana, threatened with exposure to the police by Dan Aviloh, participated in the final act to force Dr. Josh Harrington into giving up his land. Eventually she was indicted for tax evasion by state and federal agencies and for operating a house of prostitution. She is awaiting arraignment. The house on Clancy Lane, according to rumor, still receives a limited number of wealthy and influential guests. A probe into possible collusion with political and law enforcement agencies has been demanded by the local press and civic groups.

Sherri Aviloh was charged with a misdemeanor under mitigating circumstances because of her cooperation with the law.

The man known as Bushwhacker was charged with aiding and abetting in the attempted murder of Dr. Harrington. He will be charged with manslaughter in the deaths of the chauffeur and escort in the crash of the limousine on Highway I-10, as well as causing severe bodily harm to Mr. Carlos Grandee.

The adobe house is to be removed from the Rancho Mirage property and relocated on a city-owned lot in Indio. It is to be used as a historical site pending approval by the Indio City Council. The property inherited by Dr. Josh Harrington off Frank Sinatra Drive is undergoing development by the multinational corporation headed by Mr. Carlos Grandee. A large estate with an adjoining heliport are on the drawing board.

Josh and Maggie Harrington have assigned a portion of their inheritance of one million dollars from the estate of the late Dr. Martin Simon to a number of charities, including various police and fireman funds.

In quieter moments, Josh looks adoringly at Maggie while her eyes sparkle with love and admiration.

ABOUT THE AUTHOR

After serving in the Pacific Theatre as a field and hospital medic in the U.S. Army, Alvin J. Harris, M.D. F.A.C.S. graduated from the University of Illinois, College of Medicine. He completed an internship and residency in Orthopedic Surgery at the Cook County Hospital in Chicago, Illinois, where he instructed medical and nursing students as well as physicians in post-graduate courses.

In Los Angeles, California, he served on the staff of the Children's Hospital, guiding residents in clinical and surgical techniques. While tending to his private practice, he served as chief of the orthopedic section at the Presbyterian Hospital in Van Nuys and the Holy Cross Hospital.

He practiced for twenty years in Washington State and founded the Sequim Orthopedic Center. In addition to private practice, he examined and treated prisoners with orthopedic problems for the State Corrections Department and learned about prison protocol. As an expert witness, he testified in litigation resulting from vehicular accidents, physical abuse, and trauma. He lives with his wife in Palm Desert, California.

When he isn't writing, Al attends lectures at the university or researches information for his novels. He occasionally squeezes in a game of golf with his wife, Yetta. His other novels include *Death Dear Doctor* and *Take Two Tabs Then Die*. His fourth book, *Death in the Saddle (Not a Western)* will be ready for the press in the summer of 2011.